FLYING ANT DAY

SAM SMEDLEY

Flying Ant Day
by Sam Smedley

Copyright © 2022 by Sam Smedley

All rights reserved.

Paperback ISBN: 979-8-83171-264-3

Find out more about the author at:
www.samsmedley.co.uk

Part One

Chapter One

Scott stood on the patio, his brow furrowed in disbelief. "Benji?"

Taking a step onto the lawn, he squinted and raised a hand to his forehead, shielding his eyes from the sun as he took a better look around. Only ten minutes had passed since Miriam, his ex-wife, had dropped Benji off for Easter weekend.

"Benji!"

Scott dropped his hand and walked over to the bushes. Branches scratched against his arms as he pushed them aside, trying to find his son. His heart pounded in his chest as he stared into the shadows. He ran to the shed, opening the door and checking behind the lawnmower.

Still no sign of Benji.

"Benji, this isn't funny," he called as his phone rang.

Scott pulled it out of his pocket and stared at the caller ID.

'Government'

Scott sighed and continued to scan the garden for his son as he answered the call. "Hello?"

There was a pause before a deep voice said, "There's a car outside. If you want to see your son again, get in."

Scott sprinted to the front garden, sweat beading on his forehead and his blood rushing as he noted the black car idling in the street.

These days, there was no point in hiding the fact that it was a government car. They didn't care. They wanted you to know.

A thin man sat behind the steering wheel, glancing at Scott. In the passenger seat, a large man stared at the road with a solemn look on his face.

After taking a deep breath, Scott got into the backseat, and the car pulled away before he had the chance to shut the door.

"What's happening, where's my son?" Scott asked, his voice gruff and full of false bravado as he grabbed the back of the driver's seat.

"I'll explain when we get there." The thin man glanced in the mirror. "Sit back and enjoy the ride."

"Enjoy the ride?" Scott scoffed and shoved himself back, simultaneously pushing the driver forward. "You want me to enjoy the ride when you've taken my kid?"

"You'll get him back. If you're quiet, you might even get told how when we get there. So sit back, shut up, and enjoy the ride."

————

BLACK GATES ROSE HIGH, the spikes on top reaching for the sky. Armed guards stood on either side of the gate, their faces grim as they stared straight ahead.

A text from Miriam came through.

'Hope Benji is OK. I want to be able to trust you with him. Don't ruin your chance. You can lose custody easily.'

The car drove into an underground car park and pulled into a space near an entrance. Scott followed the thin man out of the car and two other men flanked him while they walked to a lift. They got inside and one of the men leant forward to press the button shaped like the number five.

Fluorescent lights reflected on the tiled floor and multiple rooms lined the corridor. The thin man led the way to one of the doors and gestured Scott inside. One of the other men forced Scott into an office chair on one side of the desk, and the thin man took the seat opposite Scott.

"So," the thin man said, picking up an envelope. "Let's make this rather unpleasant situation better."

Scott scowled and shot to his feet, slamming his hands down on the desk. "Where's my son?"

"Please, Mr. Saunders," the man said with a chuckle as he opened the envelope. "Sit down. Your son is safe, I can promise you that. But we need some help from you."

"Help with what?"

"An old friend of yours," the man said, sliding a photo across the desk.

David Newton stared back from the photo; the man who stole Scott's girlfriend twenty years ago, married her ten years ago, and now, four years after 'The Change', when a right-wing authoritarian dictatorship had taken over the country, led the resistance movement. 'The Change' had come suddenly. Following a pandemic and subsequent civil unrest, a group of MPs, right-wing activists and military leaders had led a coup, overthrowing the elected Government and ushering in a brutal autocratic regime.

"An *ex*-friend," Scott said, "we haven't spoken in years."

"No, I don't suppose you would have. He stole Angela from you, didn't he?"

"What does a girlfriend from twenty years ago have to do with my son?"

The thin man looked up. "Mr Saunders, I'll be blunt with you. This man is an enemy of the Government, and we want him dead. We kept him alive to avoid any blowback, but things have changed. Unfortunately, the security around him is insane."

"You overthrew a government, killed the Prime Minister, but you can't kill him?" Scott threw the photo back across the desk.

"We've certainly tried, but we had the element of surprise in those operations. Mr Newton has had plenty of time to prepare."

Scott ran a hand down his face, sinking back in his chair. "How do I even know you have my son?"

The man reached for the phone on the desk and punched in a number. He handed the receiver to Scott, who tried to ignore the shaking of his hands as he took the phone, his breathing shallow as he brought it to his ear.

"Benji, are you there? Benji?" Scott's eyes burned as he blinked away the tears.

There was movement on the other end of the line. "Daddy?"

Scott breathed a sigh of relief. "Are you alright? Are you hurt? Daddy is going to be with you soon, OK?"

"When are you coming to get me?" Benji asked, his voice wavering and cracking. "They said you don't want to come and get me."

"Don't listen to them, Benji," Scott said around the lump in his throat. "I'll be there to get you soon, OK? You be a good boy for the nice men, and we will go and get an ice cream later, I promise. Don't worry, Daddy loves you, OK?"

The call dropped before Benji could answer, and the thin man smiled with a finger on a button. "Soon? I like the sound of that."

Scott jumped to his feet and tossed the receiver at the man. "What do you want?"

"Mr Saunders, some people are harder to get rid of than others. And your friend, sorry, *ex-friend*, is one of the hard ones. Again, I'll be blunt: you kill him, you get Benji back."

The man pulled a bag from a drawer and flung it at Scott, who caught it easily. "In there is Newton's address and phone number, a gun, and a vial of poison. I trust your skills with a gun are still as good as they were when you were in the police force. The poison is colourless, tasteless, and fast-acting. It will kill a man in under a minute."

"And what about Angela? She'll know *I've* killed him."

"You will be fully protected by us. No charges will come your way."

"And when it's done?"

"You call us, and you get Benji back."

"Unharmed," Scott said, his eyes narrowing at the man. "I get Benji back *unharmed*."

"Fine. Benji back unharmed."

Scott felt the weight of the bag in his hands. "How do you expect me to do this? I've never killed a man before."

The thin man smiled again. "Oh, it's liberating."

"You're sick," Scott spat.

"Sick or not," the man said, his grin spreading across his face. "You have until midnight on Sunday."

Two days, Scott thought as the guards escorted him from the office. He had two days to kill a man.

Chapter Two

Another Government goon drove him home.

The quiet house unnerved him. Benji's football still lay on the grass. Scott spread the contents of the bag on the table, and whilst inspecting the eyedrop bottle housing the poison, his phone rang. Scott sighed; he couldn't ignore Miriam forever. She would drive over and demand to see Benji.

"What?" Scott snapped down the receiver, his tone as harsh as the gun glinting in the dim light of the dining room.

"There's no need to be like that," Miriam barked back. "Why didn't you pick up before?"

"I was busy," Scott replied.

She sighed. "Is Benji alright?"

"Of course." Scott squeezed his eyes shut, hating himself for lying.

"What's he doing?"

Scott looked out of the window at the lone football still on the grass. "Playing with his football in the garden."

"Isn't it raining there?"

He stared up at the rain pounding against the windows.

"No, it isn't. Miriam, please let me have time with my son this weekend without having to talk to you every five minutes."

Miriam scoffed. "Are you kidding me? Have you been drinking? I thought you had quit, but apparently, you're back on it. Typical Scott."

"Miriam, everything is fine. I'm not drinking and Benji is alright. Now leave it."

Scott hung up and tucked the phone back into his pocket. He looked at the items on the table.

It had been ten years since he had last spoken to David. They fell out after he had stolen Angela from him, but that was history.

In the news, there would be stories about David; how he had come into money and funded anti-regime propaganda, though it was hard to know the truth anymore.

Scott poured a glass of rum, the amber liquid breaking his three months of sobriety.

The stress of being a policeman in the new regime had become too much, and the drinking spiralled. Now on sick leave, but expecting to be sacked any day, he had managed to wean himself off the drink.

After necking back the drink, Scott pulled out his phone and dialled David's number.

No answer.

Another drink.

Another call. No answer. And no ability to leave a message.

After the third attempt, Scott sent a text.

'Hey Dave, it's Scott. Been a long time. How are things?'

There was no response.

After an hour, Scott sighed and looked at the phone

again, but slipped it back into his pocket, annoyed at the lack of messages or missed calls.

It was time to take matters into his own hands. He tucked the gun into the back of his waistband and pulled his shirt down to cover it. After pushing the vial of poison into his other pocket, he left home.

———

David had money, there was no question about that. The large house stood tall and imposing, more like a compound than a home. The huge gate matched the bars that covered the windows.

Scott pressed the button for the intercom and stared at the little ring he knew would be a camera.

"Hello?" Angela said, her voice soft.

"Hey, Angie, it's Scott Saunders."

"Oh?" She paused, a soft sigh coming through the speaker. "How can I help you?"

"It's been a while and I was just passing through. I thought it might be nice to catch up with you and Dave. Is he there too?"

Scott could make out a muffled man's voice in the background before Angela said, "He, um, no. No, sorry. He can't see you right now."

Scott smiled and leaned against the gate. "Come on, Angie. It will be nice. Like the old days. I've missed you both."

"Scott, it's not appropriate."

There was a dial tone as the intercom disconnected. Scott pressed the button again. No answer. He stepped back and looked at the gate; it was too high to climb and covered in barbed wire and cameras.

He peered at the house and pressed the intercom again. Still no answer and no movement or light behind the curtains, at least, not any that he could see.

He kicked the gate before walking away.

————

At 7 pm, after three missed calls from Miriam, Scott poured what he estimated to be his fifth rum and coke. The phone buzzed again.

"Please let me say goodnight to Benji," she said as soon as Scott answered the call. "It's his bedtime soon. You *are* putting him to bed, right?"

"He's already in bed," Scott said as he leaned back in his chair, swirling around the contents of his glass.

He leaned away from the phone and swallowed the last of the drink before bringing the phone back to his ear.

"This early? Is he sick?"

"No," Scott snapped, irritation clear in his voice. "He was playing in the garden and wore himself out. You know what he's like."

"Right. Well, at least let me say goodnight to him tomorrow night."

Scott rolled his eyes. "I can't promise that Miriam. This weekend is about me and Benji, not the three of us."

Miriam paused, suspicious. "Is something wrong? Are you drunk?"

"Nothing is wrong. I just need you to please step back a little bit and let me have a chance at being a better father."

"Fine," Miriam said, pausing as if she wanted to say more. "Don't get too drunk."

Scott scowled as he chucked the phone onto the table beside him. She knew. She always knew.

He stared at the gun on the table, imagining bringing it to his own temple and ending this misery. Instead, he picked up the phone and called David again.

Still no answer. Scott sighed and sent another message.

'Dave, let's meet up ASAP. Been wanting to chat lately.'

He got up to fix another drink, leaving the phone abandoned on the table. When he returned, it buzzed with a new message.

'OK, Scott. Come round tomorrow. 7 pm.'

———

SCOTT WOKE UP EXPECTING A HANGOVER, but his head and stomach felt fine.

I suppose when you wake up not knowing where your son is and have to kill a man, you don't have a hangover, he thought.

He spent the day thinking about what might happen, though it was so unreal that no scenario seemed plausible. Even though Benji's life was at stake, the thought of killing someone horrified him. Could he even go through with it?

At least Miriam didn't call, he thought as he left home with the gun and poison once more, along with two bottles of merlot in his hand for David.

The wine had been his favourite drink in the old days, and though this evening would be far from nostalgic, it might help David relax.

Scott paused in the park, smoking a cigarette to calm his nerves and watching normal life carry on around him. A child Benji's age raced by on a bike.

After another cigarette, Scott got up and left the park.

Security cameras turned to face him as he strolled up

the drive to the large house. The gun holster dug into his chest, the weight of the gun a comfort.

Angela pulled open the door, looking barely a day older than the last time he had seen her.

Over the years, he had often thought about her. He could never explain it to anybody else, but she had a magnetism that drew him in, a *force*. Despite all the years that had gone by, Miriam, Benji, everything, he would frequently find his mind drifting to her. She was as pretty as ever in her long grey dress that clung to her waif-like body, her short, springy curls framing her face.

"You look good, Angie."

She faked a smile and kissed his cheek before stepping to the side to let him in. "Thank you."

A metal detector loomed ahead of him.

"You can never be too careful these days," Angela said, a smile on her face at Scott's concerned gaze. "Especially in our situation. Don't worry though. It's just a formality."

She passed through the detector, a beeping sound emitting from the machine. A man appeared; a gun visible on his hip. He stared at Scott for a moment, his lip curling.

"This is Piotr. He searches the visitors," Angela explained.

Scott's heart pounded against the gun strapped to his chest. "Understandable, I guess."

Angela giggled and shrugged. "You can never be too careful. Don't worry, just imagine you're at the airport."

Piotr took the bag containing the wine from Scott and handed it to Angela. She grinned, her face lighting up as she saw what was inside.

"I can't believe you remembered!" Angela exclaimed, setting the wine on a side table.

She gave a nod to Piotr.

"Empty your pockets in here, sir," Piotr said, his eastern European accent thick as he held out a tray. "And remove any metal objects."

Scott threw his wallet, keys, and phone onto the tray, but there was still the matter of the gun strapped to his chest. Before he could say anything, the security guard shoved him through the metal detector. It beeped and both Piotr and Angela fixed him with a heavy stare. Scott held his hands high, palms facing out.

"Caught me. I have a gun," he said as Piotr patted him down. Scott went to remove the weapon, but Piotr was faster. "Can't be too careful these days, as you said."

Angela narrowed her eyes but said nothing as she inspected his wallet. She took out the little bottle of eyedrops and squinted at it. Scott held his breath, not knowing what to do. After another moment, she put the bottle back into the wallet and handed it to Scott.

"Sorry," Angela said as she passed him the rest of his belongings. "But we're going to have to keep the gun. You can have it back when you leave. Don't worry though, you're safe here."

Angela led the way into the house where David stood by the fireplace in a battered jacket with a cigar in his hand. His long hair was streaked with grey, and jazz music played in the background. He looked every bit the academic he had always wanted to be.

"Scott!" he exclaimed, bounding forwards and bear hugging him.

Scott smiled and embraced David. "Thanks for inviting me round. I thought it would be good to meet again."

"You rather invited yourself round though, didn't you?" David replied.

"Well, I suppose."

"Don't worry, it's always good to see an old friend. Please, take a seat."

David pointed to an armchair and Scott sat down.

"Sorry about the security stuff, but since the change, there's many people who want me dead I'm afraid," David continued. He laughed and shook his head. "I couldn't help overhearing, but it's best not to bring a gun to a wanted man's house..."

"I like to make sure I'm safe as well, Dave."

The tension eased from David's face as he waved a hand. "Of course, of course, it's no issue. Now, Angela, why not open one of those merlots, sweetheart?"

"Certainly," she murmured, shooting a glance at Scott as she left.

David turned serious. "You haven't come here with ulterior motives, have you, Scott?"

"Of course not, I was thinking of the old days and..."

David cut him off. "Good, and I take it the whole Angela thing is water under the bridge now?"

"Yeah, it's ancient history."

David chuckled and relaxed into the armchair. "Like democracy."

"Exactly."

Angela returned with the wine, and though awkward at first, she relaxed the more she drank.

"How come you're suddenly interested in seeing us again?" she asked, perching herself on David's chair.

Before Scott could answer, David held up a finger and patted her leg. "Angela, please."

She slugged the wine and stared at Scott. "It seems strange, that's all."

David rolled his eyes. "She's more paranoid than me sometimes, I swear."

Angela stared at Scott, her eyes roaming over his face. He wondered if she could see through him, see why he was really there.

"I'll finish up the dinner," she said finally, getting up and disappearing once more.

David was quick to follow, heading to the bathroom and leaving Scott alone.

Scott pulled out the eyedropper bottle. David had taken his glass with him, but as long as Angela kept the wine flowing, his guard would come down at some point in the evening.

A few seconds alone with David's glass was all it would take.

His phone started buzzing in his pocket and Scott sighed. He knew it was too good to be true. Miriam would never trust him.

"Benji should be asleep soon," Miriam said, not bothering with pleasantries. "Are you listening to jazz? You hate jazz."

"I listen to it now. It's calming."

"Scott, what is going on?"

David walked back into the room and Scott pressed a finger to his lips before pointing at his phone.

"Miriam, this is getting ridiculous."

"Send me a picture of Benji after you tuck him in. I miss him and I need to know he's OK."

"You don't get to tell me how to be a parent."

"This isn't what this is. I want to know that my child is safe. Send me the bloody picture and lay off the damn booze. Don't make me come over there."

"Don't you fucking dare. This is my weekend with him."

"Send me the picture."

The call ended and Scott was left staring at his phone.

"Wife problems?" David asked.

"*Ex-wife* problems."

———

Angela watched him like a hawk during dinner. The poison bottle was like a lead weight in his pocket.

"So," David said, pouring himself a drink. "You and Miriam have a son, right? How old is he now?"

Scott's heart sunk. "He'll be ten in a few months."

"Oh lovely, sadly we can't have children," David replied, reaching out for Angela's hand, but she moved it away.

David finished the food on his plate and excused himself to go and get more, leaving his glass behind.

Angela leant forward in her chair, her elbows on the table. "Why are you really here, Scott?"

"Why not? It's good to meet up with old friends."

"Hmmm. You think I'm paranoid, don't you?" she said as she sat back in her chair, crossing one leg over another.

Scott's head was spinning, the wine starting to lower his inhibitions.

"Frankly, yes."

She shrugged. "We can't trust anyone these days. And if you think anything is happening between me and you, forget it. I love my husband."

Scott laughed and shook his head, though that did little to aid the drunken spinning sensation. "It's not about that. Jesus."

Angela gave a sharp nod. "Fine. I'm going to check on dessert since he's probably in there having that instead of getting more food."

Scott waited for her to leave, then quickly reached across the table and grabbed David's glass.

"Isn't that my glass?" David asked, appearing in the doorway.

Scott's hand closed tighter around the bottle of poison as he set David's glass down. "Shit, sorry. The wine is going to my head."

David stumbled back to his seat and peered at the glass. "I don't think I can drink any more of this anyway. It's time for a brandy, don't you think?"

———

THEY MOVED to the living room after Angela served dessert. The once feisty woman he had known, now so subservient to her husband.

David produced a box of cigars. "These are straight from Cuba. You'll love them. I should be careful though; you know they tried to kill Castro with poison cigars."

He laughed hard and started coughing. For a second, Scott thought his job might do itself.

Angela appeared at the doorway, looking from David to Scott.

"Everything OK?" she asked.

"Nothing another brandy can't handle. Drink up, Scott," David said, grabbing the glass and chewing on an ice cube. "Angela, go and get some more brandies for us."

Angela left the room again, and David turned back to Scott.

"Don't you want in again, Scott? Bring these fuckers down. Your problem was that you had a family and got soft. But we must do something. The trouble now is you want democracy and you're labelled a, what do they call it?"

David pulled hard on the cigar. "An enemy of the state. Christ, it's like something out of some God-awful Hollywood film. But using an excuse of a global pandemic to overthrow the Government? It was bullshit. Once they developed the vaccine, things would have returned to normal, anyway."

Scott nodded. "I'm with you, Dave."

David pointed at him. "And the anti-Semitism is a disgrace, and I say that not just as a Jew myself, it's bad for everyone. Your wife, Miriam, she's Jewish, isn't she?

"My *ex-wife*, yes."

"It must have affected your family then?"

"It has, she lost her job teaching last year," Scott told him.

Twelve months previously, a raft of laws came in, including one that banned Jews from any public jobs, reducing Miriam to working part-time in a supermarket.

"Well, there you go. Can you believe it's been four years already? Four years of fascism in Britain. All I can say is... things are happening." David tapped his nose. "We can bring an end to it."

He stood and Scott followed his movements.

"Get this country back to normal." David shouted. "And if they call me a traitor, then so be it. They called Mandela a terrorist. You have to do what you can."

Angela returned, drinking from a tumbler. "David, calm down. This isn't good for your blood pressure."

Scott's phone buzzed, and a message from 'Government' appeared on the screen: 'TICK TOCK, JOB DONE YET?'

"Miriam again?" David said, guiding Angela onto his lap. She sat on him and nuzzled his neck. "Let me ask you a question, Scott. Do you still want to fuck my wife?"

Angela slapped him on the leg and they both laughed.

Scott squirmed and sipped the brandy. "I need to go to the bathroom."

———

He looked at his reflection in the bathroom mirror, studying the lines that creased his face. He ran a hand through his thick dark hair and rubbed his stubbled chin.

How long could he stay in the house without arousing suspicion?

The alcohol dulled his senses as he scrolled through pictures of Benji on his phone. There were three missed calls from Miriam and two voicemails.

He texted her, squinting to make sure the spelling was right. 'Everything is fine M, Benji in bed and I'm going to bed now. I promise. Goodnight.'

Before he put his phone away, he looked at the time. Midnight.

Only twenty-four hours left.

———

When he returned to the living room, David and Angela exchanged a glance.

"We think you should stay here tonight," David said, raising his cigar. "There's plenty of room and you don't want to be caught leaving after curfew."

A wave of relief washed over Scott as he accepted their invitation. The act of kindness cut through him though, knowing he had to kill David, a man trying to bring down the brutal regime, to get Benji back.

After that, the drink flowed more freely, and a sense of

relaxation fell over him. It had been a long time since he had gathered with people and drank for fun instead of for forcing himself to forget.

"Time for bed," Angela said after a while, pulling David to his feet. "I'll get this one to bed and then I'll make up your room."

————

ALONE IN THE LIVING ROOM, Scott examined David's glass. The alcohol was a different colour from the one he had been drinking. Scott picked up the glass and took a sip.

Apple juice.

"Scott!"

He picked up his jacket at the sound of Angela's voice and lumbered up the stairs. She apologised for David's drunken ramblings as she showed Scott to his room.

"He's got you well-trained, hasn't he? Bringing him his, what was that drink again?

"Brandy," Angela said without missing a beat.

"You're like a servant."

Her smile disappeared. "Not really."

She turned away and showed him the room. He hung his jacket on the back of the door. The poison bottle made a bulge in the wallet.

"Night, Scott," she said.

"Night, Angie," Scott replied as she walked off down the hallway.

————

Scott slept little, and soon woke from a dream about Benji as sunlight streamed through the gap in the curtain. Angela knocked on the door. "Are you awake?"

Last night's events flooded back. Scott sat up, noticing it was nine o'clock.

"Yeah."

"If you need a shower, there is a towel in the bathroom."

"Thank you."

Her footsteps padded away.

After showering and dressing, Scott reached for the wallet containing the poison. The wallet was there, but no poison. He searched every pocket, the wallet again, the floor, the bed, but to no avail.

Sitting on the bed, head in hands, Scott punched the pillow.

How could he have lost it?

He turned on his phone. Two missed calls, a voicemail, and three messages from Miriam.

'Scott, why no photo? I'm not asking a lot. Please.'

'Why can I not trust you to do anything!!!!'

'Bastard!'

Then one sent this morning: 'I'm coming round at 1 pm today if I don't hear from you.'

Finally, a message from 'Government,': 'FINAL DAY! AT LEAST YOU'RE STILL AT THE HOUSE. TICK TOCK...'

———

Angela stood at the kitchen table in a long green dress and her hair wet. She turned to him. "Sleep well?"

"Yeah, like a baby."

She studied him and raised an eyebrow. "Good. We're

having coffee on the patio. It's such a sunny morning, David is out there now."

David sat facing away from him, wearing a Panama hat and sunglasses.

"Morning Scott," he said without turning away from his newspaper. "Take a seat."

Scott sat down and they both looked out at the garden. David put the paper down but didn't look at him.

"I hope you're not too hungover."

"No, I'm OK, you were pretty drunk last night. How do you feel?"

David put a hand in his pocket and gazed into the garden. "Oh, I've felt better. I was just thinking of an old saying in the Talmud, actually."

"Oh, what's that?"

David pointed a gun at him. Scott's gun. "If a man comes to kill you, rise early and kill him first."

Chapter Three

Time stood still. The garden disappeared; the world evaporated, leaving only the gun barrel visible. Scott tried to speak, but nothing came out. David had no such problem. "This is a government issue gun. You come to my house out of the blue with a government gun. What the fuck's going on, Scott?"

In fear, before he could even think, he began blurting out the truth. "David, listen, it's not what it seems, I..."

Angela appeared from the kitchen and gasped. She ran towards David. "Put that thing down, David, what the hell?"

He continued to point the weapon at Scott. "This man has come to kill me, and maybe you, too."

She loomed over David. "If that's what you think, fine, but I think you're being crazy, I'll get Piotr."

"No, I've got this, Angela." David snapped.

"Please," Angela pleaded, "put the gun down."

He relented and put it down.

Shaking, Angela returned to the house.

David ripped off his sunglasses and stared into Scott's eyes. "Tell me the truth."

"Dave, I have not come to kill you, I..."

"Why a government gun? Where did you get this thing?" he snapped.

"I got it on the black market. I don't know where it came from, I swear."

Angela brought out three espressos and placed them on the table with hands still trembling.

"Can we please calm down, have a coffee and talk this through?" She knocked hers back in one shot. "Come on, boys, drink up."

Scott drank his and Angela looked at her husband. "David..."

David did as he was told and took a deep breath.

"Good," Angela said, pulling up a chair, eyes still on David.

Within seconds, David began to choke. His face bulged and he writhed in the chair.

Scott leapt up, horrified, and Angela reached out to hold him back. David tried to reach for the gun, but his arms were seizing up.

"Sit down," Angela said to Scott. "It'll be over soon."

She pulled the eyedrop bottle from her bra and held it up in the sunlight. "We've both got what we wanted, Scott. Now get out."

David collapsed in the chair, motionless and frothing at the mouth.

"I'm serious, Scott, go, go now... it's done. You have to leave... now." Angela walked over to David's body and took the gun, shoving it into Scott's pocket.

"Give me your phone," she demanded.

In shock, Scott passed it over. She took a photo of David and handed the phone back. "Proof."

Scott took the phone with a deep frown, confused by what she had done. "But..."

"Go!" she shouted.

Scott rushed down the hallway, the metal detector beeping as he went. As he got onto the street, he took out the phone and sent the photo, along with a message: 'JOB DONE.'

Seconds later, his phone rang, and the thin man spoke. "There'll be a car coming down the road in five minutes. A black car. Get in."

———

THE DRIVER GREETED him with a wink. "Nice job. We'll make some checks and then your boy can come home."

As they drove away, taking the slow route back to his house, an ambulance passed, sirens blaring. The driver looked in his rear-view mirror and smiled. A man in the passenger seat wore an earpiece and said nothing.

Pulling into Scott's street, the man in the passenger seat removed the earpiece. "Confirmed," he said to the driver as they parked outside the house.

"Once again, Mr. Saunders, thank you, we won't forget this, I can assure you." They made him hand the gun and phone back. "Where's Benji then?"

"He'll be along shortly."

A minute later, another car cruised down the street and parked in front of them. A woman stepped out, holding Benji's hand. The doors unlocked. "See," the driver said. "Now get out."

Scott jumped out of the car and bolted towards Benji,

picking him up in a swift motion. "Are you OK, are you hurt?"

"No, Daddy I'm OK."

"You promise?"

"Yeah," Benji replied as Scott cried tears of relief and pain.

Once Scott hurried inside with Benji tight in his arms, he placed him onto the sofa, not letting him go.

"I've been so worried about you," Scott said. "Where did they take you?" Benji wouldn't answer his questions, so he let him sit in front of the TV. This time, Scott *did* have a hangover.

He poured the bottle of rum down the sink as the doorbell rang, and when he opened the door, Miriam stood there.

"So, what the hell's been going on?" she demanded.

Scott sighed. "Come in."

Benji ran into her arms, and they all walked down the hall. Scott put his hand into his pocket and felt something. A slip of paper with a scrawled message.

'Happy Easter. Hopefully this one won't be resurrected... DO NOT tell anyone I did it. Angie xxx'. Scott turned the paper over. The writing on the back was larger. *'But you owe me a favour now. Big time.'*

"So?" Miriam barked. "What happened?"

Her green eyes glared at him, and she stood straight, hands on hips, accentuating her height. She was a tall woman, and even without heels, she stood nearly as tall as Scott.

He explained that Benji had been kidnapped, that the government had forced him to kill David, but didn't tell her that Angela ended up committing the murder. Angela's threatening note worried him. Plus, if the government found out that he had lied to them, the repercussions could be brutal.

Miriam erupted. "What the hell, Scott?"

"What could I do, Miriam? I had no choice. I..."

Miriam grabbed his arm. "You're a psycho, you are *never* having Benji again, I swear to God. Ever."

Benji burst into tears, and she held him close.

"It's OK, sweetheart. You're safe now. Go upstairs and get your bag. We're going home."

Benji ran up the stairs crying and Scott put a hand on Miriam's shoulder. "I had no choice, don't you understand that?"

She pulled away from him. "Get your murderous hands off me, you sick bastard."

"You cannot tell anyone this, Miriam." Scott hissed. "Promise me that."

Miriam scoffed. "I'm not staying in this house for one more second." She darted to the door and looked up the staircase. "Benji. We're going now," she shouted as tears rolled down her face. "This was your chance, Scott, and look what happened. You are never, *ever* having him again."

"Please, you don't get it..."

"Oh, I get it, Scott. You can't keep a job, you can't look after your son, *and* you're a drunk."

Benji ran down the stairs and Scott knelt to him. "I'm sorry about what happened..."

But Miriam took Benji's hand and pulled him away. "It's time to go."

She opened the front door and charged to the car. Scott followed.

"You have to keep this a secret." he insisted, but she said nothing and opened the car door. Benji jumped into the back seat. "Miriam, calm down and think about this. I had no choice, you must get that?"

She slammed the door and started the engine. Scott banged the window, and she opened it. "You're never having him again, and I'll tell who I want."

Benji, bawling with tears, waved to him. Scott waved back. The window closed, and she hit the accelerator.

———

THE EMPTY RUM bottle sat by the sink. He regretted pouring it away and took a beer from the fridge.

The two years since their divorce had been tough. After twelve years of marriage, they had drifted apart. He blamed her control; she blamed his drinking. She was probably right. Telling Miriam what happened wasn't the plan, but Benji would say something.

To tell the truth, that Angela killed David, crossed his mind, but he feared a reprisal from Angela. Miriam now thought he was a murderer, but *Angela* was a murderer, and he didn't know why.

Scott picked up the laptop and loaded the news.

LEADING DISSIDENT DEAD

Anti-Government activist, David Newton, has been found dead at his London home. Initial reports suggest Newton, 40, died of a heart attack. No foul play is suspected. A statement from police said an ambulance was called at 9.30 am and Mr Newton was pronounced dead at the scene. His wife, Angela Newton, told reporters he collapsed in the garden. Mr Newton, an outspoken critic of the government, is believed to be behind a series of cyber-attacks on government websites last year. In 2023, Newton was sentenced to 6 months in prison for circulating pamphlets claiming that top officials were corrupt. A story since proven false. Newton, a Jewish citizen, also claimed that the 2021 pandemic was exaggerated to enable the current government to seize control. Despite the eradication of the virus and successful measures to protect the population, Newton continued to attack the leadership. More as it follows...

Scott snapped the laptop shut. *'No foul play is suspected'*. A Government lie in which he was now involved.

He left the house to buy a bottle of rum.

————

THE NEXT MORNING, Scott awoke to the ringing of his phone. He rolled over, on top of the duvet and still clothed, and glanced at the screen: withheld number.

"Hello?" he said.

"Scott, it's Angela."

Scott lay back and groaned into the receiver.

"Well, that's charming," she said.

He shielded his eyes from the sun and said, "What's going on?"

"I'm playing the grieving widow now. You must have seen me on the news. It's so tiring."

"You sound as if you don't have a care in the world, Angie," Scott replied.

Angela snorted. "Oh, I can assure you I do, Scott. We need to talk."

"About what? Can't we leave this for at least one day?"

"No, we need to talk today, and not on the phone."

"But we're talking on the phone now, if anyone's listening, it's too late to..."

Angela cut him off. "This is a secure phone, so I'm ninety-nine per cent certain it's safe, but I want to be a hundred per cent sure. I'm going to send you details of where and when to meet me. Read the instructions carefully and make sure you're not being followed."

Scott leant on the pillow and reached for a glass, finding it half full of rum. "Angie I can't, not today I..."

"No, this is serious," she pressed.

"Ok, let me think about it."

Angela raised her voice. "There is no time to think about it, Scott. I'm not asking you, I'm telling. We're in this together now."

"Angie, I have stuff going on. I..."

"No, this is imperative, Scott." she interrupted. "I can tell the whole resistance that you killed their leader if you really want. I can tell them you're going to kill me. Trust me, you don't want that."

Scoff huffed, relenting. "Ok fine. Message me."

"Thank you."

He threw the phone across the bed and took a sip of rum. Mouth burning, he rolled over and screamed into the pillow.

Scott was curious to speak to her, to find out why she killed David, and to stop her from spreading the word that he had poisoned him. But he also wanted the weekend's events behind him. His priority now was to get Miriam back on side, not getting dragged into Angela's issues.

She had been all over the news, playing the grieving widow as she had said. In a video of her making a statement outside the house, she cried, stopping every few seconds to wipe the tears away. Scott couldn't help but smile.

———

HALF AN HOUR LATER, her message came: 'LEAVE ASAP. Get the 159 bus towards Marble Arch. Get off after a few stops and wait for the next one. Then get off after a few stops again. Cross over and get on one going the other way. Then get on the tube northbound at Brixton. Step on but jump off at the last second and get the next one. Get off at Pimlico, turn left and walk down the high street. Next to Hirst Estate Agents, there is a blue door. Press the bell quickly three times. MAKE SURE NO ONE IS FOLLOWING YOU.'

He hadn't processed the events of the last two days and Angela wasn't helping by dragging him into something new. But he had to stop her from revealing that he had gone to kill David. Maybe she would explain why she had killed David, and it would all be over.

Scott's finger hovered over Miriam's number; maybe she would have calmed down by now. Not being allowed to see Benji again would kill him.

He hit dial. It rang out.

A few seconds later, she text back: *'MURDERER!'*

———

SCOTT STOOD at the empty bus stop.

Although Angela's instructions seemed excessive, he had no choice but to follow them.

When the bus arrived, he sat near the doors. The only other passenger on board was a middle-aged man with long hippy-looking hair and a red tartan shirt, his head pressed against the window.

As Angela ordered, he got off a few stops later and

waited for the next bus. Again, it was virtually empty. He got off and crossed the road, cursing the heat.

After ten minutes, he got on the next bus, and a man in a red tartan shirt sat on the back seat. It was the same man from the previous bus. Scott tried to stay calm and not stare, but when he got off at Brixton Station, so did the man in the tartan shirt. Scott paused and pretended to study the bus timetable. The man strode past him towards the station. Scott walked in the opposite direction, then doubled back, and rushed into the tube station and down onto the platform. A few metres away, reading a magazine, sat the man in the tartan shirt.

A few minutes later, the tube hurtled into the station. He got on, so did the man. As the doors slid shut, Scott jumped off. His shirt caught in the doors, and he wrenched it free before landing on the platform. The man stood a few metres away from him. Scott ran to the escalators, pushing through people and taking three steps at a time.

When he reached the top, the man had climbed halfway. Scott ran out of the station and hailed a passing taxi.

"Pimlico Station," he said, stumbling into the back.

As the taxi pulled away, he glanced behind and watched the man in the tartan shirt leap into a taxi behind.

The driver looked at Scott in the mirror. "Going anywhere nice, mate?"

"Oh, just meeting a friend," he replied, eyeing the other taxi a few cars behind.

The driver continued. "Nice area that. Since this change come in, they got rid of all the homeless and druggies and all that. Back how it used it be. Can't be too tough if you ask me. They've been good, ain't they?"

Scott tried to appear calm. "Yeah, I suppose."

The driver looked into the rear-view mirror and

adjusted his glasses. "Bringing back the death penalty was the best thing they ever done. They've got my vote for life."

"If there's ever an election again," Scott muttered.

The driver grunted and stared at him.

Scott got out of the taxi at Pimlico Station and ran into an Irish themed bar. He ordered a Guinness and sat facing the street.

A minute later, a taxi pulled up and the man in the tartan shirt stepped out. Scott downed his drink and watched him, then to his horror, the man entered the pub.

Scott sprang from his seat and shuffled past a jukebox to a door labelled 'Toilets'. He hurried to a fire exit and pushed the bar, but no matter how hard he pushed, it wouldn't budge. Terrified, he darted into the bathroom, searching for a way out.

There wasn't one.

He went into a cubicle and tapped out a message to Angela: 'I'm being followed.'

When she didn't reply within a minute, he returned to the bar. The man stood a few feet away at the jukebox with his back to Scott.

As Scott moved to the door, *"Every Breath You Take"* by The Police started to play. The creepy lyrics about being watched echoed through the bar.

As he reached the door, he broke into a run.

Scott hurtled down the street and straight into the chest of a soldier. "Steady on, mate, in a hurry, are we?"

"Yeah, running late for something, I..."

"Card," the young soldier demanded.

Scott fumbled for his ID card, trying to see over the soldiers at the Irish pub. The soldier took Scott's ID card. Another soldier, this one older, approached.

He produced a device and scanned the card. "Where are you going, sir?"

"Meeting a friend for lunch," Scott lied, still glancing at the road behind them.

"Look at me, not the street, sir." the older man shouted, gripping Scott's arm. "I said where are you going?"

"Meeting a..."

"WHERE?" he bellowed into Scott's face.

Passers-by stared at them.

Scott recoiled. "That Irish pub."

The device checking his ID beeped twice, and the soldiers gave it a double take. The older one passed the ID card back.

"Well, you just ran past it. We'll walk you in there, sir."

People stared as they marched up the pavement together.

On reaching the pub, the older man pinched Scott's cheek.

"Top of the morning to you," he said, smiling.

They both stood at the doorway. Scott walked in.

He couldn't see a tartan shirt, and with the soldiers still blocking the doorway, he ordered a rum and coke. His phone buzzed, a message from Angela: 'DO NOT MESSAGE ME. JUST GET HERE.'

Scott swigged the last of his drink and the soldiers left. As he stood up, a new song played: *"Angie"* by the Rolling Stones. He froze and scanned the pub once more. There, walking away from the jukebox, was the man in the tartan shirt.

Scott left and rushed down the road, checking behind him every few seconds. The address Angela gave him was only a couple of hundred metres away, but he stopped halfway there and peered into a charity shop window for a minute, then looked back up the road. A flash of red tartan appeared through the crowd. Scott broke into a jog, and within a minute, he arrived at the blue door Angela had mentioned. He continued to jog past, unsure how close behind the man had got to Scott. He stopped at the next crossing, dashed down a side street, and waited.

After a few minutes, he ambled back to the main road. Not seeing any tartan, he sped back to the blue door and hit the bell three times. The door clicked open, revealing a steep flight of stairs. At the top was a closed fire door with the glass panel covered by newspaper. As Scott went to knock, it swung open, and Angela dragged him inside. "What the fuck took you so long?" she fumed.

Behind her stood a figure; the man in the tartan shirt.

Angela looked at them both. "You've met Martin then I hear, he..."

Scott cut her off, pointing across the room at the man. "*You* sent him?"

"Yes," she said, strolling to a sofa, "to make sure you were following my instructions, and that you weren't being followed by the government."

The man held his hand out to Scott. "Sorry if I scared you, mate, it was for the best."

Scott turned back towards Angela who smiled at him.

"Do you think this is funny, Angie?" Scott shouted. "You scared the shit out of me."

Angela put her finger to her lips. "Keep your voice down, we need to be careful."

"What the fuck is going on here, and what do you want from me?" Scott demanded.

Angela produced a bottle of brandy from beside the sofa and patted the cushion. "Sit down, Scott. Have a drink and calm the hell down."

Martin passed him a glass of brandy and said, "You did good, Scott, followed the instructions well, and I hope you like my taste in music."

Scott took a swig of the drink. "Not apple juice then."

Angela laughed and patted his knee. "David liked to keep his wits about him. Anyway," she said sternly, "as they say in the movies, you're probably wondering why I've invited you here today?"

Scott jutted his chin towards Martin. "Firstly, I want to know who he is." Angela held up a hand. "All in good time, Scott."

"No, I want to know what is going on."

"Martin is my right-hand man, my fixer. But he's going to leave us alone so we can talk in private."

"Yes, boss," Martin said, taking a gulp of brandy before leaving. "Good to meet you, Scott."

They listened to him walk down the stairs, and when the door swung shut, Angela spoke. "He doesn't know I killed David by the way, nobody does, so let's keep that our little secret, eh?"

"What's going on, Angie, why am I here?"

Angela smiled. "Well, it's been a funny old weekend, hasn't it?"

"Funny? Do you have any idea the shit this has caused me?" Scott snapped.

"Please keep your voice down," Angela insisted, "Not funny ha-ha, funny strange."

Enraged by her blasé attitude, Scott got to his feet and headed for the door. "You know what, I'm off, this is madness."

"Scott, for God's sake, calm down."

He stopped with one hand on the door handle. "No, this is too much." Angela grabbed his hand. "Scott, listen to me. You've come this far, don't you want to know why you're here?"

Scott let go of the handle and she pushed the door shut. "Well, give me some answers then."

"What do you want to know?"

They sat down in silence.

Scott fumed, still unsure whether to leave or hear her out. "Why did you kill David?"

Angela ran a hand through her curls and took a deep breath. "He was too cautious with our operations. We are on the cusp of overthrowing this government, yet he dragged his heels, biding his time. If we wait any longer, we will lose our momentum. Every day we wait is another day they could kill us all." She leaned towards Scott, "And he was a terrible bore." She laughed. "I'd been thinking about it for a while actually, then you turned up and I saw the perfect opportunity. Clearly someone had sent you to kill him. I could let you take the blame."

Scott frowned. "How did you know I'd come to kill him?"

"Where do I start? Turning up out of the blue, the gun, the poison, God it was obvious as hell, Scott. David was suspicious, but I *knew*. The bottle of eyedrops? Please, I know how these people work."

"What are these operations you talk about?" Scott asked.

"No, I've got a question for you, Scott," Angela shot back. "What did they do to make you do it? Blackmail, money?"

Scott sighed and paused before saying, "They took my son."

"Bastards. Is he OK now?"

"He's fine. I don't want to get into it now." Scott held his glass out and Angela poured more brandy. He took another swig, then continued. "So, the operations?"

"Resistance operations."

"Like?"

"Come and work with us, Scott."

Although the resistance was something Scott nominally admired for their bravery, he wanted no part of it. Risking his life for a slim chance of victory wasn't worth it.

He closed his eyes and groaned, "No way, Angie, I want a simple life."

Angela scoffed. "Your simple life is over."

"I can at least try to get it back."

"You think the government will leave you alone now?" she thundered. "They won't. Now they know you're a willing assassin for them they'll come knocking again and again. There'll be more blackmail. I've seen it before." She lowered her voice. "Especially now they think you're such a ruthless assassin. You can't be OK with this regime. If only for what they've done to you. They took your kid and forced you to kill a man. Doesn't that make you sick?"

"Of course it does, but..."

"The army on the streets, the anti-Semitism? We both married Jews, Scott, and look how they treat them. Miriam presumably lost her teaching job?"

Scott nodded and Angela carried on.

"God knows what they teach Benji at school now. It's hell. The censorship, having to go through ridiculous hurdles to get a passport, and if you do, what country will give you a visa? Britain is a pariah." She shook with rage. "And it will only get worse. How does that make you feel, Scott?"

Anger rose inside him, and the alcohol had kicked in. "I

need to sort my own life out before sorting out everyone else's."

"No, Scott. It is your life as well. They will never leave you alone now. You're fucked. This regime is weaker than you can imagine. The show of force is a front. There are thousands of people in the resistance, all over the country. We have people high up in the government and the army. It's a house of cards. You wouldn't believe how close they are to falling."

"So why do you need me then?"

"Because they will come back to you and that could be useful to us." Angela had worked herself up and stood, her face turning red. "Look at what they've done to you, look what they've made you do. Join us, work with us. Get rid of these bastards. So, what do you say, Scott? There's something we're working on right now. We'd love to have you on board. I'm sure your police experience could come in useful as well." Scott closed his eyes again and rubbed his temples. "Can I think about it and come back to you?"

"This isn't a bloody job offer, Scott, this is the future of the country, the country *your son* is growing up in."

"I get that, but this is a serious thing to get involved in and..."

"It would be a shame if the government found out you didn't kill David, and that you lied to them," Angela whispered.

Scott raised an eyebrow. "Is that a threat?"

"Maybe," Angela murmured.

"Are you for real? You're threatening me now? Jesus Christ, Angie."

Scott stood and shuffled to the door. Angela didn't move.

Opening the door, he stepped out and stared back at her. "You make me sick."

———

A GROUP of schoolchildren blocked the pavement as he left, and he stepped into the road to pass them. Then everything went black. Something had been placed over his head. He shouted and struggled, arms and legs flailing about. Multiple hands gripped him, and within seconds, he was in a moving vehicle. Scott screamed into the bag covering his head and kept writhing to get free.

Another hand grabbed his arm and then a needle stabbed him. As the liquid entered his veins, Scott became lightheaded and unable to struggle. His head swam, and he fell into unconsciousness.

———

SOME TIME LATER, Scott awoke into darkness, his head still covered. But as he groaned with grogginess, someone ripped the covering away from his head, leaving him blinking into a brightly lit room.

A man appeared in front of him. The man who had asked him to kill David.

"Hello, Scott, we've got some questions for you."

Chapter Four

The man sat on a chair opposite Scott and said, "I never introduced myself before. My name is Henry."

His voice echoed around the small metallic room. Scott stayed silent, staring at the wall opposite, his vision slowly returning to normal.

Henry continued. "My job is to keep this country safe," he threw out his hands and shrugged, "simple as that."

The sharp metal handcuffs dug into his skin as he moved slightly. Henry shifted forward and pointed a long finger at him. "And your job, your one job, was to keep quiet. Which it appears you cannot do."

Scott kept his eyes fixed on the wall. "I don't know what you're talking about."

Henry jumped up and punched him hard across the cheek. The sharp tang of blood filled his mouth.

"Yes, you do, Scott, yes you do." Henry sat back down and rubbed his knuckles. "Who did you tell about our little deal?"

"No one."

"Scott, you don't get it. We know you told someone. This is the time to confess."

Scott looked into the man's eyes. "I. Did. Not. Tell. Anyone."

"Miriam?"

"No," Scott lied.

"Angela?"

Scott scoffed. "Of course not."

"Well, why did you see her today?" Henry pressed.

So, they knew.

Scott closed his eyes, wishing he had never agreed to meet her.

"What did she talk to you about?" Henry asked, but Scott didn't reply.

"Scott, I'm the good cop here, trust me, you don't want to meet the bad cop. So, I'll ask again, what did she talk to you about?"

Again, Scott said nothing.

"What did you tell Miriam?"

"Nothing."

Henry stood and made a beckoning gesture to the wall behind Scott. "This is tiresome, Scott, I think I'll let bad cop have a go."

Henry walked to the back of the room and leant against the wall, arms crossed. The door swung open and a short, muscled man entered the room, shirt sleeves pulled up.

"This," Henry shouted, "is bad cop."

Scott averted his eyes to the floor.

"He gets better results than me," Henry added.

The short man held Scott's throat and squeezed. Just as he began to lose consciousness, the man released his grip.

Henry smirked. "See what I mean about bad cop?"

"Seeing as we're all on first-name terms," the short man

said in a midlands accent, "my name is Bill, and I get answers."

"I know it seems vulgar, Scott," Henry said, "but sometimes we need to cut through the bullshit."

Bill reached into his back pocket and pulled out a pair of pliers. "What did you tell Miriam?" he growled.

'*I'll tell who I want*', Miriam had said when Scott told her.

"I didn't tell her anything," Scott screamed, then lowered his voice, "maybe my son said something."

Henry pushed himself off the wall and walked over.

"Your son didn't know about the deal. What did you tell Miriam?" Henry shouted, leaning into Scott's face. Then, pointing at the pliers in Bill's hand, he said, "It's not worth losing teeth over, is it? She's not even your wife anymore?"

"I didn't tell her anything, I swear," Scott pleaded.

Henry flicked his head, and Bill got Scott in a headlock, the pliers primed above his mouth. The smell of sweat and cigarettes poured off him. "We'll start with the back ones," Henry said.

The door opened and footsteps approached.

"This is Bill's friend, Ben. Another bad cop," Henry said.

Bill passed the pliers over and a fat stubby hand grasped them. It, too, reeked of cigarettes. The pliers gripped his bottom left molar.

If he confessed, what would happen to Benji and Miriam? The pliers wrenched left, then right, twisting the tooth.

In agony, Scott squeezed his eyes shut. Then, with a sharp pull, the tooth was yanked from his mouth. The men released his head, and Scott screamed, his mouth filling with blood, and pain shooting through his jaw. He spat out as much blood as he could, the rest dribbling onto his shirt and down his throat. The room spun and he slumped forward, Bill and Ben high-fived each other.

Bill stepped forward and gripped Scott by the cheek.

"Open your fucking eyes," he shouted.

Scott opened them. Bill held the blood-soaked tooth up, its long roots pointing to the floor, then dropped it into his mouth and swallowed.

"I told you I was a bad cop, didn't I?"

The two men left, leaving Henry and Scott alone. Pain surged through Scott's mouth.

Henry walked over and removed the handcuffs, then passed over a lump of cotton wool coated in a foul-smelling liquid.

"It's antiseptic. I told you I was the good cop."

Scott held it against the hole in his gums, the stinging sensation making him gasp.

"You bastards," he muttered, spitting out a combination of blood, saliva, and antiseptic.

Henry sat and fixed his gaze at Scott. "Admit you told her."

"I didn't tell her," Scott lied again.

Henry fixed him with a long, silent stare. "Let's move onto Angela. What did you discuss?"

"She talked about how she's coping after David's death."

"His *murder*," Henry corrected. "And what else?"

Scott shifted in the chair, dizzy from the pain. "Nothing."

"Did she ask you to join the resistance?"

"No."

"Oh, I think she did. Here's the deal, Scott. We want Angela alive so we can get information on what she's doing.

And that's where you can help us again." Scott's heart sank. "We want you to join with her and report back to us."

"You want me to be your mole? Fuck you." Scott shouted. "Not after what you've done to me."

Henry pondered this answer, looking at the floor, hands on knees. "Maybe I phrased that wrong, Scott, you *are* going to join with her and report back to us."

Scott said nothing as he tilted his head back in despair, blood trickling down his throat.

"I don't need to spell out what will happen if you don't," Henry said. "I'm sure you can guess. Such a sweet kid."

Scott whipped his head down to face Henry. "I'll take that as a yes."

"It's a no."

Henry gestured to the wall behind Scott. Within seconds, Bill and Ben entered, grinning like fools.

"Ok, OK I'll do it." Scott groaned.

"Good," Henry said. Bill and Ben looked disappointed. "What did you tell Miriam?"

"I told you already, nothing."

Henry reached into his pocket and pulled out Scott's phone.

"Why don't we send her a message then and see what she says?" he said, looking at the screen. "What's the code to unlock this?"

Scott scowled. "I told you I will work with you, isn't that enough?"

"Only kidding, we broke into the phone already," Henry revealed, tapping away at the screen.

He pulled the chair towards Scott, so close their knees almost touched, and turned the phone around.

'HOW DO YOU FEEL ABOUT WHAT I TOLD YOU?' the message read. Henry hit send.

"If she's anything like my ex-wife, we'll be waiting ages for a reply."

They sat in silence for a while, and Henry told Bill and Ben to leave.

"How's the tooth?" Henry muttered, fumbling with the phone. "Well, the hole?"

The phone buzzed. Henry's mouth moved as he read the message. He showed Scott the screen.

'DISGUSTED, YOU'RE EVEN MORE SICK THAN I THOUGHT YOU WERE. DON'T MESSAGE ME AGAIN.'

Henry frowned. "So you told her something. Something *disgusting*. That's interesting."

"I told her I slept with one of her friends," Scott spat out. "She wasn't happy with it."

"Good answer, but I don't believe it for one second."

"It's the truth, she..."

Henry interrupted him. "We'll leave this for now. You go home and tell Angela you want to join the resistance today. We'll be in touch."

They untied him and handed his phone back, then walked him to an underground car park, covered his eyes with a blindfold and threw him into the back of a car.

"Make sure you call Angela today, Scott," Henry said before the car door slid shut.

"Don't even think about taking the blindfold off," a gruff voice next to him ordered.

The car pulled away.

The drive took an hour, and nobody said a word the whole way. Every time the car hit a bump, the jarring caused intense pain in Scott's mouth. The wound still seeped blood.

Eventually, the car stopped, and the man removed the

blindfold. They had stopped outside his house. Scott got out and walked inside.

––––––

IN THE BATHROOM MIRROR, he looked at the bloody hole where his tooth had been. The left side of his face had swollen, either from the tooth removal or the punches. It was hard to tell. He swallowed some painkillers, then picked up the phone, unsure whether to call Angela or Miriam first.

Who had Miriam told? What had she said?

He needed to know this first, so he called her. She didn't answer.

Alone in the house, Scott paced the kitchen, thinking over the day's events. Deciding Miriam would never answer the phone, he left and took the long walk to her house.

––––––

HE RANG the bell and footsteps came down the hall. The door opened with the latch chain on, and Miriam's head poked through the gap. She looked like she had been crying.

Her face screwed up as she saw him. "What do you want?"

"Who did you tell?" Scott demanded.

She tried to shut the door, but Scott put his foot in the gap.

"Go away, you bastard," Miriam shouted, slamming the door against his foot.

He pushed hard, and the chain strained.

"I need to know what you said and to who."

"You're making a scene Scott, just go away."

Scott leant into the door. "You're damn right I'm making a scene, open up."

"I swear to God I'll call the police, Scott, leave me alone."

He stepped back, then barged his shoulder against the door, ripping the chain off. Miriam stumbled backwards into the hallway. He stepped inside and swung the door shut.

"I'm calling the police," she stuttered, and stormed through to the living room, Scott following behind.

She scanned the room and spotted her phone on the sofa, but Scott had seen it first and snatched it, holding it above his head.

"Who did you tell?"

"I didn't tell anyone," she barked, jumping to reach the phone and slapping her palms against his chest. "Get out. You're going to scare Benji."

"Look what they did to me, Miriam." Scott opened his mouth wide and pointed at the gaping hole. "I got tortured because *you* told someone."

Miriam gaped and stopped hitting him, but still tried to reach for the phone. "I swear I didn't, why would..."

"Is it your friend, the one who hates me, what's her name, Carla? You told her, didn't you?"

Miriam gave up reaching for the phone and dropped onto the sofa. "Scott, I haven't said a word," she insisted. "You need to leave. I don't think you get the seriousness of the situation. After what you told me, you have no right to come here acting like a madman lecturing me."

Scott sat on the sofa opposite her, still holding her phone. "Look, I don't want to scare you, or upset you but..."

"It's too late for that," she said, turning away.

"Miriam, please, who did you tell? I need to know."

"And I need you to leave," she said, standing. "If you go now, I won't call the police. Now give me my phone back."

She held out her hand and he passed it to her. There were footsteps on the stairs, and they both looked round.

"Stay in here, or I'll call the police," Miriam said, darting into the corridor and closing the door.

"Is Daddy here?" Benji said. She whispered something back, but Scott couldn't make it out.

The footsteps disappeared back upstairs. It took all his self-control not to walk into the hall and look at Benji.

Miriam returned to the living room.

"When can I see him again?" he asked.

Miriam shook her head and sat down, "I don't want to talk about it now, Scott, give me some space please."

"If I find out you've told anyone I'll..."

"You'll what? Kill me as well?" Scott stepped towards her, and she backed away. "You scare me, Scott. Please go away."

"Do you understand this is hard for me?"

Miriam rolled her eyes, "Oh, here we go. Poor old Scott, woe is me."

She stood and walked over to the window. The sunlight revealed a few grey hairs glistening among the dyed blonde ones.

She lowered her head and said, "I don't want to be the nagging ex-wife, you know." As she turned slightly, a tear fell from her face onto the carpet. "That's not the role I saw for myself in life."

"I don't see you like that..." he began, but she cut him off.

"But after what you've told me, how can I be anything else?" Miriam's voice cracked as she spoke, and Scott instinctively got up to put an arm around her. To his surprise, she didn't move away. "I used to be a proud woman. I had a career, a happy family, but now look." Her sobs became louder, and he held her tight. "But then this all happened, and I can't get a decent job. We fell apart and I'm the villain somehow."

"No, it's not like that. The same reason you can't get a job is the reason I had no choice in..." Scott rested his head on top of hers, "...in what I had to do. These people are evil."

"All I want," she said, still crying, "is for me and my son to be happy."

"Yes, and that includes me being in his life, surely?"

Miriam sniffed. "I don't know any more, Scott."

She pulled away, steadied herself, and sat back down. Scott lingered at the window, unsure what to say.

"When this lot came into power, I thought that was it, things couldn't get any worse." Miriam wiped a tissue across her face. "Then we split up."

Scott opened his mouth to speak, but she held a hand up to stop him interrupting.

"I don't blame you, it was both our fault. But things got even worse."

Scott moved to the sofa and took a seat next to her.

"I know," he said, putting an arm on her leg. This time, she flinched. "Then just as things were getting better, this shit happens."

"I told you, I had no choice."

Miriam composed herself and stood again, waving a hand towards the hallway. "Please leave."

"Promise me you didn't tell anyone, not even Carla," Scott pressed.

"I didn't tell anyone, I promise."

————

Scott walked home to clear his head.

Years ago, he would have fought to get back with Miriam and to have that stable family life again. He still cared for her, but these days, he wanted his own life, to be independent. As long as Benji was happy. Miriam seemed to be telling the truth about not telling anyone. Maybe Henry was bluffing and wanted him to admit to something they didn't even know. Scott's hatred for the government had grown, but for Benji's sake, he had no choice but to work with them against the resistance.

The adrenaline had held the pain at bay, but as he got home, the agony returned. As he trudged through to the kitchen, Scott spotted a package sat on the table. Worrying it might be a bomb, he stopped dead.

Eventually, he gingerly unwrapped the package and found a box inside with a note on top that read: *'Cameras/mics. We will be in touch to set up.'* Underneath were various small pieces of electrical equipment. He tossed it aside, took some painkillers with a glass of rum, and called Angela.

She answered on the second ring. "Yes?"

"I've thought about it, Angie, I want in. I want to work with you."

She inhaled on a cigarette, "I've thought about it as well, and I've decided that you shouldn't."

"But..."

"Sorry, Scott, we don't want you."

Scott dipped his eyebrows and scoffed. "You were practically begging me before. What's changed?"

"It's a no. We don't need you. Bye."

She hung up.

Chapter Five

Miriam tugged Benji's hand as they passed Buckingham Palace. "Come on, we're late."

"Who lives in that big house?" he asked.

"The Queen used to live there, but it's empty now."

"Why did she move?"

"Please, Benji, we don't have time for this," she snapped, pulling him along the street.

"Where does she live now?"

"Canada."

"Why?"

Miriam yanked his arm, and to her relief, he didn't resist.

As they rounded the corner, a young man clambered onto the roof of a parked car. He waved a placard that read: '*NO MORE DICTATORSHIP*'.

"We've had four years living under fascism. Rise up and get rid of our unelected leaders," he shouted.

Benji looked on in awe. Some passers-by stopped and watched. Others, wary of being too close to this display of treason, hurried away.

"This is no better than Stalinist Russia or Nazi Germany. Look around you, look at what we have become."

A crowd had formed, and Miriam went to leave, but found her way blocked by the onlookers.

"I can't see, Mummy," Benji pleaded, jumping up and down to get a better view.

She tried to barge her way through the crowd again, but with no luck. Two soldiers appeared and shouted at the man to get down, but he ignored them and continued his rant.

"This regime is on its last legs, rise up now and..."

The soldiers seized him by the ankles and he hit the car roof with a thud. Some of the crowd cheered. Then the beating began; vicious blows rained down on the man, slamming him against the side of the car. Blood sprayed the air, mixed with shattered glass from the car window.

As the crowd swayed to one side, Miriam saw the man's face, bloodied and broken, barely recognisable as a face at all. Benji could still not see, thankfully, but begged to know what was happening. She ignored him and tried to find a way out of the mob. An elderly woman beside her held up a phone, recording the spectacle. Miriam headed for a gap in the crowd behind her. Somebody screamed. The old woman was being pulled out by a soldier.

"Give me that phone." he shouted at her, his face red from the exertion of beating the man.

"No," the woman said, "I'm old enough to remember a time when..."

The soldier struck her in the face with a stick. She hit the ground with a *crack,* and the soldier began beating her as well. Those closest backed away to avoid the upswing of the stick. A siren wailed. People dispersed, stumbling over each other in the stampede.

Miriam, now at the back of the crowd, clenched Benji's hand and pulled him away down a side street.

"What happened?" he asked, trying to look back at the scene. Miriam hurried him along. "Nothing, Benji, just forget about it."

———

She did her best to forget about it as they walked away. As shocking as it was, it served as another reminder of why they had to leave the country. They hurried along in silence, and by the time they reached the address, she had calmed down. She took a deep breath and pressed the bell. Benji fidgeted as she removed her sunglasses.

A voice came from the intercom, "Hello?"

"I have an appointment at three o'clock."

"Name?"

"Miriam Roth."

The door buzzed open, revealing a woman stood at the end of a long corridor.

"This way, Mrs Roth," she said, leading them into a small room, almost entirely taken up by a full-body scanner.

After being scanned, she asked them to sit and wait, and within a few minutes, she reappeared and heaved open a heavy door. "You may go through now."

Two men stood behind a desk. Behind them, an Israeli flag hung from the wall.

"Please take a seat," the older man said. She sat and lifted Benji into an adjacent chair. "How can we help?"

"I need to get out," Miriam replied, putting her hand on Benji's knee. "*We* need to get out."

"Jews are free to leave anytime, Mrs Roth. Why do you need our help?"

Miriam took a sip of water and said, "They won't let us leave. Last night, I applied for an exit visa online and got rejected."

To her shock, the routine system for Jews to leave had been denied instantly.

The younger man picked up a pen. "Tell us your situation, Mrs Roth."

"The government kidnapped my son and blackmailed my ex-husband to do something."

The men frowned. "Blackmailed him to do what exactly?"

She pointed to the pen and the man passed it over. 'KILL SOMEONE' she wrote and slid it back.

He raised an eyebrow. "Hmmm. Anything else?"

She repeated her practised lie in her mind and finally recited it to the men, hoping it would speed things along. "Last night, somebody tried to break into our house. There's a car outside most days. We're in danger. We need to get out, I'm begging you. I..."

The older man interrupted. "You believe you are in imminent danger?"

"Yes."

"Do you have any relatives in Israel?"

"No."

"Are you on the List of Jews?"

She winced at the mention of the seemingly innocent census carried out after the change. A census that led to easier persecution. Friends had recommended that she lie on it, but the penalty was ten years in prison, and she hadn't wanted to risk it.

"Yes," she said.

The older man cleared his throat. "How did you find us, Mrs Roth?"

She had memorised the address after an acquaintance had told her of it at a dinner party a year ago. "A friend."

"OK. Fill out these forms and we'll see what we can do."

He passed over a stack of papers.

"No, you don't understand. This is an emergency. My life..." She stopped herself and wrote across the first page: *'OUR LIVES ARE IN DANGER.'*

The men looked at Benji.

"Would you like to watch some cartoons?" the older one asked.

Benji made a face.

"Or play some computer games?" the younger man ventured.

Benji looked at Miriam.

"That would be fun, wouldn't it?" she said.

They waited as the woman reappeared and led Benji away.

"Do you have PRO SOCCER 2026?" he asked her as they left the room.

———

"WE CAN GET you both on a cargo plane to Israel this weekend. But..."

"Thank you, thank you so much," she said, raising both hands to her chest in a show of appreciation.

"What about your home?" the older man asked.

"I can put it up for sale."

"That would be a good idea. We expect a law soon prohibiting Jews from owning property."

A shiver ran through her. "Another reason to leave then."

"Indeed. But we still need a few bits of information from you."

He slid over a smaller stack of papers.

———

AFTER COMPLETING THE FORMS, Miriam handed them to the older man. "Done. Now please get us out."

He rifled through the papers. "We'll check this and call you later."

"I told you, our lives are in danger. I need to know now," Miriam demanded.

"We will call you, Miss Roth."

Miriam slammed her fists on the desk. "I'm not leaving this building without you telling me we are on that flight."

With a sigh, the older man took the papers and said, "Ok, wait here."

Miriam drummed her fingers on the desk, staring at the Israeli flag.

What did she know about Israel? Nothing. But at least she could be free there. Free from government hassle and Scott's bullshit. Free to let Benji grow up safely.

She walked to the mantelpiece and picked up a few of the photos: the Israeli Prime Minister shaking hands with the US President, the Russian President, the Queen. One of the desk drawers had been left open slightly, so she listened for any approaching footsteps and slid it open wider. A folder lay on top with a label that said: '*Application for emergency exits.*' She opened it up and flicked through the files, names and photos of recent applications, scribbled on each one an estimated date of exit. None were sooner than two weeks.

She snapped it shut and hurried back to her seat just as

the door opened. The older man entered and strode over to the desk. "Good news, Mrs Roth, you're good to go. Tomorrow morning, City Airport. All sorted."

Miriam let out a huge breath and got to her feet. "Thank you so much."

"No problem." He handed her an envelope. "These are the details. The flight is tomorrow at 8am. A driver will pick you up at 6am. He will use the word *'Luxembourg'*. Be ready."

The older man stood behind the desk for a moment, glanced at the drawers, then back to her looking at his watch. "You have twenty hours. Stay safe."

Chapter Six

"What do you mean she won't let you in?" Henry questioned down the phone.

"She said she doesn't need me," Scott replied.

"Well, you're going to have to change her mind. And fast."

"But..." Scott began, but Henry hung up.

———

SCOTT LAY ON THE BED, drifting in and out of sleep. A doorbell rang, and he sat up, unsure if it was a dream.

It rang again and Scott realised that it must have been real. He strolled down the stairs, jaw hurting, and prayed it wasn't Henry or some other government goons. Through the frosted glass stood a figure in bright orange clothing. He swung the door open to a man holding a crate of groceries.

"Evening, sir, supermarket delivery."

Scott stood, confused. "You must have the wrong house. I didn't order anything."

But the man turned and called out to a waiting van, "Bring it up."

An older, much skinnier man wearing a baseball cap climbed out of the vehicle, clasping a sheet of paper. "Scott Saunders, right, that's you?"

"Yeah."

The old man whacked Scott with the crate. "It's me, you idiot."

Before Scott could respond, Angela barged past him and marched into his house, dropping the crate in the hallway.

"Quite a good disguise, don't you think?" she said, taking off her hat. "I make quite a good old man."

She slipped a hand under her chin and pulled off a latex mask, revealing her tired-looking face. Her curls sprang free, and she glared into the hallway mirror.

"I swear every time I put this thing on it ages me a few years." She looked back at him. "You look like you've aged a few years yourself." Still surprised, Scott stuttered out a reply. "Er, do you want a drink?"

"Fuck yeah."

She walked towards the kitchen to where Scott had left the government equipment spread on the counter. "Angie, come into the living room," he called out.

Angela kept walking, but with a quick step, Scott reached out and grasped her arm, gently pulling her back. "This way."

"Something embarrassing in the kitchen? I know how you bachelors live," Angela teased.

"Yeah, something like that," Scott said with laughter in his voice, and to his relief, she followed him. "Make yourself comfortable. I'll get the drinks."

———

IN THE KITCHEN, Scott shoved the electronic devices into a cupboard. The chances she had seen them were slim, but not impossible.

"Is wine alright?" he called out.

"Perfect."

"Red or white?"

"Surprise me."

With a last check of the kitchen, Scott took a deep breath and returned to Angela. She looked ridiculous in the delivery uniform, a baggy luminous jacket over a massive polo shirt.

"How do you know where I live?" Scott asked, pouring the wine.

"I know a lot of things," she replied, removing her shoes.

Scott sat beside her and sipped his drink. "How come you're here? I thought you wanted nothing to do with me?"

She held the wine glass to her lips and said, "I didn't say that."

Scott knitted his brow. "You weren't interested in me joining the resistance."

Angela took a large gulp of wine. "Are you *sure* you want to?"

"Yes, that's what I said."

"What changed?" she said, slipping off the jacket.

Scott explained the kidnapping and the tooth removal, but left out the small detail that Henry had asked him to spy.

When he finished, she put a hand on his knee. "See what we're dealing with, Scott? They're evil."

"Tell me about it."

"Did they ask you to inform on me?"

For a moment, Scott considered telling her the truth, but he put his hand on hers and looked her dead in the eye.

"No."

Angela raised her brow and said, "They will at some point."

She descended into deep thought, her eyes moving upwards, head tilting from side to side. She gripped Scott's leg.

"I needed to know you really wanted it, Scott, you can't be half in this, you know?" Her hand slipped away from him. "It's all or nothing."

Scott held her gaze. "I want in, Angie, I swear."

Angela took the bottle from the table and filled both their glasses. "Ok, here's the deal. Meet me tomorrow evening." She took a card from her pocket with an address written on it. "This is the place, 7pm. I want you to meet some people."

"Who?"

"Don't worry about that until tomorrow, it'll be fun."

She finished the drink and stood up, pulling the latex mask over her head.

"Isn't that uncomfortable?" Scott asked.

"Not as much as the strapping. I know I'm not exactly Dolly Parton, but still."

They both laughed and walked to the door, stepping over the crate. Angela put on the baseball cap and said, "Enjoy the free food, and I'll see you tomorrow." She opened the door, then turned back to him. "Take the usual precautions on the way and tell reception you're there to see Rachel."

A moment later, the same supermarket van appeared on the street and Angela stepped out.

———

The man held up a wire attached to a button.

"This is all you need tonight." He ripped a button off Scott's shirt and threaded the wire through. "The battery pack is tiny, but it will last for thirty six hours, camera, sound, the lot. Amazing piece of equipment."

The man took out a sewing kit, unpicked the seam of the shirt, then slid the battery in and sewed it back up.

Scott shuffled nervously. "And no one can discover this, right?"

The man looked up from his task. "Nothing is one hundred per cent safe, but this is as good as it gets. Just be careful. A pat-down search is fine though. They'd have to take your shirt off and look at it in detail."

"But what if..."

"They're not going to do that," he replied, working the needle through the cotton. "And it sends it all back to us in real-time, beautiful technology."

He held the shirt up to Scott and smiled.

"You're all set."

———

A blue Neon sign lit the doorway that read: '*Leopold Boutique Hotel*'.

Scott pushed the door and entered the lobby. A man at reception raised his head above a computer screen. "Sorry, we have no vacancies, sir."

"I'm here to see Rachel."

"In that case, come this way."

The receptionist walked around the desk and guided

Scott through a corridor. The muffled sound of music got louder as they walked.

As they reached a large set of doors, the receptionist produced a key, unlocked them, and thrust one open.

"Enjoy," the receptionist said.

Scott stepped into the large hotel bar, his eyes adjusting to the gloom as the door locked behind him. Everyone stared at him, and as he stood hoping the camera would pick anything up in the low light, Angela appeared. She wore tight blue jeans, knee-high leather boots and a sparkling blouse, her face thick with make-up.

"Thanks for coming," she said, taking him by the arm and walking them to the bar. "Don't worry, they always stare at the new people."

She held a finger up to the barman and placed her glass on the bar. "You're just in time for my little speech. I'm a tad nervous, to be honest." Angela scanned the room with suspicion and turned back to Scott. "You weren't followed, were you?"

Scott had taken similar measures as before, almost certain no one followed him. But did it matter when he was working for the government, anyway? He'd only done it in case Angela's people had him followed again.

"I don't think so," Scott replied, shrugging.

"Good, good," she murmured, looking away, more concerned about her speech than him being followed.

The barman slid over a tall sky-blue drink with black dots floating in the liquid.

Scott narrowed his eyes. "What's this?"

Angela giggled. "Our signature cocktail; Flying Ant Day." He took a sip.

"Gin, Curacao, tonic and tiny chunks of blackcurrant.

Sounds vile, tastes divine." She clinked her glass to his. "Now, speech time."

Angela patted him on the arm and strode towards a small stage where a man pulled her up. The music stopped, and a spotlight followed her as she strode to the middle of the stage. A curtain fell behind her, revealing a red and black logo of a large, winged ant. The man passed her a microphone. The assembled crowd moved towards the stage and started clapping. Scott stayed at the bar.

"This is our first meeting since David's death," she began, looking at Scott for a second. "And though we mourn him, we must continue our fight."

A murmur of approval spread through the room.

"The continuation of our plan is vital. We know the risks we take. We know not everyone will make it to the end."

On stage, Angela became a different person. She had the audience in the palm of her hand, and as she went on, her voice grew louder, whipping them into a frenzy. They clapped and cheered after almost every sentence.

Scott relaxed, taking in the atmosphere, then after a few minutes, she pointed at him.

"And tonight, we have a new member I would like to introduce to you, an old friend of mine, Scott."

Everybody turned to face him. He held up his glass and smiled.

Angela smiled back. "Please treat him as a friend. I vouch you can trust him."

A few people shouted welcoming phrases.

"We can and will bring this government down," she bellowed, her voice becoming hoarse. "The ants will take over the house, no matter how many times they stamp on us, or pour boiling water on us. There will always be more to attack them. We are strong, we are many." She stepped to the front of the stage and lowered her voice. "Flying Ant Day is sooner than they can imagine." She paused for a few seconds, then raised her voice again. "Now we party."

The crowd burst into applause. Scott found himself joining in as the music started again, louder than before, and scores of people headed towards the bar. A few shook Scott's hand or patted him on the shoulder, welcoming him. As one man offered to get him a drink, a tall woman in a suit appeared and leant into Scott's ear.

"Mrs Newton would like to see you backstage," she said.

————

'Backstage' turned out to be a private room, better lit than the bar and guarded by another woman in a suit. Inside, Angela, still flushed with adrenaline, held court, talking with three other people. A large black man, who appeared to be in his fifties; a younger pink-haired woman, even thinner than Angela, and Martin, the man in the tartan shirt, today smartly dressed in a blue suit with his long hair tied back in a ponytail. Angela stopped mid-sentence when she saw Scott and waved him over.

"What did you think of my speech?" she said, pulling a bottle of champagne from a bucket.

Before Scott could answer, she handed him a glass and put her arm around his shoulders.

"This man here is going to be very important to us," she announced to the group. Scott sipped the champagne. "He's the one I've been telling you about."

"All good, I hope," Scott joked.

"Of course," Angela replied, squeezing him. "Let me introduce you. This is Sarge. He used to be in the army."

The large black man held out a hand, and Scott shook it. "Nice to meet you."

"Still has lots of very important contacts in the army," Angela said. Sarge smiled. "Oh yes I do."

Angela turned to the pink-haired woman. "And this cutie is Lauren." The woman clinked her glass against Scott's. "She's our finance guru...numbers and all that. And of course, you've met Martin before."

"Yeah," Scott said, shaking hands with him, "Nice to meet you guys." They eyed Scott suspiciously and an awkward silence fell upon the room. Angela's arm fell from his shoulders, and she put down her glass. "You can trust him, I promise."

"You should mingle outside now, Angela," Sarge said.

She rolled her eyes. "I can't think of anything worse, let's at least have a few more drinks before all that nonsense."

Right on cue, a waiter appeared at the door with a tray of 'Flying Ant Day' cocktails. Scott took one, relieved there was no search, not even a pat-down, yet here he was, in the inner sanctum, camera rolling.

Martin came and stood next to him. "She speaks well, right?"

"Yeah, she seemed like a different person up there."

"She's amazing, a real asset to the movement, heart of gold, and steel." They watched her as she laughed with Lauren.

"What was David like?"

"Oh, a different kettle of fish. He got us where we are now, and that's not to be sniffed at. But we needed a change of direction."

Scott moved, so the camera faced Martin. "What's the new direction?"

Martin laughed. "More aggressive. But don't worry about that now, mate. Just enjoy tonight," he replied, slapping Scott's shoulder. "Parties like this are few and far between. Chill."

As they spoke, Sarge and Lauren kept flashing glances towards him.

Scott raised an eyebrow and said, "Those two don't look so chilled."

Martin laughed again. "No, it's true, but you have to be a bit suspicious of everyone. Don't worry, Angela vouches for you one hundred per cent. She just needs to convince everyone else." Angela skipped over and took Scott by the hand. "Come with me, I'm going to initiate you."

She led him across the corridor and knocked on a door. A low female voice from within answered, "Enter."

"I do this to all the new recruits, you'll love it," Angela said, giggling and striding inside.

As they ventured through the door, the pungent scent of marijuana hit them. Through the darkness, Scott could make out a figure lying on a couch, smoke billowing around her.

Angela whispered to him, "Have you ever had your tarot cards read?"

"No."

"Really? I like to know what fate has planned for people."

They sat on the floor in front of a small table. The woman pulled herself up to a sitting position. "Good evening, mistress."

"Hi," Angela said. "I have a new one for you to read."

The woman passed a joint to Angela, who inhaled deeply before handing it to Scott. Eight years of being in the police force, with random drug tests and the now Draconian drug laws, meant he hadn't touched marijuana since university. "I haven't done this for years, Angie, I..."

"Oh God, just do it, it won't kill you."

Scott inhaled, slowly at first, then took a second, stronger pull. The room swam for a moment, then settled down. He stared at the woman, noticing how young she was, her gaunt face disappearing and reappearing through the smoke. Angela nudged his knee and the tarot reader held out her hand. He passed the joint back.

"This isn't my usual tarot reader," Angela said. "She couldn't make it, but this is her daughter. It's in the blood."

"Really?" he said, stifling both a cough and laughter.

"Yes, really."

They passed the joint around for a few minutes in silence.

"This is like our Uni days, isn't it?" he said after a while.

"I suppose so," Angela muttered.

The adrenaline from the speech had gone, and coupled with the joint, she was a shadow of the Angela on stage.

The girl looked at Angela. "Let's begin the reading. Don't worry, this won't take long, it will be a simple one card spread." She gestured for Scott to lean forward. "You first, sir."

She spread the cards face down and asked him to pick one. The weed, drink, and strangeness of the situation were funny to him.

"Is this where I pick the death card and the episode ends?" he laughed. Angela nudged him again.

"Pick a card, sir," the woman repeated.

He tapped a card and she flipped it over.

"The two of pentacles," she announced. "This card is about balance; you have two factors in your life which are hard to maintain equally."

Angela leant forward and studied the card.

"You are doing a good job of it," the woman said, then took a long draw of the joint, "so far."

Angela looked from the girl to Scott. "Does that sound right?"

Scott shrugged and said, "I suppose so."

He imagined Henry watching the video of this somewhere.

"Ensure you keep the energy to adapt, nothing can be in perfect equilibrium," she droned on, "but done correctly, it can be in near harmony."

She stared at Scott and passed him the joint. He inhaled deeply and coughed.

The girl nodded at Angela. "One for you, madam?"

"Oh, go on then."

She held a hand above the spread-out cards and picked one. The girl turned it over. "The Empress."

"Sounds about right, now come on, let's get out and meet the people." Angela got to her feet and thanked the tarot reader. Scott spun his head as he stood and walked to the door.

"Why don't you pick one?" he asked, turning back.

The woman flipped over a card. A rider on a white horse.

"Death," she said dramatically.

Scott laughed and followed Angela out of the room. She pulled a pocket mirror out of her bag and touched up her makeup.

"Interesting," she said, applying blusher to her cheeks, "a balancing act, eh?"

Scott leant against the wall, his head swimming. "You believe that stuff?"

She snapped the mirror shut and looked him in the eye, "Yes I do."

A swarm of people engulfed Angela the moment the door opened. Everybody wanted a piece of her, and within seconds, they became separated. The music pounded in the background, red and green lights spun around the room. The Flying Ant logo on the stage loomed over everything. A waiter passed and Scott took a cocktail from the silver tray, then staggered to a booth in the corner and sat down. Sarge sat there sipping a beer. "Strange innit, what card did you get?"

"The two of pentacles."

"Interesting."

"Is it?"

"Fuck knows, mate, it's all nonsense to me." Sarge laughed, a loud deep sound booming above the music. He held up his bottle and said, "welcome."

"Thanks."

"I hope we can trust you," Sarge said, getting up. "I really do."

Sarge excused himself and disappeared into the crowd. A waiter came over and he took another drink as Angela mingled with her followers.

Soon, Scott couldn't see her anymore. A woman appeared in the darkness in front of him. He squinted to make her out; the tarot card reader. She wore angel wings on her back, glittering as the lights hit them.

She extended a hand. "Dance?"

"No, I..."

She grabbed him and he let her pull him to the dance-floor. They danced for a couple of songs, any inhibitions slipping away by the second. Her dancing became more manic as they went. The atmosphere had shifted, and no one paid any attention, everyone looked intoxicated. Scott looked around for Angela, but still couldn't see her.

The tarot reader took his head and kissed him on the lips. "Follow me. I'm Olympia by the way."

Before he could answer, she took his hand again and led him to the door.

———

THE BRIGHT LOBBY and ringing in his ears sobered him up for a second. Olympia pressed the lift button and jumped up and down, clapping her hands.

"This is so much fun!" she screamed.

The lift doors opened with a ping. She dragged him inside and pushed him against the mirrored wall.

"But the real party is upstairs."

She kissed him again, and this time, he kissed her back, holding her waist. She lifted her leg against his and grasped his belt as the lift stopped.

Reaching a room, Olympia tapped the card against the handle, pushed the door open and ran to the bed. She picked up a bag and produced a large bottle of rum from inside, swigging from it. Scott walked over, took the bottle from her and guzzled a large mouthful.

Olympia eyed him curiously. "You and Angela aren't, you know, fucking?"

"Oh God no," he said, wiping his mouth.

"Good, I don't want to intrude on anything," she said, rummaging through the bag. She took out a needle and spoon and glanced at Scott. "Before you ask, yes, this is heroin, but I'm not an addict."

Her arm was covered in needle marks.

Her wings crumpled as she leant against a stack of pillows. "Don't judge me."

Though it shocked him, he tried to sound casual. "No, it's fine, whatever."

Olympia took out a small bag of brown powder and a lighter, and Scott drank some more rum.

"I'm going to use the bathroom."

Scott looked in the mirror, his reflection spinning as he held the button camera to his mouth.

"Thanks guys," he said.

When he came out, Olympia stood on the bed in her black underwear, a finger held out, beckoning him towards her.

———

Scott awoke to silence and rolled over. Olympia sat in a chair, naked except for his half-unbuttoned shirt, lit by the bedside lamp.

She injected a needle into her arm and said, "Enjoy?"

"God yeah," he groaned, sidling across the bed towards her.

She put the needle down. "This shit is gonna hit me in about thirty seconds and it's going be glorious." She crossed her legs and picked up the rum, spilling some as she drank. "Oh God, I got some on your shirt."

Olympia wiped at it, catching the top button as she did so. She stopped suddenly.

"What the fuck?" she exclaimed.

She gripped the button and ripped off the shirt, her hands following the wire to the battery in the seam.

Olympia scowled. "You fucking arsehole. Who are you?"

He scrambled across the bed, "No, listen..."

"You're a spy." she realised, and her tone grew. "There's a spy here! A spy, Scott is a spy!"

Olympia hammered her fists against the wall as she shouted. She reached for the bedside phone, but Scott wrenched it from her and threw it into the corner. He held a hand across her mouth.

"Be quiet, I can explain," he said through gritted teeth, straining to hold her still.

Olympia kicked out, and Scott struggled to hold her, but her kicks eventually slowed until she fell unconscious onto the chair. He stood, terrified, his heart pumping, not knowing what to do. She slid onto the floor and began convulsing, her body twisting, foaming at the mouth.

Automatically, he knelt to begin CPR on her, but paused. She had seen too much. He stepped into the bathroom, retching with fear, and turned on the taps, shutting out the sounds of her body thrashing against the floor.

When he came out, Olympia lay still. Scott pressed two fingers to her neck, feeling for a pulse. She was dead.

He took the shirt and put it back on, shaking, and a loud knock at the door broke the silence.

Chapter Seven

As the banging at the door intensified, Scott ran to the bathroom, locked himself inside, and flushed the wire down the toilet.

"Open the door now."

"One second," he shouted, watching in horror as the button, wire, and battery pack floated to the surface.

The main door opened, and somebody gasped as he fished out the wire. "Who's in there?" a female voice shouted as they knocked at the bathroom door. He opened the cistern and dropped in the wire before opening the door.

———

Lauren, in a pair of shorts and t-shirt, her pink hair ruffled, looked him up and down. "You? What the hell happened here?"

"She must have overdosed; I woke up and found her like this," Scott said, his lips trembling as he spoke.

In the corner, a suited woman knelt over Olympia and then stood up. "She's dead."

Lauren smacked her palm on the wall. "Fuck. I heard a commotion from next door, shouting and banging. What was that?"

Scott shrugged. "I don't know, it woke me as well."

He lifted his head and Lauren watched him. "I'm going to have to call Angela, don't move an inch."

Lauren instructed the suited woman to guard the door and left. Olympia lay in the recovery position, her open eyes staring at him. Scott shuddered and reached for the rum.

Lauren returned in a hotel dressing gown, a mobile phone clamped to her ear.

"She's not picking up, but Sarge is on his way." She stopped and looked at the body. "Did you take any?"

"Any what?"

"Heroin."

"No, of course not."

"This doesn't look good, Scott, does it?"

"You think I had something to do with this? She over-dosed. Anyone can see that. You think I killed her?"

Lauren shrugged. "I'm not a detective. But we'll find out."

———

"WELL, THIS IS A SHIT SHOW," Sarge declared, taking in the scene. "Any sign of Angela?"

"Can't reach her," Lauren said, "but we'll keep trying."

Sarge stared at the body, then turned to Scott, "So, what happened?"

Scott rubbed at his temples, looking at the carpet. "I

woke up and she was hitting the wall, screaming, then collapsed and started shaking."

Lauren frowned. "And you didn't call anyone?"

"I freaked out. She started convulsing. I just ran to the bathroom."

"You didn't try to save her?" Sarge questioned.

"I couldn't have done anything."

"You could have tried CPR, mouth to mouth or something. You're an ex copper? No wonder they got rid of you." Sarge stood over the body. "Such a shame, her mum's gonna be distraught. But at least you had your fun, eh?"

Scott scowled. "What's that supposed to mean?"

"Calm down, lover boy, don't worry."

Scott reached for his shoes and said, "This is bullshit."

Sarge stiffened. "You're not going anywhere, Scott." He kicked a shoe across the room. "Not till Angela gets here."

"She's on her way," Lauren announced, looking at her phone with trembling hands.

Sarge looked up. "Does she know what happened?"

"No, I just said it's an emergency."

———

THE SUITED WOMAN opened the door to Angela.

"So, what's worth dragging me out of bed at 2 am for? This better be..." Angela stopped, noticing Olympia's naked body. "Oh my God." She raised a hand to her mouth. "What happened?"

Nobody said a word.

"What happened?" Angela demanded.

Sarge broke the silence. "Scott?"

Angela looked at him. "What the..."

"Angie, look, she overdosed. I couldn't do anything about it."

Angela flew into a fit of rage. "Why were you here in the first place? I bet she's young enough to be your daughter. Did you sleep with her?"

"Well..."

She moved towards him, her face contorted with anger.

"Did you sleep with her?" she screamed.

"Yes."

Angela covered her mouth again and turned away. "I don't believe it."

Scott told his story again, that he woke to find Olympia overdosing and panicked. Angela didn't say a word as she stood with her back to the room, staring at the wall.

"So, what do we do now?" Sarge asked.

"We get rid of the body," Angela hissed. "No way we can call an ambulance, we'll give away too much."

She stopped, then looked at Scott.

"This whole place," she said, flinging her arms into the air, "is a front for us, Scott, for the resistance. Do you get that? You're in danger of jeopardising everything with this." A tear rolled down her face. "I don't believe it."

"She overdosed. What could I do, Ang?"

"Shut up," she screamed.

Everyone stared at her. She composed herself and looked at the body.

"Sarge, call down and ask for one of those big laundry baskets. Lauren, call Martin and tell him to bring a van, some spades and a bag of quicklime."

She leant forward with her hands on her knees, her face inches from Scott's, twitching with anger. "You're going to bury her."

———

Angela put the phone into her pocket.

"He's here," she said.

Sarge lifted Olympia's body into the basket, folding a leg down to fit her inside, and covered her with sheets. Angela watched on in disgust. "You guys search the room, clean it up," she ordered. "Scott and I are going on a drive."

"I don't know what to say, Angie, please understand, this was a terrible accident," Scott pleaded as he pushed the basket to the service lift. "Don't talk to me," Angela said through gritted teeth.

They reached the car park where Martin leant against a van, smoking. Scott could just make out the writing on it: '*Smith's Catering: For any occasion.*'

"Help us get this in," Angela said.

"Yes, boss," Martin replied, sliding the doors open.

They lifted the basket into the back, wedging it between wooden boxes. Martin secured them with ropes and covered them with a tarpaulin sheet.

"We'll take it from here," Angela said.

"Ok, good luck," Martin said, "and be careful."

He threw the keys to her, which she immediately passed to Scott. "You're driving, I'll direct you."

As they climbed into the front seats, Angela took an ID card from the glove compartment. A perfect forgery, his face, with the name Scott Smith.

"Use this one," she said, putting on a blonde wig.

"Don't I get a disguise?"

"No one knows who you are, just shut up and drive."

"What about roadblocks?" he asked, starting the engine.

Since the change, roadblocks surrounded London, checking everyone who came in and out of the capital.

Angela adjusted her wig in the rear-view mirror. "I've got that covered."

They drove in silence through the empty streets, Angela occasionally telling him which road to take, the anger etched on her face in the orange glow of the passing streetlights.

"Angie, she took too much heroin. Can you blame me for that?"

Angela didn't move a muscle.

The horror of Olympia's convulsing body would not leave him for a long time, and he worried what Henry would think about the bug being destroyed with Scott still in the company of Angela and the resistance. They headed to the outskirts of the city, and he tapped the steering wheel nervously.

"Are you sure the checkpoint won't be a problem?"

"Our people man checkpoint 206," she said, stroking the wig. "Drive."

As the checkpoint came into view, she held up a finger. "Let me do the talking."

They rolled up to the barrier and Scott opened the window. Angela looked at the soldier.

"Unusually warm night for May, isn't it?" she said, leaning over Scott, the wig brushing his face.

The soldier looked back at her, confused. "ID please."

Angela whispered as she leant back, "Shit, this is wrong, these aren't our people."

She scrambled around in the glove compartment as Scott handed over his ID card.

"What's your business and what's in the back?" the soldier enquired.

Angela fiddled in the glove compartment. "My husband and I are coming back from an event. We're caterers."

"Does your husband talk, Madam?"

"When she lets me," Scott replied.

The soldier laughed. Angela was still bent over, her hands shaking.

She whispered again, "Something's wrong, we're fucked."

Then, sitting up whilst pushing the wig out of her face, she smiled and passed the soldier a card.

He examined both and handed them back. "Ok, let's have a look then. Keys, please."

"Do it," Angela whispered.

Scott passed over the keys and the soldier walked to the side door, slid it open, and stepped inside. After lifting the tarpaulin, he looked through the boxes.

As Scott started to ask what they should do, Angela reached under the chair and pulled out a gun, fitted with a matt black silencer. She spun and fired; the soldier slumped forward over a box. Ahead, the two other soldiers looked up, then continued talking. She took a set of keys from the glove compartment and plunged them into Scott's hand.

"Floor it, aim for the middle of the barrier, I'll deal with those two."

He started the engine and hit the accelerator. The two soldiers charged towards them, guns at the ready. Angela opened the window and fired, hitting one of the soldiers in the chest. He fell to the ground as they hit the barrier, the van momentarily slowing before bursting through. Gunfire rang out. The wing mirror on Angela's side exploded. Keeping her body in the van, she reached outside and fired again. In the rear-view mirror, Scott saw the other soldier collapse to the ground.

"Gotcha." Angela shouted.

They flew down the road, Scott driving on pure adrenaline, eyes fixed ahead.

Angela leant back into the van and said, "No one seems to be following us, but we need to get rid of this van ASAP."

Words caught in Scott's throat as he tried to reply.

"I don't know if we can make it to the forest," Angela said. "Let's try Plan B. Take the next left and keep fast."

As they skidded around the corner, she took out her phone. "Mutt, it's me. Change of plan. We're coming to the farm first. See you soon."

"Mutt?"

"We were going to his after you buried her." She pointed a thumb towards the back of the van. "But now, we'll have to go first."

"Yeah, but Mutt?"

"That's not his actual name."

"I gathered that."

"Keep driving, you're still in my bad books."

————

THEY PULLED onto a muddy path by a farmhouse. A man, well over six feet and with a bushy beard, embraced Angela as they stepped from the van.

"It got a bit hairy back there. Slight issue at the checkpoint, we need to lose this van," she explained.

"You can put it in the barn. What's in it?"

"Couple of dead bodies."

"Right," Mutt said, unphased.

"Can we take your tractor?"

"Anything for you, dear," Mutt replied, and he eyed Scott up and down. "Who's this fella?"

"This is Scott, he's got us into this mess tonight and he's going to get us out of it."

Scott drove the van into the barn, and they rolled out the laundry basket containing the bodies. Mutt helped him lift it onto a trailer along with the shovels and lime.

"You still remember how to drive one of these, love?" Mutt asked as he attached the trailer to a tractor.

Angela gave a twitch of a smile. "It's like riding a bike."

On the main road, two military motorcycles shot past, lights flashing. They watched them disappear over the hill.

Mutt explained the route to take, and they climbed into the tractor's cab, waving him goodbye.

"We'll be back before you know it," Angela said to Mutt.

She pulled a lever and the vehicle shuddered into life.

"I need a quiet night in soon," she said as they bounced along the field. Scott couldn't make out if her mood had changed.

"Angie, I can't believe you just killed three people."

"I'm not entirely sure the other two are dead," she said, nearly falling out the cab as they hit a bump. "And I can't believe you had sex with a 25-year-old drug addict."

"Oh, please..."

"Don't 'oh please' me."

Scott started to reply, but Angela shushed him. They bounced along for a few more minutes, the sky ahead lightening all the time and birds beginning to sing. The sun would be up soon. Dressed as he was in a torn shirt, with only one button holding it together, the cold air made him shiver. Angela couldn't have been much warmer in her leather jacket, jeans, and white trainers, still in the blonde wig.

"We don't look much like farmers, do we?"

The hint of a smile crossed her lips. "No, I suppose not."

They reached a wooded area, and Angela stopped the tractor, keeping the engine running to provide enough light. The beams shone into the forest.

Angela pointed ahead as they stepped through the trees. "Here."

"Have you done this before?" he asked, rubbing his hands together, trying to keep warm.

She wrinkled her face. "What do you think I am?"

"I don't know, Angie."

Scott started to dig. Angela sat on a fallen tree trunk, smoking. When he had made a shallow grave, he sat against the trunk, his body aching. Despite the cold and lack of suitable clothing, the sweat dripped off him. Angela shivered as she watched. "Hard work, isn't it? Now get the bodies."

Scott trudged back to the trailer and lifted off the cover. Olympia's body lay half covered by the sheet. He wretched as he looked at her. "Hurry," Angela shouted, "It's getting light."

Scott wrapped the sheet around the body, then slung it over his shoulder. He hurried into the forest, desperate to be rid of her stiff body. As he threw her into the hole, a foot poked out from under the sheet. He knelt and wretched, then returned to the trailer, not looking back at Angela. The soldier's body was heavy, and he dragged it by the feet before rolling it into the hole beside Olympia.

"Don't forget the lime," Angela said. "It'll stop the smell."

Returning to the trailer, Scott dragged the bag of lime, pouring it onto the bodies before covering them with earth. After finishing, he lay on the ground, exhausted.

Angela put her hand on his. "It's OK, Scott."

"It's not OK, this is a nightmare," he said between sobs, "a fucking nightmare."

Angela helped him up, and they darted back to the tractor, then drove back to the farmhouse in silence, the sun rising above the fields. Mutt let them in and made tea before disappearing upstairs.

"I need to sleep so bad," Scott said, finishing his cup.

Angela lit another cigarette. "I can imagine. Have a shower first though, please."

Scott showered, and she showed him to a room.

"Mutt always keeps some rooms free for us," Angela explained, sitting at the end of the bed and looking out the window as he drifted into sleep. "I'm sorry I got so angry before."

"It's OK," he murmured.

He wanted her to leave, to shut everything out and go to sleep, so he faked snoring.

After a few minutes, Angela stirred.

"I got jealous," she said.

He continued the snore as she got up and left.

———

Scott awoke from a nightmare of Olympia's distorted body staggering across the room towards him, and screamed out, soaked with sweat. The horrors of the night before came rushing back, and his entire body ached.

Angela's face appeared at the door, "Everything OK?"

"Bad dream," he said, stretching out. "What time is it?"

"Nearly midday, you'd better get ready. We're leaving soon."

———

THEY SAID their goodbyes to Mutt and got into Martin's car.

"This checkpoint thing, it's all over the news," Martin said as they pulled away, "except they didn't mention the dead soldiers."

Angela snorted. "I bet they didn't. Where were our guys at 206? I don't get it, they've never let us down before."

"Maybe they were compromised. Who knows?" Martin said.

"Where are we going?" Scott asked.

Angela folded her arms. "A safe house. We need to stay out of the city for a bit. We can't risk another checkpoint for a while."

They arrived at a cottage on the outskirts of an Essex village with ivy growing up the front wall, black and white Tudor style timber, and the front garden full of rosebushes. Under other circumstances, it would have looked idyllic.

Martin hauled two suitcases from the boot.

"This is your home for the next few days, guys." He looked Scott up and down. "Jesus, bro, thank God we bought some clothes for you."

"Call us when you think it's safe," Angela said, her boots crunching the gravel as she walked to the door.

"Will do," Martin replied.

They stood on the drive in silence as he drove away.

———

SCOTT EXPLORED the cottage while Angela unpacked a laptop at the dining table. He passed her a cup of tea, holding his own tightly to warm his hands. "How many of these safe houses are there?"

She tapped away at the keyboard. "More than you can imagine."

He pulled up a chair opposite her. "What are you doing?"

"Our computer people sent me some files to look at. They hacked the government server or something."

Scott raised an eyebrow. "Anything interesting?"

"It's footage from their undercover spies' cameras. Recorded last night."

He choked on the tea. "Do you need to look at that now, can't we rest for a bit?"

"We can rest when the government is brought down," Angela said. She hit a button and leant forward. "So many files, so many files."

Scott stood and walked around to look at the screen, his heart racing.

Angela put down her teacup. "Oh, I can search by location."

She loaded up a map. Above the Leopold Hotel, a blue dot appeared, 'ONE FILE.'

She clicked it and the video played.

"Damn it, no sound," she muttered.

Scott watched in horror as the black and white video played at double speed. The receptionist greeting him, being led down the corridor, the doors opening, Angela welcoming him, taking him to the bar, getting him a drink...

She slammed the laptop shut. "You bastard."

Chapter Eight

When Miriam got home, she considered calling the estate agent to put the house up for sale, as the Israelis had suggested. But she didn't want anyone to know she was selling the house, least of all Scott. It could wait until she was settled in Israel. She had enough savings for the immediate future. Her parents' healthy inheritance, despite being drained by the loss of her teaching job, would be sufficient for a while.

She called Carla, an old work colleague who lived nearby, asking her to come over for a 'quick chat'. Then she sat down and wrote a letter to Scott.

Dear Scott,

It breaks my heart to write this letter. I never wanted it to come to this, but I'm leaving with Benji. I cannot tell you where we are going, but as soon as it's safe, I promise I will contact you. This is for me and Benji's safety. We are not safe here. Please try to not be angry with me, maybe one day we will come back. I loved you truly, Scott, and you will always have a place in my heart, but try to understand. It brings me no joy to take your son away, but I genuinely fear for our lives.

Goodbye,

Miriam.

She wiped a tear away, sealed the envelope and climbed the stairs. Benji stood at the top, looking at her inquisitively. "Where are we going, Mummy?"

"We're going on a holiday."

"How long for?"

She climbed the stairs to him and rubbed his head. "I'm not sure."

———

CARLA ARRIVED before Miriam could begin packing. "I came as quickly as I could. You sounded worried on the phone, is everything OK?"

Miriam shrugged. "Come in, I'll explain."

Carla shook the remnants of the freak summer shower from her umbrella and followed Miriam inside. "What's happening, M?"

"Come and sit down first."

"Oh no," Carla said, taking off her hat and letting her afro hair spring loose. "This sounds serious."

"It is."

She sat Carla down in the kitchen and began making two cups of tea. "I'm going away, with Benji. I don't know how long for, but I needed to tell someone."

Carla blew out her cheeks and drummed the table. "I always knew this day would come. Israel, I take it?"

"I can't say. Sorry, but I really can't."

Carla cocked her head. "Why now, after everything that's already happened?"

"I can't say that either, but I don't feel safe here anymore."

"When they brought in the rules that Jews couldn't teach any more, I expected you to leave then. I'm surprised you stuck around so long."

Miriam sat opposite her, sliding a mug towards Carla. "How are things at the school now?"

"Same old, same old. The curriculum is a joke. Everyone is on tenterhooks about saying the wrong thing, but at least I still have a job, right? I thought if anything, they'd get rid of us first. Don't know why they bothered with you. No offence, but we're a more visible minority, right? The whole Anti-Jewish thing is so 1930s."

There had been rumours of a coming crackdown on other minorities, but though the country expected it to happen, it never came. One theory was that the government feared race riots, an eruption of both anger from the black community and subsequent retaliation from whites.

"Are you worried you won't have a job for long?" Miriam asked.

"As I always say, M, they need us. There's more of us than you guys and they need all the workers they can get. I'm not saying it's easy, racism is practically legal now. The whole atmosphere is tense. The Britain First agenda breeds racism. But it's not like it was great before, anyway. I worry about my children. Everyone's children, in fact." Carla shook her head. "Anyway, that's my shit. Are you ever coming back?"

Miriam had considered this, and whilst she would like to return, it would be impossible under the current regime.

"I don't know. It's happened so fast I haven't had time to

process it. But it could be forever, well, until this government goes. I'm leaving tomorrow morning. The only people
I'm telling are you and Scott."

Carla rolled her eyes at the mention of his name. Miriam
regretted venting too much about their breakup to her and had
never been able to pull it back. Carla had started at the school
around the time of the breakup, and they had become close fast.

"How are things with him?"

"Not good."

"You're better off without him in your life, M."

"He's Benji's dad, he's always going to be in my life."

"Well, keep your distance. Think about it, he's got no
job, he drinks too much. Total waste of space. It's better to
have no father than a role model like that. He's a drain on
you mentally."

Carla's criticism of Scott stung. She had never met him,
only heard via Miriam what he was like. The breakup had
been painful, and Miriam knew deep down that Scott was a
good man, but the circumstances had changed him.

"His parents' deaths hit him hard. He was never the
same after that. Then the change happened...but you're
right, we're not compatible anymore."

"I'm pleased to hear you say that. A few months ago,
you sounded like you wanted to try again with him."

"I did, but not anymore."

"OK, well I hope so. Anyway, did you hear that David
Newton got killed? Or..." Carla made inverted commas
with her fingers. "...had a heart attack."

"Yeah, I saw."

Carla tilted her head. "Didn't Scott used to date his
wife or something?"

Scott's long-ago relationship with the woman married to

the resistance leader had caused huge problems when the change came. The new regime had interrogated both Scott and Miriam at length, before eventually clearing them of any resistance activity. Yet Miriam always felt they were being watched closely.

"They were together at uni."

"God, I saw her on the news yesterday. There's something not right about her either. If she's our best hope, then we're finished." Carla laughed. "So, will you be able to contact me once you get out?"

"As soon as I can, I'll let you know we're safe." Miriam leant across and hugged Carla. "Don't tell anyone I'm going away, even if they ask. I need to keep this quiet until I share it."

"Your secret is safe with me, M."

They finished their tea in silence, Miriam thinking about the enormity of what she was about to do and trying to read what Carla was thinking.

As Carla left, they hugged again at the door. "Remember to let me know when you're safely out, M."

Miriam nodded. "I will, and you stay safe as well, Carla."

"Don't worry about me, if they come for us, all hell will break loose."

———

ALL NIGHT MIRIAM tossed and turned, unable to sleep. With every sound, she sat up, worrying the government would stop her fleeing.

Right on six o'clock, a silver Mercedes van pulled up outside. A short man stepped out. He stopped, looked up and down the road, then headed towards the house. The doorbell rang as she walked into the hallway.

She put her face to the door. "Yes?"

A cheery voice answered. "Taxi to the airport, flight to Luxembourg."

She took a deep breath. "OK, one minute."

Benji stood in the hallway, rubbing his eyes. "Are we going now?"

Miriam turned to him. "Yes, let's go."

The man helped them carry the suitcases and boxes to the car. She paused, gave the house a last look, and got into the car.

"Ready?" he asked.

"Yes."

Then, with a long slow look around the street, he slammed the doors shut.

"How long is the drive?" Miriam asked as they pulled away.

Still cheery, the driver looked in the mirror at her. "At this time of day, about an hour."

He picked up a radio, said something in Hebrew, then turned to her as they pulled up to the traffic lights.

"Don't worry, it'll fly by," he assured.

Miriam tapped her leg and looked out the window. "What about checkpoints?"

"As I said, don't worry."

"There's a letter I need to drop off on the way. To Smedley Street, Clapham."

"Sure, no problem."

———

They arrived at Scott's house. She looked at every window for signs of life as she got out of the car. There were no lights on, no twitch of a curtain, nothing. She dropped the letter through the door and ran back to the car without looking back.

She wished she could sleep as easily as Benji did in the car. Already, the sun was warm, beating through the windows against her face. She closed her eyes and told herself that everything would be fine. For the first time in days, she was calm.

The driver's voice startled her. "When we reach the checkpoint, don't speak and everything will be good, OK?"

Miriam nodded.

"Good. I will raise this screen for a few minutes whilst I talk to them."

The driver hit a button on the dashboard and a thick tinted screen rose, fitting flush into the ceiling.

Then a crackle, and his voice came through a speaker. "It may get hot back there now, I'll put on the air-con, OK?"

There was a click and cool air rushed through two vents in the doors. It smelt strange, and after a couple of breaths, her vision blurred. Then dizziness came over her.

She shouted out, but the driver didn't move, and no sound came from the speakers. She started to slip from consciousness and held Benji, shaking him, but he was fast asleep.

The air coming from the vents was a pale yellow, and she thumped the screen. "What are you doing? Help us, let us out."

Miriam pulled frantically at the door handle, but it wouldn't open. Becoming dizzy, she pulled her jacket over her face, then took off her shoe and banged the window.

"Let us out, let us out." she screamed. "Please!"

Benji's head slumped forward. She lifted him up and her head spun. With the next breath, she blacked out.

———

Miriam awoke to being shaken with a droning sound in the background. She recalled being in the back of the car and the screen going up; the gas coming out.

As she leant forward, a seatbelt pulled her back. She was in a sitting position, and swung her head around, everything still a blur.

"Benji," she tried to shout, but her voice came out croaky and quiet.

The shaking had stopped. A few blinks and her vision returned. She was inside a plane.

Benji sat in the seat next to her, strapped in and snoring. His chest rising and falling in slow breaths. She held his face in both hands, and the plane shook again, this time harder, lifting her out of the seat, the belt straining against her lap, then forcing her back down as they dropped. Clenching her teeth, Miriam gripped the armrest in fear. Trying to focus on something else, she noticed all the other seats had boxes on them, covered in plastic. The trembling stopped as the plane burst through the clouds. Sunlight lit the cabin.

"Mrs Roth," a voice said.

Miriam looked around and laid eyes on a man stood in the aisle.

"I hope you are well," he said, glancing at Benji. "Ah, the boy is still asleep."

"What the hell happened in that car, why..."

The man interrupted her. "We find it easier to make our passengers more... relaxed during the escape."

Miriam ripped off the seatbelt and leant towards him. "By gassing us? Are you serious?"

"Please, Mrs Roth, it's for the best. And perfectly safe."

She thrust a finger at Benji. "What about him? Gassing a ten-year-old, is that 'perfectly safe?'" Benji stirred in his sleep. "I mean, for fuck's sake, we're escaping to Israel and you're gassing people. Do you see the irony here?"

The man squirmed and perched on the armrest of the seat.

"I apologise. But I have good news." He reached into the air steward's trolley beside him and handed her a glass of champagne. "We just left UK airspace." He poured a glass for himself, took a sip and clinked it against hers. "You're free."

Chapter Nine

Angela looked down at the table. "Before you say anything, get me the fucking wine."

Scott's hands shook as he fetched the glasses, nearly dropping one in the process.

A gun clicked behind him, then Angela's voice. "What's stopping me from killing you now?"

Scott swallowed hard and put the glasses down.

"I said get me the fucking wine," she shouted.

Splashes of wine hit the counter as he struggled to pour it. He turned back. She stood behind the table, both hands on the gun, pointed at Scott's chest.

"Any quick moves and I swear to God I'll shoot your traitorous face off."

He pushed a glass towards her, and she moved a hand from the gun to take a mouthful.

"I can explain, Angie."

"Oh, you can always fucking *explain*, can't you?" she barked, lips blood red from the wine.

"They forced me to do it."

"It's one thing after the other with you, isn't it? I have no hesitation in pulling this trigger now, Scott."

What he said next could be the difference between living and dying.

"I had no choice. They were threatening Benji's life. You said yourself they would come for me again."

Angela reached for the wine again and downed the glass, all the time keeping the gun fixed on him. "Well, why didn't you tell me?"

Scott couldn't find the words to explain it. "I don't know, I..."

"You don't know?" Angela yelled. "You don't fucking know? So now I'm trapped in the middle of nowhere with a traitor. Are you planning to kill me?"

"Please put that thing down, Angie."

"Fuck you, Scott," she said and pulled the trigger.

There was a deafening crack, and Scott instinctively leapt to the floor, crashing against a cupboard as he went. Pain shot through his right hand and his ears rang. Blood covered his hand, and a thick red pool spread out on the floor beside him.

Angela loomed over, her gun pointed at him. Her mouth moved, but he couldn't hear her over the ringing. His hand slipped in the blood, and he fell flat on the floor, his eyes still fixed on her. Sharp pain shot through his back. Angela bent down, dipped a finger in the red pool and licked it.

This time, he heard her. "It's not blood, it's wine. What a waste."

Scott rolled onto his side, relieved but still fearing for his life. "You tried to fucking kill me."

"No, I shot the bottle. On purpose."

She backed over to the table and perched against it.

Scott scrambled into a sitting position, wiping shards of glass from his shirt. She sipped her drink, watching him, the gun still in her other hand.

"I told you they would come back to you. Why didn't you tell me?"

"I don't know." Scott got to his feet. "Fear, I suppose."

Angela moved back behind the table. "You should have told me. Are you working for them or what?" She motioned to the chair. "Sit the fuck down and explain. And fill this up."

She held out the glass and he explained how they asked him to inform on the resistance. When he finished, she kicked the chair across the room.

"So, let me get this straight. When I came to your house and invited you to the meeting, they had already asked you?"

Scott took a pack of cigarettes from his pocket and lit one. "Yes."

"Jesus Christ, Scott, why didn't you tell me then?"

"They are scarier than you," Scott said, eyeing the gun in Angela's hand. "Well, they were then, anyway."

He offered her a cigarette, and she gestured at the table. He rolled it towards her and slid the lighter across. After swigging her wine, she lit it. "The damage you've done, Scott. You have no idea."

"I'm sorry, Angie, I had no choice."

Angela scoffed. "You had a choice to tell me."

"Will anyone else have seen the tape?"

"No, it's encrypted. Only I can open it. Luckily for you." She picked up the chair and sat down. "I should kill you, I really should."

"Why didn't you?"

"Fuck knows." Her mouth twitched; a sure sign she was

drunk. She stared at the window behind him, deep in thought. "Seeing as I didn't and probably won't, there's only one option. You're a triple agent now. You report back to them what I tell you. Can I trust you?"

Her proposal scared him, but he would rather work for her than the government, and if it got him off the hook for his 'betrayal', then even better.

"Yeah. Of course you can."

"There's literally no reason for me to believe you, but I do." Angela looked into his eyes. "I own you now."

Scott's pulse slowed at last. "Does that mean you'll put the gun down?"

Angela put the safety catch on and slipped it into the holster on her hip. A cloud of smoke hung between them, illuminated by the low sun shining through the window. She reached over and held his hand.

"You promise I can trust you?"

Scott squeezed it. "I promise."

She traced her finger across the back of his hand. The hairs on his neck raised.

"I heard what you said at Mutt's house," he whispered. Her finger stopped.

She looked like a child being caught out. "What?"

"In the bedroom," he ran his finger against hers, "you said you were jealous of Olympia."

Angela hesitated for a moment, then held his hand tighter. "Yes, I was, God knows why." She got up to get another bottle of wine, stepping over the smashed glass and liquid on the floor. "Well, this is awkward, isn't it?"

"It was awkward when you shot me," Scott admitted.

Angela snorted and turned to face him, then hopped onto the kitchen counter, legs hanging like a child. When he first saw her at her house, he had been attracted to her. Now everything about her turned him on. The way her curls framed her face, her green eyes, her pale, slender neck, her long thin legs, now with the black boots reaching her knees. She exuded power whilst being physically fragile.

Scott walked over, put a hand on each of her thighs and kissed her. She kissed back harder. As he slid his hands to her waist, she clutched the back of his head and moaned. Her legs wrapped around his body as she pulled him closer.

"Let's go upstairs," he said, moving his lips to her neck.

He could taste the bitter tang of her perfume on his tongue. She unbuttoned the top button of his shirt, and as she fumbled for the second button, she gave up and ripped it apart. A button pinged into her empty glass.

"No," she said, "stay here."

Angela grabbed his belt, frantically undoing it and unzipping his jeans. In one movement, Scott gripped her buttocks and lifted her, then spun around and placed her onto the table. He pulled her leggings off as she lay back. Her arm swept across the table, sending his glass and the cigarettes flying. He tore off her top, bent over and undid her bra, jet black against her pale skin, revealing her breasts, still as firm as they had been years ago.

His saliva glistened on her neck in the setting sun. As he took his jeans off, she rubbed a foot against him.

"You're so hard," she said, her head resting on the laptop.

She flicked the elasticated band with her toe and yanked his boxer shorts down. He slid them off. She was totally naked now, except for the gun, still holstered loosely around her hips. He pulled her nearer to him and entered her.

"Fuck," she gasped, letting her arms stretch out.

The gun knocked against the table in rhythm as he

thrust in and out of her. The table slowly moved forward as they continued until it eventually wedged against the wall. She pressed her hands on the wall, pushing herself towards him, and screamed. Her neck reddened, flushed with blood, and with every push, her head hit the wall, curls bouncing. Then, as he came, he held her legs, pulling them until her ankles rested on his shoulders. He leant forwards, panting, and kissed her breasts.

When he looked up at her, she smiled. "I needed that."

"So did I."

Scott went to the tap, stuck his head under, and drank deeply. "Scott," she said from behind him.

Angela lay on the table, legs apart, breathing heavily, holster still around her waist, gun in hand, pointing at him.

"Fuck me again," she ordered.

He laughed. "Give me some time, Angie, I'm not twenty-one anymore." She removed the safety catch, and sat up, hand on trigger. "You've got ten minutes."

———

THE NEXT MORNING, Scott awoke alone. Angela had been insatiable, they had sex on the table, in the living room, in the bed. Not once did she mention the resistance or the government. They must have gone through four bottles of wine, something his pounding head confirmed.

When he went downstairs, he found her stood by the back door, smoking.

"I've decided we shouldn't smoke in the house, it reeks in here."

She was right, the whole house stank of cigarettes and wine. They hadn't even bothered cleaning up the mess from the shot bottle.

"Yeah, it does a bit," he said, unsure whether to go towards her.

She threw a cigarette butt into the garden and closed the door.

"What do we do now?" he asked.

Angela moved towards him, ran a hand down his cheek and kissed him,

"We bring down this Government, Scott. Once and for all." She let her dressing gown fall open. "But first, let's have a bath."

———

SCOTT AND ANGELA spent the next two days in an imitation of domestic bliss. Making breakfast together, watching TV, cooking dinner together. Whilst sober, she didn't mention the resistance at all. They reminisced about their university days, talked about the weather. After drinking, she would rant about the government and how close it was to falling.

"Like all dictatorships, it's precarious. They're hanging on by the skin of their teeth," as she put it.

Apparently, David had been too cautious, cancelling a major 'plan' the previous winter at the last minute. The plan involved simultaneous resistance attacks across the country. Her mission was to replace that caution with a sense of urgency. *'Kill or be killed'* she said, describing it as a race against time, with attacks needed imminently to force the leaders to their knees. Resistance secrets spilled out of her: army generals who were on side, the infiltrated checkpoints, high ranking agents in the government, and the mysterious 'Nest', the nerve centre of the operation, located somewhere she wouldn't say.

"I'll take you there as soon as we leave here," Angela promised. "We run everything from there."

She spoke about the post revolution plans, how she would lead an interim government before free elections, when she would step down a hero. Her place marked forever in history.

"I'll probably have a statue," she said one night.

Scott had laughed, only to be reprimanded.

"I'm serious," she'd replied.

It seemed Angela had forgotten his treachery, though it must lie deep within her, waiting to rise to the surface should he cross her.

She changed the subject whenever David's name arose, other than to talk about resistance matters, but constantly asked if Scott wanted to get back with Miriam. He explained that ship had sailed, but still, Angela pried about his feelings for her.

"Fatherhood changed me, Angie, and she's the mother of my son, but that's it," he told her.

———

ONE AFTERNOON WHILST PLAYING CARDS, Angela asked if Scott was prepared to kill for the resistance.

"Well, I'd prefer not, but I suppose if I have to," he said, taken aback.

"No one wants to kill," she muttered, shuffling the cards, "but unfortunately in this line of work, it's sometimes necessary."

Scott thought of her shooting down the soldiers at the checkpoint and poisoning David. "I can see that."

"Have you ever killed anyone before?"

Scott shuffled in the chair with unease. "No."

Angela paused for a few minutes and eyed him with suspicion.

"What happened with Olympia, Scott, really?

"Oh, for God's sake, Angie."

"I watched the rest of the tape. The camera was facing away and there was no sound. I need to know. Did you kill her?"

Scott pushed back his chair and stepped away, standing for a moment and staring at the wall.

She put a hand on his shoulder and spoke quietly. "We need to be honest with each other. What happened?"

"I didn't kill her, she overdosed, but..." Scott paused, the images of her spasming body flashing through his mind. "But I didn't try to help her either, I let her die."

"Ok," Angela said, dragging him back to the table, "let's not mention it again."

———

ON THE THIRD DAY, Martin called to say it would be safe to return to London. Angela snapped out of her relaxed mood as soon as she took the call.

When she finished, she beckoned Scott to the sofa. "Scott, listen, about us, about..." she waved her hands around, "about this." She took his hands in hers. "I gave myself to you, and you must do the same for me, do you get that?"

"Yeah, of course, Angie, I..."

"No, listen, promise me you will tell me everything from now on."

Scott lifted a hand to her face and stroked her cheek. "I promise."

"You're a triple agent now, and you tell me *everything*."

Angela stabbed his knee with her finger, emphasising the last word. "And you tell them what I tell you to."

"Angie, I swear, you can trust me." Scott fixed his eyes into hers. "A hundred percent."

"Good. Now let's get the hell out of here."

Martin arrived within an hour.

As they walked to the car, Angela glanced back at the cottage. "We won't forget this place in a hurry."

"No, we bloody won't," Scott replied, and put an arm around her shoulder. She wriggled away. "Not in front of anyone, Scott."

———

THIS TIME 'THEIR PEOPLE' manned the checkpoint. Martin had made sure on the drive up, and they cruised through without any issues.

"Thank God I don't have to shoot anyone this time," Angela sighed. During their time at the cottage, she had explained the scale of resistance, how a vast network surrounded them in every aspect of life. "Probably one in ten is working with us," she'd insisted.

Her infectious optimism altered Scott's view of the world. Everything looked different now as he stared out the window at the soldiers, the police, the passers-by, knowing some were resistance fighters. The country didn't seem as bad. Things could change.

"We're taking Scott to The Nest tomorrow, Martin," Angela announced as they neared his house.

"Already?" Martin replied, warily.

"Yes, we've spent three days cooped up in that bloody cottage. It's like we've known each other for years."

Scott laughed. "We have."

"You know what I mean," Angela said, tutting with amusement. "We'll give him the tour, make sure there are some rooms set up, we'll stay over."

"Sure thing, boss," Martin said, and he turned to Scott. "You'll be amazed, mate. Everyone is when they first go to The Nest."

"Nothing amazes me anymore with you guys," Scott said.

"Oh, The Nest is something else though, mate."

They dropped him off a few blocks from home.

"I'll call you later tonight," Angela said as he got out. "Be ready to go tomorrow, pack some stuff. And if you hear anything from them, call me immediately."

"I will, and er, thanks for the last few days."

"No, thank *you*," she said mischievously.

Martin eyed them with suspicion.

Scott ambled towards his house, repeating the last few days in his mind. Was this all part of some plan Angela had or were her feelings real? They seemed real, yet there was a side to her he was unsure about. He'd seen her kill people with no sign of regret, and she was able to bend people to her will. Was she doing that to him? Either way, he didn't have any other option. Above all, he needed to ensure Benji and Miriam's safety.

————

Scott arrived home and opened the door; two letters lay on the carpet, and he scooped them up. One a gas bill, the other a handwritten envelope, no stamp. He ripped it open.

Been away for a few days? Hope you had a good time. We'll be in touch soon,

Henry.

Scott ripped up the letter. Any sense of peace disappeared. He soaked in a bath for nearly an hour, thinking of Angela, how her body looked laid out on the table. He wanted her again. They had made love that morning and he pictured it, him holding her curls as she moved on top of him.

After bathing, Scott made himself a cup of tea and sat in the living room, closing his eyes, still flushed from the heat of the bath. When he opened his eyes, the room felt different. Something was *off*.

And then he saw it.

A large black and white photograph, grainy as if taken from a distance, of him and Angela sat in the cottage hung in the gap where a print of Picasso's 'Guernica' had hung before. He stood and ripped it off the wall.

Chapter Ten

Angela had been calm when Scott told her about the photo. She had messaged him an address with instructions to walk there and arrive within an hour.

Scott set out straight away, and once he arrived, a young woman holding a baby answered the door.

"I'm here to see Angela," Scott said.

The woman looked over his shoulder and said, "You'd better come in then."

She closed the door quickly, peaking outside as she did so, then pushing Scott down the corridor. "This way, this way."

Then, leaning her head into the living room, she called to a man watching football on TV. "It's someone for Angela."

The man sat up abruptly. "Bloody hell, what do we do again?"

The baby cried and she pushed it towards the man.

"I dunno, there's a number to call or something ain't there?"

They were as confused as Scott.

The man looked up at him. "Sorry, mate, we're new to all this. Do you know what to do?"

"I don't know, she just told me to come here," Scott replied.

The woman scrolled through her phone, "Ok I think I've got it, one minute".

She held the phone to her ear and disappeared upstairs.

The man held out a hand. "I'm Andy, by the way, and that's my wife Karen."

Scott shook it. "I'm..."

"Whoa, don't tell me your name, mate, we don't know nothing. We just do what she says and take the money. Do you want a beer or something?"

"Yeah, why not?"

Andy led Scott to a small living room with a football match blaring from a television in the corner. A framed picture of Prime Minister Robertson hung above the fireplace.

"Oh, it's only for show innit," Andy said, grimacing. "They suggested we do it, makes us look less suss, you know."

"So, you work for Angela then?" Scott asked, moving a pile of magazines aside to sit down.

Andy fidgeted and placed the baby down on the carpet. "Er, we're not meant to answer questions really, you know how it is."

"No, sorry, suppose not."

They both stared at the TV for a moment.

"Who do you support?" Scott ventured to break the silence.

Andy smiled. "Chelsea, you?"

"Palace."

Andy chuckled. "Fucking hell, you've suffered enough
ain't ya? And now you're involved in all this stuff as well."

Karen reappeared, flustered, staring at her phone.
"Done. I'll stay here, Andy. You show him the tunnel."

Andy took him to the kitchen, dragged out the washing
machine, and pulled off a panel. Behind was a small hole in
the brickwork, barely larger than a cat flap.

Scott lifted his eyebrows. "I'm meant to fit through
that?"

"Apparently once you get in, it's larger," Andy said with
a shrug. He crouched down and pointed to the gap. "Put
your legs in first, they said there's a ladder or something."

Scott leant down and shone his phone's torch into the
gloom. "Have you ever been down there?"

"Nah, mate, all they said is you go down there, follow it
all the way and you'll end up where you need to be."

Scott stood to find Andy handing him a torch. "This'll
be better, I reckon."

With Andy's help, Scott clambered into the hole, feet
precariously balanced on a wobbly ladder. Andy passed
him the torch. "Good luck, mate."

"Thanks, feels like I'll need it."

And with that, Andy put the cover in place. Scott
descended the ladder, and reaching the bottom, shone the
torch ahead. He had to duck to fit, and the walls were so
narrow they rubbed against his shoulders. Spiderwebs
covered almost every surface, and the air smelt damp.
Muffled sounds came from the house above; talking, the
baby crying. He cursed Angela as the weak beam revealed a
large rat running away. The damp air made breathing difficult, and he increased his pace, desperate to get to the end.

As he trudged around a bend, the tunnel became
smaller and Scott had to duck to a ninety-degree angle, his

head occasionally hitting the wet ceiling. Claustrophobia enveloped him and he sped up. Something caught his eye, and he swivelled the torch to get a better look. Someone had daubed in white paint 'Flying Ant Day' across the wall. He stumbled whilst gazing at it.

On the floor lay a woman's shoe, half stuck in the floor, a spider crawling over it. He kept moving forward, hunched over, trying to ignore the rats and the bricks littering the floor.

Finally, Scott reached a wall with steps crudely cut into it. The bottom step crumbled beneath him as he put his foot on it and the torch smashed to the floor, plunging the tunnel into darkness. He felt around with his foot and eventually found the torch with his hand.

When he reached the top, Scott hammered against a wooden ceiling, desperately trying to keep his footing on the loose bricks.

"Angie," Scott shouted between knocks.

Finally, a sliding noise sounded and Angela's muffled voice. "Who is it?"

"It's me, Scott, open this fucking thing."

The hatch lifted to reveal Angela's silhouette in a barely lit room. A dim bulb shone through her curls from behind. She reached out a hand, and with surprising strength, pulled him out.

"Why haven't you got a torch for God's sake?" she said, closing the hatch and pushing a box on top.

Scott stretched, finally able to stand up straight. "I dropped it trying to get up those bloody stairs. Was all that really necessary?"

Angela took him by the hand. "Yes it was, lovely couple aren't they, bit chavvy, but what can you do?"

She led him through a basement cluttered with junk.

"Where are we? Is this The Nest?"

"Don't be silly," she said, pulling him towards a small ladder.

Angela climbed up and opened another hatch, this time into a fully lit room. Scott squinted and followed her up, instantly realising where they were.

"Your house?"

They came out into the conservatory, and from the window, Scott could see the garden chairs where David had lay dying. She noticed him looking out.

"Bring back any memories?"

That day came back to him. How Angela had screamed at him to go. Then running through the house, confused, relieved, and horrified all at the same time.

"Yeah, that seems like ages ago."

Angela took his hand again and led him into the living room, making him remove his filthy shoes.

"I'll be two minutes. Make yourself comfortable."

She left, closing the door.

Scott looked at the armchair David had sat in that night, and the shelves stacked with books. As he inspected one, the door opened. Angela stood in the doorway, looking different somehow.

"So, what do you think about the photo?" Scott questioned. "How did they know we were at that cottage?"

Angela furrowed her brow and held out a glass. "I don't know, Scott, would you like a drink?"

He nearly dropped the book. She spoke in a thick Irish accent, her voice deeper than usual. Scott took a step towards her and took the glass. Up close, she looked different.

"Wait, what's going on here?"

She suppressed a smile and Scott stepped back. "Angie, is that you?"

As he spoke, Angela walked into the room, laughing uncontrollably and holding onto the other Angela's shoulders to keep herself upright. Then, behind her, another 'Angela' entered. All of them dressed identically. The resemblance was uncanny, and it took Scott a moment to fathom the real Angela.

"Right, can somebody explain what the hell is going on here?"

The real Angela put her arms around the others.

"These are the Angels," she said, bursting into laughter again and addressing her lookalikes. "Did you see his face?"

Irritated by her laughter, Scott faked a smile and put the book back. "So, what's going on?"

"The Angels are my body doubles, you know, to throw people off the scent. We were having a meeting when I got your call."

"Right, well, can we talk now?"

"Scott, you have to lighten up sometimes. Jesus. OK, girls, go upstairs while I speak to Mr Serious." Angela watched them leave with a shake of the head. "They've even had plastic surgery. Amazing, isn't it?"

Scott waited as they filed out. "How did the government know we were at the cottage, isn't that pretty serious?"

"Let me see the photo."

Scott handed it to her, and she studied it carefully, holding it up to the light.

"Well, it looks real. I was rather hoping it would be a fake," she said, giving it back. "Another reason to get things moving, I suppose."

"I don't understand why they don't just kill you. Wouldn't that be easier for them?"

"They want information, and with their best mole on the case," she said, patting his arm, "it's better to keep me alive." She walked to the window and gazed out. "For now."

"So, what do we do?"

"We give them something to work with, something you can take to them." Angela turned back to him. "Hit record on your phone, but keep it in your pocket."

She motioned for him to sit as he took his phone out.

'Ready?' she mouthed.

He nodded and hit record.

"Next week, Tuesday the 13th, we're hitting three mainline stations at morning rush hour. This is going to be big, Victoria, London Bridge and Charing Cross, a simultaneous attack." Angela sat back and crossed her legs, pulling out a cigarette. "Mass casualties, mass disruption, then we call for the government to hold free and fair elections, threatening more attacks if they don't." She lit the cigarette, "A brutal show of force." She stopped and stared ahead, puffing on the cigarette. "Get your phone out, I need you to take photos of something."

Scott reached for the phone as she mouthed 'Stop recording.' He turned it off.

She let out a long breath and said, "Simple, now you take that back to them."

"I take it that's not the actual plan?"

"Of course not, the genuine attacks are somewhere else, but we'll discuss that at The Nest."

Scott laughed at Angela's calmness. "Aren't you scared?"

"I can't afford to be scared, Scott. Now, we both need some sleep, you'd better go home."

Scott frowned and stared at her, surprised.

"What were you expecting, a foursome with the

Angels?" she giggled. "Don't worry, I've got you a decent torch for the journey back."

"I'll call you tomorrow," she said as he stepped into the tunnel. "Don't worry, this will all be fine, Scott."

"I hope so," he said as she closed the hatch.

This time the journey wasn't as bad. He covered it in less time and her powerful torch made it easier to see. Even the rats didn't bother him as much. She had an ability to make everything OK, as if this were normal.

She had called the couple in the house, telling them to expect him, and when he arrived, Andy opened the hatch within a minute and pulled him out.

"What's it like down there then, mate?"

"Not as bad as you'd think."

"Well, you look the same, Karen says every time Angela comes out of there, she looks different."

The next day, Scott called Miriam's phone. Straight away, it disconnected. He tried again with the same effect, and even text messages wouldn't send.

When he called the house phone, a message simply said, 'This number has been disconnected'. The panic returned; something was wrong.

He set out for her house when his phone rang, number withheld. "Miriam, is that you?"

"No, Scott, it's Henry, there's a car outside. You know the drill."

————

THE CAR, driven by a man who said nothing the entire journey, took him to a remote reservoir. Reaching the destination, the driver pointed up a hill.

"There," he said.

A man sat on a bench, Henry, he presumed, faced away from him, looking out over the water. A warm breeze rustled the nearby trees as he climbed the hill.

"Scott," Henry said without turning, patting the bench, "take a seat."

Scott sat as instructed, and Henry turned his head, slowly taking in the surroundings.

"It's good to get out of the city sometimes, don't you think? Actually, I *know* you think that. Lovely little cottage. Romantic."

Scott leant forward, elbows on his knees. "I've got something for you."

"I should hope so. What is it?"

Scott took out his phone and played the recording. Angela's high-pitched voice, speaking of planned attacks, sounded out of place, almost drowned out by the birds circling overhead.

Henry took out a notepad and scribbled away in a spidery hand, *'Victoria, London Bridge, Charing Cross'*.

"Well, this is good, any sign that she suspects you're working for us?"

If they knew he had been at the cottage, what else did they know? Had they listened? Did they know Angela had seen the hidden camera footage?

"No, absolutely not," Scott lied.

Henry eyed him sideways. "Good. You've done well, Scott. Just like I knew you would. But I've got some bad news for you."

"Bad news?" Scott questioned, trying to appear calm despite his breathing increasing. "What bad news?"

"We've got Miriam and the boy."

Scott sprang up. "What the fuck? I've done everything you asked for." He whipped the phone back out and waved it in Henry's face. "Look at what I just gave you, specific information."

"Please calm down, Scott. We need to make sure you continue giving us information. It's our insurance policy."

"Where are they?"

"Obviously, I can't tell you that, but they are safe. No harm will come to them." Henry slipped the notepad into his jacket. "Not yet, anyway."

"Listen to me, you sick fuck," Scott shouted, pulling Henry off the bench by his collar, "Stop this shit, Stop it. I'll give you what you need, just leave them out of it."

A man appeared from behind a nearby tree, and Scott let go. Henry waved the man away, but for a second, as they stood face-to-face, there was fear in his eyes. Henry regained his composure and straightened his collar.

"Anger won't solve this, just keep doing what I ask, and they will be fine."

Scott looked back over the water, his world collapsing around him again. "When will this end?"

Henry walked up behind him. "Soon, I hope. Now let's get you back, eh?"

After being taken home, Scott called Miriam's phone, but again, it cut off. Once he was sure the car had gone, he called a taxi to her house.

On arriving, he repeatedly rang on the doorbell, shouting through the letterbox in vain. He considered breaking in when a head appeared from the house next door.

An old woman glared out at him. "Everything alright?"

"My son and ex-wife live here, do you know them?"

His urgency scared her, and she withdrew slightly. "Only to say hello to, I haven't been here long."

"When was the last time you saw them?" Scott asked.

The woman shook her head. "I haven't seen them for the last few days."

"If you see them, call me. This is my number." Scott scribbled it onto a piece of paper and put in the woman's palm. "Please."

———

SCOTT RANTED down the phone to Angela. "You have to do something. Can't you find out where they're being held?"

She exhaled, a long slow breath. "I don't know, it's difficult."

"This is my son, Angie, please. What about the hackers or whatever, if they got footage of my camera, surely there's something that can be done?"

"Ok, we'll try." She sighed again. "You know, sometimes I'm glad I haven't got children; it seems such a *hassle.*"

Scott scoffed. "Are you fucking kidding me?"

"At the very minimum, it's allowed the government to have an emotional hold on you."

"What?" he spat. "Do you have *any* empathy?"

"I do, but..." Angela paused. "Listen, just come to the house now. We'll talk about this later."

"I'm not doing anything for you unless you promise to help me with this, Angie."

"Oh, for God's sake. Yes, I promise. Now, are you going to come over or not?"

"How do I get there, the tunnel or what?"

"Not this time. And bring some clothes, I don't know how long we'll be away for."

"Is that safe, me brazenly waltzing up to the house?"

"They *want* to know you're speaking to me. Let them see."

———

ANGELA OPENED THE DOOR HERSELF, clad in a grey dressing gown, a towel wrapped tightly around her head. Behind her, Piotr, the security man, sat on a chair.

"Give me ten minutes to get ready," Angela said, ushering him inside.

Scott walked through the metal detector without a sound, but as she followed him through, it buzzed. The bulge of the gun was visible under her dressing gown.

"Remember what you promised, Angie."

"Yes, yes," she said, reaching the stairs. She spun around to face him. "Well, don't just stand there, come up."

Her bedroom was enormous, decorated in an old-fashioned style. Georgian, Edwardian? Scott wasn't sure. At one end stood a huge four-poster bed, draped in white covers. At the other end, under a gold-framed mirror, a dresser covered in bottles of lotions, creams, makeup, and wine. On one wall hung a gigantic oil painting of Angela, swathed over a chaise longue in a red dress, her leg suggestively showing through the slit.

Angela saw him staring at it. "Oh, that. David commissioned it, I'm not sure about it myself, but hey ho."

She unwrapped the towel from her hair and pointed to a chair with her hairdryer. "Take a seat."

Scott sat in the remarkably uncomfortable chair and admired the room. "Nice place."

She looked into the mirror back at him. "I hope you appreciate that chair. It used to belong to the Marquess of Denmead."

"Oh, the famous Marquess of Denmead," he replied sarcastically as she turned on the hairdryer, drowning him out.

Scott waited while she dried and combed her hair, her spindly legs sticking out the of dressing gown. She stopped to take a sip from a teacup and looked at him again.

"Scott, I will do everything I can to find out where Miriam and Bobby are."

"Benji," Scott corrected.

"Sorry, where Benji and Bobby are."

"This is serious, Angie, do you get that? It's all I can think about."

Angela stood above him and stroked his face. "I know."

He pulled away from her and said, "I don't know if you do."

Angela huffed and returned to the mirror. "How many times have I told you, just lighten up."

"You have no idea, Angie, you're in your own little world of revolution, you don't know what it's like to feel for people, especially your own child."

She slammed the comb onto the dresser and advanced towards him. "Wrong, wrong, wrong. I have to suppress my feelings for the greater good, Scott, and the quicker you understand that, the better."

Scott stood almost a foot taller than her in her bare feet, and he glared down, equalling her for volume. "How can I suppress my feelings towards my son?"

She stabbed a finger into his chest, raising her face to his, her breath reeking of alcohol. "I'm not asking you to, I'm asking you to understand me."

"I bought a life into this world. All you do is take lives out of it."

Angela sneered at him. "Oh that's a low blow, Scott, I do what I have to do for people like you," she jabbed him again, this time harder, "to make them safe."

Scott pushed her hand away. "Well, you're not doing a good job of it."

Scott's words angered her, and she gripped her long fingers around his chin.

"Well fuck you then and fuck your son," Angela shouted. Flecks of alcohol-tainted spit flew from her mouth.

"Fuck you," Scott bellowed, his pointed finger almost touching her cheek. "You're a psychopath and a murderer, you killed your husband and don't even give a shit."

She batted his hand away and punched his shoulder. "You didn't seem to care when you were fucking me in the cottage, did you? Was that a turn on, fucking a murderer?"

Scott grabbed her wrist, trying to stop the blows now reigning down on him.

"Get your hands off, Scott, get your hands off me." Angela yelled, and she stepped back and pulled out the gun, "I mean it."

A knock at the door interrupted them. "Everything OK in there?"

Angela's eyes darted from the door to Scott. "Yes, fine, Piotr, thank you." She put the gun on the dresser and drank from the cup.

"Whisky," she said in response to his look.

They didn't speak as she got dressed. Scott stared out the window, the tension in the air as oppressive as the constant worrying about Miriam and Benji.

"Come on, we're going," Angela eventually said. Scott followed her as she stomped down the stairs.

"Get your bag," she muttered and marched to the conservatory. She opened a door and flicked on a light. They descended into the basement.

"Follow me, and for God's sake, don't say anything, we have to be quiet."

She slid a box of old records away from the wall and kicked open a hatch. A different one from which he had emerged the day before; one that looked professionally built. A steep drop off point appeared before him, so he tread carefully to avoid slipping. Eventually, it levelled off. The walls, mostly tiled, were crisscrossed with wires. On the ceiling, automatic lights illuminated the way, turning on as they passed under, before turning off again. The clacking of Angela's boots echoed around as they walked. They travelled for twenty minutes before she slowed down and looked at the ceiling, searching for something. Then she stopped and pointed. In between two lights, a slight recess could be seen.

"Push it," she said, unable to reach it herself.

When Scott pressed it, the bottom of a ladder dropped out. He pulled it down and stared up into the hole, then gestured to the ladder.

"Ladies first."

Angela put a finger to her lips and scowled, then began climbing up. He followed, and they ascended into the darkness.

She stopped and rummaged in her pockets, then a small beam of light appeared as she lit a tiny torch, pointed upward where the stairs ended.

She turned off the torch, and the dull green light of an electric keypad lit her face. After pressing some buttons, the ceiling slid away, and Angela climbed inside. Scott followed her, and they emerged into a square room with a bank of monitors across one wall. Two men stood smiling as Angela shook their hands. They shook Scott's after and Angela opened a door, stepping into a darkened room the size of a football pitch.

Desks covered almost the entire space, and two or three

computer screens sat on each one, manned by black-clad figures: most tapping away at keyboards, some peering at the monitors. On the wall at the far end was a huge electronic map of Britain, covered in flashing dots. It reminded him of mission control at NASA.

The bustling sound of people working filled the room, and an air conditioning system rumbled away beneath it all. The glow of the screens lit Angela's face and she smiled.

She beckoned him to another door and swung it open into an identical room, but this one had an electronic map of the whole world on the wall.

When Angela turned back to him, her pale face looked sickly in the green and red light.

"This is where we bring down the government from, and there's not a moment to waste." She flung her arms out. "Welcome to The Nest."

Part Two

Chapter Eleven

"Heathrow," Sarge said, clicking a switch, and an image of the airport filled the screen. "The busiest airport in Britain, over one thousand flights per day."

The small group assembled in one of The Nest's rooms murmured as Sarge showed a series of photos on the monitor that filled the wall: planes taking off, planes landing, people queuing for security.

"Also, one of the most protected places in Britain." Pictures flashed up of armed police, body scanners, and perimeter fences topped with barbed wire. "However, an airport is inherently susceptible to breaches due to both the size of the site and the amount of people who work there."

"A chain is only as strong as its weakest link," Martin called out.

Sarge nodded. "Exactly, and this chain has many, many weak links." He walked to the door and pressed his palm to the scanner. "And here are some of those weak links."

Four men and a woman filed in. Angela sat in the corner, arms folded, looking serious.

"Names and job please," Sarge asked the four people, now standing awkwardly in front of the screen.

One by one, they stepped forward.

"Peter Gue, security officer, Terminal two."

"Ben Steeples, warehouse operative, Terminal one."

"Cara Grady, Manager Sid's Bar, Terminal four."

"Damien Toms, security, Terminal five."

"Michael Pannell, baggage handler, Terminal three."

Sarge grinned to the audience, "Pretty good, eh? Thank you guys, you can go now."

They marched out.

"With the help of those brave Ants, five bombs will detonate on Tuesday afternoon at 2pm. One in each terminal." He held the clicker dramatically above his head. "Chaos."

One by one, images of burning buildings appeared on the screen, speeding up until it was a blur, then abruptly stopping, leaving the Flying Ant logo. Angela clapped, and the others followed suit as she walked to the front.

"This operation is expensive," she said as the clapping stopped. "So thank you, Lauren for sorting out the funding."

Lauren gave Angela the thumbs up, then nervously stroked her pink hair.

"And thank you to Martin for giving our bomb makers a kick up the arse. They've been working around the clock for this. Now, any questions?"

A man Scott hadn't been introduced to spoke. "How many casualties do we expect?"

"Hard to say," said Angela. "These are huge bombs. A few hundred deaths, maybe a thousand if we're lucky."

Scott flinched at the word 'lucky.' Though the resistance's aims were admirable, killing so many innocent people wasn't so much.

Another man asked, "Is this a suicide mission?"

"No, the bombs are planted, set to timer, then they get out to safety."

Lauren raised her hand. "How soon after do we take responsibility?"

"Immediately. We get it out through the usual channels within moments of the bombs detonating."

Scott raised a hand. "What happens if it goes wrong?"

Sarge muttered something under his breath, but stopped as Angela shot him a severe look. She glared at Scott. "It won't go wrong."

————

AFTER THE PRESENTATION, Angela disappeared, and Scott went to his allocated room in the living quarters of The Nest.

Sparsely decorated, like a prison cell, the only luxury being a natural daylight lamp, intended to make up for the lack of real daylight.

He lay on the creaking single bed and closed his eyes, and later awoke to a knocking at the door.

"Bro, you in there?" Martin called out.

"Hold on," Scott said.

He wiped the sleep from his eyes and opened the door. Martin stepped in and closed the door behind him. "Boring here, isn't it? I can show you around if you want."

Scott shrugged. "Yeah sure."

Martin took him down a long corridor, back to the enormous room he had first came into. It still bustled with activity, the only light coming from the screens. They walked between desks, stopping occasionally for Martin to greet someone.

"This is the Domestic Room, communications come in from our agents all over the country, and we sift through it all, deciding what to act on." They reached an empty desk, partitioned from the rest of the room.

"My desk," Martin said proudly. "Take a seat. You must have some questions."

"God, I don't know where to start. How safe is this place?"

"As safe as it can be, the government doesn't know about it, obviously, and we don't think they'll find it." Martin logged into the computer. "If they do, we're fucked, there's about 200 people here at any time, day and night."

"Living here?"

"No, there's room for twenty to sleep, the rest commute. Here, let me show you something." Martin pointed at the screen. "Angela asked me to show you this."

A window popped up, and Martin typed in MIRIAM SAUNDERS.

Scott studied the screen. "What's this?"

"It's a list of people being held by the government, not exhaustive but ninety per cent."

The computer flashed: NO MATCHES.

"Try Miriam Roth," Scott suggested, but again: NO MATCHES.

They searched Benji's name, but nothing came up for that either.

"The Government could be bluffing. They've done that before. Do you think she may be in hiding instead, or gone to Israel?" Martin questioned.

"I mean, it's possible, but she would have told me, I'm sure of it."

The thought of Miriam going to Israel had crossed his mind as a possibility, but despite her anger with him, surely there was no way she would take Benji away without at least letting him know.

Martin put his hand on Scott's shoulder.

"Give us time, mate, we'll find them. We're doing everything we can." He got up and took Scott to the next room. "This is the International Room, same shit, but overseas basically. We're working with governments all over the world. They give us intel, and if we're lucky, money."

Scott struggled to take in the scale of it all. A secret base, below London, hidden from the view of the government, it was incredible. All those people above with no idea of this happening below.

"The intel coming from Israel and the US alone is mind blowing," Martin continued. "Only problem is the Russians, bastards keep trying to fuck everything up."

They carried on through to a corridor, and Martin waved a hand out like an estate agent. "These are the meeting rooms, and then if we follow it round, we get back to the living quarters."

Scott halted, noticing a grand oak door at the end, different from the other nondescript ones. "What's in there?"

Martin paused. "Her Majesty's Suite," he said, in a sarcastic tone.

"Angela?"

"Yeah, she doesn't slum it like the rest of us, now come on, let..."

Scott walked towards the door. "No, I want to speak to her."

Martin followed behind. "I don't think that's a good idea, buddy, she's, what's the phrase, tired and emotional."

Scott pressed the doorbell nestled beside the door.

"You're not really meant to..." Martin began.

"I'm her friend," Scott said, putting his ear to the door.

Martin bit his lip out of concern. "In the days leading up to an attack, she gets kind of stressed. It's best not to pester her."

"Angie," Scott shouted, banging the door. "Can we talk?"

Martin took Scott's arm and tried to lead him away. "Mate, I really don't think this is a good idea. Come on."

Shuffling came from behind the door, and it opened a crack, revealing Lauren wrapped in a pink dressing gown.

"Angela is sleeping."

The smell of cigarettes slipped out of the crack. "Tell her it's Scott and I need to speak with her."

"She doesn't want to be disturbed. Sorry."

Lauren closed the door.

Martin looked worried. "Told you. Come on, let me show you some more cool stuff."

Scott looked back at the door, then followed Martin down the corridor.

THE DAY of the Heathrow attack arrived.

For two days, Scott hadn't seen or heard from Angela. The word went around that she was not to be disturbed, but he went to her room on the off chance and a guard politely told him to go away.

He had spent the last forty eight hours wandering The Nest, eating the daily delivered food alone in his room. Without Angela, he was out of the loop; no meetings, no updates. He spoke to Martin, who only said he was still doing everything he could to find Miriam and Benji. The absence of fresh air made him either lethargic or restless, and the argument with Angela played over in his mind.

As he left his room, a man came up to him.

"Mrs Newton wants you," he said, and led Scott to a small room.

Angela sat alone, dressed in full military fatigues, Tarot cards spread on the table in front.

"Long time no see," Scott said.

She looked up for a moment then went back to studying the cards.

"I need to focus before a mission, no distractions. And you are a distraction," she said, standing up and kissing him.

"About the other day, the argument we had..." Scott said.

"Oh, forget about that, we've got bigger fish to fry. What do you think of my army clothes?"

She looked ridiculous in the camouflaged jacket and trousers, shiny boots and even a cap. A patch on her arm had the Flying Ant logo and 'Newton' stitched underneath.

"Well, it's different, I'll give you that."

"Different," she said with laughter. "I'll take that. What have you been up to over the last couple days?"

"Nothing. What is there to do here? Especially when the only person I know won't speak to me."

"Oh, please." Angela turned to the cards. "I'm trying to bring down a regime here, not worrying about poor Scotty Wotty being on his own."

"I spoke to Martin about Miriam and Benji, thank you."

She shuffled the cards. "I said we'd do everything we can. We'll find them."

"What do the cards say about today?"

"I'm about to find out," Angela said, spreading them face down on the table. "Will today's attack succeed?"

She picked up a card.

"Fuck," she yelled, holding up the card: The Tower.

Scott raised his brow. "Not good I take it?"

"Fuck fuck fuck." Angela threw the card across the room. "The Tower means no. I need a bloody drink."

"This early?" Scott questioned.

She opened a draw and pulled out a bottle of whisky.

"Time doesn't exist in The Nest. Want one?" Scott shook his head and she poured herself one. "We're meeting in the Control Room at 1.30. Be there. I need some time alone now."

Scott leant in to kiss her, but she moved her head away.

"No," she muttered, "I need to concentrate. I'll see you then. Go."

———

At half-past one, Scott arrived at the Control Room, and they all sat around a table, Lauren, Sarge, Martin, Angela, and himself. Two televisions filled a wall, one split into six boxes: Heathrow Airport CCTV. The other tuned into a 24-hour news channel.

"T Minus one hour," said Sarge, "everything is in place, bombs on timer, our people ready to get their arses out of there."

On the CCTV were hundreds of people carrying bags, going through security, shopping, eating; unaware. Angela sat dressed in her military fatigues, fidgeting with a pen. She looked concerned; they all did.

Angela stood to study the CCTV in more detail. "What about our airport guys, when do they get out?"

Sarge looked up from his laptop. "They'll start leaving soon. If all goes to plan, they will be back in an hour."

Angela pointed to a bucket on the table. "If they're lucky, we'll still have some champagne left for them."

On the screen, a mother pushed a buggy. A toy fell out, and she carried on without noticing.

"How big are these bombs again?" Scott asked.

"Massive," Sarge murmured.

"Where exactly are they?"

Sarge got up and headed to the door. "All you need to know is they're in place. I need a drink and a piss."

They all sat glued to the CCTV, the news channel bubbling away in the background, volume low.

Scott felt like an outsider in the room, aware he was only there because of Angela. He said nothing as the clock ticked slowly towards two o'clock.

Sarge returned, agitated and clutching a beer. The two o'clock bulletin began on the TV.

"It's time," Martin said, and silence fell on the room.

Another two minutes ticked by.

"Is the CCTV delayed or something?" Angela asked, taking a champagne bottle from the fridge.

Sarge looked at his watch. "Maybe a few seconds, but no more than that." He ran a hand over his shaved head. "They should have detonated by now, I don't know..."

He stopped abruptly as Angela smacked her hand on the table. "I knew it, I fucking knew it. What did the cards say, Scott?"

Their faces turned to him. He opened his mouth to speak, but not knowing what to say, he shook his head instead.

Sarge hammered away at his computer. "They said the bombs were ready, everything should be fine, they're on their way back now."

"Well, everything is not fine, is it?" Angela screamed, waving the champagne at Sarge.

Nobody spoke or even moved.

"Is it?" she repeated.

"Well, no, at the moment it doesn't..."

"For fuck's sake," she shouted, tearing away at the top of the bottle. "We needed this to go right, I can't believe this." Her hands shook as she tried to get the cork to move. "Can someone open this bloody thing?"

Lauren leant over and took it calmly, popped the cork and handed it back to Angela, who swigged from it hastily.

"Everyone get out." Champagne ran down her chin. "Now!"

Lauren pointed at the screens. "Maybe we should give it another few minutes."

Angela banged the table again. "A timed bomb either goes off on time or doesn't go off at all, unless five people are so incompetent, they all can't set a timer. Am I right?"

Lauren got up to leave, but Martin reached out a hand to hold her back. "I think she's right, boss, let's give it a few minutes."

Angela glowered at him for a second, then launched the champagne bottle into the TV screens. Scott flinched as it made contact, the noise reverberating around the room, the Heathrow footage still visible behind a spider web of cracks.

Sarge, glued to his laptop, didn't move.

"Come on, you heard her," Lauren said. "Everyone out."

They all stood, and Sarge turned to Angela. "I'm very sorry, Angela."

"You will be," she said with a shake of the head. "Just fuck off, the lot of you."

Scott made eye contact with her across the table. She pointed to the door.

————

IN THE CORRIDOR OUTSIDE, nobody knew what to do. Sarge, in his role as leader of the now failed attack, looked the most shaken. Something Scott took pleasure in seeing. Lauren cupped her face and paced in circles. Martin stood still, staring at the wall, a haunted look across his face.

From inside the room, they could hear Angela smashing anything she could get her hands on, shouting at the top of her voice, the words incomprehensible.

"This is bad," Martin said as a solid object crashed against the other side of the door. "What went wrong?"

"No idea," Sarge replied, "the guys will be back soon, we'll debrief them and then..."

He trailed off and walked away.

Martin watched him go and said, "Jeez, never seen the big guy like that. Listen, once she calms down, I think one of you should go in and check on her."

Lauren raised a hand. "No way, when she's like this, nothing gets through to her, she'll kill me." She looked at Scott, "You do it."

Scott frowned. "I gave her a look when we left, sort of to say, 'do you want me to stay?' but she told me to go."

"I know you two are *close*," Lauren said, the word 'close' dripping with insinuation. "Give it a try."

Scott scoffed. "You turned *me* away from her room and now *I'm* the close one?"

Lauren smirked. "I'm not doing it."

Scott listened at the door, the noises had stopped. "Ok."

He lifted a hand to the door.

"Don't knock. She'll say no, just go in."

Although nervous, Scott wanted to enter to see how Angela was.

"Good luck, mate," Martin said as he and Lauren walked away.

––––––

Angela sat slumped over the table at the far end of the room. Every chair lay on its side, and she had torn one of the TV screens from the wall. The other flashed on and off, covered in cracks but still showing people in the airport, blissfully unaware of how close to tragedy they had come. The room smelt of the champagne soaking into the carpet.

She didn't stir as Scott circumnavigated the table. "Angie, come on, it's not the end of the world."

She lifted her head, her eyes red and puffy. "Well it feels like it right now. Someone's going to pay for this."

Scott put an arm around her shoulder. "Come on, it'll be fine, there'll be other chances."

He rubbed her back and she collapsed into his arms, crying. Over the top of her head, he watched the CCTV.

Five minutes passed, then ten, before he lost track of time. He took in the silence and closed his eyes. Angela stopped crying. Nothing needed to be said between them. The comfort they gave each other was enough.

A knock at the door broke the tranquillity. Neither of them spoke as it creaked open.

Martin popped his head in and scanned the destruction in the room, then looked back to them. "The airport guys are back."

Angela pressed her head into Scott's chest, and he looked at Martin.

"Thank you," he said.

————

THE AIRPORT WORKERS sat on the floor in the adjacent conference room, shaking with fear.

"I want them interrogated, one by one," Angela barked at Sarge, her face still puffy. "I don't care how long it takes."

Sarge appeared more confident than when Scott had last seen him, sloping off down the corridor in shock.

"Do you want to be there?"

Angela leaned into his face, tip toeing to gain height, "No. I trust you to find out what happened with this fuck up. Be hard on them, I want to know who fucked up."

"Yes, Ma'am."

Angela turned on her heels and marched off. "Call me when you're done. Scott, come with me."

He looked at the hapless group on the floor, fear emanating from them, and went after Angela. She led him to her room, the huge oak door opening to reveal a small but lavishly decorated room. In the centre stood a four-poster bed. A huge candelabra on a table provided the only light, making the corners of the room almost impossible to see.

She reached into a dark wooden cabinet. "Drink?"

"Please," Scott replied, marvelling at the room, "Do you only sleep in four-poster beds?"

The corner of her mouth lifted in an attempt at a smile. "If at all possible, yes."

Scott took the glass of whiskey Angela held out. "What do you think went wrong?"

"I think we can rule out dud bombs. Maybe one could fail to go off, but not all five. Maybe someone got to them," Angela said.

Scott rolled an ice cube around his mouth. "But why would they come back?"

"I don't know, either way, they know too much now."

"Meaning?"

"Oh God, let's forget about this shit show for a while, Scott." Angela walked over to the bed. "Come here."

———

THE EXERTION of the lovemaking and the whiskey sent Scott into a deep sleep, and he woke to a loud ringing, and Angela's voice.

"Ok, give me five minutes."

Opening an eye, Scott watched her slam down the receiver of an antique telephone next to the bed. They lay, bodies entwined, and she wriggled free from him.

"Come on, get dressed, the interrogation is over, let's see what the hell is going on," she said.

Scott rolled over, just making out her silhouette in the candlelight. "Did they say what happened?"

"We're about to find out," she said, her voice muffled from pulling her sweatshirt over her head. "Get up, move."

Scott groaned in the warm bed, and Angela came back and yanked his arm, "Come on."

He sat up and she bustled away, searching for her jacket in the gloom. His body ached as he got dressed and drank a glass of water.

She looked at him impatiently, military jacket on. "Ready?

———

Sarge stood at the conference room door. They headed towards him, Angela almost running.

"Well?" she shouted before reaching him.

"They say they did everything right, they don't know what happened."

She scoffed. "Did you use what our American friends call 'enhanced interrogation techniques'?"

"It wasn't tea and a chat, let's put it that way."

Sarge opened the door. The five airport crew members sat naked, each tied to a chair. The woman cried, whilst the men hung their heads. Angela stood in front of them.

"Are you spies?"

The men said nothing, and the woman wept, shaking her head.

"Are you spies?" Angela screamed. Murmurs of 'no' filled the room. "I don't believe you. Close the door, Sarge."

He clicked it shut and Angela reached for her gun. The woman screamed, and the men looked up, wide-eyed in fear.

Angela passed the gun to Sarge. "Shoot them."

"Shoot them?" He looked from the five back to Angela. "Seriously?"

"Yes. What can we do with them now, even if they're not spies? They know too much. We can't use them again. They're worthless."

"But..."

"This was your mission, and it fucked up. Shoot them."

Sarge looked at Scott.

"Don't look at him, look at me."

Sarge paused. "But they're our own people, Angela, we can't kill them."

Angela loaded the gun and eyed the five crew members, now paralysed with fear. "Who's in charge here?"

"You are."

"Damn right I am. Didn't you learn to follow your superiors' orders in the army?" She pushed the gun into his chest. "Do it."

Sarge froze, and after a moment, he shook his head.

"I'm sorry, I can't do that, it's not right, I can't." He looked at Scott again. "What do you think?"

Scott opened his mouth to speak but Angela butt in. "He thinks what I think."

She pointed the gun at the first worker, who let out a rasping yell.

"Fine, I'll do it myself," Angela barked.

She pulled the trigger, and the man slumped back in the chair, blood pouring from his chest.

Scott turned away.

Four more shots rang out as he kept staring at the wall. The room smelt of urine and gunpowder. The door closed and Scott looked back. All five crew members lay dead in their seats. Sarge stared aghast.

"She went too far this time," he muttered. "She went too far."

Chapter Twelve

Scott roamed The Nest out of restlessness. He tried staying in his room, but anxiety and fear got the better of him. Angela had disappeared, and he had no desire to see her anyway. The senseless killings of the airport workers sickened him. Her ease at shooting them acted as a sharp reminder of both how ruthless she could be, and the seriousness of the situation he found himself in. Had she had killed anyone like that before?

Sarge's comment that she had gone too far rang in his head as he walked. Was she a liability now? Would the hero worship she inspired stop, or at least weaken? He didn't know.

The atmosphere in The Nest had slowed, the usual bustle of activity gone, replaced by quietness. Nobody crossed his path as he strolled the corridors. The main room was only half full, and those who were there sat in silence.

Across the room, Lauren and Martin strode towards him, deep in conversation. He ducked into a chair at an empty desk, thankful for the gloom, and pretended to study the papers strewn in front of him, head down.

"I don't care, this is too much, something has to change," Lauren said as they passed.

They continued walking, and after a few seconds, Scott lifted his head, just in time to see them leave by the main doors. He got up and followed.

He tracked them as they walked, too far back to hear their voices, and worried they would turn and see him. They got to a room and Martin held the door as Lauren went inside.

Scott had a couple of seconds to bolt into an alcove, pressing his back against the wall. The door ahead closed. They hadn't seen him.

He waited a moment, then eased away from the wall and started towards the door. Pressing his ear against it, he heard Sarge's voice. "I've always said she's too hot headed, haven't I?" Sarge said.

Lauren replied, but too quietly for Scott to make out the words. Martin spoke next. "There's no way she'll accept being pushed aside."

"We don't give her a choice, we force her. Fight fire with fire, Sarge said.

Scott held his breath as he listened. "She's a fucking liability, guys. You know it's true. We get rid of her and us three run things."

Somebody moved towards the door, and Scott stepped back, ready to flee. The movement stopped and someone leant against the door. It must have been Lauren, as when she spoke next, her voice became clearer.

"He's right, she drinks too much, and she's too highly strung, she's losing it."

Scott turned away and took a deep breath, then pressed his ear back on the door, aware only a couple of inches separated him from Lauren. "I'm not sure," Martin said.

"She's got her faults, but she's good, she knows everything, she's..."

Sarge spoke over him. "What about Scott then? We know nothing about him, and she brings him into the inner sanctum. It's madness." The door moved as Lauren pushed herself away. "Yeah exactly, I don't trust the guy as far as I can throw him. He's already fucked up big time with that girl."

"Personally, I think we can trust him, OK she's a bit crazy sometimes, but she knows the guy better than us," Martin said.

"Is she fucking him or what?" Lauren asked.

They laughed and Scott scrambled away from the door as two people entered the corridor. They noticed him, and he walked towards them muttering a 'hello' as he passed. He kept on, heading away from the room, heart racing, and hid around the corner.

He waited a minute and once sure the coast was clear, tiptoed back up the corridor and crouched outside of the door.

Sarge was talking. "We'll do this democratically, unlike she would. If all three of us don't agree, we won't do it. Let's take a few days, see what happens, and meet again. Deal?"

Again, movement came towards the door, and Scott hurried away, worried that if they deposed Angela, he would be alone.

———

THE NEXT DAY, Scott set out to talk to Martin about his search for Miriam and Benji. He found him sitting at his desk, eating and checking the football results.

"Busy?"

"Just taking a break," Martin replied through a mouthful of banana.

"How's the search going?"

Martin looked distracted. "What search?"

"For my son and ex-wife."

"Oh yeah, of course." Martin picked up the banana skin and threw it into a bin under the desk. "No luck yet, but I'll keep trying. Things have been a bit hectic around here as you can imagine."

"Hectic?" Scott asked, looking at the screen showing the football scores. "Is something being planned?"

Martin moved uncomfortably in his seat. "No, just dealing with the fallout of what happened. I'll let you know if I find anything."

Scott leant back in his chair, crossing his arms. "What exactly are you doing to find them?"

"I'm following a few leads, checking out of country stuff. Look, I'll let you know OK? I'm kind of busy now."

Realising that this line of enquiry was getting nowhere, Scott changed tack. "What's happening with Angela?"

Martin sucked in his cheeks. "Nothing, no one's seen her since yesterday."

"Is anyone planning to talk to her or..."

There was a noise behind them, and they turned to see Angela smiling, holding a huge cup of coffee. "Morning, boys, we need to talk. Follow me."

Scott and Martin followed her to the same room in which she had shot the five people the day before. Not a trace of what had happened remained.

"We'll wait for the other two to arrive, and then we'll start." She fiddled with her hair. "God, you two look tired, didn't you sleep?"

"Not really," Scott muttered.

Martin shrugged.

"Sleep is so important, especially in this sub-terranean world we live in. I slept like a baby. Feel like a new woman today."

She certainly appeared well rested, her eyes bright and eager.

"Ah, here we go," she said as Sarge and Lauren entered the room. They both looked at Scott, then at each other. "Come along, sit down."

Sarge and Lauren folded their arms as they sat, completely unimpressed. Angela stood at the front.

"This is like school, isn't it?" she joked, and then she began imitating schoolchildren. "Good morning, Mrs Newton, good morning, everybody." Angela laughed. "Who remembers that?"

Nobody spoke, and Angela raised her eyebrows.

"Tough crowd. Anyway, let's get down to business." She sipped from her cup. "I'll be leaving tonight."

Lauren glanced at Martin and Sarge. "Leaving?"

Angela noticed the look. "Yes, leaving, not forever, don't worry, only a few days." She stopped, disappointed when nobody said anything. "Well, doesn't anybody want to know where I'm going?"

"Where are you going?" Martin asked robotically.

"I'm glad you ask. It's a secret though. I'll be getting some help for our next attack and need to meet certain people." She shot Sarge a sarcastic smile. "If you want something done properly, do it yourself, eh?"

Sarge looked away.

"Whilst I'm gone, I want everything to run smoothly. A tight ship. Understand?" They all nodded in response, tight-lipped. "Jesus, you guys are still thinking about yesterday, aren't you? Move on, forget it."

Sarge refolded his arms. "How can we forget it?"

"Because I'm telling you to," Angela ordered, her tone shifting from jovial to sinister.

Sarge glanced at Lauren and Martin. Angela watched them, eyes flicking from one to the other.

"This meeting is over. Go back to work," she barked.

In silence, they got up to leave. "Scott, seeing as you have got no work to do, you may as well stay."

Lauren snorted, something Angela either didn't hear or pretended not to.

———

ONCE THEY HAD LEFT, Angela kicked off her boots and slumped into a chair. She rested her feet on the table and stared at the ceiling.

"I can't wait to get out of this place, it's so draining." She looked at Scott and frowned. "What's up with you?"

"What's up with me, Angie? You killed five people in front of me for fuck's sake, what's wrong with *you*?"

She ran a hand through her hair, "Oh God, what did I just say, move on."

"But..."

"What would you have done with them?" Angela shouted, sliding her legs off the desk.

"I don't know, but not that."

"See, you don't know. When you're in charge, you need to know." She sipped her coffee. "Now, can we talk about something else?"

Scott gaped at her in disbelief, and she kept her eyes fixed on his.

"Where are you going?" he asked.

"I can't say."

Scott slid his chair closer to hers and rested his elbows on the table. "There's something you should know."

Angela paused and flashed Scott a look, the cup held aloft between them. "What?"

"They're thinking of getting rid of you."

Angela put down the cup and stared at it for a few seconds.

"There was a meeting. I listened at the door. Sarge and Lauren want you out. Martin sort of disagreed," Scott explained, and Angela took out a cigarette and lit it. "I promised to tell you everything. I thought you should know."

She watched the cigarette smoke float into the air. "Thank you. What exactly did they say?"

"That you overacted to the Heathrow thing, that you drink too much. That you're a liability," Scott said.

Angela reached for the coffee cup and pushed it under his nose. "This is just coffee, you smell that? Little fuckers," she grumbled, pulling on the cigarette.

"They're meeting again to discuss it."

"This comes with the territory. There's nothing I can do about it now. When I'm back, I'll sort it out. Maybe Sarge has to be gotten rid of. Keep your ears close to the ground though." Angela seemed rattled and took a couple of quick puffs of the cigarette, then looked at her watch. "I have to go now. I'll be back in a couple of days. Listen out for anything and give me the lowdown when I'm back."

As she went to kiss him over the top of her head, Scott noticed a bullet hole in the wall. She stopped, millimetres from his lips, and followed his gaze.

"You're pissed off I shot those people, aren't you?"

"I understand why, Angie, but I think you went too far, yeah."

"I didn't go far enough," she whispered, then she kissed him and walked away, leaving him stood in the middle of the room.

He kept staring at the bullet hole.

————

AFTER A SLEEPLESS NIGHT, Scott couldn't take the atmosphere anymore. The lack of progress in the hunt for Miriam and Benji annoyed him, and he decided to take it into his own hands. He decided to go to Miriam's and look for clues, anything instead of feeling helpless in The Nest.

"I need to get out," he told Martin. "Being cooped up down here is killing me, I need some fresh air, I need to stretch my legs."

"Well, it's not a prison, bro. You can check out any time you want. But I don't think it's a good idea. If it was up to me, I'd say no, but I'm not in charge."

"I need to," Scott pleaded.

"I'll show you a safe way out. Give me five minutes."

Living underground was driving him mad. A physical and mental claustrophobia made worse by Angela's departure. He needed to see the real world to think straight, and to find Miriam and Benji.

Martin returned, flustered.

"We have a window of time now, hurry." Martin showed him to a heavy door in a store cupboard. "Go through here, and you'll come out in a staff area in Clapham Common tube station. A staff area we control." He looked at his watch. "It's safe to go now. Someone will meet you."

Scott nodded. "Thanks. How do I get back in?"

"When you're ready, message me on this number." Martin slipped Scott a card with a number scrawled across it in biro. "I'll tell you the best way in. How long you gonna be, bro?"

"I don't know, an hour or two maybe."

"Ok, don't go far."

———

SCOTT CAME out into a space with low chairs around a circular coffee table. In one corner, a small kitchen littered with dirty mugs, in another, a coat rack draped with navy London Underground jackets. A side door opened, and a young man appeared, looking around nervously.

"Come," he said with a flick of the head.

Without a word, the man kicked open another door and pointed towards the opening. Scott thanked him and walked out onto a sparsely filled platform. Nobody looked at him as he walked up the platform and onto the escalator.

As he reached the barriers, the daylight hitting his eyes surprised him. It had only been a few days, but his body wasn't used to it, and he squinted as he exited the station.

The high street, normally polluted with God knows what, smelled as sweet as country air, and Scott stopped to take it in. He glanced at his watch: ten o'clock, and continued weaving through the passers-by along the street, building up a sweat as he went. For the first time in his life, he actually enjoyed feeling the sweat trickle down his forehead; The Nest was overly air-conditioned, making the air far too dry.

Scott bought a pack of cigarettes in a nearby off-licence, his eyes finally becoming accustomed to the light.

He hadn't turned on his phone while in The Nest, fearing it would bring more stress than good, but as he inhaled the fresh air and took a few pulls on the cigarette, he switched it on and waited for the vibrations in his pocket. They came thick and fast, and he kept walking, ignoring it for now.

Scott reached Clapham Common, sat on a bench, stretched his legs, and took out his phone. Multiple missed calls from an unknown number flashed up on the screen. He opened the text messages, the first from Henry simply read: 'WHAT THE FUCK?', the second: 'WHAT HAPPENED TO THE STATION ATTACK THEN?', the third: 'CALL ME NOW'. Scott stopped reading them, closed his eyes and basked in the sun. The idea of going back to The Nest repelled him and he got up to strolled across the grass. Ahead stood a couple with a young child feeding the ducks.

In the old days, Scott would do the same with Benji, Miriam complaining that ducks shouldn't eat bread: *'It fills up their stomachs and makes them think they're full.'*

As he reached the pond, somebody shouted from behind, "Scott Saunders?"

He spun round and an armed policeman stood twenty feet away. "Hands above your head."

Scott held his arms up as the policeman advanced towards him, gun raised. From behind a tree, another two policemen approached, both holding guns. A few people in the park stopped to stare at the scene.

"Scott Saunders, I am arresting you on suspicion of the murder of Olympia Harrison. You do not have to say anything, but it may harm your defence if you do not mention when questioned something which you later rely on in court. Anything you do say may be given in evidence. Do you understand?"

Chapter Thirteen

Miriam stepped off Shlomo Lahat Promenade and onto the beach. Even with sunglasses on, the sun reflecting off the water dazzled her eyes. Benji ran ahead, kicking a ball across the bright yellow sand.

Keeping a close eye on him, she leant against a palm tree and removed her sandals. It had been years since she felt sand between her toes. She inhaled the salty air and took in the view.

The water seemed unreal, a brilliant blue, blending in with the sky on the horizon. The beach was crowded, and she squinted, searching for the pink umbrellas that would mark the meeting place.

It had only been three days since she arrived in Tel Aviv, but it felt like a lifetime. The apartment she had been given was only a half-hour walk from the beach, but she had spent those days making it feel like home and exploring the immediate neighbourhood.

She tried to push the negative thoughts to the back of her mind; money would soon become an issue. She would have to find a job, and the school Benji had been placed in wasn't the best.

On the second day, Miriam had returned from the supermarket to discover a handwritten note inviting her to a party on the beach; a mixture of locals and people who had got out of Britain. *'Look for the pink umbrellas, Kids welcome, bring a bottle.'*

She noticed the umbrellas ahead with clusters of people underneath, sheltering from the sun and tending barbeques.

"This way," she called out to Benji.

A woman introduced herself as Tanya. "So glad you could make it. We love to meet all the new Brits. How long have you been here?"

She fussed over Benji and poured Miriam a gigantic glass of Rosé.

"Only a couple of days," Miriam replied, looking around at the assembled group, mostly middle-aged women.

Tanya looked at Benji. "Do you like it here, little man?"

He mumbled a 'yes' and hid behind Miriam's legs.

Miriam laughed. "Sorry, he's a little shy."

Tanya pointed towards a group of older children kicking a ball around. "Why don't you play with the other kids?"

Before Miriam even said anything, Benji looked up and raced towards them.

Tanya laughed. "Not so shy after all. Now let me introduce you to everyone."

Miriam spent the next ten minutes being paraded from person to person, saying her name, saying she'd only been here a couple of days, then politely moving onto the next person.

Once this was over, Tanya ushered her to a cluster of deckchairs and took a bottle from a nearby table. "Let me fill up your drink."

Before Miriam could protest, another huge serving of wine filled her glass.

Tanya raised her glass. "To freedom."

Miriam took a sip. "Freedom."

She hadn't eaten since breakfast, and the heat coupled with the rosé had made her light-headed.

Tanya leant towards her. "What's it like in England now, I hear it's getting stricter by the day?"

"It's pretty bad, I couldn't take it anymore."

"What's the story with the resistance? We keep hearing about bombs and stuff. Is it as dangerous as we hear?"

Miriam had a flashback of Scott telling her about Benji being taken. "It's dangerous and getting worse, that's why we left."

"I used to count the days, praying we could go back, but now I don't think we will. I love it here. I still can't believe it happened sometimes. Who'd have thought it? I mean, one minute everything's fine, then the virus comes along, then it seems fine again, then suddenly, boom. At first, I thought it wouldn't last, then after a couple of years, I said to Fred, 'we have to go', a week later we were on the plane. Thank God they let us out." Tanya gazed out across the sea. "Are you married?"

Despite fully expecting this line of questioning, Miriam still flinched inwardly when asked.

"No, separated."

Tanya leant over and took her hand. "I can see you're upset, love, so I won't pry. Plus, there are plenty of men out here, anyway." She let out a rasping laugh and squeezed her hand. "Come on, love, let's get this food going."

They reached the barbecue and Tanya put Miriam in charge of the fish. She chatted to the other women whilst absorbing the sun and enjoying the rich smells of the cooking. A pair of speakers played Motown music and a few of the drunker people danced to it.

Miriam waved to Benji, now splayed out on the sand with some other boys playing, talking and drinking cokes. Miriam sipped her wine, now warm from the sun, and put some sea bass on the barbeque. For the first time since reaching Israel, she was happy. All thoughts of London and Scott melted away. The trauma of the escape seemed a distant memory. Chatting to the other women and laughing as they cooked made her feel at home.

———

THEY SAT on deckchairs and ate off paper plates as the sun set over the sea. Tipsy as she had become, Miriam took Tanya's jokes about finding a new man with good humour and joined in with the conversations, the sound of her own laughing a shock. It had been a while since she had enjoyed herself this much. The exiled Brit community all seemed to be here on the beach, and they regaled each other with stories of leaving England for a better life. Everybody was relaxed and it rubbed off on Miriam. The men sat separately, their conversation growing louder as the drinks flowed.

When the sun dipped below the horizon, they lit the candles perched on the tables and passed blankets around. Benji and the boys continued a football game on the sand, as one by one people said their goodbyes and drifted away.

Finishing her last drink, Miriam got up, slightly dizzy, and called Benji over. She wished Tanya and the others goodbye, and taking Benji by the hand, headed across the beach and onto the road. The cool sand crunched beneath their toes as they walked, sandals in hand.

"Did you have a good time?" she asked Benji.

Benji shrugged and said, "Yeah, it was alright."

Miriam rubbed his hair. "You look like you had fun, more than alright I think?"

He looked up at her. "I loved it. This is a good holiday."

They reached the road, and she spotted a bar with people sat facing the sea view.

"Mummy wants to sit and have one more drink before we go home, is that OK?"

Benji shrugged, and they took a seat next to a glowing orange patio heater. She ordered a glass of wine, and a coke for Benji. He lifted his feet and curled up into the chair.

Mopeds sped past and couples walked by hand in hand. She felt relaxed, and for the first time since arriving, she knew she would sleep well.

As she considered ordering another drink, a woman in a Panama hat and shades, despite the darkness, approached the table. She held a large glass of wine in one hand and a cigarette in the other.

She stopped and looked at Miriam, then lowered the shades slightly. "Miriam, isn't it?"

Miriam reached out a hand protectively to Benji. "Who's asking?"

The woman took off her hat, revealing a head of bouncy curls, and blew out a plume of smoke.

"Angela Newton," she said, "mind if I take a seat?"

Chapter Fourteen

Miriam had seen her on television before, most recently sobbing over the death of her husband; the husband Scott had killed. But never in the flesh.

Angela wasn't conventionally attractive, though she had something about her. Her thinness should have looked frail, but she carried it well. Her short, wildly curly bob reminded her of a nickname Scott said she once had: Medusa.

She flashed an awkward smile at Benji and pointed at Miriam's wineglass. "Not the local plonk, I hope, vile stuff. Now, I don't know if you know who I am but..."

Miriam cut her off, "I know who you are."

Angela smiled. "Good, that avoids any boring introductions then." She pointed at Benji, now uncurled and sitting upright. "This must be Bobby then?"

Miriam's heart raced and she felt her freedom slipping away. "What do you want?"

Angela took a long drag on the cigarette, her bony fingers shaking as she did so, and blew the smoke from the corner of her mouth. "Another glass of the Pinot would be a start."

Miriam slammed her palm on the table, causing both Benji and Angela to jump. "I said. What. Do. You. Want?"

The smile dropped from Angela's face, and she leant towards Miriam. "I need a favour. I'm in town on business, and knowing you were here, hoped you could help me."

"Are you serious?" Miriam's mouth hung open in shock. "Is there something wrong with you?" She looked at Benji who looked more interested than scared. "How did you know I'm here, anyway?"

"Don't worry about that. But please, I need your help."

"I came here to get away from all this shit. I'm not speaking to you for one more second." Miriam stood and gathered her purse. "Come on, Benji, we're going."

Angela tapped the rim of her glass. "If you help me, I can help you." She rubbed her fingers together. "Money. Lots of money, a good school for him, whatever you need."

Miriam moved around the table towards her, whispering now so Benji couldn't hear. "You stay away from me, do you understand?"

Angela took hold of her arm. "Please, Miriam."

"Don't 'Miriam' me," she hissed, brushing the hand away. "I don't know you, and I want nothing to do with you." She hesitated and lowered her voice, putting her mouth directly to Angela's ear. "Didn't my ex-husband kill your husband, anyway?"

Angela snapped her head back. "He told you that?"

Miriam pushed past her and took Benji by the hand, heading towards the pavement.

From behind her, Angela shouted across the terrace, "Well, he didn't. I did."

Miriam stopped, feeling a pang of jealousy that Scott

was ready to lie to make himself look like a murderer to protect Angela. She turned as Angela marched towards them, shoving her hat back on as she walked.

"If you know what's good for you, you'll help me. Israel can be a dangerous place."

"Are you threatening me, Angela Newton?" Miriam replied. Angela winced as she said her name. "I can call the police in a second."

Angela's eyes darted around the street. "Don't use my name. You haven't seen me, understand? I need your help. I can get you a nice house, better than that shitty apartment in Shapira."

Now Miriam winced as Angela named her address. "You'll be helping a lot of people, helping to get rid of that fascist anti-Jewish government. Plus, the money. It's win-win."

They stood facing each other like statues in the middle of the bustling street. A sea breeze blew at Angela's hat, and she reached up a hand to hold it in place.

"Don't tell me you're not interested."

Miriam hailed a passing taxi, turning her back to Angela. She opened the door and Benji got in, then spun around.

"I'm not interested."

She slammed the door, and the taxi pulled away.

———

MIRIAM TRIED in vain to be calm when she got home. She sent Benji to bed, dismissing his questions of who "that lady" was, and stood at the window.

In times like this, she understood why Scott always had a bottle of rum to hand. The effect of the wine had worn off the moment Angela introduced herself, replaced with a surge of adrenaline that had still not dissipated.

Just an hour ago, she had been relaxed and happy, as if she had erected a wall between her and her life in England, but it had been torn down by Angela's appearance. She felt unsafe, trapped in a small country, in a small apartment that Angela *knew the location of.*

Angela Newton, a known violent resistance leader, and ex-girlfriend of Scott to boot, had somehow tracked her down thousands of miles from home, within days. And she wanted something from her. Was she telling the truth about her killing David and not Scott? If so, why did Scott say he did it? Had she seen him recently? Did she want to? And what could Angela possibly want from her? Should she do it?

All these questions swam around in Miriam's head as she looked out the window, seeing the car park across the road and her own refection in the dark glass.

———

At one o'clock the next day, alone in the house whilst Benji was at school, the doorbell rang. Miriam turned on the security app the Israelis had given her. Sure enough, a slight female figure, Panama hat pulled down over her face, stood in the passage.

She muted the television, placed the phone on the coffee table, and sat still. The bell rang again, and she peered at the phone screen. Angela took out a phone of her own, tapped it a few times and held it to her ear. Miriam's phone burst into life. The ringing echoed around the tiled room, accompanied by the rattling as it vibrated on the fake marble table.

"I can hear that," Angela's voice said from behind the front door. "I just want to talk."

Miriam tiptoed to the kitchen and slid a knife into her waistband. "Who is it?"

"Who do you think?"

Miriam put one hand on the knife. "I'm asking you politely to go away." There was a muffled muttering, and she looked at the image again. Angela looked up and down the corridor, then pulled something from her bag and held it to the camera. A stack of US dollars filled the screen for a moment, replaced by Angela's lips.

"And there's plenty more where that came from," she whispered.

Miriam walked away, unmuted the television, and turned up the volume. Her phone rang again, then the knocking started. A steady *tap tap* at first and then a pounding.

Miriam leapt up, checked the knife was in place and pulled open the door. They stared at each other. Miriam, leaving the door open, walked back inside, towards the sofa, the knife digging into her thigh.

Angela stayed in the doorway. "So, are you going to invite me in then or..."

"What are you, a vampire?"

A smile crept across Angela's face. She stepped inside and closed the door behind her.

———

Miriam picked up the remote control and lowered the TV volume. "I'm not even going to bother asking how you know where I live. Let alone how you got my number."

Angela looked around the apartment with distaste and

reached into her bag. Instinctively, Miriam felt for the knife, patting it with her hand. Angela noticed the movement.

"You don't need to fear me, Miriam," she said, rummaging in the bag. "I'm here to help you. And hopefully by the end of this conversation, you will help me." Angela pulled out a bottle of wine. "Is it too early for this?"

Miriam pointed her in the direction of the kitchen and Angela returned with two tumblers of wine. "I couldn't find any wine glasses, but I'll drink out of anything."

She passed one to Miriam.

"I haven't had time," Miriam shrugged.

Angela took a long sip. "It would have been the first thing I'd have bought. Anyway, I'll get straight to the point. I need you to pick something up for me. Simple as that."

Miriam scowled. "Why on earth would I do anything for you?"

"The money, Miriam, I mean... look at this place, wouldn't you be happier in a nicer flat in a nicer part of town? I can make that happen for you..." Angela clicked her fingers. "Overnight."

Miriam sipped her wine and hesitated. "I came here to get away from this shit. I'm sorry, but I just cannot entertain it."

Angela rolled her eyes. "What is it you want then? Tell me, I'll make it happen."

"A peaceful quiet life, and you are single handily fucking that up."

Angela came towards her. "Do you ever want to go back to England?"

"I don't know, I..."

Angela pounced on her. "Because I tell you something, until we get rid of those bastards in charge over there, you can never go back." She downed her drink and wiped her mouth with the back of her hand. "And believe it or not, this skinny half-crazy bitch in front of you is the best chance of toppling them. So, help me out and you can thank me later when you're living in your own country, raising your kid without anti-Semitic bullshit, which, trust me, is only going to get worse. If you don't want to do it for me, or the money, or your people, or your country, do it for your future."

Angela opened her bag and threw down a wad of notes onto the coffee table. Miriam glanced at them, not wanting to appear interested.

"That's ten thousand US dollars there. You'll get another ten thousand for doing the job. And Bobby gets a place in the International School. I work with important people here, Miriam. I have clout."

Angela stopped and drew a deep breath, her face crimson with anger. Angela's rant stunned Miriam.

"Why me though? Surely your 'clout' means someone else can help you? This doesn't make any sense."

Angela sat next to her, shaking as she poured another drink. She went to top up Miriam's cup, but she held her hand over it.

"Listen, sometimes the Israeli Government helps me, sometimes it's non-governmental; this job for you falls into the latter category. I'm too inconspicuous to do this. If I'm seen, it jeopardises everything, so I must be incredibly careful. It's not safe for me to…"

"But it's safe for me?"

Angela threw her hands into the air. "Yes, it is."

"If I'm to help you, I want you to answer some questions."

"Shoot," Angela said, getting up.

They stepped onto the balcony and rested their elbows

on the wall. The sound of the busy street below engulfed them; car horns, people shouting, a dog barking.

"If you killed your husband, why did Scott tell me he did it?"

Despite the noise, Angela spoke quietly. "The government told him to kill David. If it came out he didn't, Bobby would still be a hostage. Or worse." She took out a cigarette. "He did it for the kid, and you I suppose."

Miriam took it in, shocked. Angela continued to stare ahead. In profile with her sunglasses on, she looked almost glamorous. Almost.

"Why did *you* kill him?" Miriam asked.

Angela pulled on the cigarette. "He was putting everything we worked for in danger. Someone else had to take the reins."

"So, you killed him?"

"Yep."

"Jesus Christ. How can you stand here and talk about killing your husband as easily as chatting about the weather?"

"The road to hell is paved with good intentions, I suppose. Everything we are discussing here is not being done for selfish reasons, it's being done to help people. Nothing has been for my personal gain. Nothing. Do you understand that? Not one thing. I have brought suffering onto myself trying to get rid of these bastards. And you know what, Miriam?" Angela held up her smoke-stained thumb and forefinger. "They are *that* close to falling."

"I don't believe that."

"Look at the Nazis, the Soviet Union. These things look strong then suddenly fall apart. That's what's happening here. When you're an old woman, you don't want to sit thinking you could have done something, and you did nothing. You help me, you're doing something."

"So, what exactly do I have to do?"

"There's a businessman, Uncle Shai. He owns a yacht currently in the harbour in Jaffa. There's a casino or something on it. You go there, tell them I sent you and they will hand you a briefcase. You leave, you give it to me, you get the rest of the money."

Miriam began to consider it. "And this is perfectly safe?"

"One hundred percent."

"And you make sure Benji and I are safe out here, the school, the money?"

Angela took off her sunglasses and faced Miriam, eyes red and squinting into the sunlight. "I promise."

"What's in the briefcase?" Miriam asked, fanning away Angela's cigarette smoke.

"I can't tell you that. I'm not even sure myself."

Miriam fiddled with her hair. "When?"

"Tonight."

Miriam gaped. "Tonight? What am I meant to do with Benji?

Angela threw her cigarette butt down onto the street below, watching it tumble before answering. "I can look after him."

Miriam scoffed. "That is not happening."

Angela scowled, irritated. "Well, you need to sort something out."

Miriam held out her cup. Angela refilled it in silence as Miriam gazed at the apartments opposite. "OK, I'll do it."

Angela exhaled. "Phew, I was worried you were going to say no. You don't half ask a lot of questions, it's like being on *Who Wants to be a Millionaire*. Come on."

They went back inside, and Angela pointed at the money on the table.

"Ten thousand dollars, and another ten thousand when I get the briefcase. I'll be back tonight at seven to help you get ready."

She walked to the front door.

"Angela, can I ask you one more thing? Have you seen Scott since the day your husband died?"

"No," Angela lied, one hand on the door. "I promise."

Chapter Fifteen

"You'll be well aware that this crime carries the death penalty, Mr Saunders, so it's best you answer honestly."

The man, late forties, unshaven and smelling strongly of sweat, hit play on a tape recorder.

"Did you kill Olympia Harrison?"

On the way to the police station, Scott had gone over his options: tell them the truth and hope they believed him; lie and say he knew nothing; or refuse to comment. Since the takeover, he had no legal right to a lawyer, but his past as a police officer gave him some knowledge of the best thing to do.

He looked his interrogator in the eye. "No comment."

The man closed his eyes and rubbed his temples. "Where were you on the night of May 15th?"

"No comment."

"Have you met Olympia Harrison?"

"No comment."

"Have you ever been to Willow Farm, Essex?"

"No comment."

The man stood. "Mr Saunders, you know we have a DNA profile of you, yes?"

One of the first things the government did upon taking power was to gather the DNA of as many people as they could. The first wave was the vaccinations. On being vaccinated, they also took a DNA swab; the next wave was all government employees, then slowly, almost all the population had a swab. New-born babies had their DNA taken at birth. The plan was to have everyone in the UK on the database within ten years. His DNA would be all over Olympia, and they wanted to charge him. Speaking wouldn't help.

"Let me show you a picture of a man who says you *have* been to Willow Farm."

The interrogator placed a photo on the table. Mutt, the man on whose land they had buried the body, beaten to a pulp.

"He says you borrowed a tractor on the night of the 15th. He says you went out onto his land with it."

Images of Olympia's pale body flashed in Scott's mind. Bile rose in his stomach.

"As you can see from the pictures, he took some persuading to tell us."

He threw another picture onto the table. Mutt, with wires attached to him, bleeding.

"We found a body on that land. We found your DNA on that body." The man took Scott's chin in his hand. "Still no comment?"

Scott stared and the man, and he produced a photo of Angela.

"Do you know this woman?"

Scott didn't even bother speaking. The man sighed.

"Don't make this harder than it has to be, Mr Saunders. The only reason we are treating you well, so far, is that you're one of ours. Sort of." He opened a file. "You're still technically a police officer I can see." He turned the page. "On long term leave though. Interesting. Are you involved with the resistance?"

Scott said nothing. The man stared at him.

"Listen, you're in a right pickle here, and things can only get worse unless you help us out."

The door opened, an officer entered and put two cups of coffee on the table and left.

The man gestured to the cup. "Have a drink. And a think."

He left the room. Scott took stock of the situation. How much had Mutt told them? Angela's picture suggested too much.

Scott picked up the photo. Angela looked back at him in black and white. *Where are you?* The bitter smell of the coffee filled his nostrils. He pushed it away. God knows what they had put in it. The abolition of jury trials meant he was on a one-way road to prison. The door clicked open again, and his interrogator entered, frowning.

"Seems like you have friends in high places, Mr Saunders. You're free to go."

After being led down a warren of staircases, Scott entered a courtyard. Henry stood by a car, his suit jacket flapping in the breeze.

"Get in."

———

HENRY STEPPED ON THE ACCELERATOR. "Charing Cross, Victoria and London Bridge, eh?" The aroma of his aftershave filled the car. "What happened? Something go wrong?"

Scott caught his sneer reflected in the windshield. As they pulled out onto the street, Henry hit a button. Sirens blared from the car. He hit another and lights flashed from the roof. Cars pulled aside as they sped up. Scott hastily fastened the seatbelt.

"I don't know, that's what I was told."

They took a corner too fast, hitting the curb as they went. Scott gripped the dashboard.

"We found," Henry shouted above the roar of the engine, "some piss poor bombs at Heathrow yesterday. Was that the actual target?"

As they hit Edgware Road, the speedometer hit 60 mph.

"Are you feeding me bullshit, Scott?" Henry swerved past a bus, heading towards the stationary cars at the traffic lights. "Because if you are, Miriam and Benji won't be safe for much longer."

Scott pushed an imaginary brake pedal as they reached the stopped traffic. The car didn't slow down. Henry squeezed them through a gap. Scott flinched as a sudden bang rang out, and the passenger side wing mirror shattered. They avoided a bus by centimetres as they crossed Marble Arch roundabout. Hitting Park Lane, Henry accelerated again.

"They will die." Henry shouted. "Do you understand that?"

He looked at Scott, holding his stare. The speedometer hit 80mph. "Keep your eyes on the road, for God's sake." Scott yelled.

Still, Henry looked at him. "They'll move."

They zoomed towards a car in front, Henry still not

looking at the road. Scott reached over and pulled the wheel just in time to avoid it.

"What do you want?"

Henry snapped back into the moment and took control of the car.

"I want you to tell me the truth," he roared above the siren, spit flying from his mouth.

"I was told those stations were the target. I knew nothing about Heathrow, I swear."

Henry pumped the accelerator, pinning Scott back in his seat as they sped up again. The next roundabout loomed ahead. Scott clenched his eyes shut as they took it at speed. A bump, then a screech, the stench of burnt rubber. A hard jolt, and the wheels lifted off the tarmac.

For a second, they floated in the air. They crashed to the ground and spun. Scott raised a hand to his head, the other gripping the dashboard, awaiting an impact. None came. Instead, the car spun, the tires screeching again, piercing through the siren's whine. He opened his eyes. The car faced the oncoming traffic, steam pouring from the bonnet. The sirens had stopped, but the lights still flashed.

Henry breathed heavily and looked around, disorientated.

"I'll tell you what you're going to do, you're going to kill Angela." A passer-by approached the car, Henry waved them away. "And if you don't, then I will personally kill Miriam and your son." He turned the engine off. "And you."

Scott let go of the dashboard. "I don't even know where she is."

"I don't care. You find her, and you kill her. She is not more important to you than your son. So I'm sure you'll find a way."

Scott wiped a bead of sweat from his forehead. "OK, fine."

He unclipped the seatbelt, and Henry reached over, placing his hand on Scott's arm.

"You have one week to kill her. Now get out of my car."

Chapter Sixteen

Miriam lay on the bed as the clock ticked towards seven. What she was about to do was absurd. Angela had been convincing, but could she really trust her? How would she react if Miriam backed out now?

But she wouldn't back out. Here was a chance to make a lot of money, get Benji into a decent school, and help deal a blow to the brutal government that had taken over her country.

Fear jolted her upright as the lift in the corridor opened. She worried about Benji staying with Tanya for the evening.

When she left England, she vowed to never let him out of her sight, yet here she was, less than a week in and doing just that.

Miriam rose just as the doorbell rang. Angela bustled in, struggling under a heap of clothes slung over her shoulder, and a large holdall in one hand.

"What's all this?"

Angela placed them on the table. "You can't go to a

billionaire's yacht wearing..." She looked Miriam up and down. "Mum clothes."

Miriam took a step back and looked at her jeans and t-shirt self-consciously.

"Excuse me, mum clothes? I have a couple of nice dresses with me."

Angela unzipped the covers. "Well, *nice* won't cut it." She looked up. "What size are you, ten?"

"Yeah."

"That's what I guessed." Angela continued unpacking the expensive-looking dresses. "Now, let's have a drink and play dress up."

One by one, Angela held up the dresses against Miriam in between large sips of champagne.

"They're a bit short, aren't they?" Miriam said.

"I saw your legs the other night. You can pull this off. This is what they'll all be wearing. It's a very Euro trash vibe at these things. You have to fit in."

"I don't know if I'll feel comfortable in any of these."

"Honestly, Miriam," Angela said, and Miriam winced again at the sound of her name, as if they were friends, "if you've got it, flaunt it. I would kill to wear any of these. Unfortunately, my legs are far too skinny. Tragic really, knobbly knees as well."

Angela pulled out the last one, an ankle length dark blue number.

"Here we go, the Chanel is long."

Miriam held it up against herself and smoothed the fabric down, revealing a full length slit.

Angela laughed. "OK, but it's still long, right?"

Despite herself, Miriam smiled.

She tried it on in the bedroom, amazed at how well it fit,

admiring her reflection before walking back out. Angela jumped up and held her hand to her mouth.

"Oh wow. Who's the hottie?" She gripped Miriam by the shoulders and turned her around. "This is perfect. Now, the shoes."

Despite all the shoes being too high to comfortably walk in, Miriam settled on a pair. Angela put them aside and pulled out a make-up bag.

"Now, final touches, make-up and jewellery. You're going to look a million dollars after this."

Angela began applying foundation to Miriam's cheeks.

"Trust me, what you're wearing isn't that far off it either." Angela giggled and looked up at the clock. "Oh God, we'd better hurry up."

Gripped by sudden anxiety, Miriam reached for a drink whilst Angela applied her eye shadow. "So, you haven't seen Scott since that day then?"

Angela's eyes narrowed. "I told you, no."

"Sometimes I wonder if he's coping alright."

Angela pressed a little too hard against Miriam's eye. "I'm sure he's absolutely fine."

"I left him a note saying I was going away. Maybe I'll contact him soon. Just to let him know we're OK."

Angela put down the makeup and peered closely into Miriam's face, their noses nearly touching. "No, I don't think that would be a good idea."

"Why not?"

She maintained the stare, her bloodshot eyes filling Miriam's field of vision.

"It just isn't," she said, holding Miriam's chin and moving her head back and forth. "Perfect. Have a look."

Angela handed Miriam a mirror, and she looked at her own heavily made-up face. "Thank you."

Angela took the mirror away. "It's the least I could do."

She took a bottle of perfume from the counter, Miriam's favourite Chanel No 5, and sprayed it liberally. "Wow, I'd forgotten how good this smells. I should get some. I always thought it was an old woman's perfume."

———

THE TAXI SLID through the darkening streets.

"So remember," Angela said, "tell someone you're there to see Shai, and that Angela sent you."

Miriam fiddled with the heavy bracelet and rings, and Angela took her hand. "Calm down, they're expecting you. Nothing can go wrong."

Miriam wasn't so sure. "I want to be in and out of there and picking Benji up as soon as possible."

Angela squeezed her hand. "I want the same, I can assure you."

The taxi emerged from the narrow street and out onto the marina. "Now look at me," Angela said, holding Miriam's face. "You will be fine, don't be scared, act like an entitled rich girl, get me the briefcase and everyone's happy."

Miriam took a deep breath and got out of the car.

———

THE 'BOTTOM DOLLAR' overshadowed the small harbour. Easily the largest yacht there, it gleamed in the setting sun.

As Miriam walked towards it, the lights strung across the decks turned on and a cheer emanated from inside. She stumbled on the cobbled floor and imagined Angela watching behind, shaking her head.

When she reached the gangway to the yacht, two

doormen in ludicrously tight-fitting suits were checking names against a list. Angela had told her to use her real name, which Miriam hadn't been happy with, but when she asked to change it, she was met with a stern, 'it's too late'.

A group of men argued with the doormen in Hebrew, and she turned to face the harbour. The taxi sat parked in the same place, and next to it, silhouetted by the sea, a thin figure smoking a cigarette, curls back lit by the sun.

"Miss," the doorman said, snapping Miriam out of her stare.

"Sorry." She tottered forward. "I was miles away."

He spoke in heavily accented English. "Your name please, madam,"

"Miriam Saunders."

He scanned the list, his mouth making shapes as he muttered the names. "No Miriam Saunders."

She fought the urge to spin around and look at a distant Angela. "There must be some mistake, I'm definitely on the list."

"Sorry, but you're definitely not." The doorman reached out an arm, ushering her aside as a group of French-speaking women entered. He shrugged his shoulders, "If your name's..."

"...Not down. You're not coming in yeah, I get it." She took a few steps down the gangway, then turned back. "What about Miriam Roth? That's my maiden name."

He scanned the list again and with a broad smile, lifted the velvet rope and flicked his head. "Welcome aboard."

As Miriam stepped forward, a waiter holding a tray of champagne approached her. She took a glass and savoured the bitter fizz.

Cautiously, she walked into the gloom of the yacht. Paintings hung where the windows should be. As her eyes adjusted to the light, the faux Asian décor became clear, a mish mash of Chinese, Japanese and Korean. The only light came from red lanterns on the walls and ceilings. From her position at the top of the staircase, she could see the gambling tables below, the lush green contrasting with the red dragon embroidered carpet.

Angela had been right about 'Euro trash'; the clientele rattled with cheap-looking jewellery. Every woman and most of the men were the same deep bronze colour. The men wore black ties and mostly hovered around the tables, living out some James Bond fantasy. The women gathered in animated groups, talking. She heard English, Hebrew, Spanish and French in the time it took to descend the stairs.

At the bottom, Miriam paused, seeing a glamorous woman staring at her, only to discover it was a mirror. She looked a second longer, amazed by the makeover, and then stopped again. Fear came over her. *This is crazy. What am I doing here? Dressed up like this on a millionaire's yacht at the behest of Angela Newton.* The absurdity made her laugh and calmed her down, thinking clearer about what to do next. *What would Angela do?*

She looked at her half empty glass and headed to the bar

———

THE BARMAN SLID her the cocktail, "Anything else?"

"I'm here to meet Shai."

"Shai? Sorry, don't know anyone with that name here."

He wiped his hands across his apron, and Miriam ran her finger around the rim of the glass. "Angela sent me."

"I just serve the drinks lady. Enjoy."

The barman stepped away to serve somebody else.

Behind her, a whooping came from one of the tables. Trying to appear calm, she walked away purposely, with no idea what to do.

Ahead stood one of the many suited staff scanning the room, earpiece ostentatiously clipped to one ear. She approached him, taking a large sip of the drink for courage.

"Excuse me." The timidity in her voice appalled her. "I'm here to see Shai, Angela sent me."

He didn't look at her, instead maintaining a watch on the room. "He's not meeting people tonight."

"Please, I need..."

"No." He turned to look at her. "Out of the question."

"But..."

"Enjoy your evening, lady."

He turned and walked away. Miriam wanted to follow him, but anger and fear rooted her to the spot. Around her, the room filled up and the multinational voices rolled into one buzzing sound in her ears. She leant against the wall to compose herself.

In one minute, she could be out of here, out of this absurd scene, taking off the painful shoes and berating Angela. Was this whole thing a set up?

She composed herself and headed to the croupier's pit.

A woman, tall and heavily made up, wearing a three-piece suit, smiled. "Can I help you?"

Angela's words stuck in her head: *Act like an entitled rich girl.*

"I need," Miriam said forcefully, "to speak to Shai. He is expecting me. Angela has sent me, and it is of the utmost importance."

The woman was taken aback. "And your name?"

"Is that important? He knows I'm coming. He knows

why I'm here, that's all you need to know." Miriam looked down at the woman's name badge. "Hannah."

The disdain with which she said the name surprised them both.

"One moment please."

She walked across the booth and picked up a phone. Feeling satisfied, Miriam allowed herself a long sip of the cocktail.

Hannah returned and said, "I'm sorry, it isn't possible. Maybe if I could take your name..."

"Miriam." she shouted.

Two Japanese women walking past looked back in shock. Hannah once again went to the phone, turning her back as she spoke.

She walked back and shook her head, smiling overly politely. "I'm afraid it's still a no, Miriam."

Enraged and frustrated, Miriam lifted her arm and watched with detached horror as she threw the drink into Hannah's face. Then, snapping back into the moment, Miriam headed for the exit, ignoring the scream behind. She marched as fast as the shoes would allow, terrified she had been set up by Angela, that it was all a trap and she would never see Benji again.

As she reached the first step, a hand grabbed her shoulder, but she twisted away and kept walking. Another hand gripped the other shoulder and pulled her back. She tried to wrestle free, but both arms wrapped around her waist and lifted her off the floor. Miriam kicked her legs, one shoe flying off as the man bundled her through a side door. She gave up struggling as the grip tightened around her, and she hung limply in the arms of a thug who reeked of too much aftershave.

They reached a set of golden sliding doors and he let go, dropping her to the floor. She kicked the other shoe off.

"You want to talk to Shai, get in the lift," he said.

The doors slid open. She turned to remonstrate, but the thug pushed her forward. Miriam stumbled, just managing to stay upright as the doors shut and the lift rose.

———

THE LIFT OPENED onto an opulent room, furnished in black and white. A fat elderly man in a tuxedo sat on a sofa, puffing a cigar. A younger man with slicked back blonde hair sat beside him.

The older man motioned for her to enter. "You must be Miriam."

From the large windows, the lights of Tel Aviv twinkled.

"I'm Shai. I hear you want to meet me. Why don't you sit down?"

"No thanks, just give me what I need, and I'll be gone."

Miriam stepped forward, her bare feet sinking into the plush carpet. The blonde man looked her up and down.

"Have a drink with us, then you get what you want." He patted the sofa. "Come on."

Shai smiled at her. "Don't upset an old man. Or Angela, you don't want to mess with her, I can tell you that."

He laughed, and Miriam sat down, calculating that she could at least overpower the older man with the crystal decanter on the coffee table if necessary.

The blonde man glanced at her leg, momentarily exposed by the slit as she made herself comfortable. Shai poured her a glass. "Macallan single malt, exceptional flavour, had it flown in from Scotland just last week." He winked. "'On the sly', as you say in Britain."

Clapping and shouting came from the deck below. Shai raised the glass. "Cheers."

Miriam clinked glasses with them and swallowed. Her throat burned as it went down. "Please, give me whatever it is."

"Why the rush, Miriam?" the blonde man asked. "Shai doesn't get the opportunity to spend time with beautiful women often."

He reached out and stroked her face, and she recoiled at his touch. "And you don't mingle with billionaires a lot, I imagine."

Miriam drained the rest of the whiskey. "Please, let's get this over and done with."

Shai reached around the armrest, then slid a silver and black briefcase around to his knees. "Here you go, it's heavier than it looks. Help an old man out."

As she leant over, the blonde man slid a hand up her leg.

"Get your fucking hands off me," she shouted, straining to lift the case. His hand moved up her thigh as she hauled herself upright. She swung the case towards him, meaning only to give herself room to escape, but misjudged, hitting Shai square in the face. He squealed and rolled over onto one side. The blonde man shouted something incomprehensible at Miriam as he helped Shai. Miriam panicked and ran towards the door, frantically pressing the lift button. She turned. Shai held his face, and the blonde man tried to help him.

The lift door opened, and she heaved the case inside. As the doors slid shut, the last thing she saw was Shai falling to the floor.

Following the route she had been dragged through, she came back out to the staircase. To her surprise, no one stopped her as she burst out, barefoot, dishevelled and carrying the case. She barged her way past the oncoming partygoers and outside, the suitcase becoming heavier as she descended the gangway.

Ahead, a car horn honked, and lights flashed. The vehicle moved towards her, then stopped. A beaming Angela got out in her Panama hat.

"Well done," she clapped.

Miriam shoved the suitcase into her chest. "Here's your fucking stuff. Now take me to my son."

Chapter Seventeen

Martin put his drink down.

"You got arrested? Fuck. What for, and how are you back here?"

Scott told him everything, except the order to kill Angela. He had presumed Angela had told Martin about Henry, and from his reaction, or lack of it, this seemed to be correct.

A silence fell as Scott finished.

Martin broke it. "Angela's gonna go nuts." He picked the label of his beer bottle and shrugged. "More nuts."

Scott took a beer. "We have to find where they're holding Miriam and Benji."

"I'm trying, bro, I'm trying."

Martin's casualness riled Scott. "You need to try harder."

"Jesus, don't get stroppy with me, mate, I promise I'm doing all I can."

Scott pushed his chair back. "I'm sick of this laid-back attitude. This is life or death we're talking about for fuck's sake."

"Are you serious? I'm doing everything, Scotty, I don't see anyone else doing anything." Martin stood up, raising his voice for the first time Scott could recall. "Don't piss me off or they won't get found for sure."

Not wanting to lose the only thing close to a friend he had in The Nest, Scott changed the subject. "Any idea where Angela is?"

"Fuck knows."

"What's going to happen when she comes back?"

Martin stepped to the door, opened it a crack, and looked through. He closed it. "We're giving her one more chance. If she's true to her word and comes back with a new attack plan, all is well."

"And if not?"

"All is not well." Martin leant back in his chair and puffed his cheeks. "It's her last chance. Sarge and Lauren think there should have been a vote when David died, anyway. She's living on borrowed time."

"What do you think of her?"

"As a leader?"

"Everything."

Martin went to speak but stopped. He shuffled uncomfortably. "I know you two are close. I..."

"Don't worry about that."

"Personally, I think she's great. I think she's strong. She's an iron bloody lady. But she needs to reign in her temper, and drink less. Definitely drink less."

"Do you think she's an alcoholic, or it just the stress?"

"Oh, an alcoholic for sure."

"Is she worse since David, er, died?"

"No, it's always been like this. But listen, she's a functioning alcoholic, and as long as she keeps functioning, it's all good." Martin leant forward, elbows resting on the table. "How close are you two, by the way?"

Footsteps passed the door. Scott waited for them to pass whilst weighing up how to answer. "I don't know. But I feel drawn to her. And I think she feels the same."

"I see the way she looks at you. And when she talks about you, there's a spark in her eyes, mate. Be careful though."

A spark? Scott pondered that for a second.

"All I can think about right now is my son, though. This is a mess, this whole thing is a fucking mess."

———

OLYMPIA STAGGERED TOWARDS HIM, *soil pouring from her as a full moon loomed behind her. Her matted blonde hair stuck to her face, and the smell of rotting flesh was overpowering. From beneath the skin, parts of her skull showed, glowing brightly in the moonlight. One eyeball hung from its socket, the other looked at Scott. He backed away and lost his footing, falling into what he knew was her grave. She leapt down towards him, somehow falling faster than him. Within seconds, she was on top of him, gripping at his neck and shaking. However much he tried to raise his hands, he couldn't. The shaking intensified, and he screamed.*

Scott woke in his bed, covered in sweat, still being shaken. The aroma of Chanel No.5, Miriam's favourite perfume, hung in the air.

"It's only me," Angela said, "calm down for God's sake."

She flicked on the bedside light. He covered his eyes from the glare as the dream faded away.

"When did you get back?"

"Just now."

Angela kicked off her boots and passed him a glass of water, which nearly slipped through his sweaty palms.

"Where did you go?"

"A secret mission," she whispered dramatically. "Meeting the proverbial man about a dog." A scratch on her face glowed red in the harsh beam of the lamp, contrasting with the beginnings of a black eye. "Or rather a dog about a man."

"What?"

"Nothing." She stroked his chest. "It was a success. That's all you need to know. I'm calling a meeting for 9am."

"What time is it now?"

She squinted at her watch. "3.33."

Her hands ran down his chest. *A spark.* Scott pulled her towards him.

———

Afterwards, she sat on the edge of the bed smoking a cigarette. "What I got from my trip will change everything, you know. Big stuff."

Scott rolled over, propped up on one elbow. "What did you get?"

"I'll tell everyone all together, it's only fair."

The smoke swirled around the light bulb.

"At least tell me where you went," Scott pressed.

"Israel."

"Israel? How did you get in and out of the country?"

"Knowing the right people. Anyway, I'll explain tomorrow, what have you been up to?"

Scott pulled himself up and sat next to her, their thighs touching. "I got arrested for Olympia's murder."

Angela spun around to face him. "You what?"

"I went for a walk. I needed to get out of here and..."

"You fucking idiot." She pulled a sheet around herself and stood up. "Have you fucked everything up again?

"No, listen, they tortured Mutt, the guy from the farm. They showed me a photo." He shuddered at the memory of the image. "They had my DNA on her as well."

"Mutt? Oh God, the poor bastard. I wonder what else they got out of him." The lights dimmed for a second before coming back on. "He's been such a help to the resistance. I can't..." Angela's head dropped, and she shook it slowly. "He knew the risks, I suppose." She stared at the floor. "But how the hell are you sitting here, then?

"Henry got me out."

"What does he want in return?"

Scott looked up at her. "He wants me to kill you."

She crushed the cigarette into the ashtray and grinned. "Are you going to do it?"

"If I don't, he will kill Miriam and Benji." He touched her arm, "We need to find them Angela."

"You could just kill me."

He ignored her comment. "We have to find them. He gave me a week."

"We are doing everything we can. But they could be anywhere. They could already be dead for all we know."

"Angie..."

"And even if we find them, then what? There's no guarantee we can get them and keep them safe." Angela pulled the sheet tighter to her body. "You need to kill Henry. We'll find out where he lives, and you kill him. End of problem. I'll get Martin onto it."

"Me?"

"Yes, you. You got yourself into this shit, you get yourself out of it."

Scott rolled over and closed his eyes.

"I'm going to my room," Angela said as she got dressed. "I need some sleep and this bed is way too small and uncomfortable. See you at nine in the War Room." She leant over and kissed him. "Goodnight."

———

SCOTT GOT to the room early, unable to sleep after Angela's visit. Martin, Lauren, and Sarge filed into the room at nine. Angela sat at the head of the table with a silver and black briefcase in front of her, and a grave look on her face. She gestured for them to sit. Scott exchanged a look with Martin as he took a seat. Angela stood up.

"As you can see, I'm back...with this," she said, patting the briefcase. With a sudden shove, she slid it across to Sarge. "I'll let the military man see if he can tell what it is."

Sarge studied the combination lock, then looked back up Angela.

"Six-six-six," she said. Sarge spun the numbers around until it clicked open. His eyes bulged in shock. Angela grinned. "Well, what is it?"

His eyebrows furrowed as he took in the contents. "Looks like some sort of radioactive device, and TNT. A dirty bomb?"

"Bingo."

Lauren shuffled in her chair. "Are we safe in here with that?"

"The active ingredient, Cesium-137, is encased in lead, which will be removed prior to detonation. Packed around it is 5kg of TNT." Lauren and Martin got up to look. "A gift from our Israeli friends."

Martin backed away. "Jeez."

Angela smiled. "I'm reliably told this will contaminate everything in a ten-mile radius."

"We've gone nuclear," Sarge said. "I'm impressed."

"This will scare the life out of the authorities. It's a game changer," Angela continued, giving Scott a 'told you so,' look. "I propose that we put it in the military barracks in Colchester. We don't want it making London uninhabitable. That's where we want our future seat of power."

She looked from face to face, unable to hold back the smugness. They all knew this was a major coup.

"Put a plan together, Sarge, I want it on my desk in twenty four hours with the attack to take place twenty four hours from that. We have no time to lose."

Sarge nodded. "Yes, Ma'am."

"Any questions?" Angela asked.

Lauren cleared her throat and spoke. "How did you get this?"

"I went to Israel. I met a contact. They gave me this. Simple."

"Gave? How much did it cost? Nothing went through the account."

"We pay after use."

"How much?"

She closed the briefcase. "We'll discuss that later."

Scott raised a hand. "How's the hunt for my ex-wife and child going?"

Angela rolled her eyes. "Martin is in charge of that. You can speak to him later." She stepped back to her seat. "Why is everyone not ecstatic? Do you understand how huge this is?"

Lauren stared at the briefcase. "I'm smiling inside, I promise you that. It's just..."

"Just what?"

"Dangerous."

"You're damn right it's dangerous. Once they know we've got this stuff, they'll come running to us for an agreement. And then we move. No agreement." She clapped her hands together. "Regime change."

Scott shared their cautious optimism, as well as being amazed that she had disappeared under a cloud and returned from Israel with such a powerful weapon. The thought of using such a horrific weapon worried him, but the more he saw, the more he knew this government needed to be removed from power.

Angela pointed at Sarge. "Forty-eight hours till the attack. No excuses. Then we can forget about the Heathrow shit show."

Scott ran his hands around the briefcase before clicking it open. Inside, a lead case covered in yellow and black 'RADIOACTIVE' stickers nestled in the black foam casing, with an orange block wedged next to it. Angela leant over him from behind and rubbed the small of his back, out of view from the others.

"Impressed?"

"Yeah, definitely."

"So you should be, so should everyone." She turned to the others. "I risked my life for this."

"We appreciate that, Angela," Lauren said, "Really. This is big."

Martin stoked the briefcase. "Fuck yeah, good job, boss."

"Good," she said, beaming. She closed the briefcase and picked up a phone on the wall. "Ready."

A woman wheeled a trolley into the room with a bottle of champagne on top.

Angela raised her hands. "I propose a toast. I know

what you're going to say." She adopted a monotone voice. "It's too early, she drinks too much, she's getting too excited blah blah blah." She giggled to herself as the woman opened the bottle. "But this deserves it."

They all took a glass as Angela held hers aloft.

"To Operation Bottom Dollar." They raised their glasses and repeated back. "To Operation Bottom Dollar."

Chapter Eighteen

The horizon oozed red, yellow, and purple. Scott closed his eyes against the low sun. The motion of the car and the white noise of the tyres on tarmac made him sleepy. It reminded him of Benji as a baby; he would drive him around in the car to get him to sleep. Would Benji be asleep now wherever he was?

The car hit a pothole, and Scott opened his eyes.

"You guys still awake?" Sarge said.

Scott and Martin both murmured "yes".

"So, let's go over it one last time."

For what seemed like the hundredth time that day, Sarge recounted the plan.

"Once we're near the base, we find a nice off-road spot. Then we camouflage the car with some greenery." Sarge adjusted the rear-view mirror to make eye contact. "The first army vehicle that passes, we stick the briefcase to it. Those magnets the guys at The Nest used are as strong as anything. Once it pulls up to the gates, we hit detonate, before they even give it the once over for bombs. Gas masks on and scarper. Top speed. Got it?"

I had it the 99th time, Scott thought.

Martin nudged him. "You know you said that out loud, bro?"

"This isn't a school trip," Sarge boomed. "This is a military operation."

Martin exhaled. "We're chucking a briefcase on a truck, mate, it's hardly D-Day."

Sarge cleared his throat, a sure sign he was about to begin another serious tirade. Ringing came from the speakers and Martin laughed. "Saved by the bell."

Sarge sighed and hit 'answer'. Angela's voice boomed out.

"How's it going? You get through the checkpoint OK?"

Sarge readjusted the mirror and said, "Checkpoint cleared successfully, boss, currently twenty minutes from target."

"Call me when you're done," Angela replied, her voice wavering with nerves.

"Yes, Ma'am."

"Good luck and come home safe," she said, and she hung up.

"Well, that was short and sweet," Martin drawled. "I was expecting the Queen Elizabeth armada speech."

Two army trucks passed in the opposite direction. Sarge waved at them. "Old habits."

———

IN THE DISTANCE across the flat landscape, the towers of Essex University stood silhouetted against the sunset.

Scott tapped on the window and pointed. "That's where I met Angela. Twenty years ago."

Martin sat up. "Go on."

"Halloween 2005. Fancy dress night in the Student Union bar."

"What were you?"

"A skeleton," he said, sniggering at the memory. "I was sitting with some friends, drinking the cheap beer. A pint was about £2 or something. Probably a few whiskey chasers as well. Boiling hot in that stupid costume. The whole place reeked of smoke and booze. Must have been just before the smoking ban. On the other side of the bar, through a crowd, I see this girl dressed as the devil. Tight red outfit. Horns. Even skinnier than now, if you can imagine. That hair. One of my mates caught me staring. *'That's Medusa,'* he said. Turned out that was her nickname. She was in his politics class. He shouted, and she came over. Trident in one hand, wine bottle in another."

Martin laughed. "The more things change, the more they stay the same, eh?"

"So my mate introduced us. I'll never forget what she said."

"What?"

"I'm Angela. A devil with an Angel's name."

Martin slapped his thigh. "Too right. Look what that moment wound you up in, mate. What's it they say, *'The devil doesn't come to you in a red cape and horns, he comes to you disguised as everything you've ever wished for.'*"

"She was in a red cape and horns," Sarge pointed out.

Martin shrugged. "Fair point."

"One thing led to another, and we ended up dating." The towers disappeared behind trees. "Seems like a lifetime ago."

Scott could picture it as if it was yesterday, though. How she sat on his lap and whispered dirty things in his ear. The night in that tiny single bed in the halls.

HE SNAPPED out of it and stared at the towers, now reappeared, the windows reflecting the colours of the sunset. What random meetings were taking place in there now that would change people's destiny for decades?

Sarge picked up the speed. "Well, let's think about the present now, we've got a job to do for that devil."

They pulled over into the woods, the vehicle shoving aside sapling and shrubbery, then scraping between two larger trees. A squirrel leapt from a branch and dashed across the bonnet. The forest enclosed them, lit by a purple glow as the sunset's dying light seeped through the leafy canopy.

Sarge unfurled the camouflage netting and they set about covering the car. The sound of a coming vehicle droned above the crunching of twigs, and they ducked down as it passed.

Martin took a hip flask from his pocket and held it to Scott, out of view of Sarge. The whiskey burned pleasantly. He took another mouthful. Martin shoved it back it into his pocket as Sarge turned around.

The briefcase, resting on a carpet of moss, looked innocuous. What a journey it had taken. From a lab somewhere in Israel to being smuggled into London by Angela.

Running a hand across it, Scott wondered how many people had held it on its passage here.

Sarge crawled along towards them. "I'm going to get back in the car, ready to start her up and get out of here. You two move to..."

He halted. Eyes opened so wide the whites showed. He turned his head a millimetre to the left and held up a finger. Then Scott heard it too. Footsteps. He held his breath, not daring to move. Then he saw it. Martin must have seen it at the same time.

A soldier, alone, walking up the road, only metres away from them. His hand firmly on an automatic rifle hanging by his side. Sarge, facing the other way, could see the alarm in their eyes.

The soldier looked through the trees in their direction. Had he heard them?

Sarge turned around, swivelling on his foot, remaining hunched over. The soldier stepped forward into the wood and raised his gun. It wasn't clear if he had seen them. Yet. He took another step forward, and momentarily let go of the gun to hold the radio clipped to his shoulder. Sarge leapt up, gun drawn. He stood face to face with the young soldier. Martin stood and pressed his finger to his lips. Sarge moved towards him, gun pointed at his head. The branches underfoot cracked.

Scott now stood, his knees creaking as he did so. Birds continued singing. Sarge had reached the soldier. He caught him and spun him around, handcuffing him as he did so, then led him towards the car. Martin reached for the hip flask. "Bro, good shout with the handcuffs."

Sarge bundled past them, shoving the soldier to the ground.

He crouched down, put his head against the soldiers and whispered. "Are you on your own?"

The soldier looked up in terror from Sarge to Martin and Scott, eyes bulging under the force of Sarge on his chest. He said nothing.

"Are you on your own?" Sarge repeated.

Again, the soldier didn't respond. Sarge twisted his head round and motioned to Martin and Scott to get down. They knelt, and Martin passed the hip flask to Scott.

Sarge reached for it. "Give me that."

He drank long and hard, then pushed his head back into the soldiers. "We're the resistance. We have no issue killing you. The regime you support is responsible for the deaths of our brothers. So, I'm going to ask you one last time, are…" The radio crackled. "Four-two-four-one, everything OK, do you copy?"

Sarge nodded at the soldier and loosened his grip. The soldier gripped the radio. Martin pointed his gun at him, and with the other hand gave a thumbs up.

The soldier spoke into the radio. "Copy, false alarm. Everything good."

Scott breathed again.

Sarge ruffled the soldier's hair. "Good boy."

"What are we going to do with him?" Martin asked, pacing nervously. "Should we call the boss?"

Sarge tied fabric around the soldier's head as a blindfold and removed his gun. "God no, we know what her answer will be."

"We can't let him go back. He's seen us. This is fucked. Any ideas, Scotty?"

"I don't know. The only options we have are to leave him here, take him with us, or kill him."

"For now," Sarge said, "we're going to put him in the car whilst we do what we have to do. Scott, you're going to sit with him, OK?" He pulled the soldier up to a standing position. "How long till they come looking for you?"

He said nothing. Sarge punched him in the stomach, causing him to double over in pain.

"You need to start answering my questions. Or it's going to be option three. This sick regime you protect deserves everything it gets." Sarge pulled aside the camouflage on the car. "We need to be done fast. They'll come looking for him soon." He pushed the soldier into the backseat and turned to Scott. "Make sure he doesn't go anywhere. We'll work something out."

Sarge closed the door, shutting out the sounds of the forest. The tinted windows and camouflage blocked out most of the light. The doors clicked as Sarge locked them. The soldier moaned as he moved into a sitting position.

Scott looked at him. "What's your name?"

The soldier rested his head against the window and didn't reply. "Well, my name's Scott."

The soldier stirred. "Fergus."

Scott patted him on the arm. "Listen, Fergus, we don't want to hurt you, but you've put us in a difficult situation."

"Yes, you do."

"No, we don't."

"What are you planning to do here, then?"

"Surveillance."

"For what? Some sort of attack? Your mate said it himself. You'd have no problem killing me. We have families, you know."

Scott glared at him. "You want to talk about families? Do you know what your sick regime did to my family? They kidnapped my son, blackmailed me, then took him again along with his mother. They have made my life hell. We couldn't even bring him up properly because she lost her job as a teacher because you fuckers decided Jews couldn't have public jobs anymore." Scott found himself hitting the soldier, punches raining down on him, and pulled himself away. "Don't talk to me about family. I used to go along with this new regime, because what else could I do, but not anymore. You deserve everything you get supporting it."

Scott rubbed his fists, amazed at his own outburst, and wished he could take a drink from Martin's hip flask.

The soldier's radio crackled to life. "All patrols return to base. Repeat, all patrols return to base."

Scott tore it from the soldier's jacket. It reminded him of his police radio as he turned it over in his hands.

It crackled again. "Four-two-four-one, what are you doing in the forest?"

Scott whispered to himself. "What the fuck?"

The soldier coughed. "Transponder innit."

He pushed the radio back to the soldier. "Say something."

"No."

It vibrated in his hand. "Four-two-four-one, do you copy?"

Scott pulled out the gun and placed it against the soldier's head. "Say something. I'm pushing the button now."

He pressed it, but the soldier didn't speak. Scott put his finger on the trigger and released the button.

"Say something now or I swear to God I will kill you."

Scott pressed the button again.

The soldier cleared his throat and spoke into the radio. "Sorry, thought I heard something, but it was just foxes."

A second passed, then another. The person on the other end of the radio didn't reply.

Then it crackled again. "Foxes?"

"Yeah, foxes."

"Copy."

Scott relaxed and leant back in the seat. He stretched his legs and let out a deep breath. Then he pondered the words. Foxes. He'd heard the phrase before. He recalled a meeting from when he was a still in the police force with an army captain. *"We call the resistance foxes,"* he had said. *"Urban vermin."*

A bead of sweat formed on Scott's lip. "Is that code?"

"Is what?"

"Foxes?"

"Dunno what you're talking about, mate."

Scott kicked him in the shins, made sure the handcuffs were secured, and pulled the door handle, but it didn't budge.

"You piece of shit." Scott shouted, kicking the soldier again.

He spun around and looked out the back window. Martin stood behind a tree, briefcase in hand. He couldn't see Sarge. He banged frantically on the rear window, but Martin didn't move. He kept banging.

There was a rumbling as a vehicle approached. As it passed, Martin slipped from behind the tree and flung the briefcase. It sailed through the air, missing the truck and skidding on the road surface. Again, Scott banged on the window. Nothing. He shouted, but his voice echoed around the car and Martin or the unseen Sarge didn't hear.

Martin scampered into the road and collected the briefcase. Scott stared at the radio, now silent, then clambered over the front seats, reaching for the horn. As he went to press it, another truck trundled along the road.

He stopped, unsure if hitting the horn now would be the right move or not.

Once again, Martin flung the briefcase, and this time, it shot low and true towards the vehicle. It stuck to the side, and the truck disappeared up the road. Martin punched the air and ran towards the car, then Sarge emerged from the undergrowth and followed.

Scott jumped back into the backseat and took the soldier by the collar. "You'll pay for this."

The doors clicked and Scott opened the door as Sarge

and Martin ripped the camouflage from the car. Darkness had fallen now. He grabbed Sarge by the shoulder.

"The radio's got a transponder on it," he said, holding it up, "they know something's wrong."

Sarge took the radio. "That's new, they never had that in my day." He threw it into the trees. "OK, let's go."

"What do we do with him?"

"He's seen too much. He's coming with us."

Sarge climbed into the car and started the engine as Martin leapt into the passenger seat. They crashed through the foliage in reverse, the last remains of the camouflage falling from the roof as they did so. The car hit the road, and Sarge shifted it into drive and plunged his foot onto the accelerator. The tyres screeched.

"Woo-hoo!" Martin yelled. "What a shot."

"Second time lucky," Sarge said, taking a corner at speed.

Martin laughed. "I dunno what happened on the first one."

Outside of the tree coverage, a small amount of light still came from the recently set sun. The moon hung above like a glowing coin. Martin threw a small metal box to Scott.

"The detonator. I'll let you do the honours."

"Now?"

"Now."

Did he want to be responsible for that? A radioactive attack on British soil. The deaths, the injuries, the long-lasting effects. He thought of Benji and Miriam, then pushed the soldier's finger on the button.

At first, nothing happened. Then came an explosion behind. Sarge hit a button on the dashboard. A dialling tone gave way to Angela's voice. "What's happening?"

"Mission accomplished, Ma'am."

"Well done. Make sure you get away fast. Did everything go to plan?"

Sarge looked in the rear-view mirror at Scott and the soldier. "Yes, Ma'am."

"Wonderful stuff. See you soon."

Angela hung up.

Sarge pointed a thumb at the prone soldier. "So what happened? Did they radio him?"

"They asked why he was in the forest. He said it was a false alarm and that he had just seen foxes. Foxes is code for the resistance. They are going to come looking for him."

Martin looked out the back window. "They've got bigger things to worry about now."

"We should have told Angela."

"Didn't want to ruin her special moment," Sarge said. "We'll deal with this when we get back."

Behind them, a plume of smoke rose above the trees.

Chapter Nineteen

Miriam poured a cup of tea and scanned the apartment.

After two days of unpacking and cleaning, it finally looked how she wanted. The sun beamed through the windows that stretched from the floor to the ceiling, and she raised a hand to block out the bright rays and get a better look at the view.

A speedboat rushed across the sea, leaving a foamy white wake in its path, and a palm tree swayed in front of the window.

She picked up the air conditioning control and clicked it up a notch. The low hum increased, and the cool air blew onto her.

She walked to her bedroom and stood in the doorway, marvelling at the light and the clean lines. Through the open wardrobe door, the dress Angela had brought over poked out, sparkling in the sun. She recalled that evening on the boat with a shudder and pushed the door closed. Angela had kept her promise, despite being on the receiving end of a torrent of abuse and a few badly aimed slaps.

Miriam lay on the bed and smiled as she remembered berating Angela by the marina, before being bundled into the back of a car to calm down. The smile increased as she recalled the journey away from the marina.

———

"CALM *the fuck down and drink this," Angela said, producing a can of premixed gin and tonic. Miriam gulped half of it down in one and wiped her mouth.*

Angela looked up. "Don't smear your lipstick, this is probably the best you've ever looked."

"I beg your..." Miriam started, but Angela held up a finger.

"Let me send you this money and we can be done, OK?"

Miriam finished the rest of the can and searched for another. "That guy with him was an absolute sleaze. I can't believe you sent me in there with him. God knows what would have happened if I didn't get out in time."

"I'm sure he was harmless," Angela muttered, tapping away at an iPad.

Miriam scoffed. "Harmless?"

The slit in the dress fell open, and she pulled it back. The comparison with Angela's bony leg was stark.

"Maybe harmless to you with your skinny little boy legs..."

Angela held a hand up and made a scratching motion. "Miaow."

Miriam crossed her legs and looked away. They were near her apartment.

"Done," Angela said, holding up the screen.

Miriam took her phone from her handbag. "I'll check it myself."

She checked her bank account, and there it was: 'Payment received £10,000 from Miriam Roth.'

Miriam frowned. "Why does it say it's from myself?"

"It'll look less suspicious that way, as if it's from one of your own accounts." The car slowed to a stop. "And I've messaged the school for Bobby. They will be in touch soon."

She held up an email to the private email address of the school's headmaster.

"What happens now?"

"I take the briefcase back to London. You spend your money. Everyone's happy."

Miriam saw the briefcase chained to the driver's wrist. "Come on, what's in it?"

Angela stared out the window. "Freedom."

Miriam paused before getting out. Angela looked at her.

"Well..." she said awkwardly, "...thank you, Miriam."

She held out a hand. Miriam batted it away and hugged her.

"Thank you, and good luck."

They stopped the embrace, and Miriam got out of the car, flashing a quick glance at the briefcase again. She leant into the open window. "Sure you can't tell me what's in it?"

"I told you, freedom. And remember, you tell no one you have seen me here. No one."

Angela blew a mocking kiss at her, and the window closed. Miriam pulled away just in time to avoid getting her hair caught. She lifted a hand to wave, but the car pulled away into the night.

———

MIRIAM JOLTED upright as the doorbell buzzed.

She opened the door to an immaculately suited man smiling at her. He looked familiar.

"We meet again, Mrs. Roth."

"Sorry I don't..."

"From the flight to Tel Aviv."

It came back to her. She recalled him handing her a glass of champagne before disappearing again, but she had not seen him since. A different man had dealt with all the formalities once they landed in Israel.

He looked behind her, into the apartment, then back at her.

"Sorry, I don't think I introduced myself. I'm Chaim." He extended a hand, "May I come in?"

Reluctantly, Miriam let him inside.

Chaim spun around and admired the apartment in awe.

"Wow, this place is quite something. Much nicer than the little place we set you up in, eh?" His smile held in place, but she sensed something else in his eyes. "How does a *refugee* afford such a place?"

She held a hand to her chest, something her mother would do when thinking about what to say. "Some of my savings from London."

"You sold the house then?"

"Yes," she replied, but then corrected herself. "No, actually this is other money."

"I see," Chaim whispered, then turned to the windows. "Wow. Look at that view. Spectacular." He raised his hands in mock wonder.

She reached for her cold cup of tea and said, "So, how can I help you?"

"Just checking you're safe and settling in well," Chaim said, and he motioned to the sofa. "Take a seat, Mrs. Roth. I need to ask you a few questions."

"Questions?" Miriam said, her voice wavering as she replied. She made a point of looking at her watch. "I hope this won't be long. I need to pick my son up from school soon."

"Oh no no no, won't take long," Chaim assured, and he pointed to the sofa again. "Please."

Miriam's hands shook as she put down the teacup and sat. "How can I help?"

"Don't be nervous, Mrs Roth, there's nothing to worry about." Chaim straightened his tie. "Or is there?"

"What do you mean?"

"*Is* there anything worrying you?"

Miriam shook her head and frowned. "No, why should there be?"

"There shouldn't be. Things are looking up for you, only a few weeks here and you have a lovely apartment in Neve Tzedek." Chaim looked around again. "I'm envious." His smile hit full beam again. "Are you making friends, meeting people?"

"Yes," she said, her feet tapping the rug.

"I'm glad to hear that. Met anyone interesting recently?"

Miriam stopped tapping her feet and swallowed. "Not particularly."

His smile waned. "Are you sure? You seem, how do you say in England, *on edge*."

Did he know about the meeting with Angela, and even if he did, would that be a bad thing?

"Mrs. Roth?"

"Sorry, I'm fine. Just..."

"You have to pick your son up from school," Chaim said flatly.

She made a face as if to say sorry.

"I take it you've seen the news?"

"No, what happened?"

"An attack in England. Hard to get details, but the explosion is emitting radiation," Chaim explained.

"My God, in London?"

"No, somewhere close by. Have a look. I can't imagine how anyone involved in an attack of such magnitude must be feeling now." He stared at her, then stood to leave. "I'll be in contact again, Mrs. Roth. Hopefully, you'll have more time then."

He looked at her knowingly, then back at his watch.

"Schools must finish early around here," he flashed a smile. "It's only one o'clock."

"Yes, they do."

"Hmm." Chaim stepped into the hallway. "Till next time."

He bowed slightly and walked away. She fell back against the door and breathed heavily as she loaded up the news on her phone.

RADIOACTIVE EXPLOSION IN UK

Sources inside the UK have reported an explosion at a military facility 50 miles from London. Reports claim to have seen personnel in radiation protection suits rushing to the scene in Colchester, Essex. The country has seen a lull in resistance activity recently, but this may suggest a return to attacks. No group has yet claimed responsibility, and the government are yet to comment. More to follow...

Miriam paced the apartment, thinking about friends and family back in England.

This is why I got out, she told herself. *I am safe here.*

But then it clicked. Did the briefcase have anything to do with this? The man's comment came back to her: *I can't imagine how anyone involved in an attack of such magnitude must be feeling now.* Was she involved?

Full of nervous energy, she put on her shoes to get out, to walk, to clear her head. Then the noise started. A piercing siren.

She scrambled to finish putting the shoes on, presuming it was the building's fire alarms, took her purse and headed into the hallway, but the sound came from outside the building. She turned back and got into the lift.

As the doors opened on the ground floor, a wall of sound hit her from the building's entrance. In the street, people hurried about, faster than usual. She approached a middle-aged woman carrying a bag of groceries. A little girl with her had a Minnie Mouse t-shirt on and covered her ears with her hands.

"Excuse me, what are these sirens for?"

The woman looked at her as if she were stupid.

"Rockets," she shouted above the noise. "You're not from here, are you? It's alright, dear, Palestinian rockets are not very accurate. We will intercept them anyway. Just go inside and don't worry."

Of course, she should have known, but being so wrapped up in events back home, the Israeli Palestinian issue had slipped her mind.

She thanked the lady who walked off in the opposite direction, and suddenly, Israel didn't seem such a safe place.

Miriam started running towards Benji's school, fearing how scared he would be without her. She turned into a normally empty street, today filled with a market. Rushing through the stalls and crowds, she stumbled and knocked over a tray of oranges. They spilled out onto the pavement. She held up a hand in apology and kept running. A man on a bicycle nearly hit her as she continued. The back wheel skidded, and he shouted at her in Hebrew. Then, as she turned a corner, a whining noise even louder than the sirens came from above.

Before she could look up, the ground shook beneath her. Her ears rang as the road lifted, throwing her into the air. Now her senses came rushing back. Suspended in the air, she screamed, and saw the bright blue of the sky, as the road flung her around and dropped her back onto the floor with an agonising crash.

Her ears rang, and her vision blurred.

Above her, the front of a building collapsed. She opened her mouth to scream, and it filled with smoke and debris. Then a sound so loud she could feel it filled the air. She lost consciousness as the building tumbled on top of her.

Chapter Twenty

Angela looked at the soldier with contempt. "We have to kill him."

He didn't flinch, just turned his head away from her.

They had got back to The Nest easier than Scott had expected. The right checkpoint and no stop and search. For the first half hour, there were no signs of panic along the roads. No emergency vehicles heading to the scene, nothing. There was no news coverage about it, but that was to be expected. They would try to keep it quiet. Until they couldn't anymore. And that time would be soon.

Angela had sent an admission of responsibility to the government, along with a threat for more attacks until elections were called. Now they waited.

"Let's throw him in the cell for now and talk about this later," Sarge said.

Angela's nostrils flared. "There's nothing to talk about. He knows too much. You just set off a bomb that will kill God knows how many soldiers and you're worried about one more? It doesn't make sense. God, I'll do it myself."

She reached for her holster, and the soldier flinched.

Scott stepped forward. "Sarge is right, let's lock him up and deal with other shit now. Debrief the mission."

Angela took her hand off the gun. "Fine, whatever."

———

SARGE RAN through the details of what happened. Angela listened and sipped her drink. She looked as if she was excited but didn't want to show it.

When the expected casualties came up, one hundred dead, another hundred mortally afflicted by radiation poisoning, Scott didn't feel that dread in him anymore. There was no guilt. He wanted the government brought down as much as anyone in the room now. Through whatever measures. What they had personally done to him had changed him, bringing the horrors closer to home.

He thought of Henry and his sneer, of the trauma inflicted on himself and his family, and of Miriam and Benji held captive somewhere, if they were even still alive. Bring on the bombs.

Lauren burst into the room. "Put the news on. Our sources say they're making a statement soon."

Somebody turned on the TV, and Prime Minister Robertson's face filled the screen; a jowly fifty something year-old man. Once a minor right-wing MP, now the leader, the dictator, of Britain. He stood at a lectern in Kensington Palace, a forest of microphones in front, and spoke.

"Good evening. Today, our great nation, our heroic military and our way of life came under attack from evil terrorists. A crude radioactive device was placed in a military base, filled with your fathers, sons, and brothers. The initial explosion killed scores of heroes, and the ensuing radiation has critically infected many more. Using a radioactive device on British soil is a new step for these terrorists and our retaliation will show no mercy..."

Martin threw a piece of screwed up paper at the screen. "Blah blah blah."

Scott had seen many a speech by the Prime Minister, but this time it was different. He looked shaken. His voice faltered as he continued, lauding the regime, and threating to hunt down the perpetrators. The camera zoomed in slowly as Robertson finished his speech.

"This is a day when Britons from every walk of life unite in our resolve for justice and peace. Britain has stood down enemies before, and we will do so this time. We go forward to defend freedom and all that is good and just in our world. Thank you, goodnight, and God save Britain."

Angela jumped to her feet. "Did you see him? He's scared to death. We've got them on the ropes."

Martin threw a pen at the screen. "He didn't mention our ultimatum, the sneaky fucker."

Lauren muted the television. "It's out there. Anyone who can get round the Netfilter can read it. Every nation abroad can read it." Angela's photo appeared on the television. Then the screen split, with her face on one side and footage of burnt soldiers being stretchered away on the other. Scott let the feeling sink in, the feeling of total devotion to bringing down the government, through whatever means, with no guilt.

———

HE LAY on the bed as Angela enthused about the attack, her wine glass spilling over as she waved it around.

They had gone to her room whilst the others got to

work, trying to find out what and when the government's response could be.

"Two things," she said, pointing drunkenly at him. "What do we do with our soldier friend, and this."

She threw an envelope onto the bed. Scott pulled two sheets of paper out as she sidled up next to him.

"Henry."

The papers showed his photo, address, workplace and personal details. "He's a creature of habit, luckily for us. Gets to his office at 8am every morning, returns between 6 and 7."

Scott scanned the biography. Oxford, MI5, the usual. Divorced. No children. "So, what's the plan?"

"As you'd expect, his house is fully alarmed. If we cut electricity to the property, it will trigger the alarm, so that's out." She lay on the bed next to him. "But he's careless with the code for his front gates. Just taps it in, not realising there's an Ant with a high-powered zoom camera in the house opposite."

"How do I get in the front door? It's got to be locked, right?"

"Henry had an unexpected delivery yesterday, a very heavy one." Angela giggled. "The delivery men had to carry it into the hallway. Whilst this was going on, they stuck a blank key into the lock, wiggled it around a bit and used the impressions on it to make a key."

"And that will work?"

"Ninety percent certain I'm told."

"Clever. But what about the alarm?"

"The Wi-Fi isn't as secure as you'd think. The alarm system is connected to the Wi-Fi. We've hacked it. We have full administrator rights in the system. All we have to do is reset it and choose a new code. Then you use that code and you're in. We'll reset that and the gate code to the original one for when he gets back."

"So I still have to do it?" Scott questioned.

"You still have to do it."

That new feeling of intent flooded through him again. "Good."

"You get in and wait for him to come home. Glock 19 to the head and leave."

"You make it sound so simple."

"It is. This time you have to enter a house and kill a man *without* his wife doing it for you though," Angela teased, winking at him.

"And when do I do this?"

"The day after tomorrow. Time is not our friend."

"OK, what about Benji and Miriam?"

"What about them?"

"We need to find them."

"We are doing everything possible to find them, Scott, I promise you that."

"Maybe I ask him before doing the job, get him to tell me where they are."

Angela's eyes widened. "Absolutely not. Don't get into a conversation, just kill him. It could give him time to raise an alarm or kill you first. We will find them, Scott. Look what we've done, look what we're capable of."

The thought of killing Henry excited him, and he pulled Angela towards him, kissing her forcefully. She flung the glass across the room and pulled him on top of her.

———

THEY LAY in the half-light after making love.

"What about this soldier, then?" Angela said, lighting a cigarette. "What do you think we should do with him?"

Scott puffed on his own cigarette. "I think we keep him hostage, it may come in useful."

"We can never release him, Scott," she said, sounding apologetic. "He's been in The Nest."

"Blindfolded all the way."

"Still."

"What if he's a good person, forced into this mess?"

She scoffed. "A good person? He tried to get you killed. He's one more casualty in the attack, that's all. It gives me no pleasure to kill him, but we have to."

"Let me talk to him."

"If you insist." Angela moved a hand down his chest, over his stomach and down. "But not now."

———

A GUARD SWUNG the cell door open.

The 'cell' was really another bedroom, the same as Scott's. Single bed, desk, toilet in the corner. It looked like the cheapest hotel room in the world.

The soldier lay on the bed. "I figured I'd be having a visitor."

"Why?"

He lifted his arms and rattled the handcuffs. "They just put these on me." Scott leant against the wall; his mouth dry from the hangover. "I'll be blunt with you, Fergus; we're deciding on whether to kill you. Give me one good reason why we shouldn't."

Fergus hung his head forward and shook it slowly. "What can I say? I was just doing my job. I don't want to hurt anybody."

He was scared but composed.

"You don't want to hurt anybody? But you're in the army. You're in the wrong job. How old are you?"

"Twenty-five," the soldier replied.

"How long have you been in the army?"

Fergus paused a long time. "Three years."

"So you joined *after* the takeover?"

Fergus shrugged. "They offered decent money. I was working in a factory before. It seemed like a good idea." He grimaced. "Not now obviously."

"Do you believe in what you're doing? This government?"

"I'm not into politics. I just needed good money and a secure job. My parents died in the pandemic and these guys seemed to have sorted it out."

Scott knelt in front of him. "My parents died in the pandemic too, so did my wife's, so did many people I know. But these people who have taken over have no respect for life. They only care about power. I could sit here and reel off all the things that have happened to me because of this regime, but that won't help anyone. The problem we have right now is that you've seen too much. What can we do?"

Fergus looked and pleaded, his voice trembling. "Let me go, please, I have a fiancé. I don't know where I am. I'll say I was blindfolded the whole time, that I never saw any faces."

Scott sighed. "I wish I could believe you."

"You can. I'm just a lad from Solihull who wanted a career. I'm not a bad person. I don't know about all the politics and stuff."

"You should know about it. 'All the politics' has people killed, has people living in fear, families separated. It's disgusting. And you work for that."

"Please, let me go, dump me by the road and I'll say nothing, I swear."

"If it was up to me, maybe."

"Who is it up to? That Angela woman?" The soldier stopped and stared at the wall. "You know they have pictures of her for target practise at the base."

Scott raised an eyebrow; Angela would probably get a kick out of that.

"Please, help me, I just want to live."

Scott turned and left the cell. "I'll see what I can do."

———

"I SPOKE TO HIM," Scott told Angela back in her room.

She sat almost totally horizontal in an armchair with her feet up on the table.

"Who?"

"The soldier."

"And?"

"And I think we should let him go, he's only..."

"Scott," she groaned drunkenly, "you're too soft. I'm worried it might rub off on me. You killed a hundred people yesterday. Don't worry about the hundred and first."

Scott was about to reply when a knock at the door and Martin's voice interrupted him.

"Boss, it's me, urgent news." Angela waved a finger at the door and Scott opened it. Martin held an open laptop and looked stressed. "Hiya, mate."

Angela lifted herself up. "What's happened?"

Martin pulled up a chair and pointed at the laptop screen. "Israel has been attacked. Multiple missile attacks on Tel Aviv."

A CNN news reader relayed the news with an image of destruction in the background.

Angela instantly sobered up. "Tel Aviv? Fuck."

"Yeah, and these aren't the usual rent a rockets from Gaza." Martin flicked to a new window. "Shin Bet reckon these are cruise missiles fired from a submarine in the Med."

Angela put a hand to her mouth. "Oh God."

"Must be retaliation," Martin said, "They must know Israel helped us out."

"Maybe they're just guessing," Angela suggested.

Martin shook his head. "No, this isn't a guess. They've never acted like this so quickly, and never directly attacked Israel. It's a proxy war, funding the hardcore Arab groups, etc. This is a step up."

"What do we know?"

"Lots of casualties, including British citizens, but it'll be a while till we have more details. The news reports don't mention the submarine. Not sure when Israel will go public with that info."

Angela got to her feet, staggering as she headed for the fridge.

"I need to contact people over there." She pulled out a can of gin and tonic. "Our allies, people who have helped us."

She drank long and hard, then looked at Scott. She opened her mouth to say something.

"Shall we put out a statement?" Martin asked.

Angela closed her mouth again. She shook her head firmly. "Not yet. Thank you, Martin, I need to think this over."

The moment Martin left, Angela flew into a rage,

kicking the bed and throwing anything to hand about. Scott held her and she writhed in his arms like a child.

"These bastards, these fucking bastards," she shouted, her elbows smashing into his ribs.

"Angie, calm down."

Scott let go of her. Her face was red, and her eyes brimmed with tears.

"They won't get away with this." She leant against the wardrobe. "God, what I have done."

"What do you mean?"

"Nothing," she composed herself. "I need to take this out on someone, but not you." She smoothed her clothes down and headed for the door. "I'll be back in a few minutes. Stay here."

Scott let her go without asking any questions and turned on the television to the illegal foreign news channels. A wide shot of Tel Aviv showed plumes of smoke against the blue sky. An interviewer talked to a man covered in blood and ash. The segment ended on a poignant shot of a bloodstained child's Minnie Mouse t-shirt in the rubble.

Shouting came from outside and Scott opened the door, heading towards the commotion. Angela stormed towards him, a gun in her hand. Her cheeks were bright red, and she wheezed.

He held an arm up to stop her. "What have you done?"

"Taken it out on someone."

Scott pushed past her and ran down towards the cell. It was open, and the soldier lay there in a dark pool of blood seeping out from a hole in his head. Scott wretched, steadied himself against the wall, then walked back to Angela's room. Sarge stood in a doorway.

"It's too much, man," he said, but Scott kept walking.

Angela's door was open, and she lay on the bed crying.

"What the fuck is wrong with you?" Scott shouted, kicking the door closed behind him.

"I love you," she sobbed, "that's what's wrong with me."

Scott stood over her, disgusted by what she had done and her drunken state.

"I love you too."

Chapter Twenty-One

It was 5 o'clock when Scott walked onto Henry's street.

According to Angela's intelligence, he wouldn't be home for at least an hour.

He ran over the plan again: type in the new passcode for the gate, hope the fake key works, type in the alarm code. Then lie in wait.

It was a pleasant area, old three-story townhouses with brightly painted doors. According to the internet, the area was "popular with the hierarchy".

He continued down the even side, looking for number 58. To arouse less suspicion, Angela had sent somebody out to get him "decent clothes", so, he looked smart in the blue suit and white shirt with no tie as he approached the house.

An armed guard stood outside the front door. This wasn't in the plan. He strolled straight past the house, and when he got to the end of the road, he pulled out the burner phone and called the number saved. The number to call if something went wrong. Martin answered on the second ring.

"Give me a tree."

"Oak," Scott replied. Any other tree meant he was under duress.

"Ok, jeez, what's fucked up already?"

The sun beat down and he moved into the shade. "There's a guard outside his door."

"Oh, for..." Martin trailed off and exhaled loudly. "Give me a minute."

Martin started talking in the background, the phrase 'Plan B' audible at one point.

Martin came back on. "I'll call you back soon. Bye."

What else could go wrong if the first stage had failed?

Scott's heart pounded. He took out a cigarette and went for a walk around the block.

———

MARTIN CALLED BACK within two minutes. "Get near the house. The guard will leave any second. Be quick, and don't help damsels in distress, OK?"

Martin hung up before Scott could ask any questions. Scott turned back onto Henry's Street. On the opposite pavement, a young woman strode along in a short minidress and heels, then dropped to the floor screaming for help.

Scott darted across the street, then stopped as the security guard opened the gates of Henry's house and looked out. Scott ducked behind a parked car just in time, and the guard gingerly stepped out onto the pavement, unaware of Scott, and shut the gate behind him.

The woman lay on the floor, still screaming, her long legs writhing against the floor. She tried to get up but only made it a metre before lying behind a parked car. The guard crossed the road.

Scott stood up and moved towards the house. Still, the screams echoed around. The guard took one last look back at the house, then crouched down behind the car to attend to her.

Scott reached the house. He didn't look behind as he typed in the code: 1933. The screams stopped as he pushed open the gate. He wanted to look back but kept focused on the sky-blue door, covering the short path in seconds, fumbling for the key as he went.

The screaming stopped. Every sinew in his body told him to turn around as he slipped in the key.

It wouldn't turn.

His sweaty hands slipped around it as he tried to make it turn.

"Please, please," he muttered.

His hands shook, sliding around the key. A car approached and he frantically wiggled the key. It turned. Scott pushed against the door with a shoulder and stepped inside.

As he turned to close it, for a second, he could see across the road. The woman stood facing him, making a show of thanking the guard. She made eye contact with Scott. The guard turned around and Scott clicked the door shut just in time.

He leant against the hallway wall, trying to control his breathing. Wiping the sweat from his hands, he flicked open the alarm panel and typed in the code. It flashed green and a smiley face appeared on the screen. A message popped up: WELCOME HOME HENRY. Then the worrying started. What if it was linked to Henry's phone? What if he was getting a notification now? Why didn't Angela think of that?

The gate outside opened and footsteps came down the

path. Scott shuffled into the living room. The curtains were open. Why didn't they think of that, either? It would only take one glance into the room from the guard, and it would be over.

Scott moved into the kitchen and sat at the table. The house was old, but the interior had been decorated in a futuristic minimalist style. It was like being in a spaceship. On the fridge was a photo, held in place by a magnet in the shape of a clog saying: 'Amsterdam'. It was a faded photograph of Henry in a café with a young boy, no more than 10 years old, both smiling at the camera. Could it be his son? Did Angela purposely not tell him Henry had a son? Did she think that would make him less likely to go through with it?

Scott opened the fridge and took out a half empty bottle of Sauvignon Blanc. *How am I going to get back out and past the guard?* he worried.

He found a wine glass and filled it to the brim, then messaged '555' to Martin; the code meaning he was inside, and they could reset the alarms back to the original codes.

He was under strict instructions not to message any words or call once inside. They must realise he was now trapped in the house?

Scott took another sip and opened the back door. The garden was immaculate; freshly cut grass, tasteful flowers, and a sundial in the middle. He didn't step out in case the neighbours saw him, so examined the back wall as well as he could. There was a door in it, and the wall wasn't too high. Surely he could get over it, or at least hide somewhere. He drank more wine and calmed down.

———

As THE CLOCK ticked closer to six, Scott fretted about having to kill Henry, about getting out, about all the things that could still go wrong. He finished the wine, went to the backdoor and lit a cigarette, careful to make sure the smoke didn't blow inside the house.

Angela had told him to stay downstairs, but Scott worried Henry would see him and make an escape out the front door, or at least raise the alarm. He stubbed out the cigarette, crept through the kitchen and went upstairs.

There was another living room on the second floor, furnished in black and white. Edward Hopper paintings of lighthouses and white clapboard buildings hung on the walls.

Up the next flight of stairs, Scott found the main bedroom. More Hopper, and more black and white. He headed into another bedroom, used as an office, with shelves full of history books and crime novels. Scott walked to the window and carefully looked down, seeing the top of the guard's head below.

————

SEVEN O'CLOCK PASSED with no sign of Henry. Scott went back downstairs and found another bottle of Sauvignon. He took it back to the bedroom and lay on the bed, staring at one of the paintings. A house, stark white against a blue sky, with wisps of white clouds. In the foreground, a breeze blew across the yellow and green grass.

Scott closed his eyes, and when he opened them, darkness had fallen. He looked at his watch. It was nearly ten o'clock. Downstairs, the front door opened.

Scott rolled off the bed and reached for his gun. Henry hummed along to music downstairs. Scott didn't know whether to stay in the bedroom or move. The plan seemed complicated again, but he reminded himself all he had to do was shoot him and get out.

He screwed the silencer onto the gun as footsteps came up the stairs. Henry's humming got closer as he climbed the second flight of stairs. Scott snuck behind the door and peered through the gap, gun ready.

Henry paused on the landing, looking at the doors as if something were wrong, which it was.

When Scott had come in, they were all closed, now they were open.

The humming stopped. Henry turned and went into the bathroom. A minute later, the shower came on and Scott stepped out onto the landing. The bathroom door was open, and although it was steaming up, he saw his own reflection in the mirror. Henry's clothes were piled up on the floor, a blood red tie poking out from underneath like a snake.

He took one last deep breath, checked the gun, and stepped inside.

Henry faced away from him, rubbing shampoo into his hair. Scott pointed the gun with one hand and yanked the shower door open with the other.

Startled, Henry spun around and screamed as he saw Scott. Then he raised both hands above his head. "Don't shoot, please."

"Where's my son?"

Henry looked pathetic, naked and shaking. "I don't know, honestly. I was bluffing. I don't know where they are."

Angela's instruction came to him: *'Don't get into a conversation, just kill him.'*

Scott aimed the gun at his temple. "I don't believe you."

Henry stepped back into the shower's flow and spat out a stream of water. "Wait. In the other room, there's a safe. There's a letter. I..." he shook hard. "She went away somewhere."

"What's the code for the safe?"

"1989."

Scott hesitated, and they stared at each other.

Henry pointed towards the other room. "I'll show you, please just let..."

Henry could be bluffing, but it didn't matter, Scott had one job to do and now he had to do it.

"You make me sick," he said and pulled the trigger.

The recoil was stronger than he expected, jerking his arm back painfully. Henry flew back against the wall as the bullet entered his forehead. A spatter of blood from the exit wound hit the white tiles and Henry slumped down the wall, leaving behind a thick red smear as he went. He ended up crumpled on the floor, as the blood and water mixed. The pink liquid flowed down the drain.

Scott backed away and went to the office. Bile rose into his mouth, and he spat onto the floor. His hands trembled as he unscrewed the silencer and put the gun away.

In a wardrobe, he found the safe, typed in 1989 and popped it open. He flicked through the stack of papers inside: lists of names, pictures of people, addresses. He was about to stash them in his pocket when he came across a letter in familiar handwriting. He moved into the light to read it.

"Dear Scott,

　　It breaks my heart to write this letter. I never wanted it to come to this, but I'm leaving with Benji. I cannot tell you where we are going, but as soon as it's safe, I promise

I will contact you. This is for me and Benji's safety. We are not safe here. Please try to not be angry with me, maybe one day we will come back. I loved you truly, Scott, and you will always have a place in my heart, but try to understand. It brings me no joy to take your son away, but I genuinely fear for our lives.

Goodbye,

Miriam."

Scott fell to the chair, stunned, then read it again slowly. The handwriting was, without a doubt, Miriam's. Her childlike script and looping letters were instantly recognisable.

So Henry *had* lied to him. She had got away. Or was the letter written under duress? Judging by Henry's last words, with a gun at his head, the letter must be genuine.

Scott folded up the letter along with the other papers and put them into his jacket pocket before taking a last look in the bathroom. The liquid flowing into the plughole was totally red now, and the water pouring from above made Henry's hair cling to his head. His jaw hung open and water flowed inside.

Scott closed the door and headed back downstairs. He peered out the living room window, seeing the guard still in place. For a moment, he considered opening the door, shooting him and leaving out the front. He was halfway to the door when he stopped and turned back.

———

IN THE KITCHEN, he took out the letter and read it again. If he'd received the letter as he should have, there would have been no need to kill Henry. Scott laughed to himself. The moment Henry stole the letter, he signed his own death warrant. A piece of trickery for which he deserved to die just as much as if he really had taken them.

Scott opened the backdoor and hurried across the garden. It was dark, but the lights from the houses gave enough light to see. The door in the back wall was padlocked, but after a few swift kicks, the timber broke enough for him to squeeze through. He emerged into an alleyway. A metal door stood on the left, so Scott walked the opposite way towards an opening onto the street, a hand on the gun. He was metre away when a guard appeared, blocking the exit.

The guard reached for his gun. "Hands up."

Scott was too quick and fired once into his chest. Even with the silencer, the noise echoed around the quiet streets. The guard staggered back before reaching for his own gun and stepping forward.

Scott fired again, this time to the head. The guard collapsed and Scott dragged him by the feet into the alleyway. He peeked out onto the street. It was clear both ways, so he walked out, brushed his jacket down and headed to the station.

He touched Miriam's letter and smiled.

Chapter Twenty-Two

Scott messaged Martin to say he had completed the job and went straight to the tube station. Nobody looked twice at the man in the blue suit, tapping his feet and reading a letter repeatedly.

Within an hour, he was back at The Nest. His pride about killing a man sickened him, but that's how things had become.

He passed Martin's office space and hoped he might be there, hunched over the computer, so he could show him the letter. Sure enough, Martin sat at the desk, with Sarge and Lauren, the three of them deep in conversation. The conversation stopped abruptly as he entered.

"Here he is," Martin said jovially, "the assassin."

Sarge leant over and turned the computer monitors off before Scott got any closer. Lauren smiled and uncharacteristically hugged him whilst manoeuvring him away from the desk.

"Well done, Scott, how did it go?"

Sarge stayed seated and rubbed his chin. They were obviously hiding something.

"He came back later than hoped, but I did what needed to be done. Thanks for the distraction."

"No worries, mate," Martin said, "he must have got the guard since the barracks thing."

"Well, thanks again."

He wanted to show Martin the stash of papers, especially Miriam's letter, but not in front of the other two.

"Where's Angela?" he asked.

Martin shrugged. "In her room, I guess."

Sarge stopped rubbing his chin. "Hopefully she's not too drunk to see you."

Scott ignored him and walked away, feeling their eyes on him all the way to the door.

SURPRISINGLY, Angela wasn't drunk. She welcomed him into her room and listened as he relayed the story of killing Henry. Occasionally, he had to check she was still listening when she gazed off into the distance. She didn't speak until he finished.

"Good job, I'm proud of you." She shuffled her Tarot cards. "What was in the safe then?"

Scott flourished the papers from his pocket. "Well, this one is very interesting." He laid them out on the table. "They aren't holding Miriam. She got away somewhere."

Angela stopped mid shuffle and looked up, eyes wide. "What?"

Scott tapped the letter. "Look, read this."

She put the cards down and read it. "Oh, well, that's good news, isn't it?" She tried to smile. "I wonder where they could be."

"She must have left the country, see how she says, 'We are not safe here'. That must mean Britain. She's gone abroad, I know it."

"Maybe, maybe not." Angela tilted her head and raised her eyebrows. "It's hard to get out."

"She could have got to Israel if she really wanted."

"Israel? What makes you think that?" Angela questioned, passing the letter back to him.

"Jews can always get to Israel, the government let them for God's sake."

"Not if the government wants them to stay, as leverage," Angela said, leaning back in the chair. "Anyway, this is all speculation. We don't know."

Scott took the letter back. "What's the matter? You seem like you're miles away. I thought you would be ecstatic. I *killed* Henry. Are you not even interested in this?" He waved the stack of papers at her.

"I'll look through them later, but yes, there is something on my mind."

"What?"

She looked into his eyes. "Flying Ant Day. The Revolution. It's on. We have to move imminently, and we will."

"Imminently?"

"Yes, they're going to crack down hard now. We have run out of time. It's going to be next week. I'm going to give a big speech tomorrow." She drummed her fingers on the table. "It's happening, Scott, this is it. Endgame. Checkmate."

Scott thought of Martin, Sarge and Lauren huddled round like witches plotting something, but said nothing.

"Come to bed with me," she said, taking his hand. "Revolution turns me on."

———

THEY HAD CLEARED one of the main rooms of desks and computers. In their place sat a dozen round tables, laid with white tablecloths and sparkling cutlery.

"It looks like the bloody Oscars," Martin said as he sat next to Scott.

A makeshift stage stood in front of the world map, now covered with a huge Flying Ant banner. It looked just like the room in the hotel when Scott saw Angela give her speech. Now she prepared to give another one, holed up in her room all day completing it whilst she banished Scott elsewhere.

He had rested away from the commotion and chaos, sitting in his room reading a book he had found on Angela's shelf; *Darkness at Noon*. At one point, he got up to give Martin the papers from Henry's safe, but sat back down. He could do it later.

In between chapters of the book, he re-read Miriam's letter for clues as to where they might be, but there were none. Israel was the primary location, but she could be anywhere. It angered him that she had not told him she planned to take his son away, though at the same time, it filled him with relief that he was away from this country.

Now, in the main room, he passed Martin the papers. "These were in Henry's safe, they mean nothing to me, but they might to you."

Martin flicked through them and put them into his pocket.

"Thanks, I'll look over them later. What's that one?" he asked, seeing Miriam's letter still in Scott's hand. Scott handed it over, relishing the surprise on Martin's face as he read it. "So they didn't have her? Shit, they must have broken into your house and taken this, right?"

"Looks like it."

Martin gave the letter back. "Well, I'll start looking in other directions then. Where do you think she might have gone?"

"Israel's a possibility."

"Hopefully not Tel Aviv. That was bad. The Israelis don't know how to respond. I'm sure they'll hit the Palestinians pretty hard just for the sake of it, but they must have an idea it's Britain. It's a dangerous situation."

Nameplates for Sarge and Lauren were on the table and Scott wanted to speak with Martin before they got here. "Do you know what this speech is about?"

"No, but I'm guessing it's serious judging by the set up. Did she tell you?"

Angela had given strict instructions not to say anything. "No. What were you three discussing when I saw you yesterday?"

Martin looked around before leaning towards Scott and lowering his voice. "They still want to get rid of her. Sarge is pissed, Lauren is basically on board."

"What about you?"

"I think it's the wrong time to change leaders, even though she's gone a bit crazy. No offence, mate." Martin looked over Scott's shoulder. "Here they come."

Sarge and Lauren took their seats with minimal greetings, both looking serious. As the room filled up, the noise intensified, and suited staff brought food and drink to the tables. What had once looked like NASA's mission control room now looked like a wedding reception.

They devoured the food, gossiping about future and

past attacks, and what the subject of Angela's speech could be. Scott played dumb.

———

AFTER THEY TOOK the plates away, the waiters returned with the signature Flying Ant Day cocktails and the lights dimmed. Stirring classical music played, and the spotlight shone on the Flying Ant logo as a lectern bearing same the logo was brought onto the stage

"Christ it's like the Nuremberg Rally in here," Martin said.

Then the lights dimmed. Angela appeared from the side of the room, clad in her ludicrous military jacket, and bounded onto the stage. The music stopped as she reached the lectern.

"Friends," she said, adjusting the microphone, "today I bring serious news. Good news, I think you'll agree." She looked around the room and smiled. "This country has suffered four years of rule by fear, intimidation and cruelty. Well, no more. Next week, Tuesday the 16th of June, we will launch the fightback. Flying Ant Day."

There were a few murmurs. Angela revelled in the shock of her announcement.

"For years, we have been building to this day, and it is finally upon us. We have tried to get this corrupt, evil regime to listen to us, but they have not. As a great man once said, 'Those who make peaceful revolution impossible will make violent revolution inevitable'. And so it is. To those who say it's too soon, I say it's too late. It is never too soon to free millions from fear. Never too soon to depose of evil." She banged her fist on the lectern, and the micro-phone wobbled. "Everyone in this room has suffered at the hands of this government, but this revolution isn't based on personal grievances, it is based on the good of all. I have discussed with our military moles, our spies within the government, and next week, we will unleash the full force of the Ants." Her voice grew louder. "As another great man said, 'There are decades where nothing happens; and there are weeks where decades happen.' Well, next week is one of those weeks. I have set in motion a plan which will bring freedom to the country, and glory to the Ants. Though we will inevitably suffer losses, we..."

Angela halted mid-sentence and stared forward. Scott followed her gaze. Sarge stood pointing at her.

"Stop this!" he shouted.

The entire room looked at him in surprise. Angela didn't know what to do.

"This is ridiculous," Sarge bellowed. "I agree with the sentiment, but the timing is wrong, it's too soon."

"Somebody take him away!" Angela yelled, pointing at him.

Her voice came out high pitched and her cheeks turned red. She looked at both sides of the room, expecting some-body to deal with Sarge, but nothing happened.

"It is too dangerous to launch Flying Ant Day now." Sarge turned and addressed the crowd, his back to Angela. "We are not ready, it would be an act of gross incompe-tence, we would lose everything we have built up."

"Traitor!" Angela screamed into the microphone, her eyes wild. "Take him away. Now."

"We should have a vote," Sarge shouted back. Even without a microphone, his voice was as loud as hers. "After all, this revolution is about bringing democracy." He waved a finger at her. "Let's have some democracy here for once."

Angela was panicking now. In her oversized large military jacket, she looked like a scared little girl. Scott wanted to help her, but maybe Sarge was right. He sat still, unsure what to do.

Sarge turned back to Angela. "Let's put it to a vote."

Angela stepped out from behind the lectern, taking the microphone with her. "We need democracy yes, but we also need leadership. And I am the leader."

"David would have had a vote."

Angela smacked her hand to the lectern, and screamed at Sarge, "David is not here!"

Sarge smirked, "And why is that?"

Gasps came from the crowd.

"What are you implying?" Angela shouted.

Sarge let the accusation hang in the air for a moment, then took a step towards her. "You are a drunk and hysterical, and you should not be in charge."

More gasps and mutters filled the room.

"Somebody take him away! I am the leader, and what I say goes," Angela yelled. She looked at Scott helplessly. "Please, somebody."

She returned to the lectern and slammed the microphone back down, then shouted into it. "I am in charge and the revolution goes ahead next week."

"You are not fit to lead a revolution," Sarge roared as Angela stormed off the stage, shaking her head rapidly.

Her curls bounced as she charged away. Scott wanted to run after her, but thought better of it.

In the silence that followed her departure, Sarge walked to the stage and took the microphone.

"All those in favour of a leadership election, raise your hands."

Scott turned to see the crowd's reaction. An enormous thump shook the room. Everything on the table jumped an inch before falling back down with a clatter. Then another bang and the smell of smoke. Towards the back of the room, screaming and shouting started. Then the gunfire started, causing people to scramble under the tables. Scott pushed himself to the floor. He could see them now; government forces swarming in and firing indiscriminately. The lights flickered, then went out, plunging the room into darkness.

Disoriented, Scott tried to work out which way to run, and where the exits were. All around, the sound of gunfire and screaming was deafening. If he stayed under the table, he would be as good as dead. So, overtaken by fear and adrenaline, he crawled away from the noise.

Shafts of light from the soldiers' guns spun around the room, piercing the dark. Without thinking, Scott stood up and ran, crashing into tables, chairs, and fleeing people. He tripped over a body and fell onto it. As he put out a hand to break his fall, he touched the body and came away covered in warm, sticky liquid. Scott grimaced, hoping the blood wasn't his, then got to his feet again. Light came from under a door, and he crashed into it.

He raced down the lit corridor and kept running, trying to remember the location of the emergency exits. They had shown him once, but he had paid little attention to it.

Behind him, the gunfire was unrelenting. Scott turned a corner and spotted two government soldiers wrestling some-body to the ground at the end of the long, straight corridor. Scott noticed the hair. It was Angela.

She kicked and screamed, desperately trying to fight them off, but they were too strong for her. He ran towards them as they pushed her to the floor. Scott was ten metres away when one of the soldiers put a gun to her head and fired.

The sound echoed around the corridor. Blood sprayed out in every direction and her kicking stopped.

Scott stopped running and fell to his knees. Her body lay limp on the floor, half her face had gone, blown off by the gun.

The soldiers shook hands and one of them spoke into his radio. "Target terminated."

Part Three

Chapter Twenty-Three

Miriam opened her eyes. The light was intense. She moaned; a long involuntary sound that came from deep within her, and shut her eyes. There was no pain. It was as if all her senses had stopped working, except for sight.

When she tried to move, her body wouldn't respond. Her brain responded, though, trying to figure out where she could be and how she got here. She remembered talking to a man in her apartment, then a siren, then going out into the street. Then nothing.

After a while, her senses returned, a tingling in her muscles, a dull throbbing headache and a dry scratchy throat. A steady tone beeped in the distance. When she opened her eyes again, a figure loomed over her.

"Mrs Roth, can you hear me?"

She tried to reply but could only make a rasping sound. The figure moved closer.

"You're in the Sourasky medical centre in Tel Aviv. You're going to be OK. Do you understand?"

Miriam nodded. The simple act of listening and nodding exhausted her, and she closed her eyes again.

———

WHEN SHE WOKE the second time, she felt different. More alert, aware of the oxygen mask on her face, of the pain in her legs and of movement around her. Again, she tried to recall how she got there, but her memory stopped at the point she got out into the street.

A figure came towards her. She blinked, and the figure became a doctor, an old man with round spectacles and white curly hair.

"Good afternoon, Mrs Roth, how are you feeling?"

This time she croaked out a reply. "OK."

The doctor removed the mask from her face. "Can you breathe properly?"

"Yes."

"Do you remember what happened to you?"

"No."

"There was a missile attack. You were buried under a lot of rubble, but luckily, the rescue team found you within a couple of hours." He smiled. "It may not seem it, but you're one of the lucky ones."

"Where is my son?" Miriam asked, her voice clearer now.

"Your son is safe and well Mrs Roth."

"But where is he?" She pulled the mask away from her mouth. "Can I see him?"

"When you feel better. There are some people who would like to talk to you."

"I feel better now." She shifted into an upright position. "Where is he?"

"It's not my business to..."

"It is *my* business, and I want to see my son. Get *these people* in."

"As you wish, Mrs Roth, I need to make a call. Excuse me."

The doctor fiddled with the drip next to her, then left.

Miriam could see the room more clearly now. With a TV on the wall, flowers in each corner of the room, and an enormous window looking out over the city, it must be a private hospital.

As she took in her surroundings, an image came to her; being flung onto the pavement before a building fell on top of her. Then darkness. A sleepy sensation overcame her. She tried to fight it, but eventually succumbed to its embrace.

———

SHE AWOKE to find two men in suits sat by the bed. They looked at each other, each goading the other one to talk first.

"Miriam," one finally said. "How are you?"

"I'd be better if people didn't keep asking me how I am." The men smiled uneasily. "Where's my son?"

Their smiles faded. This time, the second man took over.

"Your son, Benji, is it?"

Miriam didn't respond, just stared at him.

He cleared his throat and continued. "Benji is being looked after by the same person paying for all this."

He waved an arm around the room and smiled again.

Miriam sat up. "Go on."

The other man interrupted, speaking in a rapid American accented staccato. "Listen, here's the story. Two days ago, a barrage of missiles struck the city. Scores of people died, hundreds are injured. You got pulled out of the rubble and taken to the hospital. We saw your name in the reports and contacted the hospital."

"Who are you?"

"We are from the security services; we know your story. Then somebody contacted us. A very influential person who paid for you to be taken here, the best private hospital in Israel." He smiled, as if having said something impressive. "Benji is staying at that person's house, being looked after and given the best care. When you can leave, this person would like you to stay with them. Since you have no home, we are happy to accommodate this."

Although clear-headed now, she struggled to understand what had happened. "Who is this person?"

"They are on their way now, Miriam." He reached out and touched her hand. "Everything will be OK. We will be in contact again."

"I need to know who has my son," Miriam shouted as they left.

A nurse came into the room and touched the drip.

"Leave that alone," Miriam snapped, reaching for the nurse's hand.

The nurse backed away, and the sleepiness washed over her again.

This time when she awoke, she didn't open her eyes. She lay there, letting the tiredness wear off and thinking about what the men had said.

Israel doesn't seem safe anymore. But I can't return to England. What can I do? Where can I go? And who is paying for this hospital? Is it Angela?

As she ran through everything in her head, somebody

coughed. She opened her eyes to see the old man from the boat hobbling towards her with a walking stick.

"My name is Shai, do you remember me?"

It took a moment to gather her thoughts and know how to react. After all, the last time she saw him, she was running away after hitting him with a briefcase.

"What the hell is going on? Have you got Benji?"

"Benji is being looked after by my daughter, yes. He's at my country home and..."

"Don't you dare touch me."

"Ah yes, I am sorry about that. My friend was out of order, he'd had a few drinks and... well, I apologise." Shai had a large yellow bruise above his eye. "Honestly, you and your son are safe with me and my family."

"What are you doing here? How did you... I don't get it?"

"I saw your picture in the papers, a list of survivors. I recognised you as Angela's friend." His demeanour changed as he mentioned Angela's name. He looked forlorn. "Any friend of hers is a friend of mine. Please be my guest. Come and stay at my estate. Sadly, your apartment is destroyed. We can look after you. My daughter is the same age as you. It will be nice."

"With respect, Mr?"

"Zahavi, but please call me Shai,"

"With respect, Mr Zahavi, I don't know you from Adam, and the one time I met you..."

"Again, I am sorry. But please, let me make amends. We are comrades, after all."

"How do I know isn't a trap?"

"Trust me. Please, you know I help fund the resistance. I am on your side, Miriam."

She stared at the ceiling. Could she trust him?

"What was in that briefcase?" Miriam asked.

"These are all questions I can answer later when you are safe. Come on, rest up, then come and see your son. He is happy."

"It doesn't look like I have any choice, does it? I don't need to rest, I feel fine. I have enough rest when they keep putting me to sleep. Tell the doctors I'm discharging myself."

———

SHAI'S HELICOPTER raced over the desert landscape, and a smear of bright green stood out against the yellow ahead.

"There it is," Shai said, pointing. "I told you it would be quicker than driving."

The pilot gave a thumbs up and they descended. As they got closer, the estate became visible, poking out of the palm trees; a large white building beside two smaller ones and two swimming pools.

They banked sharply to the right, and from this new angle, Miriam could see Benji holding a woman's hand and waving at them. She wiped the tears from her eyes and waved back.

As soon as they touched down, Miriam unbuckled the seatbelt and jumped out. She ran to Benji and picked him up, smothering him with kisses as she whirled him around. She cried as she buried her face into his hair and stood weeping in the burning sun.

Eventually, she let him go. "Are you sure you're alright Benji?"

"Yes Mummy. I like it at this house. Esther has been looking after me."

Esther beamed and shook Miriam's hand. She was a tall, attractive woman with a fashionably short haircut, dyed red.

"Thank you, Esther," Miriam said.

"Oh it's no problem, Miriam. It's been a pleasure."

Shai led them into one of the 'outhouses', a detached house twenty metres from the main building.

"This is where you and Benji will stay. Get settled, and I will see you back at the big house for dinner this evening," he said.

Miriam thanked him and he ambled back to the 'big house.'

Benji seemed unphased by his latest ordeal, but Miriam worried about the effect recent events must have had on him. She felt guilty. He explained to her what had happened on the day of the attack. How they had heard explosions from his school and were ushered into a shelter. But no missile came near. After being unable to reach Miriam, the school had arranged for him to stay with a teacher and her family. The next day, when the hospital identified Miriam, Shai had got in touch, claiming to be a family friend, and whisked him away. Relieved he was safe, Miriam told him everything would be OK. She didn't believe this herself but needed to comfort him.

———

SHE RESTED, sipping a sparkling water with her painkillers and examined the damage. Her legs were covered in cuts and bruises and her hips ached any time she moved, but miraculously, other than that, she felt fine.

In the helicopter, Shai had explained the attack that resulted in her being buried in the rubble for six hours, an iron beam above her stopping further collapse.

For the first time since waking up, everything had sunk in. She didn't feel safe in Israel anymore. Her sanctuary had now become another prison.

———

OVER A VAST MEAL of never-ending courses, washed down with the best wine Miriam had ever tasted, Shai waxed lyrical about Miriam and Benji's bravery. Esther, picking at her food but not eating a lot, peppered her with questions about life in Britain. She had studied in London, leaving for New York just as things began to "turn nasty".

She seemed surprised that Miriam hadn't seen it coming. "Didn't living in a dictatorship alarm you?"

"Of course, but my priority was to raise my child," Miriam explained, annoyed that she had to justify herself to a billionaire's daughter. "If you had children, you would understand."

Esther pushed an olive around her plate. "So, what was the final straw?"

"I don't want to go into it."

"To be fair, Esther," Shai said, "it didn't seem all that bad at first, did it?"

"No, it didn't," Miriam replied. "They got rid of the virus. The first country on Earth to eradicate it completely. There was no sign of anti-Semitism at that point. I will not be blamed for staying in my own country."

Esther began to speak, but Shai looked at her and she stopped.

"I'm sorry," Esther said. "I can't imagine what it must have been like."

Thankfully, Shai changed the subject, and a chastened Esther stayed quiet after that.

When they had finished, Shai leant in towards Miriam.

"I would appreciate it if we could speak alone."

Esther looked up. "I can take Benji back to the outhouse."

"No thank you," Miriam said, "I don't want to let him out of my sight."

So Shai took her to the corner of the vast room, with Benji and Esther still in sight, and sat her down.

"We need to discuss a few things, Miriam."

"Yes, we do," she said, refusing another drink.

The two glasses of wine she had already drank did not mix with the painkillers and general exhaustion.

"What's going on? Is Israel safe right now?" Miriam questioned.

Shai moved uncomfortably in his chair. "I will not lie to you, Miriam. Things aren't good. We have sound reason to believe the missile attacks were a British retaliation."

Until now, she had assumed it must have been a Palestinian attack. "Retaliation for what?"

"The radioactive attack in England," Shai revealed.

A deep feeling of unease came over her. "So, is this a war?"

"Not yet."

She pointed at the bottle of brandy. "Are we safe here?"

Shai poured the golden-brown liquid into a glass. "Safer than in Tel Aviv."

"Wait, this radioactive attack. Was that something to do with you?"

Shai dropped two ice cubes into the drink and said, "I had a small part to play in it, yes."

Miriam seized the glass from him. "The briefcase, was that...?"

"I can't go into details," Shai interrupted.

Miriam scowled. "You said you would tell me what was in that briefcase."

Shai sighed. "Yes, it had something to do with it."

"So what was it?"

"The bomb."

Miriam slammed the glass onto the table. Across the room, Benji and Esther looked up from the TV. "I carried that bomb? Oh my God, I'm responsible for people dying. I..."

"Miriam, the only thing you're responsible for is helping to fight the regime."

Her head spun as she came to terms with this. "What's happening with the resistance? Angela seemed confident they were powerful, and she's the leader, right, she should know?"

Shai looked at the floor and rubbed his head. "Was."

"What do you mean?"

"Angela is dead." Shai produced a laptop from a draw. "I hope you're not squeamish."

On screen was a British news website with the headline: 'RESISTANCE LEADER ANGELA NEWTON KILLED IN RAID'.

A shocking photograph of a dead Angela with half her face missing accompanied the story. Miriam nearly wretched.

"It seems the government wanted to publish proof," Shai said apologetically. "We have tried to contact the resistance, but to no avail yet. As you can see from the story, the resistance base was discovered and attacked. All the lines are down. Our calls, emails, messages, nothing is getting through. We don't know who's left." He switched to another tab. "Well, we know a couple of survivors. This is the latest."

Under the headline read the subheading: 'SEARCH FOR RESISTANCE SURVIVORS: SAS HUNTS RADI-CALS', and three pictures stared out at her. Miriam snatched it and read the captions in disbelief. One of a 'Martin Loring: Stoner Fanatic', the other 'Edward Mulcaster: Ex-Military Traitor', and the third 'Scott Saunders: Newton's Secret Lover'.

Miriam gulped the brandy. Her head spun; from the drink or the shock, she wasn't sure.

"Lover?" she spluttered. "What? But he, he's not even in the resistance."

Shai nodded. "He is, Miriam, and he escaped."

"But how can you trust this propaganda?"

"Miriam, all my ways to contact the resistance are down. That's proof in itself." Shai scrolled the page. "There's more. I'm sorry I have to show you this, but you need to know."

Shai tapped on a highlighted passage and Miriam scanned the page.

> 'Saunders, 40, escaped from the underground compound during the raid. He is being tracked down by Special Forces, who are also on the hunt for his ex-wife, Miriam Saunders, (also known as Miriam Roth). She is believed to be in Israel and injured in a recent missile attack on Tel-Aviv.'

Miriam put the computer down and held her head in her hands. Despite the radioactive attack being against a brutal government, she couldn't help but feel sick that she had been a part of it. But she should have known the risks involved in helping Angela. Angela! Scott's 'lover'. Angela, now dead.

It was too much. The tears began to flow as it sunk in that on top of everything, she, Miriam, was now being hunted down by Special Forces.

Shai rubbed her shoulder. "They're coming for you, Miriam, but they won't find you, I promise."

Chapter Twenty-Four

Scott ran, expecting to hear a gunshot any second, but it never came. Somebody once told him that you don't hear the shot that kills you, but as he sprinted away, he awaited the loud crack.

Were they so engrossed in having killed Angela they didn't look up? Either that or they presumed there was no way out for him. There were two hidden exits, never used except for emergencies. And this was an emergency.

He reached the cupboard, pulled open the door, and flung the mops and buckets aside. With one turn of the wheel, the hatch opened. He jumped inside, pulled it shut and felt around for the steps.

If they know about this exit, this is my tomb.

He found the cold metal rungs embedded in the wall and climbed. The smart shoes slipped as he went. A combination of damp and sweat caused his hands to slip.

As he got higher, searing pain shot through his limbs. Scott wheezed in exhaustion but kept going. A whack on the head told him he'd reached the top. He bit his tongue, and his mouth filled with the metallic taste of blood. He spat down the tunnel and caught his breath. As he fumbled around for a lever or wheel, there was a thud below, then voices. A beam of light shot up towards him. He jerked the handle and daylight poured in.

Then the shooting started.

Bullets ricocheted around the concrete tube, pinging off the steps. He hauled himself out just as something struck his elbow. His whole body shook.

Scott gulped in the fresh air and slid the cover back into place. A bullet had grazed his arm and blood seeped out onto his shirt and jacket. He got up and ran.

The hatch came out in a secluded corner of a park. People milled around, sitting on the grass. A group of boys played football.

Scott bolted to the closest gate, pain from the elbow shooting through him with every footstep. Unused muscles in his arms and legs hurt from the climb, but he kept running.

He reached the gate and found himself in a side street. A car slowed down to take the corner, and he darted in front of it, waving his arms. It stopped. He hurried to the driver's window.

"I need your car," Scott said to the elderly man inside. The man was terrified. "I'm sorry, but I really need your car."

Screaming came from the park behind him.

"Get out!"

The man fumbled for the seatbelt and Scott pulled him out and jumped into the car.

"Sorry but I really need your car."

The car leapt as Scott hit the accelerator. He reached the end of the road and glanced in the mirror. A group of government soldiers stood around the man who pointed up the road. They ran towards him. Scott pulled out into the traffic and stamped on the accelerator.

The tyres screeched as he flew onto the main road. It was an old car and the lag between the accelerator pedal touching the floor and the car speeding up alarmed him. The bullet wound hurt, and it was a struggle to grip the wheel. He jumped a set of traffic lights to a chorus of horns. Then, on a long straight road, he gathered his thoughts.

He needed to get somewhere safe, and he needed to push Angela's death out of his mind until he got there. It didn't seem real that she had gone, and probably any hope of a revolution with her. The adrenalin kept him from thinking too much about it.

Scott swerved onto a side road to avoid traffic. A crucifix hanging from the mirror swung into his face as he turned. He ripped it off and threw it out the window as he flew over a set of speed bumps. The car bounced with a nasty sound of metal on concrete. He racked his brain for somewhere to go, and then it came to him.

The couple with the tunnel to Angela's house wasn't far.

Trying to get his bearings, Scott circled back out onto a main road. Their road was somewhere off this high street.

A part of the car's undercarriage scraped along the road underneath him. A siren wailed behind him. In the mirror, cars parted to let the police car through, and the cars ahead stopped.

Scott swerved, banged the horn, and mounted the pavement. A man shouted at him as the car hit the kerb and leapt onto the pavement. People screamed at him. Then a man, headphones on, strolled out of a shop in front. Scott swerved to avoid hitting him but hit a lamppost instead as he slammed the brakes. The force of the impact flung him forward, then the seatbelt pushed him back, knocking the breath out of him as the airbag enveloped his head. There was a strong smell of burning rubber. The bullet wound was agonising.

Scott clambered out of the car to a crowd of people staring at him. The police car pulled up a few meters behind with the doors already open. He pushed through the shocked pedestrians and raced into an Indian restaurant, then dashed to the back, snatching a bottle of water from a waiter as he went.

The door to the kitchen swung open, and he clattered into another waiter. Food flew everywhere, but he kept going, round the dull metal counters and out a back door. He pulled the heavy door shut behind him and turned into an alley.

His elbow, his ribs, his legs; everything hurt. Scott's whole body told him to stop. He came out onto a road, gulped from the water, and thanked God it was the right road. He dared a look back, and seeing no one, half ran, half staggered to their house and rung the bell.

They have to be in. They have to let me in.

Shouting came from somewhere and Scott knocked on the door frantically. It opened, and he pushed against it and darted inside, kicking it shut behind. Scott fell to the floor.

A man looked at him in shock. "What happened to you, mate?"

"Do you remember me?" Scott gasped in between puffs.

"Yeah, of course, what's happened?"

"It's a long story."

He helped Scott up and took him to the kitchen. Scott explained the attack on The Nest, how Angela had got shot, and his escape.

The man, Andy, dipped his brow with concern. "You

need to go to an Israeli embassy. There's a few secret ones scattered about."

"Where's the closest one?"

Andy paced about. "Let me think." He froze as the doorbell rang. "Fuck."

"The tunnel," Scott whispered, already pulling the washing machine aside.

The doorbell rang again.

"One second, mate," Andy shouted, heaving the machine aside.

Scott ripped at the wall and flung himself into the hole. Andy slid the washing machine back into place. The darkness was comforting, and he hunched against the wall, cradling his arm. He tried to slow his breathing and listen. There was muffled talking. Then footsteps came towards him. Two sets of footsteps. Then voices.

"Sure, look around. I would have heard something, though," Andy said. Then a knocking noise, and a different voice: "What's behind here?"

They were standing right by the washing machine. Inches from Scott. "Just the washing machine," Andy replied.

"Those marks. It must have been moved recently. Mind if I have a look?" There was a scraping sound as they moved the washing machine. Scott held his breath.

A burst of radio static rang out. "Alpha two zero, come back to the car, we've got a sighting." The scraping stopped. "OK, copy."

Footsteps moved away. Scott breathed again.

———

ANDY HANDED over a glass of water. "Well, that was a close one, thank God Karen's out, she'd be shitting herself. I can't believe this."

Scott winced as he wiped his wound clean. "Where's this embassy then? I need to get there soon."

Andy thought for a while, tapping his cheek nervously. "Closest one is near Buckingham Palace. I'll find the address."

"How am I going to get there? It's too dangerous? This is fucked." Scott punched the table, causing more pain.

Andy took out his phone and grinned. "I've got an idea."

———

"ONE PEPPERONI, one Hawaiian, both large. Nice." Andy put the phone down. "Be twenty minutes. When the guy comes, you take the bike and head to this address." He held up the phone. "Memorise it. I can't write it down."

"Isn't this dangerous? They'll have your address?"

Andy laughed. "That's why I didn't use the app. I ordered it for next door, and the pizza bloke always comes on a bike." He stopped and looked serious. "So, Angela's dead, yeah?"

"Yeah."

"What happens now?"

Scott shrugged. "I don't know. I don't know who survived. Big things were about to happen. I know she set things in place, but maybe this it too big a blow."

"I walk past her house sometimes. It's all boarded up now. A bunch of government blokes guard it," Andy said.

"What do you know about the resistance?"

"Fuck all, mate. We're on the bottom rung of the ladder."

They sat in silence for a while.

Andy got up. "I'll look out for this pizza."

Alone in the kitchen, the images of Angela's death kept coming back. Tears welled up, and Scott wiped them away.

"I can hear it," Andy shouted from the other room. "Come on."

Scott peered through the curtains as the bike pulled up. As soon as the rider took the boxes out and headed up next door's path, Scott walked to the door.

"Thank you," he said to Andy.

"It's fine. Good luck, mate," Andy replied, and slapped him on the back.

Scott rushed out to the bike, leapt on, and turned the handle. It jumped, and he tore off down the road.

He hadn't ridden a motorbike in years, and never without a helmet. The wind in his eyes was stronger than he expected, and he had to half close them to see. He stuck to the speed limit, trying to not draw attention to himself.

There was a heavy police presence all around, and he prayed nothing would go wrong.

Scott headed past Brockwell Park, and the traffic increased as a roadblock approached. He slowed down, calculating what to do, when the car in front stopped. Two policemen got out. Scott twisted the accelerator, and the bike slipped from under him, crashing to the floor and skidding away.

He tumbled to the ground, landing thankfully on his good elbow, and the policemen reached him. There was no way out now. This was it. Scott lay on the floor in pain as they loomed over him. One knelt beside him.

"You know it's illegal to not wear a helmet when riding

a..." He stopped, and waved to his colleague, who jogged over. "Are you Scott Saunders?"

"No."

The second one reached them and pulled out a tablet. He turned it to Scott. The whole screen was a photo of him with the heading: SCOTT SAUNDERS. HIGH ALERT. WANTED FUGITIVE.

"You're the most wanted man in Britain right now," the first one said, "and you're delivering pizzas?" He laughed. "Get in the car."

They pulled him up and lead him to the car. Scott didn't struggle. He knew this was the end.

Chapter Twenty-Five

The car doors slammed shut and one of the policemen tossed a blanket in the back. "Put this over you and don't move."

Scott did as he was told, and the car rolled forward. It reached the checkpoint, and after a brief exchange, the car picked up speed.

"Scott," a voice said, and they whipped the blanket off. "We're on your side. We're Ants. You bumped into the only patrol car we've got in South London this evening. It's your lucky day. Where are you heading?"

Thinking it could be a trick, he said nothing.

"Scott, we're not joking." The man was deadly serious.

"An Israeli embassy." Scott said.

"Sure thing, let's do it."

The car lurched forward, and the siren came on.

"We'll be there in no time," the other man said, and then looked back at Scott. "How did you get out?"

Scott told them what happened at The Nest and how he escaped. They shook their heads as they listened.

"Lauren is dead as well," the first man revealed. "You,

Martin, and Sarge are the most wanted people in the country right now. They had put us on red alert for next week. We thought it was going to be the revolution and now look. Leave the country if you can. They will find you. And don't contact the others, it could be a trap. They'll play you off against each other. Keep safe. The Israelis are your best hope."

They pulled up at a building with a gold plaque outside.

"Stay here," the driver said.

He got out and he pressed a buzzer by the front door, then waved a hand, beckoning Scott over.

"Good luck," the other man said as he got out.

When Scott reached the door, it opened. A young woman looked at him. "Oh my God."

"Told you," the policeman said as she took Scott's hand and led him inside.

———

THE WOMAN TOOK him upstairs and through a maze of corridors. The pain was intense, and despite worrying it was a trap, Scott had no other option.

Finally, they reach their destination. The woman knocked on an ornately polished door and stepped back.

"Go in," she said, and walked away.

An old man in a suit stood to greet him. "Scott Saunders, unbelievable. You realise we are risking our own lives by having you in this building, don't you?"

"Yes, but I have nowhere else to go. This seemed..."

"We will look after you," the man interrupted, "for now."

Scott raised a brow. "For now?"

"While we work out what to do with you. Please, take a seat, we'll get you cleaned up and look at that nasty wound. But first, there's someone who wants to speak to you."

The man picked up the phone on the desk, typed in a number, and waited as it rang. After a brief conversation in Hebrew, he covered the mouthpiece and addressed Scott.

"We were asked to call this number if you came to us," he said, and passed the receiver over.

"Who is it?"

"Your ex-wife, Miriam."

Scott grabbed the phone. "Miriam?"

"Scott?" Her voice cracked. "Oh my God, Scott."

———

A LIFETIME of experiences had happened since they last spoke. Scott had killed, he had nearly been killed, he had fallen in love with Angela, he had seen Angela murdered. His world had changed, and the country could be on the verge of changing.

"Where are you? Is Benji OK?"

He couldn't tell if Miriam laughed or cried when she replied. "We're in Israel, we're fine. Oh, Scott I'm so happy to speak to you." *How things had changed.* "Where are you?"

"I'm in London, in some kind of Israeli embassy. I escaped from... well, it doesn't matter. I'm safe."

Scott looked up at the old man and gestured for him to leave, waiting as he begrudgingly got up and walked out.

"How did you get to Israel? What happened?"

"I went to the embassy, and someone gave me the address," Miriam explained feverishly. "I begged them to get me out, Scott. I didn't feel safe, like I explained in my letter. I'm sorry, but I just had to leave."

She broke down, and her sobbing made him emotional.

Scott picked up the phone and took it to a chaise lounge by the window, laying down with the phone resting by his ear.

"Until yesterday, I didn't even know you had left me a letter. The government stole it from my house. That whole time I thought they had taken both of you."

"Oh my God."

Scott sighed. "They told me you were both being held captive somewhere and used it as leverage to make me inform on the resistance."

"Jesus, Scott, but how did you see the letter in the end?"

"The government agent who has been blackmailing me from the start- I broke into his house and found it in his safe. I didn't know if you were both alive or what."

"Is he still threatening you?"

"No, that problem has been dealt with."

"Do I want to know how?"

"Probably not. Anyway, Miriam, don't worry about me. Promise me you are both safe."

"We are, I promise. They attacked Tel Aviv. I ended up in hospital but..."

"You were in the missile attack?" Scott interrupted.

"Yes."

"And Benji?"

"No, it was just me. I got buried under a building." Despite everything, she laughed. "It's been crazy."

"Crazy how?"

"I heard a siren, but I didn't know what it was for, so I ran out into the street and asked someone. The next thing I know, the ground shook, and I was thrown to the floor. I literally watched the building collapse on top of me, then I woke up in hospital. Turns out I had been in an air pocket supported by an iron beam. It's a miracle I survived at all, let alone only having cuts and bruises now."

"Are you at home now? Do you even have a home?"

"I did, but our apartment got destroyed in the attack. We are staying with a friend now. We're out of the city, safe."

"I don't know what to say, Miriam, you must have gone through hell."

"Hell and back. As I said, it's been crazy."

Scott could tell she was afraid. "Oh God."

"Not as crazy as you though. I saw the news, you're the most wanted man in England. How did you end up in the resistance? I didn't think that was your thing."

He kicked a cushion away and stretched his legs. "The more things that happened, the angrier I got, Miriam, and this government has to be brought down. Look at what they've done to you, to Benji, to me..."

"And Angela."

Scott winced. "And Angela, yeah."

"The newspaper said you were her lover. Is that true?"

"Well, I..." He hesitated. "Yes, yes I was."

There was a pause, a moment too long to be comfortable. He wanted to say something to break the tension but didn't know what.

Luckily, she spoke first. "She seemed crazy."

The comment irritated him. "You have to be crazy to be in her position, but if you met her..."

"I did meet her," Miriam interrupted.

"What?" Scott exclaimed.

"You didn't know?"

He propped himself up onto his good elbow. "Know what?"

"She found me in Tel Aviv. I did a job for her. She paid well to be fair."

Scott couldn't believe it. "Wait, when was this?"

"A few days before that radioactive attack in England. I think it was something to do with that. There was a brief-case I had to get from someone. It's a long story."

"A briefcase? God, that's where she was. She disap-peared and came back with a big silver briefcase."

Angela had met Miriam in Israel and said nothing about it? She let him think Miriam and Benji were being held captive all that time? So, that explained her blasé attitude when Scott had showed her the letter from Henry's safe.

"I didn't want to do it at first, but she persuaded me. It paid for a new apartment." Miriam paused as if realising something. "Were you seeing her all these years, Scott?"

"No, of course not."

"When did it happen? She promised me she hadn't seen you."

"This is irrelevant. We have bigger things to worry about. I can see who I like and she's..." he swallowed hard and gripped the phone. "Dead anyway."

Miriam dropped the accusatory tone and softened. "I'm sorry, it must be hard."

Scott slumped back down. "It is. I saw her being killed."

"So, what now? Can they get you out of the country?"

"I need to stay in England and see what happens. They planned something big for next week."

"Scott, you have to get out, don't be ridiculous. You could get killed. Come to Israel. Come and be with me and Benji."

Did she mean as a family again? It was too late to play

happy families. Scott needed to be strong, to stay the course for himself and for the country.

"I'm a revolutionary now, I have to see through what Angela started, which can make the country safe for all kids. And since when did you care about me so much?"

"Being away has made me realise that above everything, I want Benji to be with his father, and..." Miriam paused, a long pause. "...I miss you, Scott. Do you miss me? Don't you want to be with us?"

"I don't know, Miriam, it's..."

"They can get you out, Scott. What difference can you make, anyway?"

"I can't just run away now. I need to find out what's going on with the resistance. If it's over, maybe I will come to Israel then."

"Maybe? What about Benji? Doesn't he deserve to see his father?"

"I'm not the one who ran halfway across the world," he shouted. "When the revolution comes, you can come back here."

"The revolution is not coming!" Miriam yelled, and Scott held the phone away from his ear. "Scott please, I'm begging you, for your son's sake. You'll be killed if you stay."

"I'm not saying no, Miriam."

"It sounds like it. Listen, Scott, I want you to know..."

There was a click, and the line disconnected.

"Miriam? Miriam, are you there?"

Scott called for the man to come back in, which he did surprisingly quickly.

"It cut out. Can we call her back?"

The man tried three times to get the phone line reconnected, but on each occasion, it didn't even ring.

"It appears the line is dead, Mr Saunders, there's nothing we can do. Let's get you cleaned up."

———

Scott sat in silence, trying to take in the enormity of everything Miriam had said. He was pleased they were safe, and with their safety now confirmed, he had to see if there was still any way to overthrow the government. But Angela's betrayal added to the grief of her death. Lying to him about not knowing where Miriam and Benji were. Meeting with them, *working with Miriam*.

The woman who opened the door came in and dressed Scott's wound whilst the older man, who had now introduced himself as Eli, debriefed him. He peppered Scott with questions about the resistance. Did he think the revolution is close, when is the next attack, who is in charge now?

Scott played dumb and claimed not to know anything.

"The news says you were Angela's lover though. She must have told you things?" the man pressed.

"Can everyone stop using this word 'lover'?"

Scott winced as the woman rubbed antiseptic on his elbow.

Although he knew more than he had let on, he was aware there was a vast amount he still didn't know. Secrecy had been one of Angela's major ways of running the resistance, and now, that seemed like a bad idea. She had taken too much information to the grave. Even combined, Scott doubted the others knew as much as she did. It could take weeks, months, to pool all that information and they still wouldn't know everything.

"What do *you* know about the resistance? Surely it

hasn't disappeared overnight because of what happened?" Scott asked.

Eli drew a long breath and crossed his legs. "We support the resistance, but we are *not* the resistance. I do not know what happens now."

"What do I do then?"

Eli reclined in his chair. "Well, we can get you to Israel. It won't be easy, but I'm confident it can be done." He stroked his chin and looked across the room. "If that's what you want."

Going to Israel too soon could be a waste. Scott needed time. Maybe he could become the resistance leader, if he was to stay alive, that would be his only option.

"Give me a week, I can find out..."

"Mr Saunders, you don't have a week," Eli interrupted. "You're a dead man walking. And if they find out you're here, we'll all die." The woman looked up in alarm. "You're a liability to us being here. You either leave this building or we get you out of the country."

Scott weighed up his options as the woman applied a bandage. His hand was forced.

What could he do here without Angela, and with no idea where Martin and Sarge were?

Miriam and Benji had to take priority.

"OK," Scott said eventually. "Get me to Israel. Get me to my son and ex-wife."

Chapter Twenty-Six

"Scott, I want you to know that I still care about you. I never stopped caring. Scott?"

The line had disconnected.

"Shai," she called out, "Can we call back?"

Shai entered the room and dialled the number again. "That's strange, it's totally dead."

He shook the phone and frowned.

"Can we use a mobile?"

"Sorry, I told you, it's not secure." He put it down and shouted out to Esther. "Sweetie, pick that phone up, is there any dialling tone?"

Esther lifted it to her ear and shook her head.

Shai looked concerned and put the phone down. "Anyway, how is he?"

Miriam had said too much on the call, revealed feelings she didn't even know she had anymore. She should have considered what to say before speaking to Scott. But the call came so quickly she had no time to prepare.

She fiddled with the old-fashioned curly telephone cord. It reminded her of Angela's hair. "He's alive but being stubborn. He wants to stay and overthrow the government. I asked him to come over here, to Israel, but he seems to think he has unfinished business."

"These resistance types, they're all the same."

"It's stupid."

"Not always, Miriam, the world needs people like that." Shai sat opposite her. "What did he say about Angela?"

"That bitch, she promised me she had not seen him."

"Miriam, you mustn't speak ill of the dead. Besides, she did a great deal for your country."

"Really? The same people are in charge as far as I can see. Anyway, she was a bitch to him as well," she protested. "She didn't tell him about coming over here and meeting me. Some girlfriend she was."

"She was a good woman."

Miriam fixed him with a stare. He dropped his eyes and spoke quietly. "Well, all the embassies have my number here. He will be in touch, I'm sure. Come and have a drink."

"I need a minute."

"As you wish."

Miriam put her head into her hands and cried.

She had left England for a better life, yet in a matter of weeks, it had fallen apart. Things were worse than they were in London. Speaking to Scott made it clear that she needed someone in her life. Maybe she should have given him another chance instead of leaving him to go back to Angela.

Angela had lied to her, coming to Israel being friendly whilst hiding that she was with Scott. *She looked me directly in the eye and told me she had not seen him.* The least she could have done was pass a message onto him. But maybe she was too naïve, trusting a stranger, especially a stranger trying to overthrow a government.

The hot tears ran between her fingers as she sobbed. A flashback of a memory she didn't know she had filled her mind. She was buried underground, then a hand hauled her from the ground.

She couldn't breathe and pulled her hands away from her face. When she opened her eyes, Miriam still saw rubble and heard a muffled voice calling to her. She panicked and screamed. Then she was back in Shai's house with Esther knelt beside her stroking her hair.

"It's OK, Miriam, it's OK, come and lie down."

She followed Esther into the main room. Shai stood with one of his security people inspecting the phone.

"My mobile has no reception either and the Wi-Fi has cut out."

They looked anxious. Miriam was about to sit when the lights went off, plunging the room into darkness. Esther held onto her.

"Papa, what's happening?"

There was a muffled blast outside. Benji screamed, and a hand grabbed her.

Then a man's voice, "Come this way, quickly. "

Another explosion went off and a flash of light lit up the room, revealing Benji, Shai and Esther being pulled away by security men. Through the floor to ceiling windows, she saw a figure outside. Gunfire burst out, and a security man pulled her through the dark room.

Glass shattered all around, and bullets whistled through the air. She screamed as the man bundled her through a doorway. "Benji!"

"Mummy!"

Then she was forced into a room. The harsh lights came on and Shai, Esther, and Benji were pushed in with her. The door slammed shut.

"We will be safe in here," Shai said, though his face suggested he thought otherwise. "We have five ex-Mossad guys looking after security. Just sit tight and it'll be fine."

Esther bit her nails and stared wide eyed at her father. Miriam drew Benji close to her. He was either calm or paralysed with fear.

She rubbed his head and said, "Don't worry."

Despite the room being a decent size, they all huddled together in one corner. The walls were dark green, and a small chandelier hung from the ceiling. Along one wall was a fridge freezer and a chest of drawers, along the other, a cluster of armchairs around a small table.

Shai tapped the wall.

"I've never had to use this room before, but I know all the specifications, two feet thick concrete walls and ceiling." His voice faltered with nerves. "The door is the same style as the ones in bank vaults. Nothing can hurt us in here."

The gunfire was still audible through the walls, and Miriam covered Benji's ears.

Esther, shaking with fear, ran to her father. "What's going on?"

"I knew something was wrong when the phone lines went; they must have cut them from outside, then we realised the mobile signal and Wi-Fi was jammed." Shai put an arm round his daughter. "Honestly, Esther, security will deal with this, I have no doubt about that."

Esther buried her head into his shoulder. "I can't deal with being trapped in here, Papa. I really can't."

Miriam couldn't help but wonder how Benji was dealing with it better.

Shai rubbed Esther's shoulder. "My mother and father

hid in a room much smaller than this in Budapest in the 1940s and they got out fine."

At Shai's insistence, they moved to the armchairs, and he brought over bottles of water. Miriam took one. "Haven't you got anything stronger?"

"No. I meant to stock it up but never got round to it. Let's try to take our minds off what's going on in the house."

"Tell me about Angela and how you got involved in the resistance," Miriam questioned.

Shai revelled in being asked to tell his story, and reclined into the armchair, explaining how he became a successful businessman in the 1980s, with houses in Paris, New York, and London. Then when England got taken over in 2022, he "let it be known" that he would provide funds to underground groups fighting the regime.

"Then David Newton got in contact with me." Miriam tensed at the mention of David's name. "He was the leader of the resistance and a fine man. He begged me to go to England and meet with him, but I wouldn't dare set foot in that country. I knew what was coming. Bit by bit, things would get stricter, the usual story. There was always a racist, anti-Semitic element to the government, and I knew once the sanctions began to hurt and things got harder for people, the worse that element would get."

Shouting sounded from outside and Benji put both arms round her. Esther put a hand to her head.

"We would talk on the phone as securely as we could," Shai continued. "Sometimes Angela would be on the calls. She was a strange creature. He wore the trousers, as you English say, but I could sense the burning ambition inside her. I would wire money through all sorts of complicated bank transfers when they needed it. David was a cautious man. He believed in biding the time until enough people wanted to revolt, then seizing the right moment. I was inclined to go along with it, but sometimes, Angela would press for a more aggressive policy. He strongly disagreed with her, and they fought about it." Shai shook his head ruefully. "She wanted an active, constant resistant. Ready to overthrow the regime at any moment. Whereas David favoured having as many military generals on board as possible first, especially to avoid a civil war afterwards. He would spend weeks planning minute policy details for after the revolution. A very left-wing agenda, my taxes would be through the roof." He laughed. "She would say we needed to focus on the now, and didn't seem interested in the politics of afterwards. Towards the end of David's life, their arguments got worse. Then he had his 'heart attack.'"

Shai made inverted comma signs with his fingers.

Miriam leant forwards. "You seem suspicious?"

"Well, it worked out very nicely for her. She took control of the resistance and got to do things her way."

"You think she killed him?"

"Well, he wasn't a healthy man, but I don't know, it seemed so convenient." Shai waved an arm. "Truth is, I don't want to know, anyway."

Miriam was close to telling him how Angela had confessed David's murder to her, but didn't want to get into it all with Benji listening.

"I know others in the resistance think there should have been a vote, but she took over so quickly and impressed on them there had to be unity, and they went along with it. She called me to explain that she would be in charge, and then I didn't hear from her for weeks." Shai sipped from his water. "Suddenly, she called me, begging for funds. I had become quite strict in the last year, demanding to know what exactly the funds were being used for. She knew I had been meeting with scientists here who had created small radioactive devices, but David always said it would be too dangerous. That it would kill and permanently injure too many people, that it would be an unpopular move and they would lose support. Personally, I was in two minds about it. Angela brought it up again, begged me for one, saying this was the chance, the beginning of the end and they needed one last shock to the government. So, eventually, I agreed. She was the most persuasive person I've ever known. Then, to my surprise, I discovered that she had been in contact with the scientists and was in Tel Aviv to meet them. She was too fearful to collect it in person, knowing British agents work out here. The scientists passed it to me, and I passed it to you that evening." He pointed at Miriam. "I thought you were a seasoned resistance member. She told me you were 'one of the best' they had, and you seemed it." Shai rubbed his eyes and Miriam smiled. "Then they used the device. I saw it on the news, and Angela called me to say things would move quickly and to be prepared for Flying Ant Day, as she called it. She asked for a million pounds to be wired for the final push. That was a few days ago."

"And you sent it?"

"I did, yes."

"Do you think they have a chance?"

"She seemed to think so, but she would say that. Although, I was inclined to believe her. It's always a lottery though. What happens after? Is there a civil war? Do they end up having to crackdown as much as the current regime? The hard work starts when you take power."

"Do they have any chance without her?"

"I doubt it. She kept control by only letting certain people know certain things. She was the only one who knew everything. Plus, she had the drive, the fire in her. On top of that, they've lost their leader. Put all that together and it doesn't look good. It's set them back at least a year I'd say."

Esther still listened closely, although jumped at every slight sound from outside the panic room. Occasionally, during Shai's story, a vibration caused the chandelier to sway or shake, but Shai was oblivious to it.

Miriam pointed to the door. "Who do you think is attacking the house?"

"I don't know, but I doubt it's the SAS. We wouldn't have had time to get in here if it was. Probably some mercenaries trying to make a name for themselves. Or a few shekels."

"I'm sorry."

"For what?"

"For causing all this trouble, I..."

"It's not your fault."

"No, it is, you must think if it wasn't for me, everything would be fine."

"We don't think that, Miriam," Esther said.

"Thank you."

But Miriam knew she was a liability to them. Putting their lives at risk.

They sat in silence for a while. Benji's foot tapped relentlessly against Miriam's leg.

There was a noise at the door, and they all turned to look at it. The fear came back. Esther leant over and held Shai's hand. Benji inhaled and huddled closer to Miriam. The door jolted and swung open.

A security man put his head around the door and smiled. "All clear guys."

———

THEY STEPPED INTO THE HOUSE. The lights were back on, and furniture lay everywhere. All the windows had been smashed. There were bullet holes in the wall and a burning smell lingered in the air. Shai's security lead them into another room, stepping over broken glass and bullet casings as they went.

Esther cried. Benji slowed down to take it all in as Miriam pulled him along. This room was untouched by whatever happened.

The security man stood in the doorway. "There were only two of them, but they put up a good fight."

Shai wiped the sweat from his brow. "Where are they now?"

The man looked at Benji, then back at Shai and said something in Hebrew whilst pointing to the gardens. Shai nodded and stumbled into a chair, his eyes heavy from exhaustion.

"We are evidently not safe here. Get the helicopter ready to take us to the airfield."

Miriam finally let go of Benji's hand. "Where are we going?"

"Paris. I have a place there."

Chapter Twenty-Seven

Scott awoke to knocking, and the light in his room blinded him as he peeled his eyes open.

"Get up," a voice said, "now."

He rubbed his eyes and looked at the time, 2.30am. "What's happening?"

A man, dressed in blue silk pyjamas, his hair ruffled, stood in the doorway.

"Intelligence says the government might know about this embassy; we need to get you out. Now."

Scott got up and dressed, all the while watched by the man in the pyjamas, who tapped his fingers anxiously against the wall.

The man pointed towards the door. "Let's go."

———

THEY TOOK him outside into a courtyard. The full moon gave enough light to make out a large 4x4. The man in the pyjamas, now wrapped in a dressing gown against the cool night, opened the door.

"We're driving you to Birmingham, you're not safe in London."

The driver got out, and together with the other man, lifted the back seats.

"Birmingham? How will we get past the checkpoints?"

The driver shone a torch on the lifted back seats and said, "This is how."

He lifted a panel and took out an electric screwdriver and unscrewed the four corners. After finishing the final one, he gave a firm yank to reveal a space, just large enough for a person to fit. The beam of the torch moved, showing an oxygen mask connected to a tank strapped to the side of the box.

"Are you serious?"

It was a claustrophobic nightmare, essentially a coffin hidden inside the car. A padded material lined the bottom.

"Yes, I am serious. There's enough oxygen for four hours. It's perfectly safe."

"How long is the drive?"

"Half of that. Make sure you breathe steadily and don't panic. Even with traffic or delays at checkpoints, you have enough air to make it to Birmingham."

Scott looked into the box again. He had no other option. He was the most wanted man in the country and these people were helping him. If this was what it took to stay alive, then so be it.

The man pointed to the corner of the courtyard. "If you need a piss, do it now."

Scott walked over, and when he finished, he climbed into the car. He had just enough to space to stretch out flat, with a few inches either side of him. The driver turned on the oxygen tank and Scott pulled the mask over his face, taking a deep breath. He gave the thumbs up to the driver, who leant into him.

"If anything happens, the embassy address is 44 Young Street, Edgbaston. Repeat it back."

"44 Young Street, Edgbaston."

The driver gave him another thumbs up and stepped away.

A full moon illuminated the sky. Maybe somewhere in Israel, Miriam was looking at it too. A cloud swept across it, then they slid the panel over the top of him. Scott tried to breathe steadily as the screwdriver started up.

When it stopped for the last time, there was a sliding sound above him, then a clunk as they put the seats back into place. His heart raced, and he tried to block out the claustrophobia by concentrating on his breathing.

His mind drifted to the image of Angela being shot. Her legs flailing, then the blood spatter as the bullet went into her head.

He opened his eyes, but it made no difference in the pitch black. He saw Angela's legs stop moving.

The engine started up and with a jolt, the car began to move.

———

EVERY BUMP in the road and every turn of the car was exaggerated, making it impossible to get comfortable. The stale smell of the oxygen mask, coupled with the movement and darkness made him nauseous. He couldn't tell how much time had passed, but it didn't feel as if the car was on the motorway yet, and certainly hadn't stopped long enough for a checkpoint.

Scott had lost track of time when eventually, the car rolled to a stop. It must be the checkpoint.

There was a scraping sound below him, presumably the mirror checking for car bombs. The box was too well sealed to hear any voices outside, yet despite all common sense, Scott held his breath, breathing slowly and quietly when he ran out of air.

Then the car pulled away again. Relieved they were through the checkpoint, Scott tried to lie on his side and sleep, but no sleep came.

He thought about Angela, struggling to come to terms with not only her death, but her lies. Was leaving Britain for Israel the correct decision, or should he stay and fight? Where could Martin and Sarge be? Surely, they must have gone into the Israeli embassy system as well. Would Sarge try to control the resistance now, after his denouncement of Angela in The Nest? If he did, would Scott be in the inner sanctum anymore? He was only in because of Angela. Now they would banish him to a lesser role.

Maybe Miriam was right, escaping to Israel may be the best option. Was there any chance of being happy with Miriam again? They had drifted apart before, only staying together because of Benji. Although they never expressed it in words to each other. Eventually, it became too much, and they had to separate. Why should things be any different now? But what about Angela hiding that she had found Miriam and Benji safe in Israel. Was she truthful about anything with him? Did she really love him, or had she been using him as part of some bigger plan? He'd never know, but despite her betrayal, her death left him empty inside.

He mulled over the positives and negatives of being with Miriam when the car screeched to a halt. It threw him forwards, smashing his feet against the bottom of the box and hitting his head on the top. His elbow crashed into the side, sending pain coursing through his body. The oxygen mask came off, and he fumbled around trying to find it. The car stopped, and he lay in agony, straining his ears for any sign of what was happening.

Gunfire sounded and the car surged forward, throwing him back. Then an enormous bang to the right-hand side startled him, and the car flipped over and rolled. It tossed him around the box, hitting the sides, the top, the bottom.

This time, he held the mask to his face as best he could, but still lost hold of it. Every part of his body hurt, and the car rolled over again before crashing to a stop.

There was silence.

He found the mask and placed it back over his mouth. There was a final clunk as the car settled. The rolling had left Scott on his back, and he stretched his limbs to see if anything was broken. Everything was in working order. His neck hurt as he moved it, and he lay still for a moment.

Then, to his horror, heat came from below him. The padded sides of the box were warm to touch, and a crackling sound came from outside. The car must be on fire, with a loaded petrol tank and an oxygen cylinder.

He banged desperately at the sides, kicked as hard as he could at the top, but nothing moved. The heat intensified. He was sweating and the air coming through the mask was hot.

The car could explode at any minute, and if it didn't, he would burn to death inside.

Every kick hurt his feet, every punch at the box hurt his hands, but he kept going, and with one powerful kick, the wood splintered. He kept kicking until it came apart, and found himself kicking metal. The heat was unbearable, and as the wood splintered more, a smooth, rounded metal object rolled on top of him. It was hot to touch, but he could make out the cylindrical shape of it.

The oxygen cylinder.

Scott twisted around as much as he could to face the hole, then held the cylinder, using it as a battering ram against the metal base of the car. On the third go, it broke. He continued pounding the metal base until he saw the orange light of a road lamp above him. He couldn't move around enough to crawl through the hole or squeeze through headfirst, so instead, Scott pushed his feet through as he pressed his hands below him onto the padding of the box, the jagged twisted metal ripping at his trousers and skin as he did so. His legs, from the knee down, were outside the car. The smell of burning metal and rubber wafted through the hole, then with one huge push, he got up to his waist and pushed again.

The thin metal of the bottom of the car bent easily, and within seconds, he was out on top of the upturned car. There were flames all around him, coming from below. The car lay in a ditch by the side of the road, and he leapt off into the long grass. He landed in soft mud by the car and staggered towards the trees.

As he reached them, an enormous blast behind threw him to the ground. The car had exploded. He covered his ears and pressed his face into the mud.

A few seconds later, parts of the car hit the surrounding ground. He got up and stumbled into the forest.

———

THE GROUND WAS damp beneath him as Scott lay down. From his spot just inside the tree line, he was hidden from view but could see the road lit by both the overhead lights and the fire still flickering from the wreckage of the car.

There was no sign of what had happened, no other car near, and everywhere was silent. Occasionally, a car passed, slowing down to look at the smouldering wreckage.

Scott retreated farther into the wood in case emergency services, or worse, arrived on the scene. He crawled along, partly to avoid being seen and partly because his aching limbs hurt too much. Eventually, he stopped and collapsed under a huge tree. He had no idea how far they had travelled before being attacked.

A breeze started up and wafted the smell of burning car towards him. He wanted to rest, but moving by night would be safer, and getting to Birmingham and the embassy as soon as possible was vital.

Walking parallel with the motorway gave him enough light and ensured he was heading in a straight line. Above him, owls hooted in the trees.

A road sign appeared ahead, and he moved towards the road again, but he had to emerge from the cover of the trees to get a full view of it.

When Scott was sure that no cars were approaching, he stepped out. The sign was illuminated, its white lettering reflecting the lights: BIRMINGHAM 8.

———

TRUDGING over the tree roots and mud underfoot was exhausting, and Scott's thirst became a problem.

After a few hours, the sun appeared from below the horizon, illuminating the motorway. A deep yellow glow through the trees. The traffic increased, first huge lorries, then more cars. The forest ended and Scott came out into open fields.

The most wanted man in the country walked in clear sight. It was dangerous, but the alternative, hiding in the woods until nightfall again, was unthinkable. So he kept going, keeping as close to any hedges as he could for what seemed like hours. He was too tired and thirsty to worry, and almost in a trance, only seeing the few metres in front of him.

An eternity later, Scott took a step forward and hit a suburban street. He must be on the outskirts of Birmingham.

He hurried with his head down, and when he reached a bus stop, the clock told him it was 7.15am. The bus map showed the direction to Edgbaston, but it would involve changing in the city centre, and that would be too risky, even at this early hour. So he kept walking.

As time passed, the streets got busier, and he got more worried about being spotted. His mud-splattered clothes would draw attention as well. The birds were singing in the trees, and Scott was still so thirsty. It reminded him of being young and coming back home after being out all night.

He reached a strip of shops, and outside the newsagents, the newspaper had a picture of him on the front. For a moment, he considered stealing one to read what they knew, but stopped. Getting caught would be the end. They would be outdated as well, anything could have changed overnight.

Scott had no money to buy water, so he stared at the drinks inside the shop. A man behind the counter stared back at him, and Scott hurried away.

He continued to walk, stooping his head every time someone walked past him. Then, at the entrance to a park, he saw an old Victorian water fountain. It was the kind of thing you wouldn't normally notice, but in his state, it was the most amazing thing in the world.

He pressed the button, his mouth salivating. Nothing came out.

Continuing, Scott was aware that there were too many people around to be walking openly. His tiredness and thirst focused him but also made him lightheaded and unable to think sensibly. Beside the playground, a bicycle had been left propped against the green painted railings. It was unlocked, with nobody near it. He made a dash for it, jumped on and rode away. Someone shouted from behind, but he kept pedalling towards the exit.

He left the park and sped off toward Edgbaston.

———

Scott arrived in Edgbaston out of breath, scared and thirsty. All he had to do was find Young Street. It was rush hour and the streets were busy, kids going to school, parents taking kids to school, people dashing to bus stops, to stations.

At any second, somebody could recognise him, but Scott hoped he looked too unimportant with the bicycle and dirty clothes. He rode around randomly, hoping to see the sign for Young Street, but it was hopeless, he had to ask somebody. It could be the most stupid decision he would ever make, one which could end his life, but he had to do it.

Scott pulled up to the pavement where two schoolboys ambled down the road in ill-fitting burgundy blazers.

"Morning, lads, do you know where Young Street is?"

The boys stared at him for a moment, then looked at

each other. He panicked but tried to look calm. They broke into laughter.

"Are you joking, bruv?" the taller one said.

"No, I'm not joking," Scott replied, mildly irritated.

The boy pointed to the houses on the corner of a road next to where they stood. There was a sign against the red brick that read: 'Young Street'.

Scott laughed, louder than intended, a spontaneous laugh of pure joy. The boys exchanged glances as if he were a madman. Scott went to thank them and leave when the other boy said something.

"Where do I know you from?"

"Nowhere," Scott stuttered. "I don't know you."

"I swear I've seen you. Do you know my dad or something?"

"Your mum more like," the other boy joked, and they started punching each other on the arm and laughing.

Scott hopped onto the bike, pedalled a couple of times and freewheeled down Young Street.

Number 44 was the largest house, a detached two storey building at the end of the street. Unlike the other houses, it had high hedges in front and closed security gates.

Scott wheeled the bike around the corner and left it, not wanting to draw any attention to the house. He pressed the buzzer.

"Hello?"

"It's Scott," he whispered. He glanced down the street to make sure all was quiet and leant towards the camera. "Scott Saunders."

The gates clicked and opened.

Scott darted down the path, towards either sanctuary and water, or a trap. A man opened the front door and glanced nervously over Scott's shoulder. He waved his hand as if to say *hurry*. Scott jogged over and the man shut the door behind them.

It was a normal 1930s suburban house with light green painted walls and a wooden floor.

"What happened?" the man asked, eyeing Scott's filthy clothes. "We were expecting you hours ago."

"It's a long story, but I need some water first."

The man pointed towards a kitchen and Scott bolted straight to the sink. He put his head under the tap and drank deeply, letting the water cascade over his cheek as he took huge gulps until he couldn't drink any more.

When he finished, Scott kept his head bowed over the sink in relief. There was a cough behind him, then a voice. "You could have used a glass you know?"

Angela's voice.

Scott spun around. She was sat on a bar stool at the kitchen island, hands grasping a mug. With a wry smile on her lips, she got up. "You didn't really think I was dead, did you?"

Chapter Twenty-Eight

Scott's legs turned to jelly, and he had to hold the counter to keep standing.

"But I saw you get killed. They blew half your face off."

She hugged him and said, "No, you saw one of the Angels being killed."

Scott gaped in disbelief, and Angela held him tight as she ran her hands up and down his back.

"Her name was Evelyn. Such a shame, but that's what they were for, I suppose."

Scott moved back to look at her face, to see it was really her, that she was alive. She pushed her face into his chest and cried. Her chest convulsed against him, and she buried her head even deeper into him.

"I thought *you* were dead," she said through the sobs. "I thought you were gone."

Her emotion overwhelmed him, and Scott began to cry. She pushed back and looked up at him, her eyeliner smeared around her bloodshot eyes.

"Don't tell me you're crying as well. This is silly, look at us." Angela fanned her face with her hands. "We've got a revolution to run. We can't be standing here bawling our eyes out."

Scott wiped a tear from his face. "How did you get out of The Nest, what happened?"

"I hid behind a curtain, one of those huge drapes by the stage. They were shooting everyone. It was chaos. I saw them shoot one of their own guys. He dropped dead right next to me. In the confusion, I pulled his body behind the curtain and dressed in his clothes." Angela smiled at the thought of it. "Luckily, he was on the smaller size, but I was still swimming in them. I put the helmet on and stepped out from the curtain. There were bodies everywhere. It was hideous. I saw Lauren dying on the floor. They had shot her in the chest, and she was bleeding out. I knelt beside her and removed the mask. She smiled at me. Then a soldier came over and I quickly put the mask back on. *'Finish the job,'* he said to me, *'remember what we were told.'*

"Did you?"

Angela put a hand to her temple and rubbed slowly. "I had to. It was best for her, though. Put her out of her misery, I suppose."

"Jesus, Angie." Scott could see that she was hurting telling the story but didn't want to show it. "Then what happened?"

"I stepped into the doorway and saw them grabbing one of the Angels. The poor girl was fighting for all she was worth, but they pinned her to the floor and shot her in the head."

"I saw it too. I thought that was you."

Scott watched the replay in his head again, the image that had been haunting him ever since.

"At that point, it went crazy. All their training went out

the window, they got too excited. I saw two soldiers guarding the main entrance to the tube station leave the door and come to see 'Angela' being killed. So I went to the door and just walked out. It was empty. They must have closed the station, and when I got to the top of the stairs, a soldier opened the cordon and let me out. He didn't say a word, just nodded, so I nodded back and out I went. Then I went round a corner and raised my gun at the first car. They jumped out in fear, thinking it was being commandeered by the army, and I drove straight to an embassy. They hid me in another car, and I was here within a couple of hours." She stroked Scott's face. "What about you?"

Scott told her about his escape, omitting the part about speaking to Miriam, and Angela listened with intense interest.

"Quite a last twenty four hours we've had," Angela said, reaching into a cupboard. "Let's have a drink to escaping."

She pulled out a bottle of red wine and poured two glasses.

"What about Martin and Sarge, how did they get out?"

"I have no idea. I hope Martin can get to safety, but Sarge? I hope they find him and shoot the bastard." Angela's eyes filled with rage. "How dare he threaten me in front of everyone. He's a traitor. If they didn't kill him, I will."

She drank heavily from the glass, then lowered it, her lips ruby red and quivering.

"Don't look at me like that, Scott, he's a fucking traitor, and he needs to be dealt with."

She walked to the window and stared out.

"Oh, one other thing actually," he said, taking a sip. "I spoke to Miriam."

"Really?" Angela turned to him. "When?"

"When I was in the embassy, she's safe. She's in Israel."

"Oh, that's good."

"Angie, I know you met her. I know what happened over there."

She turned back to the window.

"Why didn't you tell me, why did you lie to me? And to her, for that matter?"

There was silence. Angela took another sip.

"Well?" Scott pressed.

"It was for the greater good. We needed to focus on the revolution."

"Bollocks," Scott shouted. "I could have focused more knowing they were safe. You betrayed me, Angie, it's out of order. You said you loved me. Is that another lie?"

She spun around. "Scott, I'm not having this conversation. Can't we just be happy?"

She walked past him and towards the kitchen door. Scott pulled her back.

"No, we are having this conversation now. Why didn't you tell me that Miriam and my son were safe and well? Didn't you want me to be happy?"

Angela looked up at him, her eyes sad, and vulnerable. "Maybe I should have told you."

"Maybe? *Maybe?* You're damn right you should have told me. So, answer the question, do you love me?"

The way Scott had felt when he thought Angela was dead told him he loved her more than he even thought. He couldn't bear to think that she didn't feel the same, despite her lies.

Angela put her arms around him and buried her face into his chest again.

"Yes," she sobbed, "I do love you, Scott. I'm sorry. I'm so sorry."

Scott didn't know how to deal with this; him being the

strong one and her in tears. "Is this an act as well, Angie? I don't know what to believe anymore."

She pushed back and moved her face close to his, her mascara smeared all over her cheeks. "I love you. I promise I do."

Scott turned away from her and drank his wine. "Well, don't lie to me ever again."

She put a hand on his shoulder. "Remember what happened last time we had an argument in a kitchen?"

"Yes, you tried to kill me."

"After that." Angela's hand moved down his back, then around to his front. She reached under his shirt and scratched his chest. "Let me make it up to you."

"No."

Scott stepped away. Angela closed the kitchen door and approached him. He recoiled as she touched him, but he wanted her, and she knew it. He heard her taking off her clothes and tried to block out his conflicting emotions.

"What's happening with the revolution now, anyway?"

"I'll tell you later." She put her hand down his jeans. "Oh, I knew you wanted me."

Scott turned. She stood in her underwear, with her shiny black boots still on. Black like the day in the safe house with the gun holstered around her waist.

He pushed her against the wall.

She scratched his back. "Do it like you hate me."

———

ANGELA STOOD at the open window, puffing the smoke from her cigarette out into the cool Birmingham sky. She shivered underneath her silk dressing gown. They had gone into the living room after Scott had obeyed Angela's orders.

A sly look from the Israeli man in the corridor didn't bother her, but made Scott feel self-conscious. Weren't they guests in this place?

His resentment for her had disappeared and transformed into a raging lust he couldn't control. Now, as he reclined in a chair watching her, it came back.

"I know you're still pissed off with me," she said as if reading his mind. "But I can't change the past. We cannot afford to argue, not now."

"You lied to her as well. You told her you hadn't seen me."

Angela erupted. "What was I meant to tell her? *'I'm fucking him?'* I didn't know how she would take it, and it would have delayed getting the bomb from Shai, delayed everything."

"Did you go out there planning to use her all along?"

"No, I only found out she was there when I got to Tel Aviv. My contacts there showed me a list of names who had recently arrived. So, I had somebody clean in the city I could use."

"You put my son's mother in danger."

"She wasn't in any danger, Scott. *I* would have been if I did it, but not her. Anyway, she made good money out if it."

"That's not the point."

"Listen, hate me all you want, but we have a government to overthrow, *this week*, and we can't be fighting each other."

"So, it's not over, you still think it can be done?"

"I know it can be done. I am going to be totally open with you, Scott, and tell you things only a handful of people know."

Angela paced the room, kimono flowing as she did, her spindly legs jutting out like sticks.

"It's all about the military. It always has been. And they are still on board. We have several generals onside as well as special forces. They don't want power themselves, but they will help us return this country to normality. I have a deal with them; elections within a year and they'll help us, then leave us alone."

Scott hoped this was true, considering it had been large factions in the army who helped facilitate 'the change' away from democracy in the first place.

"Tomorrow, a group of those special forces will assassinate Prime Minister Robertson. At that point, the military will seize control of all communications, I will go on television announcing the PM is dead, and that I am in control and for people to take to the streets." She buzzed with excitement as she spoke. "By now, the government must know they didn't kill me, that it was a lookalike, but they haven't told the public yet. So, it's a double reveal, one, that I'm still alive, and two, that they lied."

Scott frowned. "You said several generals, so not all the army are on side?"

"No, but enough."

"It sounds like a civil war waiting to happen."

"Once they see the PM is dead and half the army have turned, the rest will follow, I'm sure of it."

"I hope so."

"Listen, lives will be lost, there will be violence, yes, but that's what we have to do. You can't make an omelette without breaking a few eggs."

"And then what? You ride into London on a white horse?" Scott questioned, more sarcastic than he meant.

Angela nodded. "Basically yes. We seize the capital, announce any of the old regime to be enemies of the state, and form an interim government."

"Are you sure this can work?"

"No, I'm not sure. There's certainly a chance we all get killed and fail, but we have to take the chance. Those fuckers did it four years ago, so why can't we? We will have the people on our side. We will be heroes, Scott."

"OK, so say it works, and there are elections in a year, what will you do then, just step back?"

"Yes, of course, move to the country and drink wine. I can't wait." Angela stared at him and waved her hands. "God, doesn't this excite you, Scott?"

"No one wants this revolution more than me, Angie, you know what I was like at first, but now I'm fully on board. This government is pure evil. I'm just worried it could all go wrong."

"Well, we have to make sure it doesn't. Now get dressed. We have a conference call with the generals in ten minutes."

————

THE FACES of the generals filled the computer screen. Greying, old-fashioned, austere-looking men, some in military wear, most in shirts or polo tops. They appeared anxious, off guard and reticent; probably because of being hectored by a woman.

And Angela did hector. She impressed on them the importance of this moment for the people, in a historical sense, and playing to their patriotism, for Britain. She reeled off a list of famous historical victories and placed this firmly among them. Insisting victory would be in their grasp, and anyone who didn't give it their all would be remembered forever as a traitor. Hints of recriminations on those who didn't give everything littered her speech. But when they spoke, they were confident of succeeding, of how with the many men under their control, they could seize power. None gave any impression of wanting the army to have any role in the future government, something Scott worried about. Mainly due to how Angela might react to that rather than the good of the country. Any government would be better than this one.

"One year and then elections," was the mantra of the call.

General Forster-Gallagher summed up the feeling. "We are convinced of success, Mrs Newton, the operation to assassinate the Prime Minister is in place for 06.00 tomorrow morning, and everything is in place for after that. We will view the body cam footage live as they storm his country home. Then once we have confirmation that he is eliminated, control of television will pass to you, and you can make your statement. Currently, the only people who know you are alive are us on this call and the Israelis with you. When the country, indeed the world, finds out, momentum will swing to the military and to yourself."

"The government knows I'm alive," Angela said. "They will have checked DNA or something by now. The fact they are hiding that is a lie that once exposed will also swing momentum to us."

"Indeed," General Forster-Gallagher replied.

The others concurred.

As the call continued into details of strategy and numbers, Scott drifted off, thinking how seismic the next few days would be for the country and his place within it.

With no doubt, Angela was a fearless leader of the resistance. A strong focal point and figurehead, but the army held the trump cards. The Kingmakers. What was once a feeling deep down of wanting to overthrow the government was now a burning passion. He felt it as much as she did, though his worries of what may happen were more than hers. Her confidence had always been infectious, but it could only go so far. Nerves came to the fore. But not hers. She was convinced the moment was upon them.

She ended the call with a call to arms.

"This is the last day of a corrupt regime, tomorrow is our day. Flying Ant Day."

The generals signed off.

———

SHE TURNED off the computer and they sat in silence after the call, Angela busily scribbling notes on a pad and Scott trying not to fall asleep in an armchair. The lack of sleep and pure adrenalin of the last twenty four hours had got to him.

"I want to call Miriam," he said, breaking the quiet.

Angela didn't look up from her notes. "You can't. She cannot know I'm alive. Not until tomorrow."

"I won't tell her."

"Scott, it's too risky. Please don't jeopardise anything at this stage. Leave it one day for God's sake."

"No, Angela," Scott said, rising. "I need to know my son is safe."

"Fine, whatever," she mumbled and picked up a phone. "He wants to call her."

A man appeared at the door and took Scott upstairs. He said nothing as he dialled a number. From the phone came a long tone and a recorded voice in Hebrew. The man frowned, then the message repeated in English, 'Sorry, the number you are calling has been disconnected.'

"Sorry," the man said and replaced the handset.

"Is there any other number you have for her?" Scott asked.

"No, sir, this is the number of the residence she was at, a secure line, there is no other number."

"What does that mean?"

The man shrugged. "We don't know."

"Keep trying," Scott said as he left the room. "Please."

————

"WELL?" Angela said as he came back.

"The line is disconnected. Should I be worried?"

She kept her head down, examining her notes. "Probably."

"You don't give a shit, do you?" Scott barked, but Angela didn't reply. "I need to sleep."

"Upstairs, first on the left."

Scott slammed the door and headed back upstairs. He fell into a deep sleep, untroubled by dreams, and awoke to Martin standing over him.

"Wake up, bro, it's Flying Ant Day."

Chapter Twenty-Nine

Martin hurried Scott down the staircase, refusing to explain how he got to the house.

"I'll tell you later. Come on, we can't miss this. I don't know why you're still so tired. Angela says you've been asleep since yesterday morning, bro."

Angela sat on the living room floor, cross-legged in her military jacket, which she had notably not worn on the call with the generals. She looked up as they entered, then turned back to the TV. The two Israeli men sat on the sofa. Martin sat on the floor, gesturing for Scott to sit in the armchair.

Black and white static filled the television screen. A regular thudding boomed from the speakers. Angela tapped a microphone.

"We can't see anything," she said.

There was a clicking sound, and the static cleared to reveal a night vision image from a camera mounted on a soldier. All Scott could make out was another soldier in front, stern-faced, facing the camera. "They're in the helicopter now," Angela said, "heading to Robertson's house.

They should arrive in..." She looked up at the clock on the wall, "five minutes."

"So, what's the plan exactly?" one of the Israeli's asked.

Angela kept her eyes fixed on the screen. "Fly in, blow the doors open and start shooting. Remember the Bin Laden raid? It's like that."

The green light from the television screen glowed on Martin's face. He had no scars or cuts and bruises on his face. His escape from The Nest seemed to have left him unharmed.

The heavy black curtains were drawn, letting no light in or out, and tension hung in the air. Angela barely moved an inch as she stared forward. Even Martin, usually so laid back, rested his head on his thumbs and tapped his fingers together anxiously. On a table by the sofa were two bottles, glowing dully in the dim light. Scott squinted to make them out: Gin and Curacao.

"This is it," Angela proclaimed.

Scott flicked his eyes back to the screen.

The helicopter doors were pulled open, and within seconds, the camera was bumping along towards a large house. Lights on the side of the house flashed on, saturating the screen in bright green. Shooting started. It was impossible to tell what was going on. Two explosions boomed from the speakers. Still, Angela didn't move.

"Who's doing the shooting, us or them?" Scott asked.

Angela held up a finger to silence him.

More explosions, then clearly, the soldier with the camera was inside the house. There were shouts, and Scott could make out the soldier in front running upstairs. More shooting, more shouting. Bouncing green tubes of light pointed in front of the guns. A split-second view of a man pulling a gun before being shot. Then a clear image of large white double doors. The soldier kicked it. Nothing happened. They fixed something to it and the camera turned away, another explosion. The camera spun back, revealing a gap. The doors were gone. There was jostling in front, and it was clear that they were in a bedroom. They shone a torch towards the bed, to show a figure half running, half tumbling towards the window. Angela leant forward. "That's him."

Scott and Martin leant forward. The Israelis stood for a better view. Two of the soldiers pinned him to the bed and held a device up to his face.

"Go ahead, Ma'am," one of them said.

Angela lifted the microphone to her lips.

"Mr. Robertson," she said mockingly. "This is Angela Newton, alive and well, as you surely know. You are about to be executed. Do you have any last words?"

The Prime Minister's face filled the screen. Scott had never seen anybody look so scared. Not even Henry when he pointed the gun at him in the shower. The Prime Minsters' eyes bulged, and his lips quivered.

"Well?" Angela shouted.

"No, don't do this," Robertson begged, shaking and barely able to get his words out. "We can compromise, an agreement, something surely."

Angela scoffed. "Sorry, no can do." She got up and looked at the screen in triumph. "Come on, let's hear some famous last words."

"What about our talks?" Robertson stammered out. "My meetings with your husband. He said I would get immunity, that I could go somewhere safe. I..."

One of the soldiers broke in. "Ma'am, we do not have time."

Angela was in shock, her mouth hanging open. Her

bony fingers shook as she held the microphone. "What talks?"

"He didn't tell you? That was the agreement we made before he died."

"Ma'am," a soldier shouted.

"I killed him and now I'm killing you," Angela roared. "Do it."

The camera moved back, and the soldier aimed a gun at him and fired twice into the temple. Blood spattered everywhere. It reminded Scott of "Angela's" killing.

Everyone in the room gasped. The last thing they saw on the screen was Robertson's body being bundled into a bag before the camera shut off, plunging the room into darkness.

For a few moments, nobody moved or spoke. Scott was trying to process what he had just seen when the lights came on. Angela stood by the door, her finger on the light switch. They all turned to her. Her face was pale and taught.

"First," she said, looking at Martin, then the Israelis, "you didn't hear what I said about killing David. Second, if he held talks with that parasite, he deserved it even more than I thought, and third," she relaxed and smiled at the Israelis, "seeing as we're guests here, fix us all drinks please, gentleman, Flying Ant Day's all round, please."

———

THERE WAS a celebratory mood in the house. Angela, after instructing the Israelis on how to make the cocktails, disappeared upstairs to get changed.

"How did you get out of The Nest?" Scott asked Martin.

"That's for me to think about," Martin replied, peering through the silt in the curtains. "Let's just say it wasn't easy. I thought you'd be a goner. How did you do it?"

Scott related the story.

"Shit," Martin said when he finished. "We're the lucky ones, though. God knows how many died. You know Lauren didn't make it right?"

"Yeah, and we don't know about Sarge."

"It's probably best for him that he got killed. He signed his death warrant after his little interruption before it all kicked off. Hey, did you know about Angela killing David?"

Scott wasn't sure how to respond. It was out there now, so what did it matter? "Yeah, I did."

Martin whistled. "Jeez."

He walked to the door and listened for a moment, then turned. "So Sarge was right." He lowered his voice. "He made some good points to be fair bro. I mean, look, it's Flying Ant Day, and Angela's doing cocktails at four in the morning. Haven't we got kind of big day ahead of us?"

"Did you know Miriam and Benji were in Israel?"

"Israel? No, how did you..."

"Yeah, Israel, and *she*," he pointed to the ceiling where they could hear Angela moving about, "knew all along."

Martin widened his eyes in surprise, making it hard to tell if he was bluffing or not.

"I didn't know, bro, I was doing all I could to find them. Israel was certainly a possibility, but we thought they were probably in England somewhere."

Martin stopped as Angela descended the stairs. She came in, freshly made up, with bright red lipstick. She had changed into black jeans and a black t-shirt emblazoned with the Flying Ant logo with the military top over it.

"Here," she said, throwing a package on the coffee table, "put these on for the speech."

Scott picked up the package. Inside were t-shirts similar to hers, black with the logo in the centre.

One of the Israelis returned with a drinks pitcher and a tray of glasses as Scott and Martin put on the t-shirts.

"Before anyone says it's too early, this is like an airport. Normal drinking hours are out the window," Angela said.

She lifted a drink from the tray, and Scott and Martin took theirs.

"This is it," she said, "the day we've been waiting for, to Flying Ant Day."

The glasses clinked together.

Scott wanted to ask Angela about David meeting with Robertson, but it could wait until the drink's effects kicked in.

Around them, the Israelis set up a camera and fiddled with wires, coming in and out of the room with a table and chairs.

Martin beat Scott to the question.

"What Robertson said about meeting David, do you think that's true?"

Angela's eyes dimmed. "Fuck knows. I wouldn't put it past him. He was too cautious, too ready to appease them. That's why he had to go. We wouldn't be here today if he were still alive. We'd be sitting around discussing this day but not living it." She took a long sip and her eyes glazed over. "Part of me doesn't believe it's real, though. Today, all the Ants will come out, in the army, in the government, in every walk of life and destroy this regime." Angela finished her glass. "Beautiful."

Whilst the Israelis tested the camera, she took a call from one of the generals, downing another cocktail as she spoke, sat on the sofa, legs crossed, gesticulating as she spoke. She fired questions at General Forster-Gallagher; times, places, locations, numbers. It was exhausting listening to her, and Scott slumped into the armchair and poured another drink.

Martin excused himself and went upstairs.

Angela pontificated and drank. She was in her element. He sympathised with the poor general on the other end, and eventually, she ended the call and perched herself on the edge of Scott's chair, pouring them another drink. "Ideally, we would take over the TV a bit later in the day when people are actually awake, but we have to act quickly. We're showing it on a continuous loop all day, anyway. We have hacked the news websites and it'll be up there."

Angela talked for a long time, still animated, still drinking. Talking about the country, the Ants, the look on Robertson's face. She only stopped when one of the Israel's stood up from the mass of wires.

"Mrs. Newton, It's ready."

————

SCOTT AND MARTIN sat on either side of Angela's seat. She had one last look in a pocket mirror, one last slug of the drink, and walked over, unsteady on her feet. She sat, cleared her throat and nodded to the Israelis.

Maybe somewhere, wherever they were, Miriam and Benji would see this.

As Scott looked into the camera, a red light came on. The television in front of them switched from a children's cartoon to the image of the three of them at the table.

"Good morning," Angela began. "I am Angela Newton,

leader of the resistance. Alive and well despite what the government has told you."

She wasn't using any notes and Scott worried she would mess up.

"I am speaking to you from an undisclosed location in the UK." She cleared her throat. "This morning at 6am, Prime Minister Robertson was killed by an elite group of special forces loyal to the resistance."

Angela slurred her words as she went. Scott tensed, already nervous and unsure of where to look. Sweat formed on his brow.

"Unlike the heinous government he led, we do not lie to the people of this country."

Footage of Robertson's face appeared on the screen, glowing white and green, then being pushed onto the bed and shot. The camera went back to Angela.

"As we speak, forces loyal to the resistance are taking control of key infrastructure, government buildings, and as you can see, television. For those of you involved in the resistance, I ask you to carry out your given duties for Flying Ant Day. For those who are not, I ask you to stay in your homes safely. Today, this country will once again become free. Within a year, we will hold free and fair democratic elections. I will head the…"

She stopped.

"Oh, what's the word?" she said to Scott. "Where it's like a temporary government?"

Was this really happening live in the middle of the speech?

"Interim," Scott whispered.

"Yes, an interim government, that's it," she continued, looking back at the camera, "I will head that until we stabilise this great nation. I ask all foreign nations to support this revolution against a vile dictatorship and to provide support and halt sanctions immediately. Thank you, and you will hear from me again in due course."

The red light clicked off.

Angela banged her head on the table. "I can't believe I fucked that up. Why didn't we prerecord it?"

Scott put an arm around her. "You did fine, don't worry."

She didn't raise her head.

"You did good, Angie," Martin said. "Listen, I need to stretch my legs. I'm going out for a run."

"No," one of the Israelis said. "You can't leave, it's too dangerous."

"With respect, I think we're in control now, mate, and anyway, I'll be wearing these."

From behind the sofa, Martin picked up a hoodie and put on a large pair of glasses.

Angela lifted her head up. "Don't be a fucking idiot, Martin. If anyone sees you, it'll blow our location. We just appeared on live TV together."

"No one will see me. It's 6.30 am, I'll make sure. I got here, didn't I?"

"Martin, no."

He shrugged. "Fine, I'll just jog round the back garden."

Martin walked out. The Israelis were uneasy.

"We'll monitor the intelligence assets, Mrs Newton," one said as they left.

Angela got up and poured another drink from the pitcher.

"Now what?" Scott asked.

"We wait for the army to do their stuff and get back to me."

She tore the curtains open. The sky was getting lighter as sunrise approached.

"Please stop hating me, Scott, I can't do this without you."

"Don't push me away then."

Angela walked to the door and locked it, then came over to him and straddled him, kissing his neck.

"You know what revolution does to me, Scott."

She nuzzled his neck, and he gave in to her.

————

THEY LAY ENTWINED on the floor, exhausted.

If she was trying to win him over with sex, he worried it might be working. The birds sung outside, and light crept in around the curtains.

Angela looked over at the window and said, "I wish we could watch the sun rise on this day."

There was a knocking at the door.

"One moment," she shouted. "Who is it?"

"It's Noah. Important news," he said, sounding nervous.

Angela jumped up and covered herself in the rug, rolling Scott off it as she pulled it up. Scott reached for his clothes as quickly as he could.

"This is my Marianne Faithfull look," she said to Scott as she pulled the door open to one of the Israeli men.

"Oh, sorry, I didn't realise," Noah said, apologetic.

"Don't worry, we have more important things to worry about. What is it?"

"It's Martin, he's gone."

"Have you looked everywhere?"

"Yes, I think he jumped over the fence," Noah replied.

"For fuck's sake, give us a minute."

Angela came back in, and they both got dressed frantically.

"He's risking everything for a jog, the idiot," she said, pulling the t-shirt back on.

They got out and searched the house again whilst the Israelis searched the garden, but there was no sign of him. As Angela lit a cigarette and made a drink, Noah came out of a room, pale and shaking.

"I have more bad news," he stuttered. "We intercepted radio chat from the government air force. Well, what's left of it."

"And?" Angela said.

"They're launching a drone attack somewhere in Birmingham."

Scott took the cigarette pack and fumbled for a lighter. "When?"

"Now."

Noah looked at the pack of cigarettes and Scott slid it over to him. Angela looked up. They all stopped. Then they heard it; a high-pitched whine, barely audible at first, then increasing in volume.

Noah dropped the cigarettes. "Oh God, that's a missile."

Angela jumped towards Scott as the whine intensified. She hugged him. "I love you!" she shouted.

Scott could barely hear her above the screeching. "I love you too."

He closed his eyes as the sound became unbearably loud, ending in an enormous explosion.

Chapter Thirty

Miriam stood on the balcony. Below her, Paris stirred. The pre-rush hour traffic had started, and she marvelled at the patriotism of French car owners, as a Citroen, a Renault, then two Peugeots drove by.

Outside the café across the street, two men dressed in white shirts and jet-black waistcoats put out chairs. The sun hit the pools of water on the pavement. She gripped the cast iron railing, black as the waiter's waistcoats and wet with the morning dew.

It had been raining when they landed at Charles de Gaulle Airport in Shai's private plane. The relentless drizzle continued on the drive into the city, past a shimmering Eiffel Tower, and here to the apartment on the Rue de Bac.

It didn't look much from the entrance, but as they entered the second-floor property, it became clear that a multi-millionaire owned the place. Housekeepers discreetly melted away into the background as Shai, Esther, Miriam and Benji dumped their bags and headed straight to bed.

Now, Benji snored, sprawled out on the enormous bed. No matter how safe Paris was, she had insisted that they sleep in the same room. The relief at being out of Israel, itself once a sanctuary, was palpable, but after everything that had happened, Miriam couldn't shake the feeling of danger.

A knock at the door startled her, and Esther called her name. Before Miriam reached the door, Esther had cracked it open.

"Miriam, sorry to wake you, but you need to come and watch the television."

"It's fine. I was awake anyway. What is it? I'll be five minutes."

Esther's face suggested that she did not have five minutes. Miriam looked back at Benji and followed her down the hallway.

———

As THEY ENTERED the palatial main room, which looked more like a hotel lobby than a living room, Shai, already in a full suit complete with a pink silk tie, asked them to sit down. He held the TV remote control, and on the screen, currently on live pause, sat a serious-looking news reporter with an image behind him. An image of Angela Newton.

"You will not believe this," Shai said. "Are you ready?"

Miriam, preparing for whatever the shock would be, carefully sat down.

"I'm ready."

Shai hit play. Miriam covered her mouth in shock as she listened to Angela, flanked by Scott and another man, drunkenly explaining that not only was she alive, but had just ordered the assassination of the Prime Minister and was attempting to seize power.

Esther smirked as Scott had to help Angela remember her lines and gasped at footage of Robertson being shot.

When the broadcast ended and returned to the reporter, Shai paused it again.

"My God, she's done it. I don't know if I'm more surprised that she is alive or that they killed that bastard."

Miriam swallowed hard, unable to be as happy as Shai and Esther. However glad she was that the government appeared to be falling, selfishly she was concerned. Did this mean any chance of a reconciliation with Scott would be over?

Shai turned to her. "What do you think, Miriam, isn't that marvellous?"

She tried to smile. "Yes, it's incredible."

"I'm trying to reach my contacts over there, but can't get through, it's radio silence I'm afraid."

Esther smiled at her. "Maybe one day soon you can go back to London."

"Well, let's wait and see what happens next," Miriam replied. "It all seems very much up in the air."

Shai rewound and played it again with a chuckle "This will be about the tenth time I've watched this."

"Was she drunk?" Esther asked as it replayed. "I swear she was, how bizarre."

This time, Miriam focused on Scott's face, filtering out Angela's slurring rhetoric and watching his eyes, wide like a deer in the headlights, staring into the camera. He looked scared; they all did. Even Angela, in her moment of glory, was half drunk and half scared, eyes wide and stumbling over her words. Scott was holed up in the midst of this somewhere now. With *her*.

Benji's voice interrupted her thoughts. "Is that Daddy? Daddy's on TV?" He ran towards her, still in his pyjamas. "What's happening?"

Shai stopped it and looked awkwardly from Benji to Miriam. Benji looked at the paused image. "That's Daddy with your curly friend. What are they doing?"

"They have done something very brave, young man," Shai said. "They are making your country safe again."

Benji tilted his head with confusion.

"Yes," Miriam said. "Let me make you some breakfast and I'll explain."

———

THE HOUSEKEEPER SEEMED BOTH amazed and pleased that Miriam insisted on making breakfast herself, and disappeared around a corner, curtseying as she went.

Miriam turned back towards Benji as he climbed up into a chair. "I think you're old enough to understand, Benji, so I'm going to explain why Daddy was on TV to you. If you don't understand anything, just stop me and ask, OK?"

Benji nodded.

"When you were born, Britain was a happy country," Miriam said, as if telling a fairy tale. "There were a few problems, but on the whole, everything was good. Then we had a recession, which means the country ran out of money, a lot of people got poorer, and they got angry. Some people blamed other types of people for their problems and the country became more divided."

Benji listened, the same look on his face as if she were reading him a bedtime story.

"This went on for a few years, getting worse and worse.

Then a virus spread through the whole world and made things a lot worse. Lots of people died, especially old people and everyone got scared."

Miriam paused, remembering her parents, both of whom had succumbed to the virus.

"People got even more angry with each other and with the government. It was chaos. One day, a group of bad people took over the country. But they created a cure for the virus, and because they got rid of it, people turned a blind eye to the bad things they did because nobody was dying anymore. Then they did more bad things, but nobody could get rid of them because they didn't have elections anymore. A group of good people, brave people, called the resistance, were trying to get rid of the bad people. They had to do bad things as well to win. Daddy is one of those good people trying to defeat the baddies. And today, it looks like they might be winning. Does that make sense?"

Benji nodded. "So, Daddy is a goodie?"

"Yes."

"And the curly haired lady?"

"She's the leader of the goodies."

Benji looked at her wide-eyed. "Wow! That's a cool story."

"Yes, it is."

"Is that why we had to go away until the bad people are gone?"

"Yes, and when the goodies win, we can go back home."

Explaining it to Benji in these simple terms gave clarity to recent history. A simple story of good and evil. And right now, it looked like good was winning.

For the rest of the morning, no more news came from England. They mentioned unconfirmed reports of fighting and explosions, but nothing concrete.

At around noon Shai stood and addressed Miriam, Esther and Benji. "I'll be meeting an old friend to discuss the situation. Why don't you three get out of the building, have a stroll round the city then meet me for lunch after?" They jumped at the idea, bored and impatient as they were sitting watching the same news on television.

———

SHOPPING IN PARIS with a billionaire's daughter was not something Miriam expected to be doing at any point in her life.

"If you see anything you like, let me know," Esther said as they strolled onto the Rue Saint Honoré. "I would like to buy you a present." She knelt to Benji. "And you as well, little man, anything you like." Esther stood up again and reached out for Miriam's arm.

"It's the least I can do, Miriam, for helping my father and his cause."

She didn't want to be seen as a charity case, but there was no point in arguing. "Thank you."

Esther swanned around the boutiques as if she owned them, whilst Miriam gasped at the prices. Champagne was brought out, and immaculately dressed assistants fussed over Benji. Esther spent an obscene amount of money on clothes. Miriam, still thinking about Scott and the situation back home, tried to pay attention but became distracted. It felt wrong to be in these luxury shops whilst her country was in the throes of revolution.

She kept thinking about Scott, sat next to Angela staring into the camera. What was going through his mind, knowing millions would see him? What if the government fought back and won? They would kill Scott.

"Miriam?" Esther said.

She turned back from staring out the window. "Sorry, I was miles away."

"I was thinking this would look good on you."

She held up a garish fur-lined jacket. It felt like the time Angela appeared at her Tel Aviv apartment, brandishing expensive clothes at her.

"Oh no, I couldn't wear fur."

Esther leant close to her and whispered, "It's faux fur. But everything else is the highest quality. Something for those chilly Autumn evenings when you go back to London. The autumn collection has just come out this week."

Benji stood by a mirror as a young woman tried various hats on him.

"It's not my usual style," Miriam muttered.

Esther followed her gaze to Benji. "Ah, the thing is, I don't have a man in my life, I don't have children, shopping is all I have." She laughed a little too loud, looking at Benji. "It's sad really, but that's life."

"Do you want children?" Miriam asked.

"I'm too old now, don't tell anyone, but I'm forty-two in October."

"Did you ever want them?"

Esther sighed. "I used to, like every young woman does, I suppose, but the right man never came along. There were lots of 'suitors', as Papa called them, but it never worked out. I was engaged for a few years in my early 30s but..."

She trailed off and stroked the fur of the jacket. On the outside, Esther appeared to have everything going for her, the money obviously, and a life of luxury with some unspec-ified job in Shai's business that didn't appear to be too demanding. She was certainly attractive as well, but it was obvious that something was missing.

As Shai's only child, Miriam suspected that she had been even more cosseted and spoilt than most rich men's daughters.

"I will die alone," Esther said. "But in the finest clothes."

She laughed that hollow laugh again and dragged Miriam to the mirror, forcing her to put on the jacket.

———

After visiting the last shop on the street, Shai called Esther to say that he would meet them at the Angelina Paris for coffee before the driver took them home. Miriam laughed to herself at the name of the café, and they started down the street.

Benji, in a brand-new Louis Vuitton baseball cap, looking like a spoilt rich brat, skipped along the pavement in front.

"What do you make of this Angela Newton?" Esther asked as they followed his lead. "Papa says you met her in Israel."

"I don't know enough about her, she seemed very secretive."

"Was she drunk on that video do you think? Apparently she likes a drink."

"It looked like it. Surely you must have met her before?"

"Oh yes, a few times. Her husband was an awful bully, had to dominate every conversation, but when she was alone, I could tell she was a fighter. Strange woman really, never knew where I stood with her. I don't know if she's got what it takes to run a country, but who has?"

"Indeed."

Benji stopped at the corner as instructed, but had turned back to them waving.

"I can see Shai!" he shouted.

Esther weaved her arm into Miriam's. "Papa loves this place, the coffee is amazing."

They reached the corner and up ahead, they spotted Shai strolling towards them, a black briefcase in his hand. He raised a hand to wave at them, and as he did so, a motorcycle raced past from behind Miriam, heading towards Shai. It swerved towards the pavement, and two cracks rang out.

Shai fell to the floor, letting out a piercing howl. Time slowed down and Esther dropped her shopping bags and ran towards him. Miriam grabbed Benji's hand as Esther's sharp screaming drowned out both Shai's howl and the motorcycle.

Before she reached her father, the man on the back of the bike leapt off and snatched Shai's briefcase. Within seconds, he was back on, and sped away.

A crowd of onlookers surrounded Shai, some backing away, others kneeling next to him. Miriam had stopped, fixed to the spot, gripping Benji's hand so tightly he tried to release it. He was staring at the scene in front. If it were not for Benji, she would have ran ahead, but the thought of him being traumatised again stopped her. Benji pulled her forwards.

Shai lay splayed out on the pavement, deathly pale and still. A dark red patch of blood seeped out from underneath him. She knelt next to him. Esther clutched his head, speaking rapidly in Hebrew.

His eyes fluttered, then opened. "I love you Esther."

Miriam turned Benji away from the horror. She felt sick, and as she took a step forward, she stepped in a pool of

Shai's blood. Telling Benji to keep looking away, she spun round and knelt back down.

"The briefcase," Shai murmured. "Tell Angela the briefcase is gone." He convulsed and coughed. Blood spattered from his mouth and Esther screamed. One of the passers-by was on the phone to the emergency services. He said something in French to Miriam.

"English," she shouted.

"Does he have a pulse?"

Miriam put her fingers to Shai's neck. The pulse was weak. "Just about."

The man spoke in French down the phone. Then Shai's eyes closed, and his head fell to the side. Esther let out an animalistic sound, a horrifying deep screech, then dropped to the floor.

"Papa, no!" she wailed.

Benji cried as Miriam placed her fingers back on Shai's neck. This time, there was no pulse.

Chapter Thirty-One

Scott pushed Angela to the ground, falling on top of her as the explosion hit. He clenched his teeth, waiting for the pain and death. His life didn't flash before him as he expected. No pain came. No death came. Angela wriggled beneath him.

"You nearly broke my neck," she said, reaching out a hand to hit his shoulder.

The lights still shone, and the house still stood.

"I was protecting you!" he protested as she shoved him off.

Angela sat up and looked around. "What use would your body do against a missile, anyway?"

Scott pushed himself into a sitting position, hands propping him up from behind. "They must have missed."

Angela climbed to her feet. "Ten out of ten for observation, Scott."

Noah appeared in the doorway, looking sheepish. He held out a hand to Scott and hauled him up off the floor.

"Are you both OK?"

Before Scott could reply, the back door slid open, and Angela strode into the garden. About a hundred metres away, a plume of smoke rose from behind the trees. They followed her out.

"Maybe they didn't miss, maybe they had the wrong target," she said.

An acrid burning smell hit them as they went outside. The sound of car alarms wailed all around them. Black smoke twisted in the air.

"They must know we are here, though. But how?" Scott said.

Angela turned back to them. "Yes, how indeed, that's the question."

The other Israeli came out and Angela stared at them. "How could they know our location?"

They shrugged and looked at each other. She took a step towards them. "Well, any ideas? Because right now it looks like one of you fuckers isn't telling me something." She stood, hands on hips, her lips pursed. "Are you working for them?"

Noah cracked his knuckles. "No, why would we do that? We're in the house as well, it would have killed us."

"Martin," Scott said, "Martin wasn't in the house."

Angela met his gaze for a second, then stared at the floor. "No, it can't be."

"Think about it, Angie, he turns up out of the blue and then suddenly disappears just before a missile attack. That's a pretty big coincidence. Did he tell you how he got out of The Nest? He was hesitant to tell me."

Angela continued to stare at the floor, deep in thought.

"He gave some sort of vague description," she muttered, barely audible over the car alarms.

The smoke wafted towards them.

"Come on," Scott said, "let's go inside."

———

THEY SAT in the living room with the television playing their own announcement over and over in the background. Angela grilled the Israelis about whether the broadcasting of the video could have given away their location. They insisted there could be no way. She paced the room.

"If Martin is a spy, it must be recent. There's no way he could have been working for them all that time. I would have known. They must have turned him after The Nest attack. Maybe they forced him." She flung her glass across the room. "Damn it!"

"We need to decide what to do now, surely we cannot stay here," Scott said. "Is there another place we could go to?"

Noah broke in. "The situation is too volatile. We cannot move around. Our only hope is they have the wrong intelligence, and think they've killed you already."

"Find out what's happening. If we're winning, what the situation is in London, get in contact with the generals. We're sitting ducks here," Angela barked, "and get me another drink."

They left the room, looking relieved to be out of there.

"So," she said to Scott, "Martin. Really?"

"I don't want to believe it myself, Angie, but it's a real possibility. And you'd think he would be back from his jog now, especially seeing as there's been a missile attack nearby."

She sighed. "Any resistance is built on trust. You put your life in the hands of everyone you recruit. The people at the top, like Martin, I trust with my life. I just cannot believe it."

"But what if they got to him? Look what they made me do before? I spied on you, remember. It might be against his will."

Angela leant against the wall, rubbing her temples. Scott feared another attack and every noise in the house sounded like the start of another whining missile. The nagging fear that the revolution would be a failure had always been there, but now it had come to the fore.

Scott looked up at the television and watched Angela stumble over her words. What would Miriam's reaction be if she had seen the speech?

"Where's this fucking drink?" Angela shouted.

Scott kept his eyes on the screen, at his own scared face, at Angela's stuttering delivery, and deep into Martin's eyes. Could he really be behind this?

There was a knock at the door.

"So, they've learned to knock at last," Angela said as she hurried to the door.

She spoke to one of the Israelis, asking about the generals, and as Scott looked back at the TV, it flashed and went blank, then returned to a white screen with bold black lettering: 'A MESSAGE FROM YOUR GOVERNMENT.' It flashed again to show the Deputy Prime Minister, Simon Nicholson, a short fat man, behind a desk. The camera slowly zoomed in on him. Scott reached for the remote and turned up the volume.

"Angie," he shouted.

———

THE DEPUTY PM looked directly into the camera, and they looked directly back at him.

"Today, terrorists have assassinated the Prime Minister and are attempting to take control of the country," he began. "John Robertson was a good man who saved this country from the grips of anarchy and a devastating pandemic. I am sure you will all join me in commemorating his memory."

"Too fucking right we do," Angela said, knocking back a glass of Flying Ant Day and holding it up.

The Deputy PM paused before continuing, looking down at the table in front of him. "We implore all citizens of this great country to stay indoors and stay safe whilst we deal with the menace in our midst. We now have full control of the country, the airways, and are implementing a crackdown on all terrorist activity. Within the last hour, multiple strikes against terrorist locations around the country have taken place, with more to follow. Two days ago, we located and destroyed their base, resulting in what we believed to have been the killing of the leader, Angela Newton. It has since come to light that she escaped, using a lookalike to fool government forces. This poor woman was used for the sole purpose of being murdered in place of Newton. Another despicable act by the group." He thumped a fist on the table. "Angela Newton is not a saviour. She is a ruthless, murderous, degenerate radical who will stop at nothing in her lust for power. She is responsible for the deaths of hundreds of innocent people and must be stopped. Following the shocking death of Robertson, I will now take charge in leading the search for any remaining terrorists, including Newton herself and her accomplices, many of whom are Jewish I might add. Please be assured that anyone connected to her and her group will face our full might. This includes traitorous army generals hell bent on destroying this wonderful nation. The country is in safe hands and will not be taken back to the dark days before Robertson came to power. So please, stay at home, and stay safe. I promise you that this threat will be dealt with swiftly and harshly. Thank you."

The screen cut to a photo of Robertson, and 'Land of Hope and Glory' swelled underneath.

Angela slumped back on the sofa, despondent. "Fuck, how did they get back on the TV?"

After the high of seeing Robertson being killed and Angela's speech to the nation, things had gone rapidly downhill. The missile strike, Martin potentially being a spy, and now this. Maybe the revolution would not be happening now. Scott feared for his life.

Angela stood. "I need to talk to the army, find out what's really going on. Come on."

They went to the communications centre, a box room upstairs where the two Israelis sat, headphones on, staring at computer monitors. An ashtray between them overflowed with cigarette butts. The glowing computers in the dark reminded Scott of The Nest.

Angela startled them as she barged in. "What's going on? Are we winning? What is the army doing?"

Noah took off his headphones. "As far as we can tell, everything is still going to plan. That broadcast was clearly an attempt to discredit you and encourage people to turn against you. It's propaganda. Like your man Orwell said, 'The first casualty of war is the truth.'"

The other man took his headphones off and said, "All units are in place and engaged in action against the remaining government forces. They're not putting up as much fight as expected. Almost certainly because of more military deserting to our side."

"Get me one of the generals on the line," Angela demanded.

"We're trying, but they're kind of busy," the man said, grinning.

Scott worried what Angela's reaction would be, but she grinned back. "Are we expecting any more missile attacks?"

"There is some aerial activity from the government, but we can only hope they had false intelligence."

"We wait. War is about waiting and hoping you don't get killed. Call me when you get a general on the line," she said, and turned on her heels. Scott followed her out.

———

ANGELA INSISTED on decamping to the garden. The sun beat down on them as they sat on rickety garden furniture on the patio. Scott chain-smoked, barely able to hold the cigarettes in his shaking hands as he inhaled deeply. Angela took a pack of tarot cards from her pocket and laid them on the table, a bottle of Sauvignon Blanc next to her.

The sound of car alarms had ceased, replaced by an eerie stillness. The smoke from the missile attack had cleared, revealing a clear blue sky. Over the fences and through the trees, it was possible to make out the nearby houses. What were the residents of those houses thinking? Whose side they were on? Would those in the resistance get scared now and stay home as the Deputy PM had instructed or carry out their instructions as Angela had asked.

"Do you think people will believe him or you?" Scott asked.

Angela didn't look up from her cards. "Me. This is the day they have been waiting for. I have faith."

"How many people are actually in the resistance?"

"Thousands. As well as the army and people in the government, there are thousands of ordinary people primed and ready for this day. Carrying out multiple acts of sabotage. Don't worry."

"Is there a list of everyone in the resistance?"

"There is, but not in England. It would be too dangerous. Can you imagine the names and addresses of every Ant at work? There would be a massacre if it fell into the wrong hands. One of my Israeli contacts has it, the same contact who got the radioactive material. I've already asked for it to be sent over as soon as we take power. As soon as I went on air, moves were made to get it. That's one of the many plans in place for Flying Ant Day." She drank straight from the bottle and flipped over a card. "But I tell you what, anyone who worked against us will suffer. We'll round them up. The prisons will be full of them. My God, they will suffer."

Scott drew on the cigarette, alarmed by her lust for vengeance. "We'd be no better than them in that case though."

"Who gives a fuck? Maybe we don't even have elections for a few years, until we've purged everyone we need to," Angela replied, her mouth twitching as she spoke.

The scream of a jet plane above drowned out what she said next, and Scott looked up, alarmed, but Angela didn't stir, focusing on her cards.

"That doesn't sound good," he said. Then he saw them; three jets in formation shooting across the sky. "Maybe we should get inside. They must have drones or something as well."

"No," she snapped. "We will be fine, Scott, look."

Angela held up a card in between her shaking thumb and forefinger. An image of a naked woman, a ribbon wrapped around her, holding two sticks. Underneath were the words 'The World'.

"This means we win."

The sounds of the jets faded away. Scott wanted to go inside, to hide, to drag her indoors and pray no more missiles came. Instead, he leant over and took the wine bottle. The taste of her lipstick gave way to the fruity liquid, and he gulped at it. A calmness came over him. He tilted his head back and let the sun hit his face. He stayed like that for a few minutes, unsuccessfully trying not to think of anything.

He thought about Miriam's offer of a reconciliation, of being a happy family again instead of being tied to a drunken Angela, which could lead to God knows what. But he loved Angela, and there was nothing he could do about that.

The doorbell ringing brought him back to reality. Angela gave Scott a flick of the head and he followed her into the house.

Noah was already at the bottom of the stairs, head-phones around his neck. "It's Martin."

Angela gave Scott a nervous glance, then looked back at Noah. "Get the handcuffs and let him in."

They watched on the CCTV panel by the door as Martin trudged up the path, his head covered by the hoodie. Before he reached the front door, Angela swung it open.

Martin pulled down the hoodie and held his hands up. "Look, I had to get out OK, nobody saw me, I promise."

Angela blocked the doorway. "You took your time."

Martin stopped, looking anxiously at them all. "I was on my way back and heard that explosion. People came out into the street, and I had to be careful who saw me. What was that anyway, a missile?"

"You tell us."

"What do you mean?"

She turned away, facing Scott and Noah. "Take him into the living room."

———

Martin sat handcuffed to a chair, tapping his feet nervously. "Nobody saw me, I swear. We don't have anything to worry about."

Angela pulled out her gun and pointed it at him.

"What the fuck?" he exclaimed, fear in his eyes.

Angela's mouth twitched. "Who are you working for?"

"Who am I working for? Are you serious-"

"Yeah, I'm fucking serious Martin!"

"Wait, you think I'm a spy or something?"

"You disappear just before a missile strike, presumably meant to kill me..." Angela flicked her head around the room, "...to kill us." Her finger twitched on the trigger. "How exactly did you escape from The Nest?"

Now Martin grasped the seriousness of the situation. "You're for real?"

Angela moved her head back an inch as if getting ready for the recoil.

"Mate," Scott said, hoping to stop her shooting, "just answer the question."

Her finger rested on the trigger.

"When the shots started, I dived under the table and stayed there. I couldn't see a thing because of the bloody tablecloth but could hear the shooting. I could hear the boots of the soldiers walking around the tables and knew I was a goner if I stayed there. So I made a run for it, just got up and legged it, knowing they would probably shoot me.

There were people everywhere, bodies everywhere, but I just kept running, head down until I got to one of the exits."

Angela didn't move a muscle, keeping the gun pointed at him.

"When I got above ground, I flagged down a car and kicked the driver out. I realised I had my fake ID in my pocket, so thought I'd try my luck at the checkpoint out of London. What else could I do? Honestly, at that point, I presumed I'd be caught, but I had to try something. At the checkpoint, I got waved through. I presume it was one of our guys because he looked at me and said 'Birmingham, avoid the M6.' So I went the other route and there was only one checkpoint, which I passed easily. Then I got here."

"How did you know to get to this house?" Noah asked.

"I saw the list of embassies every day. I worked on that shit."

Angela let out a whistle. "Well that's some serious strokes of luck there."

"I could say the same for you guys. Anyone who got out is lucky."

"Do you believe him, Scott?"

Scott had no idea. He wanted to believe him, and what he had said was true. His and Angela's escape stories could also be perceived as too good to believe. "I don't know."

Martin looked up at Angela. "Angie, come on, you know me, how could I..."

"And you know me, Martin. I'm not afraid of getting rid of traitors. The sensible thing would be to kill you now."

She took a step forward and put the gun against his head. Martin closed his eyes.

"I am not working for anybody except you," he shouted.

"You'd better fucking not be." She stepped back and put the gun away.

The sound of a jet overheard stopped her and they all looked up.

"Leave him in here," Angela said as the sound died away. "Noah, get back to work, Scott, come with me."

Martin shouted as they left. "You've got this wrong, I'm clean."

Chapter Thirty-Two

Angela held the satellite phone in one hand and a cigarette in the other. "And you're one hundred percent sure, yes?"

She listened to the response, raised her eyebrows, and inhaled deeply on the cigarette, blowing a cloud of smoke towards Scott.

"OK then, thank you, send it now. Bye."

She tilted her head back and stared at the ceiling.

"Well, what did he say?" Scott asked.

After leaving Martin handcuffed to the chair, she had pestered the Israelis until finally, through persistence or coincidence, one of the generals called her back.

Scott had returned to the garden, sipping wine, smoking, and worrying about the revolution falling apart before his eyes. He had left Angela inside, hectoring the Israelis with increasingly drunken proclamations of revenge as she veered between moods, one minute thinking they had lost and would be hunted down, the other confident of victory any minute.

No more jets flew over and the surrounding streets were

calm again, yet the laughing of children playing in a nearby garden sounded shockingly out of place. He had shut out Angela's voice and let the quiet of the garden wash over him.

Now, however, as he stared into Angela's bloodshot eyes, all that tension came back.

"The situation has stabilised; desertions are crippling the government forces. They're suggesting we go to London now and claim power."

"How would we get there?"

"They're sending helicopters, one for us and two escorts."

"Is that safe?"

"No, nothing is safe. We're in the middle of a revolution, but if we don't go now, if I don't go to London and show I'm in charge, we could lose momentum. This is a critical moment." Both the Israelis took their headphones off, Scott stubbed out a cigarette. "This is the moment we have been waiting years for. We have to seize it."

Noah coughed. "Who is going in the helicopter, all of us?"

"Yes, we can't leave you two here, we're all going."

"Martin?" Scott asked

She groaned. "I don't know. If he's telling the truth, we need him. But if he's not, we're fucked. I'll think about it whilst we get ready. The helicopters are coming from a nearby base, we haven't got long."

"And if we don't take him, what do we do with him?"

"We shoot him."

As they waited for the helicopters, the Israelis burned piles of paper in the garden and dismantled the computer equipment. A thick black plume of smoke billowed from the makeshift pyre on the patio.

Angela disappeared upstairs, asking not to be disturbed. Scott, left alone with nothing to do, went to speak to Martin.

————

MARTIN TWISTED his head around as Scott entered. "Has she sent you to kill me, or let me go?"

Scott pulled up a chair. "Nobody sent me."

Martin wrinkled his face. "God, you stink of fags, mate."

"Kind of a stressful day."

"Tell me about it."

On the television, the video of Angela's speech played. The resistance must have taken control of the broadcast again.

Scott got straight to the point. "Did they get you to? Did they force you to work for them? I've been there, Martin, I understand."

Martin pulled himself up straight. "Nobody got to me. I went out for a jog, which admittedly may have been a stupid thing to do, and clearly if I could turn back time, I wouldn't have done it. But that's all. You must believe me. Without blowing my own trumpet, I'm an important part of this resistance. You can't push me out now."

Scott leant forward and rested his head in his hands. Martin was right. They reeked of cigarette smoke.

"I want to believe you, and I'm sure she does too."

"I support her, but she can get psycho, and if she doesn't believe me, we both know what she'll do. If you think I'm telling the truth, you have to convince her, mate. She'll listen to you."

"I'm not sure she will."

"She will, Scott, I'm telling you."

"Are you sure you didn't know Miriam was in Israel all along?"

"I told you before, I swear I didn't know."

The first time Martin had told him, Scott believed him, and looking at him now, he still did. But if he was now a spy? That was a different story.

"How did Angela know, but you didn't when you were in charge of the search?"

"Look, mate, if she lied to you about it, she's obviously gonna lie to me about it as well." Martin shrugged his shoulders. "What can I say? I didn't know. Everything pointed to the fact they were here in Britain. You believe me, right?"

"I don't know, Martin, I'm sorry."

Scott looked away and left the room.

As he came out, Angela came down the staircase. "Scott."

He turned. She stood at the bottom of the stairs in her military jacket, her hair wilder than ever. Tears glistened in her eyes.

"Angie, what is it?"

"This is the day we have been fighting so long for, Scott. It's silly, but it's just hit me." She fanned her face, trying to evaporate the tears away. "I'm thinking of everything I've been through to get here. God, how did I even end up here, on the verge of running the country?"

Scott put an arm around her shoulders and guided her down the hallway. "I understand. It's been a rollercoaster for me, and it's only been a few months since I came on board. Until I met you again, I did not know how close the government were to falling, and how evil they were. So, thank you."

"All these years, all those people who said it would never be possible. This is going to sound strange, but I wish

David could see me now, not because I miss him, but so he could see I was more capable than he thought I was, than he could ever think I was." She tapped Scott's chest. "And Benji, he will be proud of you for this. You'll be his hero. If they didn't stop me having children, I would be their hero too."

"What do you mean?"

A tear rolled down her cheek, and she grimaced, trying not to cry.

"They arrested David and I not long after they came to power. They interrogated us, and..." Angela broke down, her shoulders shuddering as she cried. "They...they did something to me."

"Did what?"

"I woke up in a hospital, with a scar, you've probably seen." Scott had noticed a small scar below her belly button but thought nothing of it. "They removed both my fallopian tubes."

"Oh my God, Angie, I'm so sorry."

"Now you can see another reason I hated those bastards." She wiped the tears away and waved away his concern. "Anyway, this is the best revenge I can have."

They began walking again and reached the garden, helicopters rumbled in the distance. The sun still shone and the pyre of burnt documents and computer equipment smouldered away.

"Who would have thought what our destiny would be all those years ago at university, Scott?" Angela said, resting against his shoulder.

They both looked up at the sky, and Scott gripped her shoulder, rubbing slowly.

"I need you with me," she said, resting her hand on his, "me and you, Scott."

Scott thought about Miriam and Benji, and the potential family unit Miriam was so eager to go back to.

"I'll be with you, don't worry about that," Scott said.

The sound got louder, and now in the distance, they could see them; three double-winged Chinooks flying low towards them.

"We still have to make it to London, though. I'm not looking forward to this journey. I don't like the idea of helicopters, anyway, let alone when we could be shot out of the sky at any moment."

"Look what we've survived so far, Scott. I'm sure this will be fine. The cards say it will."

―――――

THE ISRAELIS RETURNED and threw the last couple of laptops onto the fire. The helicopters were now almost on top of them, and one descended, hovering above the garden. The downdraft whipped the smoke from the fire around and the trees bent as if in a gale. Angela's tarot cards flew around them like insects.

A man appeared at the helicopter door and threw down a rope ladder. They couldn't hear each other over the sound, so Noah ran over and cupped his hand to Angela's ear. Scott leant in to listen.

"What about Martin?"

Angela threw a hand out to catch one of the Tarot cards. A naked woman leant into a pool of water with a huge star above her. She held it for a moment, then released her grip and let it flutter away.

"Bring him with us."

The rope ladder fell towards them. Angela gestured for Scott to go first, and he grabbed it and climbed.

As he reached the top, a soldier hauled him inside, then pressed a helmet onto him. He pointed Scott towards a bench against the wall. The helmet shut out the deafening roars of the engines. The soldier strapped him in and Noah, then the other Israeli, came aboard. Martin appeared next, stumbling as he entered. He took a helmet but rejected the soldiers guiding hand and staggered towards Scott instead.

"Thank you," he said into the mouthpiece.

It crackled into Scott's ears, and he gave a thumbs up. Angela appeared at the brim of the entrance and stood, one arm on the side, looking out. The soldier pulled the rope ladder back up and the helicopter jolted, knocking her sideways. She fell to her knees, then forward towards the opening. Martin sprang over and reached for her. For a second, it looked as if he were too late, but he got a hand on her jacket just in time. She hung half out of the helicopter, and Martin strained to hold her.

Scott grasped at his seatbelt, fearing that Martin was a spy and would throw her to the ground. But he gently pulled her inside.

The soldier, oblivious to everything, hauled the ladder up, turned towards them, and slid the door closed.

Angela lay flat on her back, panting.

Martin's voice came through the earpiece. "I got you, boss, I told you I was on your side."

The soldier, along with Scott and Martin, went to lift her up, but she pushed them away as if embarrassed, and stumbled towards the benches.

The helicopter banked and climbed into the sky. Angela had a helmet shoved onto her head and looked towards Martin, then Scott.

"Thank you," she said, her cheeks flushed red.

The pilot informed them over the radio that it would

take forty-five minutes to reach London, and with the two escorts; they were safe, though would fly as low as possible to avoid radar detection and anti-aircraft fire.

Scott sat next to Noah, who had his eyes closed and mouthed what must be a prayer. The other Israeli sat on the other side, staring ahead at the round window on the wall opposite. Angela and Martin sat below the window. Angela had a serious look on her face, looking at the floor, and Martin glanced around as if he didn't have a care in the world.

Scott had no idea where in London they were going and what would happen once they got there, but as nobody spoke, he kept quiet and closed his eyes. The helicopter bounced occasionally, at one time causing Noah to reach out and grab Scott's hand.

Reaching the outskirts of London, the pilot announced that they would land soon, and Scott loosened his balled-up hands.

As the craft banked, the high-rise buildings of London became visible through the window. They levelled off, and Angela removed her safety belt and went to the window.

"Oh my God," she said.

They unbuckled themselves to look, and the destination became clear; Buckingham Palace.

———

A VAST SEA of people stood outside the gates, waving up at them. Interspersed amongst the crowd were tanks and armoured vehicles. Beyond the throng were craters, and shockingly, a smouldering wreck of a helicopter similar to the one they stood in. On the horizon, smoke rose into the sky.

They manoeuvred over the roof and touched down with a gentle bump, before being immediately instructed to get up and get out.

The pilot spoke over the radio as they took the helmets off. "Thank you for flying with us today, Ma'am, and good luck."

Emerging into the central courtyard of the Palace, two men in military gear escorted them towards an open door.

Scott spun around to take in the grand old building around him, and the helicopter sat in the middle of it all, blades slowing to a stop in the sun. The other two hovered above, creating a downdraft that billowed their clothes, almost ripping off Angela's jacket as she jogged in front of him towards the door. Above the din, the crowd whooped and cheered.

They entered a room as lavish as Scott expected Buckingham Palace to be. It was gloomy, despite the clear sunny day outside with walls covered in oil paintings of kings, queens, and the aristocracy of the past. Towering windows, net curtains drawn, reached up to the impossibly high ceiling where a chandelier hung, glittering from the lights within. A musty smell hung around them and dust clouded up from the plush red carpet.

One of the men in military uniform stopped and gathered them together. Scott noticed him from the conference call. General Forster-Gallagher. He saluted Angela, and she smiled.

"Ma'am, I trust you had a safe journey. Welcome to your home for the next few days." He looked at the others and bowed slightly. "Gentlemen, welcome." Then back at Angela. "We will give you a full briefing momentarily, but essentially, the capital is secure. There is still some fighting on the outskirts, but I can assure you, we have everything in place to protect you here. Snipers on the roof, anti-aircraft guns, the whole shebang."

Angela looked around in wonder.

Outside, a chant broke out from the crowd, "AN-GE-LA! AN-GE-LA! AN-GE-LA!"

"As you can hear, they appreciate you coming," General Forster-Gallagher said with a wry smile. "Any questions?"

"Yes." She broke into a smile. "Where's the wine cellar?"

Chapter Thirty-Three

The Rabbi finished his prayers.

Esther stepped forward, adjusted her veil, and took a handful of earth. She looked at the casket for a moment, then threw the dirt onto it. It reminded Miriam of doing the same at her mother's funeral, and tears came to her eyes. Beside her, Benji watched with interest. The other mourners consoled Esther with a few words as she walked past them. Miriam gripped her shoulder softly as she passed.

A warm breeze blew across the cemetery. It had been a whirlwind of grief and shock in the less than twenty-four hours since Shai's killing. Initially, Esther had been distraught and unable to think straight, screaming and shaking as they went to the hospital, then the police station to be interviewed.

The police had nothing to go on, but promised they would work hard, interviewing witnesses and tracking down leads. They had implored to the police how British agents must be behind it, and Esther wailed at them, asking how a man could be murdered in broad daylight on the streets of Paris and there be no leads.

With the help of staff, they swiftly arranged the funeral, and the few friends Shai had in Paris had attended. Esther, as the only immediate family member present, pushed her grief aside to organise what needed to be done.

She had now inherited the business, the money, and the responsibility of managing Shai's affairs, something that would be a huge burden on her. Angela needed to be contacted, yet the news from London suggested that she had other things on her plate, and it could wait a few days.

The Deputy PM had come on the air and announced he was back in control. A civil war seemed imminent, but as they had left for the cemetery, reports said that the situation had stabilised, and the sporadic fighting had been dying down. They didn't know if that was good or bad news.

Getting through to Angela or anybody in the resistance would prove difficult, and Shai's business partners promised that once the funeral had gone ahead, they would reach out to her.

They sat in silence, driving back through the busy streets with Esther weeping beside Miriam and Benji fidgeting with his tie. Seeing somebody up close lose her parent, no matter how old he was, gave more imperative to the thought of securing a safe and comfortable family life for Benji, possibly with his father.

Miriam ruffled Benji's hair, and he leant away.

———

THEY GATHERED BACK at the apartment, now overtly sombre in its grandeur, and Miriam kept one eye on her phone, checking for updates from London whilst making small talk with the mourners, mostly composed of Shai's business partners and a few distant family members who had got flights in time from across Europe.

The children, Benji included, had been sent to a faraway room to play. Talk of business was prohibited, yet people subtlety offered their services to Esther.

Esther made discreet enquires as to who her father may have been meeting with. Neither party received any straight answers. Miriam hoped the Paris CCTV would shed some light on it.

The guests, one by one, slipped away, offering their last condolences to Esther, and departing with bowed heads.

As Miriam opened the door to the children's room to gather them up, she saw Benji, his hands shaped like a gun, making firing noises at the other boys.

ONE MAN REMAINED after the others left. Esther introduced him as Yossi, one of her father's closest aides, who had flown straight over from Tel Aviv in a company jet as soon as he heard the news.

Esther drifted away, leaving Miriam alone with him. He looked about fifty, with bright silver hair and a glowing tan.

"Miriam, isn't it? Now the others have gone, sadly we have to talk business. Esther tells me you have a link with the resistance in the UK."

"My ex-husband, his father" she replied, pointing towards Benji, "is Scott Saunders."

"Impressive. I worked with Shai in his dealings with the resistance. I am sure we can get to the bottom of who did this despicable act. If the police do not, we will. We have a team of private investigators on the case as we speak. They will not get away with this."

"I hope so."

"Tell me, do you have any idea who Shai may have met with yesterday?"

Miriam shook her head. Yossi looked downcast. "And this briefcase, Esther says he asked her to tell Angela it was stolen, yes?"

"Yes, his exact words were 'Tell Angela the briefcase is gone'. We need to get through to her soon. Surely you have a way of contacting her?"

"I'm trying, but from what we know, it looks as if she is preparing to seize power imminently. We believe they have defeated the government, the army have backed the resistance at the crucial moment."

Esther returned, her long black dress swinging around her as she strode towards them. "Yossi, we have to put all our energy into finding who did this and bring them to justice, all the weight of the company and the family is going into this, OK?"

"Absolutely, Miss Zahavi."

"I am in charge now, and my first action will be to solve this. Step one is to reach Angela. My father's dying words were to tell her the briefcase was taken, so let's honour that."

Yossi picked up a raincoat from the seat. "Leave it with me. I'll set you up a call with her."

———

MIRIAM WATCHED THE TELEVISION ALONE.

Esther had retired to her room and Benji had gone back to his to play computer games.

Confusing reports came out of England from CNN. One minute, it seemed the resistance had won, then the Deputy PM's statement had changed the story. The news ticker along the bottom occasionally scrolled news of Shai's killing: 'PROMINENT ISRAELI BUSINESSMAN GUNNED DOWN IN PARIS STREET'. Rumours abounded online; Angela was dead, the Deputy PM was dead, Prince Charles was flying back to lead the country. Then, as Miriam had her finger on the off button, 'BREAKING NEWS' flashed up.

A helicopter hovering over Buckingham Palace, and a crowd below cheering. Angela had flown in with 'top resistance leaders' to take power. They expected a speech any minute. The reporter believed that Scott was also on board. A camera zoomed into the windows to show Angela waving.

Miriam held her breath as the helicopter, so fragile looking, slowly descended out of view. She turned to see Esther standing behind her, in the doorway, watching the TV.

"We know where she is now, Esther, we can get hold of her."

"I'll call Yossi," she said without emotion, and slinked away.

Yossi returned and occupied one of the many rooms of the apartment. He set up a laptop and two satellite phones, asked for a cup of coffee and set about trying to get through to London.

Once Esther had got him settled, she disappeared again. Miriam tried to talk to Benji, but all he wanted to do was play computer games, so she gave up and sat in front of the TV.

A reporter stood amongst the crowd outside the Palace. The people he interviewed were giddy with excitement.

'Angela is my hero' one woman declared. A man sold 'Angela Newton wigs' and at one point, the reporter stuck one on his head and the crowd cheered. People waved flags; both Union Jacks and the Resistance flag of a Flying Ant.

It was one giant street party. Surely it could not be as secure as the revellers thought?

One man spoke of seeing fighting near his house in the suburbs as he had left to come, and they quickly ended the interview. The media pushed the 'peaceful takeover' story hard.

All Miriam could think about was Scott in that grand building, and what he was thinking.

Esther appeared in the hallway, still in black. Her eyes looked as if she had been sleeping or crying. Or both.

"He got through to London. Angela is available now. I'd like you to be on the video call, Miriam."

She didn't realise it would be a video call, so as she followed Esther, she took a peek in one of the mirrors covered for mourning, pulling aside the covering and checking she was presentable before carrying on.

"Miriam," Yossi said as they entered, "Scott would like to speak to you first. Would that be alright? Angela will be another five minutes."

He handed her a phone. She looked back at Yossi and Esther.

"Ah, some privacy, yes of course."

Yossi shuffled away. Esther remained, staring into space for a few seconds before following him out. The door closed.

Miriam cleared her throat. "Hello?"

Scott's voice came back immediately. "Miriam, hi. God, so much has happened since we last spoke. Are you and Benji OK? I want the truth. If you're not, just tell me." He sounded stressed. "How come you're in Paris? What happened in Israel?"

"Scott, give me a chance to answer at least one of your questions."

Her laughter relaxed him, and he made a noise halfway between a laugh and a sigh.

"We are both fine, and that's a promise. We had to leave Israel, it wasn't safe anymore. But I'm not sure Paris is safe anymore either."

"Why?"

She told him about Shai's assassination.

"Jesus Christ, Miriam. Who is this Shai anyway?"

"Angela knows who he is, and his last words were to tell her about the briefcase, that's why we need to talk to her."

"All this stuff Benji keeps seeing. The poor kid is going to be traumatised for life. We need to do something, Miriam. I don't know what but..."

"I know what, Scott. Like I said before. We can be a family again and give him the support he needs. A loving environment, a..."

"Miriam, I'm sorry, but I can't. That will not happen."

Scott said it with regret, but with a finality that took her aback. Miriam walked to the window and looked out over the street. Neither she nor Scott had said anything for nearly a minute. She had a lump in her throat and feared she would cry if she tried to speak.

"Miriam?"

"Is it because of her? Are you throwing away your son's future because of her?"

"God, Miriam, we split up, it's over. We can't work. We tried and tried, but it didn't work. We would make each other unhappy. I know deep down you know that as well.

You're imagining a future that cannot happen. I will still be in Benji's life, but not with you."

She tried to hold back the tears and pressed her forehead against the glass.

He was right. It was a pipe dream. It made her feel like a teenager, angry that another woman had stolen her man. The truth was, he wasn't her man anymore, anyway.

"Miriam?" Scott said. "I don't mean to be harsh, you know, I still care about you."

"I know."

"Come to London. It's safe here. Not perfect, but Paris doesn't sound too safe either. Let me see Benji, we'll find a place for you to stay, and we can talk in person."

There was a knock at the door, and she lifted her head away from the glass. Yossi leant through the gap giving the signal to wind it up.

"We'll come, Scott. Listen, I have to go now. But we will come. Bye."

"Goodbye."

Yossi opened the door fully. "Sorry, but Angela is ready and doesn't enjoy waiting, we don't want to miss our window."

She placed the phone on the table, and as Yossi tapped away at a keyboard, Esther approached her. "Are you OK?"

"I'm fine thanks, Esther, I'm fine."

"You don't look fine, but who is in this house, right?"

She hugged Miriam, and they both cried, much to Yossi's obvious discomfort.

Esther pulled away and turned back to Yossi. "Put her on."

Within seconds, the screen on the far wall flashed and Angela's face appeared. From the tight shot, it was unclear if she was alone. Was Scott with her? Had she heard him on the phone?

Angela leant forward, as if looking at a small screen. "Afternoon, ladies."

"Good afternoon," Yossi said.

Angela broke into a giggle. "Sorry, and gentleman."

It was clear she was drunk.

"London calling," she said in a mock upper-class voice. "What news from Paris?"

She looked slightly to the side at something, or somebody. Could it be Scott?

"I need to talk to you about my father," Esther said.

"How are you, Esther? It must be what, two years since I saw you? And Miriam, I hope you're still showing those legs when you get a chance. Yossi, I tell you they're to die for, better than my skinny little things." She stood up, "Look! It's the one thing I'd change if I could. They're like a teenage boy's, for Christ's sake."

Her giggle turned into a full-blown laugh, and she fell back into the chair, slapping her thigh. Miriam winced with embarrassment.

"My father is dead!" Esther shouted.

Miriam had never seen a smile wiped so quickly from a face.

"What?" Angela said. "How, when?"

Esther's jaw trembled. "He was shot dead in the street yesterday. Two men on a motorbike stole a briefcase from him and killed him." Now Angela trembled as Esther wiped a tear away. "His last words were to tell you the briefcase had been taken."

Angela stared off camera, her eyes darting about as if trying to think something through. "I spoke to him a few days ago, I asked him to get that briefcase."

"What was in it?" Miriam asked.

Angela raised both hands to her head and fell back against her chair.

"What *wasn't* in it? The names and addresses of everyone in the resistance, all our cells, all our plans. Everything. We thought it would be safer not being stored electronically. Oh God."

Yossi hung his head.

Angela closed her eyes. "We're fucked."

Chapter Thirty-Four

Scott looked through the net curtains and down at the sea of humanity outside. After the conversation with Miriam, he had paced the palace, relieved yet morose.

Letting her down had been hard, but it was for the best. There was no way they could be together as a couple again. Being with Angela seemed just as unlikely, but he loved her and there was nothing he could do to change that. Despite all her flaws, he wanted to be with her, to start a new life with somebody he loved, and who loved him. To have a purpose, not merely be a bystander in his own life. Yet he wanted Miriam and Benji to come to London as soon as they could.

The absurdity of being in Buckingham Palace, a building he had seen so many times from the outside, leant a surrealness to the situation, and the speed at which it had all happened amazed him.

Angela had banished everyone, him included, out of the room to take conference calls from various people. Keeping only General Forster- Gallagher with her as an assistant.

The crowd outside had grown, waiting in anticipation for Angela's speech. Hopefully she would be sober enough to deliver it properly, having demanded a case of wine brought up for the afternoon. "Mr Saunders."

He turned to see General Forster-Gallagher, smiling apologetically. "Mrs Newton has asked you to come to see her now."

"Of course," he said, unconsciously matching the generals upper-class tones.

———

ANGELA STOOD at the window smoking, a glass of wine in her hand. She looked at him as he entered, then just as quickly turned back.

A chaotic mess of papers lay across the floor and the furniture was upturned.

"What happened here?"

"We're in trouble. Big trouble." She threw the cigarette butt out the open window. "Shai is dead, which is a tragedy. That man helped us and won't live to see our victory realised."

"Yes, Miriam told me."

"I bet she did," she sneered. "But the real problem is *why* he was killed. Remember, I told you we kept a list of agents? A list of every Ant, their addresses, everything. I sent Shai to get that list, to move it from the safe deposit box in Paris and bring it here now we can safely hold it. They stole the list when they killed him."

"Who's they?"

"The remnants of the government, their supporters. There is nothing to stop them hunting down and killing every person on that list, torturing them, getting information out of them. Anything. We may be in power now, but be under no illusions, we will have to fight a resistance, and they have an enormous advantage already. I've got General Forster-Gallagher to coordinate a hunt for it, but I'm not too optimistic. Damn it."

Angela drank long and hard from her glass.

It was clear she needed to make her speech before she drank any more.

"The most important thing you can do now is to get out on that balcony and make your speech, Angie. Show the people you're in charge."

"You're right."

She stepped away from the window and reached for the bottle beside her.

"No," Scott said, taking it away. "Not until after."

"Don't you tell me what to do, you don't own me."

"Angie, please, you can't go out there drunk."

"I can go out there however I want," Angela retorted.

She slammed the table, her glass half shattering as she did so.

Scott picked up the bottle and headed for the door, but as he walked, a crash sounded, followed by a scream. He flinched, half expecting something to hit the back of his head. He turned. The curtains billowed, and a man clad in black wearing a balaclava held Angela, a knife to her throat.

Scott dropped the bottle. It hit the deep carpet with a dull thud. She writhed around, trying to move, but the man was too strong for her.

"Don't make a sound, Angela, and Scott, don't take another step," the man said.

Scott couldn't place it, but the voice was familiar. Angela stopped moving. The blade of the knife pressed against her throat.

"If you try to raise the alarm, I will kill both of you."

Now Scott could place the voice: Sarge.

"What do you want?"

Sarge ripped the balaclava off and spoke. "I want to end this madness. This woman is not fit to run the country, we all know that. I'm getting rid of her so somebody more sensible can. As long as she's alive, this revolution is going in the wrong direction."

Angela's bulging eyes stared back at Scott.

He held up a hand. "Sarge, stop, we can sort this out."

Sarge shook his head. A bead of sweat ran down his forehead. "We fought for years to take down this government, and now what? We're replacing it with a psychotic drunk. Is this going to be any better? Step aside now or I'll kill you."

Sarge took a step back to the window, yanking Angela hard as he did so. As she twisted, Scott saw the broken wine glass in her hand.

"You fought years to overthrow them and you're destroying it as just as it happens? Surely, we can come to an agreement, a place on the counsel or something."

"No!" Angela shouted.

"I told you to keep quiet."

Sarge moved the knife into position and pressed it into her flesh. Angela flung her hand upwards, bringing the broken glass hard onto Sarge's face.

Instinctively, Sarge reached up to the wound, giving Angela room to move. In a whirlwind motion, she spun round and grabbed the knife. Even in his stricken state, Sarge was too strong for her. Blood poured from his cheek and a horrific injury to his eye. Despite falling to the floor, he kept his grip on the knife.

Scott ran forwards and kicked him. The knife fell from

his hands and Scott kicked it away. Sarge crawled towards the window, and before Scott could do anything, Angela came from behind him, kicked Sarge in the head and drew her gun.

"You know what I do with traitors," she said, pressing the trigger.

Scott closed his eyes.

Nothing happened. Scott opened his eyes to see her frantically pressing the trigger. Either the gun had jammed or it had not been loaded.

She lunged for the knife on the carpet. Scott jumped onto Sarge to stop him from getting away, coming face to face with his gruesome injury. As he wrestled him, the blood smeared against his own face.

Sarge overpowered him, throwing him off before scrambling to the window. As he climbed through, Angela ran towards him and held the knife back, ready to plunge the blade into him, but he fell as he tried to climb out and the sudden movement caused her to miss.

He grabbed a wire and slid down to the grass below, then looked up at them.

"This is not over, Angela! I will expose you as the wrong person to lead this. I know your crimes. You know what she is, Scott, and you're no better. You killed that woman, Olympia. You're both murderers, and soon, everyone will know. She'll turn on you one day, Scott, you know that, mark my words."

He fled and Angela shouted from the window, pleading for help, for somebody to catch him, but nobody came. They stood helplessly as Sarge reached a wall in the gardens and ascended a ladder propped against it.

Scott held her. "Are you OK?"

Angela collapsed into a chair, gasping for breath, rubbing her neck where the knife had been.

"How the hell could he get in here, Scott? Where is security? Are we compromised already?" She picked up the gun and opened the magazine. It was empty. "How could I be so careless, damn it, could anything else go wrong today?"

Two soldiers burst through the door, guns drawn. "What happened?"

"I'll tell you what happened!" Scott screamed. "Your new leader, who you are meant to be protecting, has nearly been killed by an intruder."

The men looked at each other in shock.

"How could you let this happen? How could you leave her so unprotected?" Scott bellowed.

They muttered apologies and Scott stormed away from them towards the open window. They followed him, but Angela raised herself up and berated them.

"I was that close to being murdered, you fools. Get General Forster-Gallager in here now."

They radioed down to security to scour the permitter walls and check the CCTV. Angela picked up the bottle Scott had dropped, found a fresh glass, and began drinking again. Scott let her, putting an arm around her as she did so.

She rubbed her neck and said, "Our first aim is to hunt down that bastard and kill him and every one of his people."

"I'm inclined to agree with you this time, Angie, but you really need to put this aside for now and do that speech."

"I knew it wouldn't be easy but think about it. We're going to be fighting any government remnants who have the briefcase with the details of every Ant, plus Sarge and his band of merry traitors." Angela fiddled with her gun, adding new bullets and looking into the chamber. "And trying to run a country."

One of the soldiers came back from the window. "Ma'am, we have alerted all guards on the perimeter, but we were on our way to get you, actually. General Forster-Gallagher sent us up here to give you some news."

She looked up. "Go on."

"The Deputy PM is in custody. We caught him trying to flee the country."

"Where is he?"

"Here, in the palace. In a makeshift cell before they move him somewhere else. General Forster-Gallagher thought you may want to meet with him."

Angela's eyes lit up. "General Forster-Gallagher is right."

———

A GUARD LED them deep into the basement. Angela's boots clicked loudly as they proceeded down an ill-lit tunnel.

General Forster-Gallagher appeared from a door, a sheepish look on his face. "I'm very sorry about what happened, Mrs Newton. I can assure you we will do every-thing to beef up security and hunt down the perpetrators."

Angela stopped so abruptly that Scott bumped into her. "You will be sorry if you don't find them, General. I want the full force of the security apparatus working on capturing Sarge, as well as that bloody briefcase." She pulled herself up straight, still only reaching General Forster-Gallagher's chin. "Do you understand?"

"Yes, Ma'am."

"Good. Now what do we have down here?"

"We detained deputy PM Nicholson at a private

airfield in Kent, supposedly heading for Russia. After being captured, they drove him straight to Buckingham Palace, the only location with the relevant security in place at the moment to hold him."

Angela scoffed. "I hope he's more secure than me."

"Apologies again, Ma'am."

She shook her head, and General Forster-Gallagher took them to a steel door.

"The Royal Family used this as a vault," he said, opening the six-inch thick door to reveal another door with thick metal bars. "There is not enough ventilation for somebody to survive more than a few hours."

"What are we planning to do with him?"

"Once we find a safe cell for him in a prison, we can move him there and conduct a full interrogation. I take it you plan to hold some sort of trial for deposed government figures, Ma'am? A modern-day Nuremberg? To draw a line under the past few years?"

"Yes, we do."

"Good, and Nicholson is the highest-ranking figure still alive. He will be a treasure trove of information. It is of the utmost importance that we keep him safe. We thought you might want to speak to him before we move him."

"Thank you, General."

"He's fully shackled and searched, but please be careful." He unlocked the door, swung it open, and gestured for them to enter. "I will wait here."

———

HIS ARMS HANDCUFFED in front of him, and legs manacled under the table, Sir Simon Nicholson, MBE, deposed Deputy Prime Minister, looked up as they entered.

Dressed in a navy suit, without a tie, and his hair neatly combed back, he looked exhausted, and older than his fifty-five years.

"So much for your little television address," Angela said. "It appears the tables have turned." She leant towards him and squinted at his handcuffs. "Gosh, those don't look too comfortable."

"Cut to the chase, Newton, what are you going to do with me?"

Smiling broadly, she perched herself on the table. "A trial, life imprisonment, hopefully. Make an example of you, that sort of thing."

"You can't keep me here forever."

"Unfortunately, re-joining the Geneva convention seems to take a while, so we can do what we want with you."

"There'll be hell to pay if you torture or kill me."

Scott broke in. "We will not kill you."

Nicholson scowled at him with disdain. "Ah, he speaks!"

"We won't bring ourselves down to your level. But you will pay for what you've done to this country."

"And what have I done to this country? Get it back on its feet again, defeat the virus, bring stability, jobs, a sense of national pride. That's not a crime."

"The secret police? What about your racial policies? You're disgusting."

"Oh, don't accuse me of racism, Mr Saunders, our government put black and Asian people back to work in their droves. They're some of our staunchest supporters, as a matter of fact."

"My ex-wife, is Jewish. I don't think she would agree with you. Or my son."

"The Jewish thing went a little far, I admit, but that wasn't my doing, I-"

Angela cut him off. "In that case, you will be pleased to know Israel has played a huge part in your overthrow. Every single Israeli I have worked with has been braver and stronger than you and your pathetic group of friends." She hopped off the table, pointing at him with rage. "You are going to tell us everything you know, and everyone involved, or we'll hunt your family down and kill them all."

"I'll tell you everything. I don't really have any other option, do I? But let me tell you this first, your new regime will barely last till the end of the year. The army will turn on you, your supporters will turn on you and the millions of people out there who backed us will never accept you." He looked her up and down. "Look at you, nobody's going to respect you."

Angela slapped him square in the face. The sound rang around the cell. "See? You're too highly strung. Hysterical. I've read the intelligence about you. I know who you are, Angela Newton, and soon, the entire world will know. The drinking, the executions, the madness."

He stared into her eyes, a red mark spreading across his cheek.

"You won't last a year. Mark my words."

She slapped him again.

Nicholson looked at Scott. "Feisty one, isn't she? I bet she's good in bed though."

Angela pulled her gun from its holster.

Scott held a hand up. "Angie, no."

Nicholson turned pale. She pointed it at his forehead.

Scott put his hand on the gun and gently lowered it. "Come on, let's go, this is going nowhere, Angie."

She watched the fear on Nicholson's face for a moment, then turned away. "You're right, let's go."

She took a step towards the exit and Scott followed.

"Stupid bitch," Nicholson muttered from behind them.

In the blink of an eye, Angela spun around and fired off two quick shots. In the confined space, the noise was deafening. Scott's ears rang, and Angela doubled over.

Nicholson's body sat bolt upright, a hole in his forehead, blood streaming from it. Scott grabbed Angela to take the gun from her, and as he did so, she stood upright and pulled up her top, revealing a bright red mark on her side.

The ricochet of the second bullet must have grazed her.

General Forster-Gallagher rushed in and said something that Scott couldn't make out over the ringing, then covered his mouth with a shaking hand.

Angela walked out of the cell, and Scott stood still, looking from Nicholson to General Forster-Gallager in disbelief.

"What the bloody hell has she done?" General Forster-Gallagher shouted.

Scott walked out. The two guards at the cell door rushed past him as he reached the now open door. Angela stormed away, and as he followed her, somebody held him back. It was Martin.

"Did she kill him?" he asked.

"Yeah," Scott said, as Angela got into the lift, "she did."

"Meet the new boss, same as the old boss." Martin rolled his eyes. "If these military guys think she's unfit to rule, they will take our revolution from us, Scott."

Scott pulled away from him and ran towards the lift.

Chapter Thirty-Five

Scott pushed Angela against the wall of the lift. "You need to get on that balcony and make this speech now, before the army decides to back someone else, do you understand?"

She twisted her head away like a petulant child.

"Everything is in jeopardy after your little stunt back there. You have to speak to your people right now."

"Stop, you're hurting me."

Scott let go, and she pulled up her top again, looking at the wound.

"It's just a graze. You could have killed yourself, you could have killed me. What the hell were you thinking?"

"His face, God, his smirking little entitled face, I couldn't take it anymore."

The lift doors slid open and they emerged onto the first floor.

"How are we meant to hold the moral high ground when you're killing them? This is insanity. We cannot be the bad guys, Angie, do you get that? Let alone the amount of intelligence he had. We are *that close* to losing everything, Angie, the military won't stand for this."

They reached her room. Two guards stood at the door, pretending not to listen.

"Give me some time, Scott."

"Time? I don't know what we are waiting for. You should have made the speech the moment we got here. I'm going to send a doctor up here, and if you're not out in an hour, I'm going to drag you out onto that balcony myself."

"Scott, come back."

"What?"

She came up to him. "Don't be like this with me, you know what scum these people are."

"I do. I know as well as anyone, but you need to rise above it for now. One hour, Angie, then you're doing this speech. I don't even know why you haven't done it already." Scott pointed at his watch. "One hour. And don't even think about drinking anymore."

Angela looked chastened and let herself into the room. He slammed the door on her and stormed away.

"Get a doctor in there," he barked at a guard.

As he went down the hallway, General Forster-Gallagher and Martin emerged from the lift. The General nodded to a door. "In here."

Scott and Martin stood like two schoolboys being told off by the headmaster as the General spoke, clearly trying to suppress his anger. "Nicholson was your biggest intelligence asset, and now he's gone. I'm not sure how she thinks that will help things. He's another martyr for their followers. That was a terrible move."

"General, she is under intense stress." Scott held up a hand as General Forster-Gallagher went to reply. "I'm not defending what she did, not at all, and I have told her in the strongest terms that I disagreed with it. This is the most intense day of her life. Her emotions are all over the place. An intruder nearly killed her minutes before. She will calm down, get out there, give the speech and we can get on with taking this country forward."

"I am a soldier, Mr Saunders, I believe in the chain of command, and as agreed prior to today, she is in charge, so she is my boss. That's not in doubt. But I must register my concerns about what just happened. Let me speak with her."

"No, she needs to be alone to relax and get into the correct frame of mind. Trust me, I know her better than you."

The General relented. "Very well, but gentleman listen." They stopped. The crowds outside continued to chant her name. "It's vital that she goes out there and shows the country she is in control, before something else goes wrong."

"I told her the same, and she will do it. I have faith in her."

"Good. Tell her she still has our backing, gentleman, I have business to attend to."

———

THEY REMAINED in the small room General Forster-Gallagher had taken them into, and Scott slid out a pack of cigarettes, offering one to Martin.

"I've got something a little better, bro," he said, producing a perfectly rolled joint from his pocket. "I heard the Beatles smoked a joint in here once. I've always wanted to do the same."

They rolled up the window and leant out, passing the

joint back and forth, looking out on the courtyard. Scott gave him a detailed rundown of what happened with Sarge, and in the cell with Nicholson.

Martin laughed. "My old mum used to say, 'If you don't laugh, you'll cry.' God, this is the day we've been fighting towards for years. When it comes, it's a shit show. Typical. I didn't think Sarge would sink that low, though. He needs to be stopped ASAP."

"So, you're definitely not a spy then?"

Martin laughed again. "No. I thought jogging was good for you. That's the last time I ever go for a run." He pulled hard on the joint. "Angela needs to chill out, maybe she should have some of this."

"I know. It worries me how she behaves sometimes. God, the amount of people I've seen her kill..."

As Scott spoke, a black limousine pulled up outside. It slowed to a stop, and a guard jogged to the door. He pulled it open, and a smart red headed woman dressed in black, stepped out, followed by a blonde woman in a fur-lined jacket. The blonde woman looked up at the palace.

Scott nearly dropped the joint. It was Miriam. Then Benji stepped out of the car.

Scott shouted out to them. "Benji, Miriam!"

They looked up and waved.

"Stay there."

Scott passed the joint to Martin and headed for the door. He raced into the hallway, flying past bemused guards and bounded down the staircase, his nostrils filled with the dust kicking up from the carpet. He paused at the bottom, racking his brains for how to get to the courtyard, then took off towards a man milling about under a painting of Queen Victoria.

"The courtyard. How do I get to the courtyard?"

The man pointed across the hall. "Nearest exit is that way. Is something wrong, Mr. Saunders?"

"No, not at all, thank you."

As he ran, Scott saw them through the enormous glass doors. Miriam was fussing over Benji whilst in conversation with the red-headed woman.

Scott burst through the doors and across the red tarmac. Miriam saw him first and froze. Scott scooped Benji up in his arms and whirled him around, pressing his face into the boy's coat. Benji's smell took him back to happier times, and the tears flowed. He held Benji at arm's length, getting a proper look at him.

"Have you missed me? I've missed you so much," he exclaimed, hugging him tightly.

"Yeah, I suppose I've missed you."

Scott laughed and put him down. He turned to Miriam. Despite everything she had been through, she looked good.

"Miriam, come here." They embraced, and the fur of her jacket tickled his nose. "I didn't know you would be here so soon. How are you?"

Tears ran down her cheeks. "I'm good. Happy to be back in England, and rather impressed with your new place." She looked up at the building. "Is it safe here, really?"

"As safe as it can be."

"We have Esther here, Shai's daughter, to thank for our quick arrival. We took a private jet from Paris to London as soon as we could."

If it was possible to look rich, then Esther did. Everything about her reeked of money. She was a striking woman, her short red hair standing out against her black clothes. She looked stricken with grief.

"Nice to meet you and thank you." Scott shook her hand. "I'm sorry about your father."

"Thank you."

He took Benji by the hand. "Let me show you around Buckingham Palace. Are you excited?"

Benji looked up in awe. "Is this our new house?"

"Sort of."

Miriam entwined her arm in his and they walked inside. He took them into one of the upstairs rooms.

————

SCOTT FRETTED over Benji so much that the boy got annoyed. Luckily, one soldier produced a football, and Scott and Benji kicked it to each other across the vast room. In between kicks, he listened to Miriam give a detailed telling of events in Paris. Esther occasionally butted in, adding to the story, despite the obvious pain it caused her.

The ball flew towards Miriam, and she held onto it.

"That's enough for now, I think. Benji, why don't you stay with Auntie Esther whist me and Daddy talk about adult things?" She looked at Scott. "Is there somewhere we can go?"

"We'll be back soon, big man," he said, leading Miriam into the next room.

Miriam looked out at the throng of people below. "So, what happens now, then?"

"With us?"

"No, I know what happens with us. You were quite clear about it. Maybe you were right, and if you're happy with her, then I'm happy for you both."

She had almost come to terms with his decision. Wanting a new start with him came from the turmoil of the situation she had been in. Craving something familiar to hold on to, rather than an actual relationship with him again.

"We've both been through a hell of a lot and need to take whatever happiness we can. I'm just glad to be here, in England, with that lot gone. If they are gone?"

"They are, it's over. The PM is dead, the Deputy PM is dead. The army has taken our side. There's no coming back for them."

"The Deputy PM is dead? I saw him on TV giving his announcement just a few hours ago."

"The army caught him trying to escape, and he, er, he died in custody."

"How is Angela?"

"Stressed, probably drinking a bit too much. I've told her she has to make a speech as soon as possible."

"Does she listen to you? No offence, but it seems she would wear the trousers in any relationship."

He laughed. "Not really. But I was forceful with her. Look, Miriam, I know this is weird but..."

"It is weird, but if you are in Benji's life, and this country is free from tyranny, then fine. But aren't you worried about reprisals? Robertson's support won't disappear overnight."

"Of course, the situation is still fraught with danger, but this is what the resistance has been fighting for. This is the dream." Scott sat on the window ledge. "How's Benji?"

"He's been through a lot. Me being nearly killed in Israel, the attack on Shai's place, and Shai's murder. It must have affected him, but he doesn't talk about it, even if I try to get him to."

"We can get him the best help. Doctors, psychologists, whatever is needed. I'll sort it out."

"The main thing he needs is his parents. Promise me you won't let your responsibilities here get in the way of being a father."

"I promise, Miriam. I don't even know what my responsibilities are, anyway. Nobody knows anything. It all happened so quick. I don't even know where I'm sleeping tonight." Scott looked at his watch. It had been an hour since he told Angela she had to make her speech. "Come on, let's go back in. Benji will wonder where we are."

They hugged a final time and went back next door.

Esther and Benji had pulled out the contents of a cabinet and the various ornaments lay spread on the floor. Benji ran up to Scott to show him one, a small golden model of an elephant. As they examined it, the door swung open. Angela entered and headed straight towards Esther, kissed her on both cheeks and consoled her.

"Your father was a great man."

She appeared calm and sober, though Scott knew she must still be drunk. Then she embraced Miriam as if she were an old friend.

"I didn't think I'd see you again after Tel Aviv. We must have a girl's night together soon. The three of us."

Miriam looked happy to see her and Scott relaxed a little.

Angela looked at Benji and gave a little wave. "Remember me, Bobby?"

He nodded. "My name is Benji though."

Angela laughed and went to Scott, pulling him close. "I'm ready. This is it." Then she addressed the room. "Come on, we're going to the balcony. Then boy are we going to party afterwards."

———

THEY GATHERED in the room behind the famous balcony. Angela maintained a stoic disposition, muttering to herself and drinking water. The chanting from outside grew louder. Scott introduced Martin to Miriam, Esther and Benji, while the General fussed over security concerns.

"We are bringing up a transparent bulletproof shield, the kind used at Presidential inaugurations, its two inches thick and-"

Angela snapped out of her trance. "No."

"But, Ma'am, you'll be a sitting duck out there. We do not know who could be in that crowd."

"There are soldiers on the roof, spotters in the crowd, a no-fly zone overhead, that's enough. I cannot be cowering behind a shield for this moment."

"It's totally transparent, no one will notice it."

"No."

The General looked around as if waiting for someone else to back up his argument, but there was no point trying to change her mind, and as risky as it may be, she had survived many dangerous moments on the road to get here.

The General looked exasperated. "Very well then, but in that case, please can I ask that it's just you out there."

A team of soldiers arrived with the shield and the General waved them away. Angela brushed down her jacket, thankfully not the military one she had favoured before, and smiled at the General.

"It will be only myself, General, and will be a brief speech announcing victory, and dissolving the previous government's limitations of freedoms and race laws within the next forty eight hours. They will hardly have time to shoot me."

He made his now familiar bowing gesture. "Very well.

There is a microphone just to the left as you exit. Keep it quick."

The General departed to the drinks table and poured a large single malt. The old oak table heaved under the weight of spirits and wine, but at Angela's insistence, Flying Ant Days were being prepared next door, waiting to be dished out after her speech.

Angela took Scott by the hand and led him to Martin. The three of them stood together. She put her arms around their shoulders, and they bent down, huddled together like players before a football match, their foreheads touching.

"We did it. This is it. This is history. This is Flying Ant Day," Angela said in a low voice. "Everything we have fought for. We must not forget those who have lost their lives along the way, every single person who gave their life so we could be here today. Thank you to you two, for everything."

"Amen," Martin said.

They hugged tightly, then followed Angela as she walked to the large doors, now swung open, a net curtain billowing in front of them. The volume of the crowd increased, and clapping started.

Angela kissed him and whispered in his ear. "I love you."

Before Scott could reply, Angela turned and marched to the door. He looked over at Miriam, who looked down at the floor.

Angela stepped onto the balcony and the crowd erupted.

"People of Britain," she began, then stopped, waiting for the roar to stop.

Scott made his way to Miriam and Benji. He held Benji's hand and stood beside Miriam.

She smiled at him. "I can't believe this is really happening."

"Me neither."

The General nervously sipped his whiskey. Martin leant against a pillar, revelling in the moment. Finally, Angela spoke again.

"Today marks the end of a long struggle for freedom. A struggle to become the great country we deserve to be once again. Today is the light at the end of that dark tunnel."

So many emotions went through Scott's mind as he listened to her berate the previous government, promise peace and prosperity, and an end to the oppressive laws, and elections within a year. After everything they had been through together, he admired her, even though a part of him worried about the future, and her murderous streak. Would she be calmer now she had power? More prepared to listen, less prepared to kill? Only time would tell.

Her voice rose to a crescendo. "This is the freedom we want, this is the freedom we deserve, and this is the freedom we now have."

If it was possible for the crowd to cheer any louder than before, they did.

"Thank you," she bellowed, and strode back into the room, buzzing with adrenaline.

Waiters emerged with trays of 'Flying Ant Day' cocktails.

She stood in the centre of the room. "Everybody please take a glass and join me in a toast."

Miriam picked a glass from a tray and frowned at it quizzically. "What on earth is this?"

"Flying Ant Day."

"What does it taste like?"

"Freedom."

Scott sipped the drink, then stopped. Benji was gone.

"Scott," Miriam said, "he's here."

Benji stood behind her, hiding from the people gathered around. Relieved, Scott leant over and ruffled his hair.

For the first time in years, he didn't recoil with embarrassment. They shared a smile as Angela stood on the table, drink in her hand, flushed with excitement. "To Flying Ant Day."

If you enjoyed this book, please leave a review on Amazon, and keep up to date on my writing at www.samsmedley.co.uk

Acknowledgments

Firstly, thank you to my wife Deepa who had to put up with me disappearing into the box room on many an evening to work on 'the book.' To Monika Mandova and Sidony Vaughan for extensive feedback on one of the many drafts, and a huge thank you to my editor Chelsea Terry at www. standcorrectedediting.com for all the magical work an editor does.

And finally, to my late father, Ian Smedley, for passing on to me his love of books.

Printed in Great Britain
by Amazon

81033525R00222